BETRAYAL
of
TRUST

B. B. Wright

To Renis

With Best Wishes

BETRAYAL
of
TRUST

iUniverse, Inc.
Bloomington

Betrayal of Trust

iUniverse books may be ordered through booksellers or by contacting:

iUniverse
1663 Liberty Drive
Bloomington, IN 47403
www.iuniverse.com
1-800-Authors (1-800-288-4677)

ISBN: 978-1-4759-5130-1 (sc)
ISBN: 978-1-4759-5131-8 (e)
ISBN: 978-1-4759-5132-5 (dj)

Printed in the United States of America

iUniverse rev. date: 11/05/2012

For my grandchildren:
Alexander, Zoe, Emma and Ethan
&
For two other exceptional people:
Nadia and Mikayla

Acknowledgments

THIS BOOK WOULD NEVER have reached completion without the constant support and encouragement of my wife, Jeanne, and her tireless devotion to reviewing each chapter and the final product.

I would be remiss not to include my mentors who provided their unique perspective and skills to inspire me to lofty goals: Miss Helen Richardson, Mr. and Mrs. Fred Bell, Dr. H. L. Ridge and Sandra Birdsell. My heartfelt gratitude goes out to you. Thank you.

To all my friends, thank you for continuing to be part of my life's journey.

To my daughter-in-law, Jamie Wright, I extend my gratitude for the time you spent editing and reviewing the manuscript before it went to print.

And, a special thank-you goes out to the staff at iUniverse for their ongoing support, insight and patience.

BUILDING 3C

CHAPTER ONE

EDWARD SLOCUM COMBED HIS fingers through his thick salt-and-pepper hair; stretched out his six foot–plus, medium-sized frame; yawned; and, using his foot, pushed away from his desk and placed his legs on the only small island vacant of paper left on his desk.

He wore a dark blue dress shirt with sleeves rolled up, the top two buttons at his neck undone, and a yellow silk tie hanging loosely down. His grey pin-striped jacket was draped across the back of his high-backed black leather chair.

At 42 years old, he had only lately seen a roll developing around his 32-inch waist. Though he had a gym at home and went to the executive gym at KemKor (one of the perks of being an executive vice president), he had barely used either of them in the last two months.

Edward glanced at his watch, shook his head in disbelief and sighed. Four hours had flown by since his return from supper at six. He pursed his lips as he looked at the stack of folders still in his in-tray and the reports and other related paraphernalia scattered about his desk. He rested his chin on his extended thumbs, his fingertips pressed together to form a steeple.

Two years tomorrow, he thought.

He took a deep breath, stood up and walked to the wall of windows overlooking the lamplit main street. His eyes followed the street to the intersection.

A soft thud caused Edward to turn away from the window and look back toward his overly busy desk. The Tuesday evening newspaper, which had been neatly folded and left earlier on the corner of his desk by his administrative assistant, Nadia, lay on the floor, the headline page facing up. He picked it up and scanned the front page while making his way around his desk toward the office door. Halfway across the room, he stopped. "Well, I'll be damned."

The heading of the article located right in the middle of the lower half of the front page read, "Norman Rattray found dead. Thought to be suicide." The article finished up on the second page with a picture from the recent staff picnic of Norman standing beside his brother William, the CEO of KemKor Pharmaceuticals.

The two of them don't look too happy, he thought. *Surely they could have found a better picture.*

He placed the paper on the table beside the door and made a mental note to convey his condolences to the CEO the next day. After looking back at the mound of paperwork on his desk, he let out a deep sigh.

Still a few hours yet, he thought, cringing with the prospect. *Right now, I need to get out of here.*

Though the July evening was hot and muggy, Edward showed a sense of relief, almost freedom, as he stepped out into the courtyard and heard the door slam behind him, imprisoning the air-conditioned atmosphere within. For a moment he took in the night sky, watching wisps of cloud drift lazily across the full moon. He reached into his shirt pocket and took out a cigarette, briefly hesitating before placing it between his lips. He fumbled through his pant pockets for the paper matches, tore one off and, striking it, held the flame up to his cigarette but did not light it. Instead, he threw the lit match onto the ground and stamped it out with his foot.

"There," he said, looking up at the night sky. "I've kept my promise, Karen." The poignancy of the moment caused his voice to crack. "This is the last one." He crumbled the cigarette in his hand and, holding the resultant debris close to his lips, he blew it away. "God! How I miss you. Whatever drew you out that evening two years ago?" It was one of several questions he still had unanswered after her death.

His attention was drawn to the light and muffled sounds at the far end of the court. He began to walk down the middle of the treed courtyard toward its source.

The only structure down the path to the left was Building 3C, and it was still not operational—at least according to the information he had been told. Building 3C was under the jurisdiction of the other executive vice president, his friend John Elkhart, and it was being refurbished to test out Edward's new filtration system.

Edward took a deep breath and slowly let it out as he continued through the courtyard. Uneasiness and trepidation unexpectedly bubbled up in him. Trusting his instincts, he moved off the paved surface onto the lawn and into the shadows, pressing his back against the wall of one of two large buildings that lay to his left. He slid along the wall until he came to the open space that separated it from the next building, and he peered around the corner.

Building 3C was in use.

He quickly traversed the open space to the next building and made his way along the wall to the far corner. Giving himself enough time to catch his breath, he finally eased forward enough to take a circumspect look at what was going on.

The effluent valve was turned on full, and whatever flowed from it spilled into the Saugeen River.

Anger swelled up in him.

He had worked the last 15 years to develop a new filtration system that screened out harmful pharmaceuticals from contaminating the water supply. His preoccupation with it had almost cost him his marriage. *Their careless indifference could jeopardize my project*, his mind screamed. *Goddamn them!*

He was about to step out to give them a piece of his mind, but he quickly pulled back and pressed hard against the wall, hoping that he had not been seen. A short, wiry individual with a ponytail stood on the loading dock with an automatic weapon while three other men loaded something from the building into a white van.

Edward reached for his cell phone to call security and the police, but it wasn't there; he had left it in his office. A surge of panic rippled up his spine as he turned and ran the distance back to the main building. He went into the main foyer to alert security and to get them to call the police, but he was shocked to find their desk was empty. The monitor that should have displayed Building 3C was blank.

When he lifted the phone to call out, the line was dead.

He looked around at the darkened offices, hoping that someone may have decided to work late, but he was quickly disappointed.

Only one elevator ran at this time, and it was on the top floor.

He started to head to the stairs when a sudden flash of movement at the front of KemKor caught his attention. A white van pulled sharply onto the main street from the side of the building, where the security hut was located, and sped past the building.

CHAPTER TWO

EDWARD LOOKED OUT ONTO the street below his office and chewed over the previous night's disquieting events around Building 3C. *What in god's name were they loading into that van?* he thought. *And why would they need automatic weapons?*

His eyes drifted along the main street to the intersection where his wife, Karen, died two years ago.

After returning to his desk, he hovered over it, his knuckles tapping on its surface as he remembered Constable Paul Dickenson's askance look and his not-too-subtle reference to the empty scotch glass and uncapped bottle on the credenza the previous evening.

It troubled him deeply, and it was then that he decided to keep a detailed diary of not only last evening's events but everything he learned or that happened to him until it got resolved—no matter how minuscule it might be.

"Shit!"

Deep down, he knew that Paul hadn't believed him. Paul had bought into the bit about one drink to settle the nerves after calling the police, but the smirk on Paul's face told him that he didn't believe that it was his only drink. He'd been barely able to restrain himself from taking Paul by the neck and throttling him, but he had relented and instead exhorted his innocence to Paul's unsavoury inference. "I took only one goddamn drink, taken after the fact, not before!"

Not surprisingly, Paul just lowered his eyes, continued to smile and nodded his head in that "Sure, I believe you" manner that meant he thought it was BS, and he had scribbled down something in his notebook.

It hadn't helped Edward's cause that not so much as a speck of evidence supported what he had seen last evening. In fact, according to Paul, Building 3C had been closed up tighter than a sardine can. That meant to Paul that there had been no break-in. Edward had also learned that Paul had tried to contact the CEO to obtain permission for entry, but his attempts had been fruitless because Rattray had turned off his cell phone. As it turned out, Rattray had travelled to Toronto to make arrangements for his brother's funeral and to visit with family.

Edward found having Norman Rattray's funeral in Toronto bizarre, because he had spent the better part of his life in West Grey. But he knew that Norman's friends probably wouldn't complain too much about travelling the two hours south to that sprawling megatropolis.

He shrugged off the thought as he walked to the table beside his office door and picked up the *West Grey Chronicle* that he had left there the evening before. He began to reread the article about Norman's death as he slowly made his way back to his desk and sat down. He opened the bottom drawer, placed his foot against its edge and began to rock back and forth, the paper lying across his lap.

His mind kept drifting back to last evening's events.

The guard at the gate house swore that only Edward had left and returned to the KemKor facility. His red Wrangler and license number had been dutifully recorded as leaving at 5:01 and returning at 6:09.

There's only one goddamn exit and entrance for vehicles coming and going, and that's through the gate house, he thought. *So how did the white van get in and out without being seen, except by me?*

He kicked the drawer shut with his foot and leaned forward in his chair.

Unless … the white van came in before the guard's shift, and the guard, for whatever reason, either was not there or was lying about it leaving. Still, Paul should have found at least one entry in the day shift's report, he thought. *Funny, there was no mention of that.*

"Both guards had to be in cahoots," he murmured under his breath.

He picked up his reading glasses from the desk, opened the newspaper to the second page and examined the pictures that went with the article on Norman. Other than Norman and William posing for the camera at the Canada Day celebrations at the Stoddard Fair Grounds in Priceville, there were two other photos. One showed John Elkhart, William Rattray and other administrative members standing in front of the ruins of Ritchie's Factory and Head Office eating clearly visible Ritchie's ice cream sandwiches. Norman stood off to the right of the group while, in the middle, William shook hands with a sombre-faced Gale Slaughter, vice president of Ritchie's. The other picture showed the ground-turning ceremony for KemKor Pharmaceuticals' Complex at the same site where Ritchie's used to be. There were four people in that picture: John Elkhart, William Rattray, company lawyer David DeLuca and Norman Rattray. Norman's eyes looked away from the camera and off to his left; he was the only one not smiling.

Sombre puss! They could have at least found a picture with the guy smiling, he thought. He looked at the photo again. *I wonder who captured his attention to plant such an expression on his face?*

There was a light knock at his door. After quickly closing the paper and folding it over, he dropped it beside his chair and placed his reading glasses on the desk. "Yes?"

His administrative assistant, Nadia Oiska, poked her head around the slightly ajar door. "Mr. Slocum?" she asked, seeking permission to enter.

Before Edward could reply, the door swung wide open, and she entered balancing an armful of binders and folders. Blowing aside wisps of blonde hair, her five-foot-two-and-a-half, petite frame figure quickly traversed the office to a small table beside Edward's desk, where she plunked her load down. After a few minutes of rearranging the material into folders and binders, she straightened her blouse, patted down her skirt and turned back toward the door.

"Hang on there! What's this?" Edward said as he pushed back his chair and grabbed his glasses, heading toward the mountain of material on the side table.

Nadia arrived just as Edward picked up one of the binders and inserted her face between his and the binder.

"Now, Eddy—I mean, Mr. Slocum—don't tell me you've forgotten? Two weeks of my life went into compiling this for today's meeting." Nadia stepped back and placed her hands at her hips, waiting for an answer.

"Oh—ah, I see. Thank you. It's just I don't think there'll be a meeting. You know, because of the recent death of Mr. Rattray's brother. Ah—you do know, don't you?"

"Of course I do. Everyone knows." She sighed deeply and clasped her hands in front of her. "You know, Mr. Slocum, he's the last person I would have thought would commit suicide." She drew her forefinger across the top binder on the table and looked up at him. "Everyone liked him. You'd have to be in a deeply sad place to blow your brains out like he did. To my knowledge, no one had a hint of him being in such dire straits emotionally."

"I want to show you something," Edward said as he rounded his desk and picked up the newspaper. "Do you know anything about these two pictures?" he asked.

Nadia took the paper from him and spread it across the top of the binders and folders. She bent down to get a closer look. "He sure doesn't look happy in any of them. I'd guess these two were taken … what, ten years ago?" Nadia said, looking up at him.

"You know anything about them?"

She smiled at him as she straightened up. "Are you kidding? I was a teenager back then. My only interests were boys, partying and sports. But, I'd bet Shirley Cooper would know. I think she still works for the *Chronicle* in the archives section." The *West Grey Chronicle* was often referred to lovingly by many in the region as just the *Chronicle*.

"I'll do just that," Edward said.

"I ordered the flowers for your wife's gravesite. You can pick them up at the flower boutique before you head home."

He quietly thanked her, and for a brief moment silence reigned between them.

To break the silence, Edward asked, "Oh, by the way, how's your stepsister?"

"Charlotte's doing just fine. You know, Edward, she wouldn't bite you if you decided to drop by. Should I tell her you asked for her?"

Charlotte Bradley had been Edward's first love. There was a time they thought their love would last forever. That all changed when they went off to university.

"I know she wouldn't bite me. It's just that … sure, if you'd like." He pointed to the binder he was perusing: "You've done a great job here, Nadia. Meeting or no meeting though, I should get working on it."

Nadia pointed at the newspaper across the binders. "Should I take it away?"

"No—just place it on the table by the door. If I have time later, I'll drop by the *Chronicle* for a chat. It might be helpful if I brought it with me. Thank you."

Nadia was closing the door behind her when Edward called out. "Nadia?"

She poked her head around the door. Edward waved at her to come back in and to close the door behind her. He put down the binder he had been perusing and came around the desk. "I guess you've heard about last night and the break-in at Building 3C?"

She looked away from him and down to the floor.

"Yes—there are rumours floating around about the alleged break-in," she replied.

"What kind of rumours?"

"Just rumours—nothing more, nothing that's worth repeating." She barely raised her head to look at him. "I guess you know that Constable Dickenson was in to see Mr. Elkhart this morning?"

"No, I didn't." He made a mental note to ask John about it. John Elkhart and Edward had been friends since they'd met at the University of Waterloo. "I wonder if I can ask a big favour?"

"Tell me what it is, and I'll decide," replied Nadia.

"Before I ask it, I wonder if you've heard anything about the readiness of Building 3C?"

Nadia stepped back a couple of paces and looked Edward straight in the face. "Why would I know anything about that?"

"I just wondered since I've seen you having lunch with Lola Albright."

A broad grin creased Nadia's face. "Edward, Mr. Elkhart's administrative assistant and I never talk about any business associated with KemKor during lunch or at any off-hour events. None of us do. It's our golden rule." She crossed her arms and asked, "Now that that's out of the way, what is this favour you want from me?"

"I wonder if you would check something for me in accounting."

Nadia's arms across her chest closed tighter. "Accounting? Sorta out of my mandate, don't you think? Wouldn't it be better if you did that? You do carry a lot more clout than me."

"After last night, I think it's best that I keep a low profile here. I think you know what I'm getting at." He raised his eyebrows and added, "Rumours."

Nadia sighed and dropped her arms to her sides. "What am I looking for in accounting?"

"That's my problem—I'm not quite sure." He began to pace back and forth. "Building 3C would be a good starting point—and anything that might remotely justify last night. Nothing more."

Reflexively, her hand slid across the back of her neck. "Nothing more? That phrase by itself makes the hair on the back of my neck stand up, since it usually means just the opposite—namely, a pack of trouble."

"If that means you won't do it, I understand."

"I didn't say that. I'm just thinking." She walked toward the door, stopped and turned to find Edward looking out the window.

"What should I say if accounting asks me why I'm there?"

"I'll leave that to your wonderfully creative mind."

"I'm not sure this is a wise decision by either of us, but I'll give it try. Mr. Slocum?"

"Uh-huh?"

"Don't forget to pick up the flowers."

As the door to his office closed softly behind him, Edward's eyes drifted back to the intersection of Main and Toronto Street.

The last thing Karen had to have heard was metal hitting metal, he thought in anguish. *And the baby! God! How could I have not known she was pregnant?*

CHAPTER THREE

EDWARD ROLLED HIS CHAIR out from behind his desk and over to the pile of binders and folders that Nadia had left earlier. On top of the folders was a large plastic envelope, and he wondered how he'd missed it earlier. Other than his name and KemKor's address, there was nothing on the envelope to indicate who the sender was.

Anonymity, at least for the time being, is essential to our arrangement, my friend, he reflected.

Seeing the envelope lying there provided him a smidgen of joy. He had waited five months to receive the contents.

He lifted the envelope up and opened it. The summary report and testing results by Grynberg Laboratories and Research Facility of Brampton for one of the small filtering devices to be used in his system spilled out in front of him.

His eyes ingested their title covers and he sighed satisfyingly. *One more to come,* he thought, *and all stages will be finished.*

Testing for each of the five critical stages of his invention had been entrusted to this Brampton Facility for no other reason than he had had a trusted relationship with its owner, Irving Grynberg, since childhood.

He questioned how much longer the CEO would let him dance around without handing over the patents. *No one bankrolls something like this without expecting substantial rewards,* he reminded himself.

"Too much of my damn life has been invested in this to let it fall into somebody else's hands without a fight," he mumbled under his breath.

His delay tactics were wearing thin with KemKor's CEO. Still—and this was his ace in the hole— he had assured himself that his relationship with Grynberg Laboratories was safely under KemKor's radar.

Retrieving a legal-sized pad of paper from the side drawer, he opened the summary report and was about to read through it when the phone rang. It was Natasha Whitfield, William Rattray's administrative assistant, calling to inform him that the meeting was still on for three o'clock. Edward expressed his surprise in light of her boss's recent loss, but Natasha remained noncommittal through her silence. He thanked her and hung up.

Damn! The only good part of the day just evaporated!

He put Grynberg's results back into the envelope

Exhausted from last night's trauma and a lack of sleep over the last couple of days, he wished he could have canceled the day outright.

He threw the envelope into the open briefcase on the credenza behind him and turned to face the wall of windows. After standing up from his chair, he walked over to the window. A young couple holding hands walked toward the intersection, and his eyes followed them. The light turned green, and they walked across the street. His eyes never left them until they vanished from his view.

Two years ago today, Karen's car had been T-boned by an oncoming truck at the same intersection the young couple had just crossed. She had died instantly. Two days after the autopsy report, he had learned that she had been pregnant. Five days later he had buried them in the same plot in St. James Anglican Cemetery in Priceville.

"Why didn't I know you were pregnant? Why?" he said aloud. He turned away from the window and looked at her picture in the tabletop frame on his desk.

"Were you hiding it from me?" He walked over to his desk and picked up the picture. "Where were you going to or coming from, so late that evening?" he asked before returning the frame to its place on his desk.

His shoulders slumped in despair with the knowledge that the likelihood of answers to any of his questions were next to impossible.

Retrieving the Grynberg Laboratories envelope from his briefcase, he sat down, moved his chair closer to his desk and pulled out the summary and statistical reports. He glanced at his watch; he still had four hours before the meeting of which he wanted no part.

His mind continued to bounce between Karen's death and last evening's events.

After several false starts, an hour and a half later he rocked gently to and fro in his chair, satisfied with accomplishing something—namely, finishing Grynberg's summary report on his filtering device. He had written a number of notes in the report's margins, and not only had he managed to fill three pages in his legal-sized notepad with more detailed comments and questions, but he had cross-referenced them with Grynberg's testing results.

His momentary respite from thoughts that wrapped around Karen and last evening's emotional roller-coaster ride came to an abrupt end, and he felt raw anger.

He had already dismissed from his thoughts Paul's reaction—he may have read too much into it—and the armed men he saw on Building 3C's dock, because at the moment he couldn't prove it. Yet the residue from around the effluent tap and its waste that flowed into the Saugeen River were a different matter because they had the possibility of being proven. He knew it was a stretch, but at the very least, he had to give it a try. With his credibility on the line, he committed to finding proof, even if it meant following this long shot.

When the phone on his desk rang, he picked up the receiver.

John Elkhart, the senior executive vice president, was on the other end. "Good morning, Eddy." John had called Edward "Eddy" shortly after they met at university. Edward preferred to be called "Edward," but he had never corrected John. "Is everything a go for today's meeting?" John asked. "You do know it's on, don't you?"

Edward rocked gently in his chair. "Natasha called to inform me." He picked up his pen and began to doodle on the pad beside him.

"You don't have to sound so excited about it. Your enthusiasm would deaden a wake, Eddy."

It had been John who had convinced him to accept the senior engineering position and vice presidency at KemKor Pharmaceuticals. His decision to return to Grey County with Karen had been more a need than a want.

"Tell me something, John: why the need for this meeting today? I'm sure it could have waited until next week. My god! He's just lost his brother."

"I can't answer for the big guy, except to say he wasn't that close to him."

"Has that always been the case?"

"Why are you asking?" John asked.

"No reason. Just curious."

"I do remember there was a big fall-out between them around the time KemKor acquired this site from Ritchie's."

"Do you have any idea what it was over?"

"Not a clue. Anyway, let's get back to why I called you. Did Natasha send the new agenda over to you?"

Edward stopped rocking his chair and sat forward. He pulled out the agenda from his side drawer and placed it in front of him. "No. Why would she? Isn't it the same as the one I received last week?"

"Eh—well, not really. In fact, Eddy, not at all."

"Not at all? In what way has it changed?" He sketched the outline of a truck on his pad as he waited for the answer.

"Are you okay, Eddy? You don't sound so great."

"No, I'm not okay. But, that's beside the point. The agenda?"

"Is there anything I can do?"

"Actually, there is. Paul Dickenson met with you this morning. Did he have anything new to add to last night's events?"

"New? I wouldn't know anything about that. He just went over what he had gathered so far, asked a few questions and left."

"What kinds of questions?"

During the ensuing silence, Edward sketched the face of a woman with large, bright eyes and long, flowing hair below the truck's outline. Then he sat back in his chair and swirled about to face the window and the cloudless, azure sky.

"I don't remember, Eddy," John replied, clearing his throat. "Let's get back to the agenda. Your filtering system would be a boon to this company, and—if you remember at the time of hiring—there was a clear expectation that all the rights would be signed over to KemKor upon successful completion and testing of the system."

"Where are you going with this, John?"

"I'm just reminding you."

"So what does this have to do with the agenda?"

"Bill 54."

Bill 54 was a landmark piece of environmental legislation awaiting third reading before becoming law. One section in the bill addressed the growing concerns about the cocktail of pharmaceutical-related contaminants in drinking water and their harmful effects on the population. If Edward's filtering system delivered on its promises, then the owner was poised to receive a substantial financial windfall.

"A lot of money has been spent putting a multitude of resources at your doorstep, Eddy. A lot more is needed to make it happen. Don't forget Rattray's making it all come together. So don't be too critical of our CEO's small oversights."

"Small oversights? What are you getting at John?" Edward angrily wrote the number 10 across the truck sketched on the pad and circled it heavily several times.

"Premier Bolsover and his cabinet will meet with our board and executive management today at three. They want to learn about your system. Now, don't tell me that you're not up to it."

"Let's just back up a bit, here. Bolsover and his cabinet want to learn about my system? With what purpose in mind?"

"I can't speak for them, but my sources tell me they want to make that system of yours the standard across Ontario—and who knows, maybe across North America and beyond. Rattray's pushing the envelope, Eddy. I know he can be a pain in the ass, but patience isn't his long suit. You'll get use to him once you've worked with him as long as I have."

"I'm not sure I want to get use to him. When is he going to begin formal negotiations with me? He has told Bolsover that KemKor doesn't own the rights, hasn't he?"

"I don't know what's been said, Eddy. Maybe we'll learn at the meeting. But as you know, those rights do fall to KemKor next Monday."

"Anything else?" he asked, pushing the pad he had been scribbling on to one side.

"No, I think that's about it. You'll be at Rattray's on Saturday for Blackwell's launch?"

Charles "Chuck" Blackwell had been the author of Bill 54 and was launching his bid to become the next premier of Ontario on Rattray's estate.

Edward replied, "I'm part of that program. Remember? I'm introducing him. Now, I can't very well miss that, can I?"

"I'd forgotten," John said with a chuckle. "Well, I'd better go. See you at three."

When John hung up after talking with Edward, he noticed the light blinking on the other line.

"John Elkhart here."

"Well, did you talk to him?" asked Chris Stedman, KemKor's manager of security services.

"Not yet. Are you sure he didn't see you?"

"Unless he's got eyes in the back of his head, yes, I'm sure. What did Paul have to say?"

"He reported what Edward said he saw, and then he added a surprising conclusion."

"And what was that?"

"He wasn't sure anyone would believe Edward." He played with the letter opener on his desk. Edward had given that letter opener to John as a gift for Christmas.

"Now that's a surprise. Did he say why?"

"If you remember from your report on Edward, at one time he had a drinking problem. Well, it seems he was drinking the previous evening."

John began to tap the point of the letter opener on his desk.

"I see. That can be useful. Regardless, we'd better keep an eye on him."

"I'll take care of my part here. Just take care of yours." He placed the letter opener down. "I sure wish I knew Eddy's next step."

"Hmm, I hear you," Chris replied. "I'll be his invisible shadow."

"Not too close, or he'll get suspicious. In the meantime, I'll try to learn what I can."

John's administrative assistant, Lola Albright, entered the room with the files he had asked for earlier.

"Keep in touch," he said to Chris before he hung up.

Exhausted, Edward went to the washroom to splash some cold water on his face. Feeling somewhat refreshed, he returned to his office and put on a clean shirt and tie. Then he settled in behind his desk and let out a long sigh. His eye caught the pad that he had been scribbling on, and he pulled it out and looked at it.

"My god! How did I do …?"

Overcome with emotion, his question trailed off to incompletion.

He had unconsciously drawn a picture of his wife and the truck that had taken her life two years ago. When Nadia entered the room, he was barely aware of her presence as she told him that he had only five minutes until his meeting in the boardroom.

CHAPTER FOUR

AFTER THE BOARD MEETING, as he mingled among KemKor's representatives and government officials—Premier Bolsover having already left—Edward couldn't help thinking that the accolades being showered on him were somewhat premature; the efficacy of his new filtering system was still untested on a large scale. Experience told him that start-up costs always exceeded projections, and he had no doubt that his system, by the time it was up and running, would be no exception.

Yet right or not, the mixed message sent by his accidental observation at Building 3C last evening had left Edward distrustful of the company's intentions.

Edward's attention was drawn to the bombastic voice of the CEO, William Wardlaw Rattray, who had conspicuously positioned himself apart from the group.

William Rattray was a short, plumpish, full-faced individual who had a full crop of wavy red hair sitting atop it. His face and neck had a tendency to redden whenever excited, and this was one such occasion. He was impeccably dressed in a navy-blue suit, white shirt, red tie and cognac-coloured, leather-laced shoes. On his lapel was an 18-karat gold pin with both the Canadian and Ontario flags on it.

"Gentlemen!" Rattray exclaimed, smiling and bowing in deference to the only female member present, Marilyn Ferguson, who stood slightly off to his left. "And, lady!" He redirected his attention to the group in front of him and continued. "This day heralds a new horizon for KemKor Pharmaceuticals and cannot go unrecognized without champagne and some mignardises. Once my assistant, Jeremy, arrives, I shall begin."

As if on cue, the door at the far corner of the room opened, and Jeremy Brown, a short, trim, middle-aged, balding man, wheeled in a cart. Behind him, a young girl pushed a cart filled with three trays of petit fours, which she placed on the conference table as directed by Jeremy. Once done, she and the cart left immediately. Jeremy took the two large ice buckets filled with ice, each containing two opened bottles of Veuve Clicquot Ponsardin Brut from the top shelf of his cart, and he placed them a short distance from the bite-size dessert trays. After retrieving the champagne glasses from their bottom location, he placed them beside the ice buckets except for three sterling silver flutes, which he placed on a small circular tray. He poured champagne into each silver flute and, picking up the tray, he delivered each personally to the CEO, Edward, and John, in that order. Jeremy then returned to the table and indicated for the others to join in.

Shortly after, with filled champagne glasses in-hand, they formed around Rattray in a horseshoe configuration. Edward stood at the edge of its opening while, to his right, John Elkhart had already edged back into the group and was whispering something into Marilyn Ferguson's ear. Once Jeremy picked up the remaining champagne glass, William Rattray began.

"One of my greatest pleasures, Edward," he said, turning to face him, "was to see the incredible success you have achieved—and, by association, the benefits our company has accrued because of it. On behalf of all of us, may I say that your ethos, training and methodology have come together today to bring us to this highly favourable crossroad. Thank you!"

A crescendo of cheers and clapping filled the room.

Once the salutatory praise ceased, Rattray raised his glass and gave a short poem.

"Here's to you, Edward, as good as you are,
And here's to me, as bad as I am;
But, as good as you are, and as bad as I am,
I am as good as you are, as bad as I am."

Laughter echoed throughout the room as the participants raised their glasses, clinked them together and quickly emptied them.

Unaccustomed to such notoriety, Edward felt a warm flush bathe his face. With a slightly shy stance, he raised his flute in gratitude and quickly thanked them, and then watched as many stampeded back for more champagne.

Rattray gave his special engraved champagne flute to Jeremy, and he walked back toward Edward. "You should be very pleased with yourself, Edward, notwithstanding, of course, that it was I who made it happen through my status, my contacts and my money. But you already know that. Putting that aside for the moment, your presentation knocked their socks off. You have arrived. Hmm?"

"Arrived?"

"Yes, my boy! You may now eat the crumbs off *my* table. And, that is a feat in itself. Most are not good enough," he said, extending his hand.

Edward smiled and took it. "I'm not sure I understand, sir."

"You will. Your preparedness and presentation for today's meeting, I deem most laudatory. I can see you are puzzled by that statement." Rattray released his hand from Edward's grip and moved closer. "You see, Edward, after last evening's … unfortunate events, I expected—how should I say it?—a performance on your part far less than I got. You were able to separate the baggage of last evening from the task at hand, and that trait I respect highly." He placed his hand on Edward's shoulder. "I know you want to talk about last evening, and we shall—just not now. Now, what I *do* look forward to is working closer with you."

Rattray signalled to Jeremy to retrieve Edward's flute, and once done, Rattray and Edward headed through the doors of the boardroom and out into the quiet solitude of the hall, where Rattray turned to face him. "It's time I rolled my sleeves up and got more involved in your project, Edward. Get my hands dirty, so to speak," he said, smiling. He took on a more sober façade before continuing. "Firstly, we shall talk directly—not through Elkhart or meetings similar to this. Like you, Elkhart is very thorough. It's always reassuring, though, when it comes from the horse's own mouth, don't you think?" Rattray stepped closer. Edward tried to step back, but because his back was already against a circular support post, he was unable to.

Rattray briefly rubbed his hands together in a washing motion. "Secondly, to make this happen, next Wednesday report directly to me at nine in the morning. I'll set aside an hour—more, if it's deemed necessary. And John, as my liaison and your project manager, will also be present. The frequency of such meetings will be decided then. From time to time, schedules *will* conflict, but flexibility must reign. Bottom line: our filtration system must be fully functional in Building 3C sooner, not later."

Edward looked down the barrels of Rattray's grey steely eyes and knew he had to acquiesce. "I agree. Our efforts must be stepped up. But at the moment, I have no idea whether the settling pool or run-off piping and valves are installed yet. Assuming nothing unforeseen occurs, prototypes of the five filters and their respective components should be in place once Building 3C is ready to receive them. But I need a final timetable to ensure a smooth run up to that eventuality, and John hasn't provided me with one yet—I'm working in the dark."

"Your component completion estimates were sent to him, and you've spoken to him?"

"I have, and he does have my specs and dates."

"Hmm, I see. Surely the two of you, being friends, can resolve this? Eh?"

Edward nodded.

"So, I assume you want to scrap my earlier suggestions?" Rattray rejoined.

"Not at all," Edward quickly retorted. "I'm suggesting daily, real-time reports during the actual testing mode. That's when it counts most, when everything's in place. It allows us to interpolate the results and extrapolate actual start-up time."

"Hmm, okay. Still, based on what you've just told me, the three of us will meet next Wednesday. At that time, the timetable will be resolved and in my hands. Natasha will call you with the time. The retrofitting of Building 3C has been much slower than I expected, and as of today, that must change." A wide smile crossed Rattray's face. "Once you're up and running, I'll want the results and your personal appraisals to come directly to me. Any meetings needed to apprise pertinent others will be left to your discretion, in consultation with me."

Edward nodded his agreement and shook hands with Rattray to cement it, uncertain what exactly that handshake really meant. "I was very sorry to hear about your brother," he said.

"Thank you. You know, Edward, only the strong survive life's nasty twists." Rattray began to play with the diamond ring on his pinkie. "I guess my brother wasn't among the strong."

Edward said, "He will be missed."

"I've been told."

Rattray looked back toward the doors to the boardroom.

"When's the visitation and funeral?" Edward asked. He slid around the support pole and stepped to one side to lengthen the distance between them.

"The visitation will be tomorrow, and the funeral is on Friday. I'll have Natasha fill you in with the particulars. It will be published in tonight's *Chronicle* and all the major newspapers."

"By the way, thank you for that toast, Mr. Rattray. It was ... quite different."

"It was an old Scottish toast."

When Jeremy Brown joined them, Edward thought the conversation had ended—until Rattray sent Jeremy to the elevator and told him to hold it.

"Edward, the R & D of your project has, for the most part, been outside this company's auspices. Sure, we've freed up your time to solely concentrate on it, and we've provided you with the site to test it, but outside of that, that's it. The rider in your contract with KemKor governing the ownership of patents is time specific, and that time, as I'm sure you are aware, is about to expire. I don't know of any other company that would have agreed to the inclusion of such a rider. Needless to say, a number of our key benefactors have voiced concerns. Now, I hope my trust wasn't misplaced. Before you came to KemKor, I understood that some of the developmental stages were being handled by Grynberg Laboratories and Research Facility. Is that still the case?"

Edward was taken aback. He'd thought this was a closely guarded secret.

"No need to answer," Rattray continued. "Your expression gave it away. See David DeLuca in Legal first thing Monday morning; he will be expecting you. Keeping abreast of such things is important to all of us, as I'm sure you are aware." The CEO patted him on the arm and said, "Again, Edward, job well done today! My filters are in good hands."

Rattray then left to join Jeremy at the elevator. As the elevator's doors began to close, Rattray yelled out to Edward. "See DeLuca first thing Monday morning, and no excuses."

Edward drew in a deep breath, and when he saw John come out of the boardroom, he looked at his watch again. He needed to talk to him, and he also wanted to obtain scraping samples from the effluent tap. Convinced he still had enough time to pick up the flowers at the flower boutique for Karen's gravesite, he waited for John to come over.

John Elkhart stood talking with Marilyn Ferguson. Her auburn hair was combed back into a bun, and she was dressed in a pin-striped grey business suit. Her meteoric climb to success had garnered much interest in the business community. She did not suffer fools well, but she was known to be as straight as they came.

Marilyn's eyes kept drifting back to Edward as she and John spoke.

When the elevator doors opened, she shook hands with John and ran toward the waiting elevator, nodding and silently mouthing congratulations to Edward as she passed by him.

When the elevator doors closed, John headed toward him. "Well done in there today, Eddy! Well done!" John exuded youthfulness in his gait. He had a swath of curly blond hair, and his large blue eyes shone with delight as he gave Edward congratulatory pats. "You won that old buzzard of a premier over. Only one way to go now, and that's up!" He stood back and surveyed Edward. "Now tell me, what did our CEO have to tell you? I'd bet after today, he's prepared to give you the whole damn world. Well, am I right?"

"Not exactly, John." Edward stepped back from him as the doors to the boardroom flung open and the rest of the people in the meeting spilled out into the hall. He looked at his watch.

"Is there something wrong?" John asked.

"Karen," replied Edward in a soft voice. He looked at his watch again. "We really should talk, John. I just don't have a lot of time."

"Oh! How could I have forgotten? It was two years ago today, wasn't it."

Edward nodded.

"Yes, of course. I should have ... I'm sorry," John said. "Your office or mine?"

"Mine."

The two of them walked down the hall toward Edward's office. Edward closed the door behind him.

"Johnny Walker Blue okay with you, John?"

John had wandered over to Edward's desk. "You need to ask?" John replied, running his finger along the desk's edge. "That will do just fine."

"Single ice, isn't it?" Edward asked, sliding the pocket door open and entering the room behind it.

"You got it, Buddy."

John lifted the picture of Karen on the desk, sighing as he looked at it.

"Sit in one of those wing chairs; I'll be out in a jiffy," Edward called out.

John put the picture of Karen down and casually wandered to the book shelves lining the wall beside the area Edward designated. He was perusing the book *The Morbid Age: Britain between the Wars* when Edward returned with the drinks.

"I didn't know you were a history buff, Eddy," John said. He restored the book to its proper place on the shelf and turned to face Edward.

"I'm not really. That particular book just caught my interest," Edward replied. He walked toward John with their drinks and, handing him his, he motioned for him to sit down.

They sat in silence drinking until John leaned toward Edward. "Look, Eddy, I'm really sorry."

"So am I." Edward swallowed the rest of his drink. "You want more?"

John looked at his glass and then looked up at Edward, who was already standing. "Not right at this moment. Go easy on that stuff."

"Not to worry. What do you say I bring the bottle back and park it between us?"

"Sure, if that's what you'd like."

With the Johnny Walker Blue between them, Edward looked at his watch, poured a small second drink and shifted toward the edge of his chair. "You spoke with Paul."

"I did."

"Look, John, I wasn't drinking that evening, except for the one after I called the police. I saw what I saw. It wasn't some goddamn drunken stupor of a dream. It happened!"

John said, "Stop beating yourself up—I believe you. I told Paul that as well."

"Thank you." Edward edged forward on the wing chair. "What's next?"

John savoured his next drink and sat back, looking at Edward. "Well, Building 3C will have to be tested for residue. Our lab will do that. I told Paul that if we came up with something, that information would be passed on to him." He placed his glass on the table beside him. "You do know, Eddy, what you said you saw last evening sounds ... well, way out there."

"Do you think I don't know that? Isn't that the problem for me?"

"Yes, I guess it is. I just hope that something shows up when our lab people go in to test."

"Do you think I don't?" Edward finished his drink and placed it on the table between them. "What do you know about Building 3C?"

"Same as you," John replied, shrugging his shoulders. "Why?" He got up, glass in hand, and crossed the room to one of the leather chairs, sitting down to face Edward.

"Is Building 3C anywhere near functional?" Edward asked, sitting back in his chair.

"If it is, that's news to me."

"How much longer?"

"Three months, max, provided your final filter is ready for testing."

As John sipped his drink, he watched Edward over the brim of his glass.

"The filter will be ready," Edward reassured him. "What about the timetable you promised? It's been long in coming."

"I know—sorry about that. It will be in your hands by the end of this week. Promise."

"I've been wondering since last evening what those men were transporting to the van. You wouldn't have any suggestions, would you?"

John shrugged and replied, "You're asking me? How the hell would I know? What colour was the van?"

"White."

John gulped his drink down, got up and went to Edward's desk. He placed the empty glass on it, picked up the phone and punched in four digits. "Chris? No, I want to speak to Chris Stedman." He played with the letter opener while he waited. "Chris, John Elkhart here. I'm sorry to bother you, but I'd like you to review the surveillance tapes between nine and eleven yesterday evening. I'm looking for a white van leaving the grounds." John looked back to Edward for confirmation and, getting it, continued. "I'm also looking for any irregularities, small or great, around Building 3C."

While listening intently, John turned back to Edward, placing his hand securely over the mouthpiece to muffle their conversation. "The cameras in the Building 3C area have never been functional. According to Chris, Rattray told security not to waste their time on a non-active area."

"You've got to be kidding," retorted Edward, exasperated.

"Activate those cameras around Building 3C immediately. Again, check your tapes for a white tradesmen van that might have come onto the grounds sometime yesterday and left during the time frame I just gave you. I'm heading back to my office. Phone me there."

John hung up the phone and turned to Edward.

"Well, I guess we'll wait and see. Is there anything else before I head off? You do know that Rattray won't want the police on this unless there's something solidly definitive."

Edward sighed deeply as he walked over to John. "I know," he said, looking at his watch.

"You appear to be in deep thought. What's up?" John asked.

"It's getting late. I've got flowers still to pick up."

"For ...?

"Yes." Edward raised his head to face John. "There is one other thing, though. The effluent taps were on full. Whatever they were dumping, I'd imagine there should still be residue."

"I'll tell Stedman to check it out personally. Our lab folks and security will take care of the rest. Anything else?"

"I'm going to check downstream from the dump site."

"Our lab people can do that."

"I know that—but I'll get samples nevertheless. It might be a good cross-check with our lab's results."

"Who's going to check your results?" John said.

"An independent lab."

"Ooo, sounds mysterious. Anyway, I've got enough here to keep me busy. I'll phone you if I get anything."

Fifteen minutes later, Edward was scraping samples from Building 3C's effluent taps into small envelopes. Neither security nor the lab had arrived at the site yet. He made a mental note to obtain the keys to Building 3C from security. As he headed back to the main building, he looked up.

Damn! The security cameras are still not activated, he quietly observed.

CHAPTER FIVE

EDWARD WALKED ACROSS THE parking lot trying to juggle the rolled-up *Chronicle* and flowers in one arm, and his briefcase and a package of baby bottles in the other. He smelled the medley of flowers that Nadia had ordered for him from the boutique and was pleased with her choice.

Before leaving KemKor, he had called Grynberg Laboratories and spoken to Irving about the viability of his idea of collecting downstream samples; he told him that he already had effluent scrapings. Irving told him that he held out greater hope for substance identification from the scrapings than from any water samples, but he added that if Edward insisted on water samples, they must be taken no later than today. He suggested that baby bottles would be excellent sample collectors for the job. Throughout their conversation, Irving repeated several times that he didn't hold out much hope for the water samples. Edward had listened patiently to Irving, thanked him and politely hung up. Believing in the long shot, Edward went ahead and bought the baby bottles anyway.

He opened the door to his Wrangler and placed his briefcase and package of bottles on the backseat. Before closing the door, his attention was briefly fixed on the package of baby bottles, and he wondered what it would have been like to be a father. Just as quickly, he pushed that out of his mind as he shut the door, went around to the driver's side and climbed in, carefully placing the flowers beside him along with the newspaper containing the photos he was interested in learning more about. He had already decided that his visitation to the *Chronicle* would have to wait until later this week or next.

Looking back at the KemKor building, he put his key into the ignition and started his vehicle.

John Elkhart had phoned just before Edward had left his office. According to John, the lab technicians had already taken samples from the effluent taps, and Chris Stedman had reconnoitered Building 3C, both outside and inside, and had found nothing out of the ordinary. When Edward had asked John when the surveillance cameras around Building 3C had been activated, he had been told that it had occurred shortly after they last spoke. Edward had found that answer more than a little disconcerting, since 15 to 20 minutes after they had last spoken, the cameras had still been down. To Edward, it was starting to sound as phoney as John's dyed blond hair. None of it made sense to him since, within the time frame John had told him, he should have passed Stedman and the technicians when he had headed back to his office with his effluent scrapings.

Edward popped in the CD *Body and Soul* and drove out of the parking lot and past the guardhouse, turning sharply onto Main Street. The classic voice of Tony Bennett in duet with Amy Winehouse filled the Wrangler, and it softened the hardship of his day, if only slightly.

The traffic lights ahead turned red, and he came to a stop. Until a month ago there was only one set of lights in Markdale, at the intersection of Main and Toronto Streets. Then City Council decided there was a need for this second set and, it seemed, and no matter the time of day, he always got the damn red light; today was no exception. Casually he looked around, impatiently drumming his fingers on the steering wheel, waiting for this interminably time-wasting traffic light to turn green. He was distracted by the sales advertisement on the Home Hardware window when a loud pounding sound on his hood startled him. The McAlistair brood of two boys and four girls were peering back at him, making an assortment of contorted faces while using the hood of his vehicle as a set of bongo drums. Their mother, Susan, tried with some difficulty to shoo them off. She was the same age as Edward. Her auburn, shoulder-length hair and contoured clothing made her look stunning and youthful.

Though crying on the inside, he mustered up a smile. Karen and Susan had been close friends, and he felt obligated to put up a good front.

He rolled down his window and called out to her. "Hey, Susan! What have those sweet muffins of yours got you roped into now?"

Emma, Susan's youngest, turned and stuck her tongue out at Edward and began to giggle. The others joined in.

The mirth in this moment momentarily assuaged Edward's troubled thoughts, and he joined in by sticking his thumbs in his ears and wagging his hands, emulating their gestures.

"Survival, Eddy," Susan called back, pointing to the Ritchie's ice cream sign in the window of Sweets 'n' Stuff, which had been designed to look like a late-19th-century ice cream parlour. "When are you comin' over?" she asked as she busily ensured her children reached the sidewalk safely. "Mo and I haven't seen ya for a while. You haven't forgotten about that horse, have ya?" Mo was the abbreviated name she called her husband, Morris.

Actually, he had forgotten. Two weeks ago, he had promised to stop by to look at a horse they had for sale. "Of course I haven't forgotten! I'll phone you early next week."

"Eddy, are you okay? I know today can't be easy for you ..." Edward shrugged and temporarily looked away. "Why don't you drop by for supper tonight? We haven't seen you for a while, and it would do Mo good to have ya around."

"Let me take a rain check on that, Susan. But I will drop by soon."

"Okay, Eddy, I understand."

"I'd better get movin'," he yelled back, pointing at the light, which had just turned green.

He continued along Main Street toward Barr Road and home. He glanced into his rear-view mirror and smiled as the last McAlistair child entered Sweets 'n' Stuff, followed by Susan. His hand reached out to the flowers beside him as he passed by the Barrhead Sports Bar and Grill tucked away at the bend of the Barr Road. It had been a location he and Karen had frequented most Friday nights shortly after he took the position at KemKor.

Rolling hills and thirsty acres of farmland filled his route in a dusty grey hue. Pesky twitch grass and weeds, the only green vegetation, flourished.

The tall grass at the side of the road suddenly parted, and a groundhog scurried across in front of him. Edward hit his brakes and swerved his

Wrangler to miss it, causing the vehicle to fishtail on the gravel before coming to a stop. While catching his breath, he watched the groundhog scurry unharmed into the opposing ditch before disappearing into its burrow at the base of an old, dead maple tree.

Placing his car in park, he rested his arms across the steering wheel and stared out the window, tears streaming down his cheeks.

In a mangled heap, lying on the floor, were the flowers he had bought for Karen's gravesite.

CHAPTER SIX

AN HOUR LATER, AFTER visiting Karen's gravesite, Edward turned into his drive, passing the Pine Meadows sign he and Karen had made shortly after they had bought this property. The wooden sign showed an unusual rate of weathering; paint had blistered like tiny teardrops across its surface. Rail fencing, five rails high, lined the front of the property and along one side of the driveway. In front of the fencing, pine and cedar trees led the way to his home.

He parked his vehicle beside the walkway to his house and opened the car door. After swinging his feet around to get out, he decided instead to sit there for a moment, deeply breathing in the welcoming warm scent of cedar and pine.

When Edward finally exited, his gaze, as always, skirted the treed boundary of his hundred-acre farm. He still had to pinch himself in disbelief that he and Karen owned this majestic property. It was a dream they'd never thought would happen. Karen had loved to entertain, and their first summer had been filled with parties here.

He noticed there were only two of his horses in the side field—a good indication that Camilo and Andres Green were probably with the other two horses in the Cover-All, back of the barn.

For a small fee, the two brothers had been exercising his horses since he and Karen had moved here. He remembered the day well when Josh and his wife, Marta, had dropped by with their two boys to welcome them to the neighbourhood. They brought a basket of homemade preserves, assorted jars of homemade pickled vegetables from their own garden, homemade blueberry pie and four bottles of homemade red and white wine. After much coaxing from Karen and him, the Greens had finally given in and stayed for supper. From that day forward he and Karen had grown fond of the brothers. He had grown especially fond of the younger one, Andres.

Edward closed the car door and walked toward the barn.

For a time after Karen's death, there had been awkwardness between him and the Greens, since it had been one of Josh's trucks that had T-boned Karen, causing her death. The driver, Steve Armor, had been cleared of criminal negligence, and after a mechanical inspection of his truck by the Ministry of Transport, Green's Egg Products had been exonerated. Based on the police report, the judge had concluded that Karen had entered the intersection at Toronto and Main against a red light, thereby precipitating the accident that had led to her death—and the death of their unborn child. The only witness to the accident, Chris Stedman, the head of security at KemKor, had been unequivocal in his dissertation. "There were no other vehicles at that intersection other than the truck and her car." At that point, the verdict was read and the file closed.

Edward never understood why she was out so late that evening. When he had spoken to her earlier that day from the Canadian Standards Association Conference in Toronto, she had told him that she was up to her neck in work, trying to meet a deadline for her drawings, and she expected to be up working on them when he got home.

He remembered the day when Karen had been offered the contract by Terri Elkhart, John's wife, to be an illustrator for the prestigious Toronto marketing company of Moyer-Hayes & Roussel. She had been so excited. That evening Edward and she had celebrated with the Elkharts, McAlistairs and Blackwells at Steven's Restaurant in Markdale.

Sighing deeply, Edward noticed that a number of the boards on the 35 by 55–foot timber-framed barn were either missing or in need of replacement—one of the many chores he had found some excuse to delay lately. As he entered the barn, he noted one of the fallen boards leaning against the wall. *Maybe, I'll put it up this weekend*, he thought.

He opened the door to the tack room at the far end of the barn and crossed the floor to the other door, entering the Cover-All.

He and Karen had decided to have this Cover-All built after visiting the Parelli Ranch in Pagosa Springs, Colorado, while on holidays. It was the best alternative to wooden- or metal-roofed arenas, which had a tendency to spook horses when rain pounded its roofing or snow slid off it. The 110 by 160–foot arena was bright and airy. Five-foot, high-tensile, metal-tube rail fencing separated him from the main arena. The gate leading to the stables was at the far end of the fencing.

Edward leaned over the rails and watched Camilo and Andres put his horses, Rosco and Tequila, through a series of jumps and manoeuvres at the far side of the arena. *Karen would have been pleased*, he reckoned. He imagined seeing Karen riding her horse, Tequila, and putting her through the same routine as Andres was doing right now.

As Camilo brought Rosco over the last jump, he cantered to the centre of the arena and then slowed Rosco to a walk, heading back toward the gate.

"Hola, Señor Slocum!"

"Hola, Camilo! I'll get the gate for you."

"Don't bother, Señor Slocum."

But Edward hadn't heard the reply and was already at the gate, unlatching it.

Camilo walked Rosco through the opening and dismounted. He was a confident young man, tall, lean and handsome. His jet-black hair fell across his olive skin face as he took off his helmet. Nodding at Edward without any further cordiality, Camilo led the horse down the hallway to the stables. Edward watched him disappear into the barn.

Why's he always so aloof? he reflected. *Doesn't he know he borders on rudeness and disrespect? Oh well—he's a damn good rider. If he only knew that's the only reason I keep him on—and because he's Andres's brother. I should be thankful; both boys are devoted to the horses.*

Edward turned his attention to Andres, who was walking Tequila toward him. Other than being shorter than his brother, Andres resembled his brother except for his personality, which was open and friendly. But, unlike his brother, he exuded a degree of vulnerability and lack of confidence.

"So, who's on first?" Edward asked with a broad smile on his face.

They both loved this famous skit by Abbot and Costello. Edward had given Andres the book *Who's on First?* by Richard J. Anobile when the boy was learning English. He remembered how frustrated Andres had been learning English with the materials he had and how often he had complained about being stupid and a failure. It had been then that Edward had decided to mentor Andres. Though he had offered equal time to his brother, Camilo had refused. Edward and Andres had read, and reread that book, often acting out the skits. The book had fit Andres's personality to a tee, as he had strived to understand the comedic essence framed in the language and how best to deliver it for effect. This had been a turning point for Andres, and his learning had reached new heights.

Whoever would have thought that words from a far-off generation would have had such an effect? Edward mused as he watched Andres.

"What's on second, I don't know is on third, and I don't care is the shortstop. Or was it, I don't give a damn?" Andres's face and dark brown eyes glowed with the exchange.

"Well, I guess it depends when you first heard it, Andres. Who worked up the greater sweat, you or Tequila?"

"Probably me—I sweat like a stuffed pig." Andres stroked Tequila's neck as he spoke. "Considering the heat, Señor Slocum, we kept the workout light. No more than an hour."

"If I haven't said it before, you and your brother have been a godsend. You care for these horses as if they were your own. Karen would have been pleased." Edward reached out and patted Tequila's nose. "Thanks."

"No problem," Andres replied before he was pushed slightly off balance by Tequila nuzzling him.

"Once you've finished grooming them and cleaning up, put them in the side pastures with the others rather than in the back paddock. And make sure the water trough is filled before leaving," Edward said. He was about to leave, but he hesitated. "You and your brother drop by the house and pick up your pay."

Andres's reaction was immediate and electric. "Sure will. And thanks!"

Andres ran off toward the barn, pulling Tequila along with him.

"Now, don't forget," Edward yelled out to him.

Edward wondered whether Andres had built up enough nerve to ask Jennifer Blackwell to the dance at Stoddard Hall Friday evening. *Well, he's still got time,* he thought.

Shaking his head and smiling, he looked back to the ring where Karen had ridden her horses. He climbed up onto the first rail and hung over. *I can still hear her telling her friends how tough a nut I was to crack,* he reminisced. *Thank god she was some hungry squirrel.*

With the boys paid, a half hour later Edward grabbed a banana and apple from a basket on the kitchen counter and headed for the front door. Time seemed to be flying ahead of him as he wolfed down the banana and discarded its peel into the recycling bucket. He took the keys from a hook on the wall and locked the door while firmly clasping the apple between his teeth.

Fifteen minutes later, Edward turned down the Valley River Gorge Road, a route canopied in cedar and aspen. He turned off the air conditioner and lowered the window on the driver's side, letting the warm air gently caress his face and arms as he drove closer to the river. He popped in an Amy Winehouse CD and listened to "Tears Dry on Their Own."

A short distance behind but far enough back not to be seen, a metallic blue Silverado followed Edward's Wrangler.

Chapter Seven

CHRIS STEDMAN CAREFULLY MANOEUVRED his Silverado along the Valley River Gorge Road far enough behind Edward so as not to be detected. After glancing at his watch, he swore under his breath and wished that he was home enjoying dinner and watching a movie on Moviepix rather than following this asshole. He wiped away the rivulets of sweat from his forehead with his forearm.

His dark complexion had a blue teardrop tattoo inscribed under his right eye, and he was proud of it. He had earned it by killing a high-ranking lieutenant of a competing drug gang for turf on the east side of Toronto.

Sneezing several times, he took a handful of tissue from its box on the dashboard, blew his nose and tossed the balled-up mixture onto the floor. Stale booze and cigarette smoke permeated his litter-filled cab.

He popped out a Contact C from its wrapper and washed it down with the dregs of cold coffee from the holder beside him, and then he crumbled the paper cup and tossed it through the open window. His eyes never left the winding and bumpy road as he retrieved a cigarette from the pack in front of him, lit it and drew the smoke deeply into his lungs before exhaling it through his nostrils.

A sudden yet welcome cool breeze washed briefly over Chris's arm as it dangled over the side of his cab. Ahead, he saw Edward's Wrangler burst out of the shade of the overhanging trees and into the clearing that swept down to the river's bank. He pulled his vehicle to the side and shut down its engine. Then he retrieved his cell phone from its pouch on his waist and pushed the redial button.

"It's just like we thought, Doug."

He fumbled about, searching for his binoculars under the passenger seat.

"Exactly where are you?" Doug asked.

"I'd think about three hundred metres from the clearing on the Valley River Gorge Road." Chris pulled out the binoculars by its straps and placed them beside him.

"We'll be there in about fifteen minutes. Stay put! I'll cut your balls off if you fuck this one up like the last job."

"Hey! Go fuck yourself."

But Chris's words fell on deaf ears because the connection had already gone dead. Returning the cell phone to its holder at his waist, he looked at his watch and let out a disgruntled moan.

Seven o'clock. I've still got to deliver that fuckin' sound system to Rattray's, he thought. *I hope Doug makes this quick. It's bad enough working for KemKor during the day, but acting like a delivery boy to the CEO? That's worse.*

He was about to throw out the half-finished cigarette but thought better of it because of the tinderbox dryness of his surroundings and angrily butted it out in the ashtray. He hated being spoken to that way, especially by Doug. He took in several deep breaths and allowed the rancor to subside. He lit up another cigarette and sat back to wait.

Edward geared down to control his advance across the loose pebbles, coming to a stop a few metres from the edge of the Saugeen River. While sitting back, he enjoyed the final few moments of the song "Rehab" as his eyes drank in the surrounding beauty of the valley.

A goshawk circled effortlessly overhead, riding the updrafts of air. White caps formed around boulders as the diminished Saugeen River coursed its way downstream. Upstream, KemKor's buildings sat high into the horizon. Before the drought, the waterfall beside it had roared; now it could barely be heard as a soft hum.

Edward needed to be here in the valley. He had to do something, anything, to get through the rest of this day. Though the effluent tap scrapings would have been all he needed, staying home alone right now was out of the question for him. It was just too tempting to drown those recurring questions surrounding Karen's death in alcohol. For him, memories here with Karen had been good ones. They had trekked, swam, camped and canoed along its shores. He knew it was a long shot getting anything meaningful in the water sample, but reliving the good times he and Karen had had here was his primary goal.

The water sample would be taken a short distance downstream where the water pooled, near where they used to fly-fish.

He grasped the roll-bar and swung to the ground, taking the package of baby bottles with him. He looked at his watch: it was 7:05. The sun was well into its journey to the western horizon when something flashed from the hill above the clearing.

What the hell! Squinting, he tried to decipher its source. *Somebody's up there. I'm sure of it.*

Suddenly it ceased. *Then again, maybe there's not.*

Paranoia was setting in, and he knew he had to shake it off. Edward made his way along the river's embankment, loose stone and sand easily giving way beneath his weight. Upon reaching firmer ground, he quickened his pace and was swallowed up by the darkness of the woods as he entered through a seething wall of bush and evergreen.

Lying on his stomach above Edward's parking site, Chris watched Slocum through his binoculars. He had been restless waiting for the others to arrive and wanted to be assured that he knew which way Slocum had gone. His attention was drawn to the sound of a vehicle coming down the path behind him.

A black Lincoln Navigator pulled up behind his vehicle and turned off its engine. Doug Irwin was behind the wheel beside another man Chris didn't recognize.

Chris pushed away from the brim of the hill and, once assured he could not be seen from below, got up and went to meet them. While brushing himself off and removing the binoculars from around his neck, he approached the driver's side of the Lincoln Navigator and, nodding to Doug, scrutinized the guy beside him.

Doug Irwin welcomed Chris with a broad Cheshire cat grin.

"Chris," he said, thumbing toward his passenger, "this here's Ken."

Clean-shaven, slightly built and deeply tanned, Ken's arms were tattooed to the shoulders with an intricate, colourfully intertwined display of dragons and demons. His coarse black hair was drawn back in a ponytail that seemed too large for his small frame. Like Doug, his sockless feet were sheathed in new Adidas cross-country runners.

Chris leaned through the open window just as Ken turned to face him. Ken's eyes were so dark that Chris wondered if he had pupils. He followed Ken as he got out of the SUV and went to the back, opening the lift-gate. Chris drew his attention back to Doug. "Why the fuck is *he* here? You and I always work alone."

"Why don't you ask Ken? He's heading up this operation. Now get the hell out of my face."

Doug pushed Chris away from the open window and exited the vehicle, joining Ken at the rear.

Ken had already pulled out his German-made Heckler-Koch SL8 and was in the process of slamming in the 10-round magazine.

"Which way did he go, black boy?" Ken asked, aiming the rifle skyward and pretending to pull the trigger.

"Downstream," Chris said. "And I'm not your boy!" Menacingly, he began to swing the binoculars at the end of its strap. "Racist pig!" he shouted, slowly moving toward Ken.

Doug stepped out from behind the SUV and pushed Chris back while Ken leaned against the corner of the vehicle with a smirk on his face. Doug warned, "Now, calm down!"

Chris tried several times to get around Doug while dishing out a string of inflammatory remarks at Ken; Ken's taunting smile just grew larger with each outburst from Chris. Finally, Ken turned his back on him and busied himself at the rear of the vehicle, unaware that Chris had flipped him the bird and spat at him.

When Chris finally settled down, Doug released his grasp on him and moved closer.

"Look, buddy, I don't care what you two do out of shop. But right now, we have a job to do."

Chris wanted to settle it here and now, but he knew Doug was right. He was on a job, and that had to be his only focus—at least for the moment.

Ken made his way to the front of the SUV along the side opposite to Doug and Chris, and he shouldered his rifle. "Let's get goin'." He headed off at a quick pace toward the clearing.

Once Ken was out of earshot, Chris got right up into Doug's face.

"What the fuck is going on? Who is he? And why is he here?"

"I told you." Doug pushed Chris back to arms length. "On this gig he's the head honcho. Now, get your rifle, shut up and do what he tells you."

"I swear I'll get that sonofabitch," Chris interjected.

"As I said—save that for later. Anyway, he may turn out to be a valuable asset."

"In what way?"

Doug said, "What does it matter? Right now, we've got a job to do. So whatever shit you've got in that head of yours, drop it. Do you hear me?"

Chris nodded.

"Good! Now, let's get our rifles."

Rifles in hand, the two of them took off at a slow trot along the same route as Ken.

CHAPTER EIGHT

EDWARD PLOUGHED THROUGH THE pungent fragrance of humus, rotten vegetation, sodden logs and moss-covered rocks on a pathway that was deceivingly simple and straightforward at first. The footpath then began to challenge his mettle as it snaked, twisted and turned, rising sharply one minute, plunging the next and banking steeply to the right and then to the left as it followed the river's course. While en route, he had found an acceptable walking stick, and now he used it to brace himself against the path's steepness.

Often the outcrop of poplars and beech, and his roughly hewn walking stick, were Edward's only supports against tumbling down to the rocky riverbed below. A slight breeze hissed through the surrounding sun-bleached cedar that tenaciously clung on to its life along the steep incline. A northern goshawk effortlessly glided overhead in ever increasing loops and he wondered if it was the same one he'd seen earlier.

He lost his footing and, unable to correct, slid head over heels down the last 10 metres, coming to rest with a thump on the soft, velvety carpet of spongy mosses and decaying leaves. A multitude of sparrows, startled by his fall, took wing, momentarily frightening him with their abruptness. Regaining his breath, he surveyed himself for any damage. He felt a sense of relief as he sat up and looked around for the package of baby bottles and his walking stick.

Everything in hand, he continued along the path, his steps now more prudent in their deliberation. He was drawing closer to the location where he would take his samples. It was the only site where the water pooled substantially before branching farther downstream into three tributaries. Because of the drought, the water had a tendency to remain longer in that location before trickling away.

The wild beauty of the river valley; the sun-dabbled ravine along the path; the unique, often interesting natural gardens notched between tumbled limestone boulders and granite faces; the mixture of fragrances and the soothing mellifluous flow of the river—these things energized him with its beauty. Bulblet and Fragile ferns and jewel-like orchids—Calypso, Spotted Coral-root and Rattlesnake-plantain—scattered up the slope beside him.

Edward stopped and drank in the surrounding beauty, remembering how much Karen had loved trekking along this trail. Once they had camped close by so she would see what it looked like at first light, but it had rained all that night and well into the next day. He recalled her declaring that it was all worth it just to inhale those wonderful after-rain fragrances—whereas he remembered only wanting to get out of his wet clothes and have a good night's sleep.

He smiled to himself.

Stepping out onto the sun-baked, dry-heat sauna of bedrock lining the shore, Edward stopped, balanced the walking stick against him and carefully ripped open the package of baby bottles. He mapped out his route to the sampling location, roughly five metres from the shore; the water had less movement in that location. Filling each of the four bottles from different depths, he closed each of them tightly and returned them to their package.

The high-pitched clatter of a mass of wood sparrows taking flight from the forest's edge startled him, and he almost lost his balance.

Poking below the water's surface with his walking stick until it struck solid base, Edward scrupulously managed his way back across the boulders to the shore, where he quietly stood listening. He thought he'd heard voices and shouting, but as quickly as the sounds arrived, they disappeared.

An eerie, unnatural silence fell over the area.

Chris stood on the rocky flat where Edward had rested earlier. The distant call of a goshawk distracted his eyes skyward as he began to descend, and he lost his footing. The path, now an avalanche of stone and earth, evaporated under him, sending him head over heels toward Ken and Doug, bowling them over. The birds, startled by this commotion, exploded skyward.

Edward looked at his watch: it was 7:30. He decided to walk farther downstream to where he and Karen used to fly fish. *She always caught more than me,* he reminisced. *I never did learn her secret.*

Letting out a long sigh, he grasped the package of sample bottles in one hand and his walking stick in the other, and he began to head downstream along the ragged shoreline.

Snap! Crack!

A section of limestone boulder to Edward's right exploded, a piece of it momentarily stunning him. The sample bottles dropped to the ground as he wrapped his hands around the walking stick to support himself.

What the hell just happened? he asked himself, staring at what was left of the boulder and rubbing the side of his head.

He picked up movement from the corner of his eye and turned to investigate.

Three men emerged from the woods along the trail Edward had just come from. All three men carried weapons. The man out front was yelling something and pointing at Edward as he ran.

Edward's gut knotted in fear. He was sure the man out front was the same person he'd seen on Building 3C's loading dock last evening.

Panic streamed through his body. Throwing away his walking stick, he grasped his sample package and began to run as best he could along the shoreline.

While rounding the face of the cliff, he heard the weapon's report. *Snap! Crack!*

The bullet ricocheted off the rock with a pinging sound, splaying Edward's forehead with fine stone particles. He kept running. Ahead, he saw a break in the rock formation and picked up his pace.

All Edward could hope for at that location was a short respite to catch his breath and evade, if only momentarily, the increasing accuracy of the shooter. Lungs aching from the effort, he reached his temporary refuge and collapsed behind a large rock formation, gulping in air and gathering himself. As he listened, he was surprised that their voices appeared more distant than he expected. Peering around the rock and half expecting the wiry man with the ponytail to pounce, he was surprised to find no one there. *Where are they?* His mind frantically searched for an answer.

Their voices grew closer.

"Shit! How could I be so blind?" he chastised himself.

He had been crouching at the bottom of a rough-hewn pathway that led to the top of the cliff. It was then he realized that he was at the site where he and Karen had gone fly fishing. Somehow he had forgotten about this pathway.

He began to climb in earnest, the burn in his thighs painful.

Snap! Crack!

A section of the trunk of a birch tree beside him splintered, and he reflexively ducked while still endeavouring to increase his upward rate. The rock face ahead zinged, spraying fine powdered dust in his face as he passed it. The top drew near. His legs felt heavy as his thighs ached with indescribable pain. He was slowing down. Though nauseated and woozy, he forced himself to keep climbing.

He hit the top of the cliff at a full run, stumbled and slammed into the ground, the package of sample bottles taking flight. Gulping in large volumes of air, he staggered to his feet, half walking, half jogging into the woods and never giving a thought to the samples he left behind. Instincts drove him forward as he reached into his memory banks to the time he and Karen explored this area. Branches whipped his face; his eyes, slits from stinging sweat, couldn't see. The profuse undergrowth of rhizomes, ferns, and low-lying brush tripped him, and he hit the ground hard, face first. His nose bled as he scrambled to his feet, willing himself forward. His legs felt like they were mired in quicksand.

Snap! Crack!

Dizzy, he fell and began to roll down the slope.

Some sort of outcrop stopped his forward motion, and he could feel himself falling backward before he drifted into unconsciousness.

CHAPTER NINE

JANET THOMPSON DRAGGED HER canoe through stinky blooms of algae to the shoreline by the Epping Road. She couldn't remember this part of the Beaver River looking like this. As she looked up, she saw Charlotte Bradley waiting for her on the shore, a sign tucked under her arm. To her dismay, Charlotte had parked her Toyota Prius right in front of her Camaro instead of on the road.

"Used to be a piece of cake," Janet called out in her gravelly voice as she slipped and then regained her footing. She blew away a wisp of white hair that had fallen across her forehead.

Charlotte grabbed the bow of the canoe and pulled it onto the shore. "What used to be a piece of cake?"

"The three-kilometre paddle, girl! What else? It's my late-day ritual before supper, weather permitting."

Standing in the water behind the canoe, Janet forced the errant hair that kept falling across her forehead under the wide brim of her camel-coloured hat. "Did you have to park there?" she asked, pointing at the Prius. "It does make it inconvenient for me leaving."

"I'm not here long. But right now, though, I want you out of that water."

"I see that look, Miss Bradley. To you I'm just some old fart. Well, I'm not." She wagged her finger at Charlotte. "I can still show you a thing or two. Just don't ask me to show you this moment."

"It never crossed my mind, Janet, but I still want you to get the hell out of that water. The longer you stand in it … Just get out. Now!"

Using the side of the canoe to guide her, Janet gingerly made her way out of the water to the beach.

"All right, all right! I'm out! Are you pleased now? What's the big deal?"

Most days—and today wasn't one of them—60-year-old Janet Thompson didn't look a day older than 50. She had a tendency to be plump, but she kept it in check by her vigorous lifestyle. She preferred pants to skirts and boots, preferably work boots, to the conventional fashion that graced a woman's foot. She liked hard liquor, preferably single-malt Irish whiskey, and she enjoyed poker with an occasional cigar. She never fit into the typical image of a teacher, but she liked that just fine, too—and so, as it turned out, did the community. With her no-nonsense approach, she was a person of integrity and fair play who met life head-on. However, lately she felt her energy level slipping—and, along with it, an important part of her essence.

"Are you sure you need to put up those 'No Swimming' signs? One look at this water along the shoreline should be a duh moment for most people."

Charlotte shook her head and smiled. "It sure wasn't a 'duh' moment for you, now, was it?" She ran her finger along the "Due to Pollution" portion of the sign.

"What's it like farther upstream?"

"There's a little along the shoreline, but nothing like this, Charlotte. Is it likely to get worse?"

"Uh-huh."

"What is this stuff, anyway? Should I be concerned? Considering all the times I've walked through it, I never much gave it a thought, at least not until now." Janet nodded toward the sign.

"The algae you just walked through are blue-green algae blooms. Its official name is cyanobacteria."

"Fancy name." Janet began to massage the back of her neck. "Um, Charlotte, what are its side effects?"

"Are you okay?"

"A bit of a headache, that's all. I don't get them often, but this one has lasted a few days. You wouldn't by any chance have some Tylenol on you, would you?" Janet straddled the bow of the canoe and sat down.

"I may have some Aspirin," Charlotte said.

After Janet encouraged her to get them, Charlotte scurried off to the Prius. A few moments later, she returned with a small bottle of Aspirin and some bottled water. She put a couple of tablets in Janet's hand and handed her the bottled water.

"Thanks. Well? Are there any side effects?" Janet asked as she popped two of the pills into her mouth, followed by a swig of water.

Charlotte took in a deep breath before answering her. "Headaches are one of them."

"Jesus! One of them? What are the others?" Janet asked, alarmed.

"Fever, abdominal pain, nausea, skin irritation and vomiting if ingested. The sooner you get into a bath, the better. You haven't ingested any of this stuff, have you?"

"Yuck! No!" Janet's face screwed up as if she had bitten into a lemon. As the colour in her face returned, she reached back into the canoe, pulled out her towel and flung it across her shoulders as she massaged her temples. "You've learned a lot during your time at University of Guelph." Using one end of the towel Janet wiped her forehead and face. "I've always been curious about something, Charlotte. Most young people with your qualifications leave this region for greener pastures. You didn't. Why?"

"You knew how ill my mom was, and with my stepdad dead, she only had Nadia and me to take care of her."

"But after your mom died, there was really nothing keeping you here."

"Perhaps. Except I've always believed my greener pastures were here."

"Are you sure it had nothing to do with Edward's return?" Janet prodded.

Charlotte looked elsewhere. "Oh, look, there's a whooping crane," she said, following its flight path with her finger.

"I guess that's my hint to mind my own business. Not too subtle, dearie."

"Don't read too much into it, Janet. My earlier answer holds—this is where I prefer to be; nothing more, nothing less."

Charlotte Bradley was of average build and height, and her satin-black hair poked out in a ponytail from the back of her Blue Jays baseball cap. Her face was milky white and flawless, except for a small scar on the bridge of her nose from a childhood accident while playing with her stepsister, Nadia. When she was 12 years old and ill with nephritis, the Board of Education had sent Janet out to tutor her; that was when they first met. Charlotte cringed with the thought of how quickly time had passed.

"Well, Charlotte, my headache has just about gone." Sliding off the bow of the canoe, Janet stood up. "Anything else I should know or do?"

"First of all, I'm glad you haven't ingested any cyanobacteria. I would strongly encourage you to have a bath when you return home. And that means scrubbing yourself head to toe until your skin wrinkles up like dried prunes."

"I've got enough wrinkles, dearie. Let's just keep it at a thorough wash. Anyway, I don't like baths; I only take showers."

Charlotte nodded her head, smiling. "Whatever, Janet. Just do a damn good job of cleaning."

"Always do, honey." Janet threw the towel from her shoulder into the canoe. "I'd better boil that damn thing, don't you think Charlotte? Ah, screw that! I'll just chuck it in the garbage." She looked down at the canoe and then back at Charlotte. "Give me a hand?"

"Of course I will. Now, Janet, you don't have to look at me that way. It's not my fault this area's polluted. I'm only the messenger."

"You misread me, Charlotte. I was just thinking that you've turned into a very competent young lady. I guess I've always known that, but I never really thought about it until now."

"It's really nice hearing that—especially from you. Thank you. Oh, by the way, once home, wash this canoe down with lots of soap and water even before you take it off the roof of your car. Then, repeat once it's off."

Ten minutes later, the canoe was lashed securely onto the roof of Janet's red and black 1978 Camaro RS.

Charlotte went to her car and returned with an open box of hand wipes. "Use these wipes for your hands and legs and any other part of your body that you think may have come into contact with that stuff."

Janet began to wipe her hands and legs. "What about yourself? Surely this isn't your only box?"

"No, I've got lots in the car. But I should wipe myself."

Janet held out the box to Charlotte, who took enough to wipe her hands.

"Janet?"

Janet had just finished wiping her legs and was preoccupied with her last-minute inspection to ensure the canoe was secure. Finally she stopped and looked back at Charlotte.

"It's just a habit of mine, double-checking and sometimes triple-checking things. So don't take it as a slight on you. By the way, Charlotte, what should I do with these?"

Janet held up the used wipes.

Charlotte returned to her car and came back with a small box. "Throw them in here." Throwing her own wipes in, she tucked the box under her arm. "Just now, I didn't think you were ignoring me. So, no slight was taken. It was just that ... I wanted to ask you something."

"Well, girl, ask it."

"Here it goes, then. Why is this car so special to you? I know there's a story around it, because you've implied that on numerous occasions."

Janet fondly patted the Camaro. "Ah, that there is. This mystery will need to be plied out of me over a bottle of good Sauvignon Blanc—maybe several. Pick the time and place, and all will be revealed."

"You said that the last time."

"Did you enjoy yourself?"

"Well, yes, but that's beside the point."

"Is it? A good mystery builds up to its own climax."

"Okay, and that means what, exactly?"

"By summer's end—you'll know by summer's end."

They heard a vehicle approaching on the gravel road and looked up to the single-lane bridge that spanned the river. A dark blue limousine hummed across the bridge, kicking up a funnel of dust as it returned to gravel surface on the other side, scattering stone and loose debris. A splay of stone hit the water's surface like buck shot, causing Janet and Charlotte to duck.

"Are you okay?" Charlotte asked.

"I think so," Janet replied, rubbing her head. "I wonder where the hell he was going to in such a hurry?"

Janet popped open the Aspirin bottle, dropped the last pill into her hand and swallowed it. She rounded the car to the driver's side, threw the towel into the backseat, got in and turned the ignition.

"Where to next?" Janet asked, leaning out the window and taking a drink from the water bottle.

"Rowns Lake," Charlotte replied.

Janet let out a long sigh. "There are a lot of fond memories there too, Charlotte. It's part of the mystery." She broadcasted a large toothy smile before taking a drink from her water bottle.

"You're just playing with me," Charlotte accused.

"Yes, I guess I am." She put the cap back on the water bottle and placed it on the passenger seat. Then she said suddenly, "What's that sound?" Turning off the ignition, she got out of the car and listened intensely.

"What am I supposed to be hearing?" Charlotte asked.

"It sounded like gunshots. Heavy calibre, I'd say, if my ears aren't failing me yet. It came from that direction." She pointed to a location behind Charlotte.

"The Gorge? Now, how could you possibly know that?"

"Put it down to years of experience, honey," Janet said, getting back into the Camaro. "I used to hunt throughout this area before government regulation and development. I developed an ear for that kinda thing. It kept me safe and away from someone else's target."

Janet cranked the stick shift into reverse. "Charlotte, it would be nice if you'd move that car of yours so I could get out."

A few minutes later, Charlotte parked her Prius on the side of the road and got out just as Janet stopped beside her.

"They're probably gone by now, but I'm going to drive over to the Gorge and check it out anyway. Probably some damn teenagers."

"You really should go home and get that shower."

"It's kinda on my way."

Charlotte shrugged and shook her head. "Look, why don't I call the police on my iPhone and have them check it out?"

"Whoever it is, I probably know them. I'll give them that 'teacher stern' look of mine and threaten to call their parents. That's all that's needed. Calling the police would be over the top."

For a moment, Charlotte stood and watched Janet drive off. Then, climbing into her Prius, she drove off in the opposite direction to place her signs at Rowns Lake.

Fifteen minutes later, Janet Thompson maneuvered her '78 Camaro down the Valley River Gorge Road. Ahead, two parked vehicles barely left enough room for her to pass. Without turning off her engine, she parked a short distance down from them and got out of her car. As she walked around to the back of the Lincoln Navigator, she looked in. Three empty rifle sleeves and a number of cartridge magazines were enough to convince her that these were probably the jerks she'd heard.

Returning to the Camaro, she retrieved her backpack from the backseat, withdrew her digital camera and began photographing each vehicle, making sure to include their license plates. Then she returned to the Camaro, threw the backpack containing the camera into the backseat and drove down to the clearing.

After parking her vehicle beside the bright red Wrangler, she sat awhile listening. No gunshots. Only the sounds of birds and the Saugeen River met her ears.

She stepped out of the car and began to take photos of the back, front and opposite sides of the Wrangler. After she returned the camera to the backpack, she leaned up against the Camaro, listening and surveying the landscape. Still there appeared to be nothing out of the ordinary.

Beginning to feel nervous, she wondered whatever possessed her to come here alone in the first place. Reassessing her situation on a scale zero to ten, she rated this fear level closer to zero. *Anyway,* she thought, *I've taught most of the parents whose teenagers are likely to be down here.* In other words, she didn't expect to encounter any problems she couldn't handle.

Opening the car door, she reached in behind the driver's seat and pulled out a cow bell. Through the top of the bell was threaded a blue ribbon that she used to tie it around her neck. She always wore this bell when she went trekking in the woods in Northern Ontario to ward off bears. She never knew if the clanging sound it made really worked, except to say she never encountered a bear. Today she wore it to alert whoever was out there she was coming and thereby reduce her odds of being shot.

Trying to ignore the rash and itch that had developed on her calves, she headed into the woods and along the path toward KemKor Pharmaceuticals.

CHAPTER TEN

PREMIER BOLSOVER'S DARK BLUE limousine pulled into the circular driveway of William Wardlaw Rattray's property and came to a stop in front of the white portico adorning the front of the house.

Rattray's 19th-century, two-and-half-story house was stately and was built of red brick from the Parker Brick and Glass Factory. The portico gave the front entrance a sense of majestic splendour while solid oak double doors, which were inlaid with decorative floral glass, conveyed terra firma. Above the door was a semi-circular piece of glass with the word "Idylwilde" etched in Lucida scroll. The original foundations for the house were laid by Joseph Parker and his wife, Yvonne Lyn Wilde, in 1888. The Parker Brick and Glass Factory, originally located where KemKor Pharmaceuticals now stood, eventually went out of business once Joseph and his business partner and wife, Yvonne, died. Rattray's wife, Diane, was their great-great-granddaughter.

Premier Bolsover slid forward in the backseat to talk to his driver, Antonio. "Don't open my door yet. I'll let you know when I'm ready."

Bolsover closed the opaque window between them and, sitting back, placed his briefcase on his lap and opened it. While whistling the song "Whistle While You Work," he took out the neatly arranged files and placed them beside him. Then he lifted up the bottom panel and turned on the voice-activated recorder fixed in the hidden compartment. Once everything was returned to its proper place, he opened the window between him and Antonio.

"I'm ready now."

Premier Bolsover took in a deep breath and sat back. *I wish I had never gotten mixed up with Rattray*, he thought. *Unscrupulous sonofabitch!*

He tapped his fingers on the broad, flat surface of the tanned leather briefcase lying across his lap. A satisfied smile crossed his face when he thought of the library of information he had recorded during his meetings with Rattray.

Antonio, his chauffeur, opened the door, and Bolsover got out.

One of the double oak doors to the house opened. "Welcome, Matthew," Rattray called out. He stepped out and made his way to Bolsover with an outstretched hand. After they shook hands, he relieved Matthew of his briefcase, handing it to Antonio.

"Here, take this to the library. It's the first door on your right through the front entrance there." He pointed to the open door behind him. "If you're thirsty, Antonio, I'm sure Mrs. Rattray will set you up with a nice cold drink. The last I saw her, she was on the terrace at the back. After you leave the library, follow the hallway to the kitchen. I'm sure you'll find her. Oh, one other thing—close the door when you enter the house. Come along, Matthew."

Rattray placed his arm across Matthew's shoulders and escorted him along the terracotta crushed-stone pathway, edged with railroad ties, to the rear of the house.

The patio ran the full width of the house with a brick wood-burning stove with a pizza oven at one corner. Pairs of Adirondack chairs were strategically placed along the front of the patio to capture different views of the garden and encourage conversation. Though the region was in drought, the manicured and lush green grass, starting at the edge of the terrace and carpeting the garden's two acres, did not whisper a hint of hardship.

A work crew was busy setting up a large dining tent and stage in the middle of the unctuous surroundings. Rattray's wife and a young girl were engrossed in conversation with a man in a hard hat. The three of them, at the far side of the property, were bent over a sheet of paper laid across a folding table and anchored down by four good-sized rocks.

Matthew needed to move out from under the unpleasantness of Rattray's heavy arm across his shoulders, and he called out several times to attract Diane Rattray's attention. When he finally got it, he made a beeline to her. "Hey! Diane." Hugging her, Matthew pushed back the brim of her sun hat and gave her a chaste peck on the cheek. "As always, it's great to see you!"

Matthew enjoyed seeing her comely figure, clothed or unclothed, and especially unclothed. It had only been two days since their last tryst, and the ardour of their love making was still tantalizingly fresh in his mind. He stepped back and refocused his thoughts. "What are you doing there?" he asked, pointing to the unfurled sheet of paper on the table.

Diane smiled demurely at Matthew, removing her sunglasses.

"Some last-minute corrections to the layout." Her mellifluent voice lacked even a hint of timorous undertones. She wore a brightly coloured flowered print dress and sandals. Her brown hair was pulled back and held in place with a hair clip. Shifting her attention to the blonde girl beside her, she queried, "I think you know Jennifer Blackwell?"

"Of course I do!" Matthew shook Jennifer's extended hand. "I remember when you were this tall," he said, placing his hand at waist level. "Tomorrow's a big day for your dad."

"It sure will be," Jennifer said. She brushed her hair away from her face with her hands before self-consciously adjusting her blouse. "I'm happy to play whatever part is necessary to ensure my dad's success." She dug both hands into the side pockets of her white shorts.

"Of course you do—that goes unsaid," Matthew replied. Patting her on the shoulder, he found her impudent self-confidence endearing. "And *you* are?" he asked, shifting to face the man wearing the construction helmet who was standing to one side listening in.

Diane stepped forward and softly touched Matthew's upper arm.

"Forgive me, Premier Bolsover, but this is Sean McVitie, owner of the Four Seasons Party Rentals."

After a polite exchange of salutations, Sean's attention returned to Diane and Jennifer. "Unless there's still something further we've got to talk about, Mrs. Rattray, I'd better get back to work. Nice meeting you, Premier."

Diane glanced at Jennifer for confirmation.

As Sean walked off to the location where the stage and dining tent were being erected, William joined his wife.

"I hope you liked him, William," Diane said.

She reached out tentatively to touch his upper arm but stepped back. "Not that it really matters—because I do. He's very thorough and very professional. Isn't that right, Jennifer?"

Jennifer nodded.

"You've chosen wisely, dear—but—where's the sound system? It should have been here by now." He looked at his wristwatch. "My god! It's almost 8:30. Surely it's not being set up in the dark? In fact, it had better not be."

"Calm down, William. Chris Stedman phoned earlier to say he was running a little late. So the cherished quietness of your evening will not be compromised in the least."

"There he is!" Jennifer yelled excitedly, clapping her hands.

Jennifer sprinted across the lawn, her red and white running shoes moving like finely tuned pistons through the grass toward the blue Silverado with a U-Haul trailer hitched to it. She arrived at the edge of the drive, parallel to the backyard, just before the vehicle came to a stop.

"Come along, Matthew," William said, clapping him on the back. "Diane, we will be in the library if you need us."

The old floor creaked under their weight as they walked through the kitchen and into the hallway that led to the library. Matthew took out a handkerchief and wiped the remnants of perspiration from his forehead and balding head.

Rattray ushered Matthew into the library. "Make yourself comfortable, Matthew. I'll be with you in a few moments." He left the room, closing the door behind him.

Matthew heard the sound of old hardwood giving way to Rattray's receding footsteps. He heard muffled voices in the hallway and the front door being closed.

Pleasant scents of leather and wood tantalized Matthew's nostrils as he wandered about the room. At one end of the room was a fireplace with a framed 19th-century map of Africa centred above the mantel. Flanking the fireplace were floor-to-ceiling bookcases. At the opposite end of the room was a bar and glassed in wine room. Sitting in front of it was a baby grand piano. Colonial style windows and patio doors, draped in champagne coloured shears, filled the wall opposite him. Two tanned leather couches, parallel to each other on an Aztec rug in the middle of the room, were separated by a mahogany coffee table.

Matthew's briefcase sat beside one of the couches.

At the bar, Matthew searched among the choices until finally pulling out a bottle of Locke's Irish Single Malt whiskey. He poured himself a stiff drink and swirled the contents in his glass as he watched the activity outside.

A crest with a rampant lion, facing a fire-spewing dragon on a red, white and green tartan background, crossed over with two swords, was located on the wall beside the patio doors, and it caught his interest. He walked over to have a closer look at the crest, and he let his fingers brush across the keyboard of the piano as he passed it. He knew Diane loved coming into this room to play it, especially when her husband wasn't home.

He put on his reading glasses and attempted to decipher the Latin script on the crest. He hadn't studied Latin since his misguided decision to join a Jesuit order in his youth, and for all intense and purposes, that was an eternity ago. He stood back and took a few sips from his drink when Rattray's voice startled him.

"Flectere si nequeo superos, Acheronta movebo," Rattray said with a hint of disdain in his voice. "Forgotten your Jesuit experience? Shame on you! Let me translate. 'If I am unable to make the gods above relent, I shall move hell.' Fits me to a tee, don't you think?" Rattray looked at the bottle of Irish whiskey on the bar and back at Matthew's glass. "Let's do business first before I offer you more." He pointed to the couches.

Matthew sat down on the couch beside his briefcase while Rattray sat on the couch opposite.

"First things first," Rattray said briskly. He opened the drawer in the coffee table and pulled out a large manila envelope, sliding it across the table to Matthew.

"Your $100,000 plus a discretionary bonus of 10 percent."

"Discretionary bonus?" Matthew repeated.

"You seem surprised."

"Well, I am."

"In time they'll be more—a lot more. Let's just call it a thank-you gift."

"Where are you with this new filtering system?"

"Would you like a Cohiba?" Rattray asked. He opened the humidor on the coffee table, took out a cigar and slid the opened box across to Matthew. "The system is still untested."

"And the patents?" Matthew asked. Without taking a cigar, he closed the humidor and pushed it to the centre of the table.

"Next Monday—they become KemKor's, whether he's alive or dead. Slocum's to see David DeLuca in Legal first thing Monday morning, to firm up the hand-over." Rattray lit his cigar and sat back, spreading his arms along the back of the couch.

"Still, that should cost KemKor one pretty penny," replied Matthew.

"Uh-huh, it will. But you see, I intend to hold those patents."

"You?"

"Well, actually, the Idylwilde Group."

"And, how do you expect to get away with that? Won't that be ill—"

"DeLuca has already worked that out," Rattray interjected. "My friends in accounting will do the rest."

"Still, I can't just see Slocum sitting idly by and saying nothing when he learns that you have the patents."

Matthew finished his drink and placed it on the table.

"Actually, neither do I. But who is to say he'll know," Rattray replied.

"So?"

"Matthew, you just continue to do your part, and leave the rest to me."

"Easier said than done. There are changes afoot," Matthew retorted.

Rattray stood up and walked over to the windows overlooking the back lawns, a trail of cigar smoke arching over his head, and he pulled back the curtains. "If you want another drink, you know where to find it. Tell me—what do you mean by changes afoot?"

"I'm a lame-duck premier, for one thing. Announcing one's retirement does that. We both know that." Matthew poured himself another whiskey and walked back toward the sitting area, but he stopped halfway. He took a sip from his glass before he continued. "Look, you're aware of the spate of adverse publicity our government had to face surrounding contract allocation. It's taken its toll. Sure, we've been hammered from a number of sides during the past seven years, but this stuff on contracts was the straw that broke the camel's back. Right now the opposition smells blood and my cabinet is in survival mode." Matthew took a long drink from his glass to give time for what he had just said to sink in. He cleared his throat and continued. "You're an informed person. You must be aware that the bipartisan committee formed to clean up the contract allocation mess has done just that. A new bill is to be introduced next Wednesday to rectify any unfairness in the meting out of contracts in the public sector. The procedural steps to acquire a contract are precise and, now, are soon to be very transparent."

"You've got a copy of the proposed bill?" Rattray asked. He continued to still look out the window as cigar smoke hovered in the air above him. "You know, Matthew, you've let me down. I hadn't realized it had gone this far. As you well know, the process of contract acquisition from *your* government has been well greased for both me and my associates. And now you're telling me that's about to change? Why do I feel like I'm about to get fucked?" He turned and faced him. "Among other sundry things, Matthew, you're paid to keep me informed."

"The bill's in my briefcase."

"Put it on the coffee table, and sit down."

Matthew quickly went to his briefcase and, juggling his drink, opened it. The binder, containing the bill and relevant documents, was too large to retrieve with one hand. Placing his glass on the coffee table, he pulled out the binder and put it along side it. The manila envelope, containing the money, was scooped up and placed in the space once occupied by the binder. He then closed his briefcase, returned it to its original position beside the couch and sat down.

Rattray went over to the coffee table, picked up the binder and began to thumb through it. "How much?" He threw the binder on the table, almost knocking over Matthew's drink.

"Pardon?" Matthew said.

Rattray sat down on the couch opposite Matthew. "How much will it cost me to make *this* go away?"

"I don't know."

"Hmm. When will you know?"

"Soon."

"Make it sooner," Rattray said. Sucking in the smoke from his cigar, he purged it through his nostrils. "Blackwell's the guy steering this fucking bill. Right?" Matthew nodded. "You told me the last time we met that you had something that would put Blackwell's balls in a vice. Well, were you shitting me, or is it true?"

Matthew swung the briefcase onto his knees, opened it, and extricating a square plastic holder containing DVD discs, he pushed it across the table toward him. "My chauffeur, Antonio, is a multifaceted individual with contacts I don't care to know or meet."

Rattray picked up the container of discs and said, "I'm intrigued. What is it?"

"Watch them—you'll soon understand." Matthew closed his briefcase and looked at his watch. "I'd better get going." He quickly finished his drink and stood up. "I'm always tardy lately getting to these damn cabinet meetings."

"Where is it?" Rattray asked.

"Talisman Resort and Spa."

"Over in Kimberley? That shouldn't take you long to get there." Rattray stubbed out his cigar and stood up. "Elkhart should be here shortly." He glanced back at the discs on the table before walking Matthew to the door of the library. "He and I have a long night ahead of us. Poor bastard—and he thought he was just coming for a quiet dinner with wine." He chortled as he unlocked the door and opened it, escorting Matthew along the hallway to the front door. "That bill's going to need amendments by morning. John and I will send over our ideas to your BlackBerry by tomorrow morning. You don't get any sleep either, Matthew. Soften the pipeline. Get it primed for whatever we come up with. Work your magic. Your cabinet meeting couldn't be timelier."

Matthew nodded his agreement.

Rattray stared at Matthew long and hard before returning to the library and closing the door. He did not shake his hand.

Matthew took in a deep breath as he opened the front door. His conscience was barely pricked by what he had just set in motion as he thought about the DVDs he had just left with Rattray, which recorded the several trysts between Blackwell and Slocum's wife.

Chapter Eleven

SWEAT DRIPPING FROM THEIR foreheads, Ken and Doug searched the edge of the embankment. Hawthorn branches and snarled cedar twigs whipped back, scratching their faces and inhibiting their frenzied quest to find Edward's body.

"I nailed him, I know I did! But where the hell's his body?" protested Ken. Ken had no sooner removed a thorn from the palm of his hand when his bushy ponytail got ensnarled on a tree branch. Untangling it, he forced the ponytail on top of his head and, pulling a baseball cap from his back pocket, forced it down over his head.

Doug stopped and shooed away a cluster of mosquitoes circling him with his hand, and he continued to plow through the jungle of foliage in front of him, using his rifle to push aside the tangled confusion of tree branches and shrubbery.

"Fuck!" Ken removed another thorn from the back of his hand and sucked on the bleeding puncture. "Between these goddamn bugs and branches …" he complained, waving his hand in front of him. "Tell me something, Doug."

"What?" Doug paused and, straightening up, wiped his arm across his brow as he waited for Ken's question.

"Back there I saw you and Chris chatting, and then he buggered off. Where'd he go? And why wasn't I told?"

"Chris's part was done," Doug said.

"I decide when he's done!"

"Actually, you don't."

"You think *you* do?"

"No, I don't. But when I tell you Chris's part was done, it's done. And, quite frankly, where he's gone is none of your fuckin' business. But I will say it was part of his cover at KemKor. As security manager there, Chris's role is a valuable asset, wouldn't you say? So nothing—absolutely nothing—should jeopardize that."

Standing the rifle against himself, Ken picked up the bottom of his T-shirt and, using it as a towel, wiped the sweat from his face and the snot from his nose before letting the shirt fall back in place. "Then I guess there's nothing more to be said."

"You've got that right. So let's keep looking," replied Doug.

Bending low to the ground, Doug continued his search using the stock and barrel of his rifle to efficiently move and separate the vegetation. Suddenly he stopped and knelt down, running his hand over the ground's surface. "I think I've got something."

Ken crouched down beside Doug and examined the same location. "It looks like blood to me. And by the looks of the depressed vegetation, he must have rolled down there."

Ken pointed to a patch of ground just behind Doug and began to shake his head. "But, I'd swear I nailed him back there." He indicated a location about 10 metres away.

"Maybe you did, and his momentum just did the rest."

"With these SL-8s? Not likely."

"Likely or not, it appears he did. You ever hunt deer, moose or wild boar on the run?"

"Why you askin'?"

Doug explained, "A wild boar, when wounded, is just plain nasty. Humans, on the other hand, are vindictive, revengeful and inventive. So I hope you've killed him."

Ken examined the ground again. "There isn't a lot of blood."

"That's my point. And if he's got a cell phone, he's probably already called the cops."

Ken looked over at Doug and then eased over to the edge of the embankment, peering over. "Fuck! I don't see the asshole."

"That's bog down there, Ken. So the way I figure it, there are only two scenarios. One, he's already under it and our job is done. Two, he's waiting for us."

Ken fastidiously scanned the area below him, looking for any kind of movement that might give away Edward's position. "Only one can go down at a time. The other stays to cover the descent."

"Leave things as they are. We've accomplished what we came here for," Doug suggested.

"Just to scare him? He probably saw us the other night."

"Probably, but I'm sure he's got the message."

"What? 'Keep your mouth shut or you're dead' kinda message?" Ken asked. Doug shrugged. "Asshole."

Sitting with his rifle cradled between his arms, Ken began to maneuver down the steep embankment on his backside.

"Where are you going to go once down there?" Doug asked.

"I'll figure that out when I get there."

Doug let go of a deep sigh. "Okay, then. Don't say I didn't tell you."

Ken held up his hand and flicked him the bird when suddenly, the ground beneath him gave way and his rate of descent accelerated. Panic grabbed him as he watched his rifle toboggan ahead of him and land on top of black slop below, quickly disappearing. His heels frantically tried to dig in while he grasped for anything to stop his slide. His hand clamped shut around one of the roots, and he stopped. Lying perfectly still and catching his breath, he waited for the scree and friable rock flowing around and over him to stop. Assured the ground beneath him had settled, he reinforced his grip around the root with his other hand.

"Hold on, Ken. I'll be right back."

Doug hacked away at the trunk of a maple sapling with his knife until it was free. He trimmed off the branches and quickly returned to the edge of the embankment, where he lowered it to Ken.

Ensuring his footing was secure, Ken grabbed on to the branch and, with Doug pulling at the other end, ascended the embankment until he was safely at the top. "Fuck! That was close!" Ken exclaimed, climbing over the edge. Hunched over and trying to get his breath, he occasionally looked back to the edge of the embankment. "I'll settle for him getting the message." His shoulders sagged in desperation. "I've lost a damn good rifle."

Doug joked, "Like your gun, he's already underground. Convenient, eh? Saves cleanup."

Chuffed with laughter, Doug slapped Ken on the back. Ken returned to the edge of the embankment and, letting his hand run across his chin several times, he surveyed the bog and the surrounding vegetation. "Maybe you're right, Doug. Whatever—we'd better get on with the rest of it."

As they walked back to their vehicles, Ken asked, "You figured out what we're doin' with that vehicle of his?"

"I've been thinking about that. If he's already called the police, then they know where he is, and there's no point in doing anything with it. On the other hand, if he hasn't called the police and he's dead—and that's my bet—there's every reason to move it. Why put the cops on the scent too early when there's no need to?"

"So we move it. Right? But where?" Ken asked.

"You're right, we move it."

"Well, you gonna leave me in the dark?"

Smiling, Doug stopped and turned to Ken. "Let me give you a hint. You trespass at your own risk."

A smirk formed at the corner of Ken's mouth. The two of them were now of one mind.

Five years ago, two cyclists fell to their deaths after a bridge collapsed under them. The municipality condemned the bridge and immediately put up "You Trespass at Your Own Risk" signs at both ends of the bridge to prevent hikers and cyclists from using it. At one time, it had been part of a logging route to the mill located on the other side. Though West Grey Council vowed to reopen it for nature trail huggers, in the end they decided to keep it closed and reroute the nature trail. Shortly after the council's decision, Chris Stedman, along with a crew of workers from outside the region, initiated the clandestine initiative to fix the bridge to provide a route for their trucks after picking up the Oxycontin from KemKor. It was called the ghost road by them because it kept their trucks off the main routes for a good two miles or more, away from prying eyes.

"We'll leave his vehicle in the mill under a shit-load of debris. And believe me, there's lots of it," Doug said. "There's even an old bulldozer on-site that just happens to work."

Ten minutes later, the two of them climbed into the Lincoln Navigator and drove toward the clearing. Circling the Wrangler and Camaro, Doug pulled up beside the Wrangler.

"Whose Camaro?" quizzed Ken.

"I don't know for sure, but it looks like Ms. Thompson's."

"Who the hell is she?"

"She was one of my high school teachers."

"That's why you're so formal with the 'Ms.'?"

"She could be one heap of trouble if she catches us here," Doug said.

"Who says she'll be able to tell anyone anything if she does?" replied Ken. He fondled the hilt of the knife on his belt.

"Let's just do what we have to do and get out of here."

Ken pressed Doug's forearm with his hand. "I bet she took down our license numbers." He got out and walked over to the Camaro.

"What makes you think she would have left it behind?" Doug yelled out after him.

"A hunch. Teachers are trusting folk."

"But they're not stupid."

Ken shrugged. "I never said stupid—just trusting."

Ken thoroughly searched the front seats and glove compartment of the Camaro, but he found nothing. Surprised not to find even a pencil or piece of paper, he took a peripheral glance into the backseat, and right before he was going to call it quits, he saw the knapsack on the floor. He lifted it out, opened it and began rummaging through it. There was a pad of paper, two unopened water bottles, a hair brush and a digital camera. He fanned through the pad of paper. Not only was nothing recorded, but there were no impressions of any kind on the pages to indicate the pad had ever been used. He turned his attention to the camera and turned it on.

"Bingo!" *So I guess this is your style of hi-tech,* he thought.

Doug joined him, and Ken shared his findings with him. Popping out the memory chip, Ken replaced it with another he found in the knapsack, and then he returned everything to its original position.

"Slocum's key was in the ignition," Doug said matter-of-factly.

"Trusting soul. He sure made your job easy."

"Common practice in these parts; I kinda expected it. Do it myself."

Ken held up the chip. "Let's hope these aren't backups for her cell phone. Otherwise, our goose is cooked."

He put the chip in his pocket and slowly walked back to the Lincoln Navigator.

"I wouldn't worry about it," Doug replied, veering off to get into the Wrangler.

"Why?" Ken yelled back.

"Later. Right now, let's just get the hell outta here."

Ken got into the Navigator and turned the ignition.

"What you just said doesn't inspire me with a great deal of confidence," Ken said, hanging over the driver's-side window.

"Just being practical, that's all."

Shaking his head and laughing, Ken slammed the accelerator down, sending a splay of stone in Doug's direction, who quickly ducked behind the Wrangler.

When Doug was assured that Ken was a safe distance away, he stepped out and shook his fist. "You sonofabitch!" he screamed.

Doug continued to shake his fist and unleash a cascade of obscenities until the SUV disappeared over the brim of the hill.

CHAPTER TWELVE

ON HER WAY BACK home from posting "No Swimming" signs at Rowns Lake, Charlotte, who was worried about Janet, decided to detour via the Barr Head Road and swing over to the Valley River Gorge Road. She felt more than a twinge of guilt for not insisting that they call the police on her cell phone. *The police should have been checking out those shots, not Janet,* she thought.

She glanced at her iPhone on the seat beside her. What troubled her most was that Janet had gone there without a cell phone. Though, if she did have one, Charlotte would have been flabbergasted because Janet was somewhat of a technological Luddite.

Janet was being slowly won over to the merits of the technological age—it just wasn't fast enough for Charlotte. When she'd bought Janet a new digital camera for her birthday, she half expected that it would never leave its box. But to her surprise, Janet took to it like a child to candy and peppered Charlotte with all kinds of questions before finally settling down to read the instructions. Janet had even signed up for photography courses at Georgian College, where her friends benefitted by receiving beautifully framed photos. Charlotte had two large framed photos hanging over her couch.

The cell phone, on the other hand, was a different story. According to Janet, it was no more than a newfangled device that had insinuated its way into her life without so much as an invitation. She had made up her mind that she would not have that bothersome appendage glued to her ear. She always said that if someone really wanted to talk to her, they would leave a message on her land-phone, and she would simply call them back.

Charlotte picked up her iPhone and was about to dial 911 when she hesitated. Not wanting to make a mountain out of molehill, she decided against the call, convinced that if Janet had thought that there had been any real danger, she would have encouraged her to do it.

Charlotte returned her phone to the seat beside her.

The temperature gauge in her car read 40 degrees Celsius. The air-conditioning had broken down several months ago and, somehow, she had never got around to getting it fixed. It was a decision that, at the moment, she dearly regretted.

Feeling light-headed, she pulled over at the entrance to the Valley River Gorge Road and turned off her engine. After taking off her Toronto Blue Jays hat, she used it to wipe the perspiration from her face and brow before throwing it on top of her iPhone. Then she reached behind her and withdrew two bottles of water from the cooler on the floor before stepping out onto the gravelled shoulder. She poured the contents of one bottle over her neck and face. The cold, refreshing liquid reinvigorated her.

Tossing the empty bottle into a blue recycling box on the floor behind the passenger seat, she meandered down the tree-canopied road toward the river. The road was not graded and had not been freshly dressed with gravel in over two years, so it was deeply grooved and worn from numerous cars that had travelled along it. Provincial cutbacks had slammed the region hard socially, economically and culturally; this road was just one of the many casualties.

At first, the ground on either side of Charlotte was flat and gently rolling, with an occasional stone outcropping poking out between a plethora of shrubs, ferns and trees. She stopped for a few moments to admire the artistry of a yellow and black spider making its web between two milkweed plants.

Ahead, the route slipped between limestone faces that crowded in from either side. Charlotte had forgotten how long the route was to the shoreline, and she wished she had driven instead of walking it. She stopped to take a drink from her water bottle and rest.

The road's shoulder was no more than a sliver now, and the decline was steeper, scarred and furrowed from spring run-off that had coursed its route before the drought.

This route amazed her with its resiliency and diversity of habitats and how well it had fared during the drought. Yet the vegetation showed signs of stress and was fast approaching its tipping point. Trees atop the limestone faces on either side spread sun-dappled shade across the path. Certain types of delicate ferns existed in the Gorge area and nowhere else in the province, like Northern Holy Fern and Walking Fern, which sprouted from fissures in the face of the limestone. Though the road's incline had made it awkward for Charlotte to keep her footing, she reached out and delicately touched and examined the ferns.

The cliffs on either side began to crowd in. Charlotte continued to scour the numerous crevices filling the face of the cliffs on either side for smaller ferns that often went unnoticed because of their size; if found, they were treats for naturalists like her. A Maidenhair Spleenwort Fern, four metres up on her right, caught her attention, and she started to climb up for a closer look.

Charlotte never heard the vehicle coming. The roof of the Lincoln Navigator slid under her heel. Its speed told her that either the driver was oblivious to her presence or just didn't care.

Hugging the wall of the cliff, she tried to capture a glance of its license plate number, but her angle and its dirty plates prevented it.

Charlotte carefully maneuvered down to the road. The distant drone of another vehicle sent her running up the road to where it widened, and she crouched behind a thick bush.

When the Wrangler whizzed by her, she gave chase. She knew it was moving much too fast for her to keep up, but she had to try. She wanted to see the person driving it.

She stumbled and stumbled again, yet she breathlessly kept going. She was unable to see the Wrangler, and then she could still faintly hear it. Then, there was nothing.

Out of breath, she stopped, bent over with her hands digging into her thighs and gulped air. Her eyes followed the route ahead. The surface was too hard to follow the Wrangler's tire tracks.

Charlotte's mind darted back to Janet.

Turning, she quickly made her way back down the road, filled with fear that something may have happened to her. She picked up speed down the slope, mindless of any possible harm that may be awaiting her. Her hand patted her pocket for her iPhone, but she had left it in the car. *How stupid of me!*

Her brain churned with worry and fear, but somehow it galvanized her forward motion. When she reached the steepest part of the decline, her speed picked up dramatically, and it took all of her concentration and agility to stop from going head over heels.

Not knowing what she was going to find in that clearing, every instinct told her that Janet was still somewhere down there and might need her help.

Charlotte barely had time to react. She was scooped up by the Camaro as it came around the corner, planting her squarely on its hood. Arms and legs splayed out across it, face pressed against the windshield, she came eye to eye with a shocked and screaming Janet.

Janet slammed her foot on the brake, her stick-shift thrown into park while turning her steering wheel sharply to the right. She forcefully pulled her hand brake up and turned off the ignition. Then she headed out to attend to Charlotte. "Oh my god!" Janet was frantically praying and half delirious as she reached her friend, who was draped over the hood of her car. "Speak to me. Tell me you're okay! Please!" She pulled back Charlotte's hair and began stroking her face while her other hand felt along her spinal column.

Momentarily stunned by the impact, Charlotte moaned. Every part of her body ached, and she hesitated to move. She could hear Janet mumbling something, and she felt a hand along her back. "What are you doing, Janet?"

"I'm trying to make sure you're intact."

"Leave me alone. Just let me lie here for a minute."

Charlotte tried to take in a deep breath, but her ribs screamed in pain. She took in a number of shallow breaths and waited it out.

"Well, are you okay?" Janet asked.

"Help me down."

Slowly and carefully and with Janet's assistance, Charlotte slid onto the ground from the Camaro. Releasing herself from Janet, she cautiously felt her ribs.

"Well?" Janet asked again. Tentatively reaching out, she withdrew her gesture to help when Charlotte waved her off.

"I don't think they're broken—just badly bruised," Charlotte replied. "Thanks for driving so slowly."

"It doesn't move any faster up a hill like that."

"If you had torn up here like the previous two vehicles had ... well, let's not go there."

Charlotte made her way to the passenger door of the Camaro and opened it.

"Right now, Janet, I need you to drive me back to my car."

Charlotte eased herself into the seat and reached for the safety belt, but the sharp jolt of pain made her quickly give up on that idea.

"Are you sure I shouldn't be taking you to the hospital?" Janet said as she attentively clicked Charlotte's safety belt in place.

"I'm sure." Charlotte adjusted her seat slightly and then turned to Janet, who had just settled in behind the wheel. "Did you find out who those shooters were?"

"I'll tell you as we drive. Right now, all my attention must be right here with my baby," she said, patting the steering wheel. Turning the key in the ignition, Janet slammed the stick-shift into first gear before she released the hand break. The Camaro stalled, causing them to roll down the hill; they came to a stop at the river's edge.

"It wasn't quite the direction I was intendin', dearie," Janet said with a chuckle, turning to Charlotte. "At least from this vantage point, we have a better run at that hill."

"I'm sure Napoleon was just as positive at Waterloo. Whatever, I can't watch." Charlotte placed her hands over her eyes.

Janet revved up the motor and floored the accelerator. First gear. Second gear. "I think you can come up for air now, Charlotte," she snickered, grinding the gear into third. "We've made it."

Janet talked nonstop as the two of them jounced along the short distance back to where Charlotte's Toyota Prius was parked. She told her about finding the empty gun sleeves and unused cartridge magazines in the back of the Lincoln Navigator. She spoke about the Silverado and finding Slocum's red Wrangler at the river's shoreline. She proudly bragged about how she had used her digital camera to record each vehicle while recognizing that since no one was caught red-handed, she really had no proof. Still, she persisted in insisting that the pictures she had taken of the hardware inside the Lincoln should be enough to push for a police investigation. She relayed why she thought Slocum was probably an innocent bystander, and she feared that he may have been hurt. Sprinkled throughout her recount were spliced-in apologies for not having gone home as Charlotte had directed.

When they parked beside the Prius, Charlotte released her seat belt, opened the door and, gritting her teeth, stepped out and walked about holding her side. That bumpy ride had taken its toll, and it was something she didn't want soon to repeat.

Walking over to the Prius, she carefully reached through the window, pulled out her iPhone and dialed 911. After she answered their questions, they connected her directly to Paul Dickenson of the Durham police, and she calmly related what Janet had told her and her own experience while emphasizing throughout her concerns for Slocum. When she finished, she dropped the phone on the passenger seat and went around to the driver's side, pulling out a pair of sandals. She sat on the edge of the seat and began to remove her work boots and socks.

Janet was in the process of getting out of her car to help her but Charlotte waved her off.

Without thinking, Charlotte held up her socks and sniffed them. Her face contorted as if she had just taken a large bite from a lemon. "Whew!" She flung the offending fetor to the ground and finished putting on her sandals.

Taking in a deep breath and using the steering wheel to steady her, she stood up.

"Now, that feels much better," she said, wiggling her toes. She looked over at Janet, who was still in the Camaro.

"You know, I never did see that Silverado—but there is something else." Charlotte continued to massage her side.

"Fire away," Janet rejoined.

"Well, how did you know the Wrangler belonged to Edward?"

"The license plate." Janet's head dipped below the car window before popping up again. "PineMed 1." Her head disappeared below the window again as she kept talking. "It's the name of his farm: Pine Meadows."

"What's the one stand for?"

Janet appeared in the open window again.

"I've not a clue."

"Well, that sure wasn't Edward driving that car," Charlotte said. "And that's what makes me think something has happened to him." She looked at her watch. "I wish they'd hurry up and get here."

"But you said you didn't get a good look at the driver," replied Janet as she disappeared below the window again.

"I didn't. But he was too big to be Edward. His profile wasn't right."

"And you should know?" Janet questioned.

"It's not as if I haven't seen him around," Charlotte shot back defensively. Charlotte moved closer to the car and peered into the window. "What the heck are you doing?" she asked.

Janet looked up at her. "My legs itch like hell."

"You'd better get home and do what I told you to do. I'll wait for the police."

"Do you think Dickenson will bring Rusty? That big, lovable Lab of his is one great dog."

"How should I know if he's bringing his dog? Go home, now!" As Charlotte looked at her watch again, she noticed a car in the distance. "I think that's Paul coming. Now get going! I'll take care of it from here."

CHAPTER THIRTEEN

EDWARD FELT A CLAUSTROPHOBIC surge of panic as he tried to focus his eyes. The stale air made him nauseous. The side of his face felt wet, and the tip of his tongue tasted a salty mixture of perspiration and blood. His head felt terrible. He slowly moved his hand up the side of his face until he felt the wound above his ear. A blood drop landed on the ground where others had preceded it, and at the back of his head was a nasty bump.

Somehow he had managed to contort his body into a very unnatural alignment, and he carefully rolled over to his back but was unable to stretch out fully.

Leaves rustled close by. He held his breath and listened intently. The tranquil sound of the distant river and the occasional flutter of wings assuaged his concerns. Moments passed, and still he sensed no human presence.

Twilight was beginning to merge with dusk.

He felt the swollen tissue around the wound. The bleeding had stopped, but the throbbing headache continued to assail him. Stretching as best he could, suddenly his legs began to cramp, and he quickly pulled them back, massaging them. When the cramping disappeared, he lay back quietly and took time to take in his surroundings.

Roots hung from the ceiling like fine lace. The dirt floor was flat, smooth and damp. The walls and ceiling showed shovel marks from a recent excavation. Coke cans, chocolate wrappers, cigarette butts and brown paper bags were scattered about. A urine smell mixed with rotting vegetation and something else, sweet and nauseating, permeated the atmosphere.

Trying to sit up, he bumped his head on the low-lying ceiling. He lifted himself up slightly with his elbows so as not to hit his head again, and he pushed his feet out of the opening. Then, rocking his torso from side to side and using his elbows and hands to aid him, he inched his way forward.

The portal to his temporary refuge looked like an open mouth with a dramatically protruding lower lip, similar to the brass head on an old-fashioned ashtray. Dappled light danced beyond the opening while the unsavoury odours within this cavity continued to assault his senses. *I have to get out before I vomit.*

Pushing with all his might, Edward propelled himself through the opening, hitting the ground about a metre below his exit.

Volumes of salty sweat dripped from his forehead and washed over his face, stinging his eyes. He pressed his knuckles into his eyes, hoping to wring out the irritating sweat, but he soon gave up and instead pulled the dirty bottom of his T-shirt up to wipe the perspiration away. He looked up to the unobtrusive opening in the face of the embankment that had been his haven.

Edward's head throbbed, and the bleeding had started again. His chest and shoulder ached as he rose to his knees. Images of what had happened rushed through his brain like a hurricane, and his fears pushed him closer to the ground as he scrutinized his environs.

Rivulets of blood trickled down the side of his face from the wound above his ear. He absently touched the spongy swelling on the back of his head—and instantly regretted doing so. The pain was excruciating, and he clasped his knee tightly, rocking to and fro until the intermittent waves of pain subsided.

Taking in several deep breaths, he forced himself to stand. The pounding pain in his head caused him to become disoriented as he staggered toward the embankment. Falling to one knee, he waited until the pain became nothing more than a persistent, dull, throbbing nuisance.

He breathed deeply several times and, finally feeling ready, began to climb.

At the top of the embankment, he lay perfectly still, listening. He could hear distant voices coming in his direction.

Goddamn it, they've got a dog!

Three kinds of emotions were triggered when he was shot at. Denial, associated with the disbelief that someone would try to kill him. Elation, the ecstatic joy he felt once he managed to live through it. Paranoia, when he expected his would-be assassins to appear at every turn.

Paranoia had Edward firmly in its grasp.

Blood from the wound above his ear channelled down the side of his face, dripping off his jawline, and he wiped it away with the back of his hand.

Crawling on his belly, he clawed his way through the underbrush. At the edge of the path, he stopped and pushed aside the tall grass, looking along the well-worn pathway, listening intently.

The sounds of breaking branches and the barking dog drew closer.

Frantically, he searched for better cover. Time had limited his options. Rising, he burst across the path into the thick hawthorn and honeysuckle bushes on the other side of the path. He was oblivious to the hawthorn thorns ripping at his flesh.

When he hit the ground, it temporarily knocked the wind out of him. Like a wild and wounded animal, Edward scratched his way to the base of the hawthorn and honeysuckle and began to cover himself with layers of dried leaves and mildew-smelling earth to camouflage his scent from the dog. Satisfied that he had done what he could, he waited.

The pain in his head returned with a vengeance. Before falling unconscious, the last thing he remembered were their voices and footsteps inches from where he lay. And that goddamn dog!

Chapter Fourteen

THE SUN HAD ALREADY begun to cross to the western horizon as Bolsover's limo sped along County Road 13 to his cabinet meeting. He slid the opaque divider that separated him from the front seat open and looked out through the windshield.

Vibrating heat waves had created several large mirage puddles ahead. It was an effect Bolsover had been fascinated with since childhood.

He watched as his route unfurled like a black ribbon, first falling gently and then dramatically as it spilled into the Beaver Valley. Alternating between the side windows, his eyes followed the slope of the valley, swooping down on one side like the path of a bird of prey only to climb sharply again on the other side to meet Old Baldy, the white exposed face of the Niagara Escarpment.

He shook his head in amazement, recalling how this valley, an indentation of the Niagara Escarpment, was formed from river erosion many years before. Sitting back, he rested his head against the doorframe and watched the landscape speed by.

Dotting his route, in various states of disrepair, were barns built of limestone foundations, quarried and cut in the region. On either side of his route, greyish and almost ashen cedars, exposed to the hot blasting winds, clung to fissures in solid rock. Parch-dry leaves and vegetation opened new hunting grounds for turkey vultures cruising overhead, hunting for carrion.

"Ugly bastards," mumbled Bolsover under his breath. "If I had a gun, I'd get you." Bolsover aimed his forefinger at the circling vulture, his thumb cocked back like the hammer on a gun. *"Pow!* Got ya, you ugly sonofabitch!"

Closing the divider, he picked up his briefcase from the floor, laid it across his lap and opened it, pulling out the envelope that contained the hundred thousand dollars Rattray had given him earlier. A slight smile etched across his face as he glanced out the window, absently caressing the envelope. He placed the envelope down on the seat to his right and removed the other documents and files from his briefcase, piling them to his left.

Using both hands, his fingers nimbly worked in opposite directions around the inner seams of the briefcase until the bottom panel came free. He placed the panel on the floor, released the Velcro that held the voice-activated recorder in place and took out the recorder. Popping out its memory chip, he took out a small, brown envelope from one of the sleeves in his briefcase and placed the chip in it. Retrieving a pen from his briefcase, he wrote the following on the envelope: "William Rattray's home, Wednesday, July 10." Below it, he wrote down the time of arrival and departure before he returned the pen to its original location and closed the case.

He began recording these meetings about five years ago, shortly after his affair began with Rattray's wife, Diane, to protect himself against any fallout that might occur should Rattray find out. In other words, he needed something to keep at bay the danger inherent in Rattray's unforgiving, vindictive and revengeful personality. As time had passed, he'd realized these tapes offered much more for him. They were an invaluable currency for persuasion that led to power and wealth. It meant he would always have the winning hand to extort from Rattray whatever he needed or wanted. The times of choosing and their frequency fell entirely within his domain.

He placed the envelope containing the memory chip on top of the package containing the money.

In the early morning hours, when he was unable to sleep—and that was often lately—he would go into the privacy of his study, open his vault and listen to some of those tapes. He knew it would have been wiser to have stored them in a safe-deposit box, but like everything associated with his relationship with Rattray, it had become an addiction, and he needed his fix close at hand. *Now, those DVDs are a whole different story,* he thought, smiling to himself. *I wonder what Rattray would do if he knew I still had a copy?* He patted the envelope containing the memory chip. *Nothing! That's what he'd do. Nothing!*

After he had listened to the tapes, he would usually lock the door to his study and withdraw the DVDs from the safe, for his personal viewing.

Lascivious thoughts of their contents aroused him and he began to massage the growing hardness in his pants. Abruptly he stopped when he passed the sign to Kimberley; he was only two kilometres away from his cabinet meeting.

Sitting up, he removed the briefcase from his lap and placed it on the floor. He then opened the cabinet in front of him. A small safe, installed to protect sensitive documents while in transit, was recessed into the cabinet's rich walnut wood interior. After dialling the safe's combination and opening it, he withdrew a rectangular teak box, hinged on the short side by gold-plated hinges. The interior of the box was lined in red velvet and divided into four rows, each with 10 slots. Two of the rows were filled with small, brown envelopes similar to the one sitting on the package beside him.

He placed his most recent recording in the appropriate slot, closed the box and returned it to the safe. Jamming in the package containing the money, he forced the door to the safe shut, spun the dial on the combination lock and sat back, closing the cabinet door with the toe of his shoe.

He had had those DVDs for several months before handing a copy over to Rattray. Not because he wrestled with some lofty moral dilemma—just the opposite! The sexual content was more than titillating to him, especially in those early morning hours. Images looped through his brain like the film on a projector as he thought of it, and he became aroused again.

He didn't care that Blackwell—dear old Chucky—was fucking Slocum's wife. Not at all! A little word to Antonio to fix it, and it was fixed. Chuck, "happily married" Chuck, was fucking somebody else's wife who just happened to be his best friend's wife. All caught and recorded. Perfect! Check and checkmate! Slam dunk!

He slapped his knee triumphantly. The memory chip and DVDs held equal weight in his extortion plans. *Chucky boy wouldn't risk humiliation and his career going down the toilet. No sir, not him. The hypocritical sonofabitch will take my place in Rattray's dirty little tangled web while I'm spinning one of my own.*

He opened the divider again and sat back.

A broad grin crossed his face as he looked at the back of Antonio's balding head. He remembered the first time Antonio demonstrated his special abilities. It had been two weeks before Christmas during his first year in office as premier. He had offered to drive a female reporter home from a party that they had both attended. Drunk, he had tried to force himself on her in the back of his limo. A nasty scene developed, and she threatened to blow the whistle on him for attempted rape. Traffic was at a standstill when she attempted to exit his limo on Hwy 401. Pursing his lips together, he shook his head as he remembered the struggle that ensued to prevent her from exiting. Somehow—and he didn't know how it happened—he had knocked her out.

Antonio had exited at the next ramp and had toured about until he found a vacant lot, parking in a location without lighting and cameras. Antonio had given Bolsover some pills to calm him down and had made a number of phone calls on his cell. A half hour later, another limo had arrived to take Bolsover home.

The apprenticing young female reporter was never seen or heard from again.

Bolsover remembered that the newscasts had been filled with her disappearance and the actions by local and provincial police to find her. There had even been a reward, though he couldn't recall the amount, set up by the local news station she had worked for and by her parents.

Within three months, the story of her disappearance had gone from the front pages of newspapers to the back, eventually disappearing altogether. Daily newscasts, once consumed by her disappearance, had moved on. *I'm always amazed by the public's short attention span,* he reflected.

He finished his bottled water and placed it in the sleeve on the door. *How easily the public becomes bored and distracted. Oh, well! That little piece of knowledge has served me well.*

That night Antonio had become his most trusted and valued asset.

He felt Antonio's dark, expressionless eyes staring back at him through the rear-view mirror. He quickly reassembled his briefcase and organized his papers. He smiled back at Antonio. A deep uneasiness, as if at the edge of some horrific nightmare about to happen, swelled up in him.

The limo entered the town of Kimberley and branched off along the road leading to Talisman Resort and Spa, where his cabinet awaited his arrival.

Soon, Antonio, he thought, *I'll keep my promise to you. Canadian citizenship will be your reward.*

He knew it was a promise he dared not break.

.

I'VE REALLY PISSED OFF SOMEONE

CHAPTER FIFTEEN

CONSTABLE PAUL DICKENSON PARKED his police van beside Charlotte's Prius at the entrance to the Valley River Gorge Road. He and his partner, Richard Malone, got out, and after the usual cordialities, Constable Malone went to get their search dog, Rusty, out of the back of the van while Paul went over Charlotte's earlier report to 911 and him. Taking out his cell phone, he tried reaching Edward at both his home and workplace.

"Hmm," Paul mumbled under his breath as he returned the cell to its holder on his belt.

"No luck?" Charlotte asked.

Paul shook his head in response.

"You know, Paul, I know this area pretty well. If Edward's somewhere down there, I can help you find him," she added.

"I appreciate your offer, Charlotte, and I can see you're concerned, but at this stage we're best trained to do that," Paul replied, patting Rusty's head. "He's a damn good search dog."

"Janet and I are concerned that Edward may have fallen to foul play."

"I know you are, but it's too early to fret about that Charlotte. Don't let your imagination get the better of you. Are you listening to me?"

"I hear you. It's just ..."

"I know," Paul interjected. "But sometimes what you think you saw or heard often turns out to have a whole different meaning. Look, we'd better get going while we still have light. If you think of anything else you may have seen or heard, call me, okay?"

Paul did not wait for her reply as he joined Richard and Rusty, who were already heading down the Gorge Road.

As she watched them disappear, Charlotte decided to take a detour on her way home and drop by Edward's property.

Charlotte turned off the asphalt-surfaced Artemesia-Glenelg Townline and onto the recently graded and freshly gravelled North Line Road toward Edward's place, just outside of the town of Priceville. The route, lined with old stately oak and maple trees, wound lazily through the countryside.

As she drove, her mind drifted back to the time when she and Edward had first met.

Along with the other grade nine students, Charlotte and her friend Susan Mueller had arrived at the high school the day before formal classes to participate in a mandatory orientation program for grade nine students in the auditorium. Upon arrival, the school's counseling department divided the students into groups alphabetically.

Once the counselor in each group explained the function of their department, they were introduced to their student leader. It was then she first met Edward.

After the principal had delivered her welcoming address and had left the stage, the approaching sounds of a marching band generated excitement among the students. The atmosphere became electric as the room fell dark and the flood lights to the stage went on. The band, student council, cheerleaders and football team marched in from both sides of the stage. Morris McAlistair, the president of the student council, came to the mike and waited for the band to finish the school song. When all had settled down, he gave a short address on the purpose of the student council and then quickly introduced his executive before carrying on to the cheerleaders and football team.

The new quarterback for the team, Edward Slocum, was conspicuously singled out by his good friend Morris. When Morris was finally done, balloons dropped down from the ceiling above the stage and cascaded onto the gym floor, where they were cheerfully exploded by the scurrying frenzy of students.

A large screen slowly lowered from behind the ceiling curtain that fronted the stage, and the lyrics to the school song were projected onto it. When the band struck up, each group in turn was encouraged to sing the most raucous, dramatic version of the school's song without getting too far out of tune. Charlotte's group, which was all girls, excelled.

She had already become attracted to the charismatic quarterback leading her group to the heights of fun-filled foolishness.

Late summer melted into autumn during her first year in high school, and Charlotte spent her weekends at Susan's learning how to horseback ride. During one of her riding sessions, Morris, who had become Susan's boyfriend, showed up with Edward. Edward hung around talking to Charlotte about the school's upcoming football game and the strategy they were going to use to beat the Hanover Devils; she tended to her horse in the stable. Then, out of the blue, he asked her to go with him to the Halloween dance at school. Immediately she knew her answer was yes, but she contained herself and refused to give him a definite answer under the pretense of obtaining her parents' okay.

She then kept him waiting almost a week before she told him yes.

He kissed her for the first time at that dance, and for the next two years, they were an item at their high school.

Their relationship began to change shortly after June graduation. Charlotte still had two more years to go, and she didn't look forward to being separated from him while he attended university. The time they spent together during that summer soon erupted into argument. About two weeks before he left for university, she was invited to his parents' cottage on Georgian Bay, about an hour north of Markdale. A fresh body of water, Georgian Bay spills into Lake Huron, one of the Great Lakes.

She remembered those two weeks spent with Edward and his parents as the best time of the summer. They boated, trekked, sang around campfires, played games and toured the area along the coast from Collingwood to Meaford.

It was also the first time she and Edward made love.

By the time she graduated from high school, their relationship was hanging by a thread. She barely saw him. Then, one evening, after a short phone call from him, it was over.

She later learned through his friend Morris that Edward had been dating a girl he had met during his second year.

A year later, Charlotte was asked to be the maid of honour at Susan's upcoming wedding to Morris. It was during the prenuptial rehearsal that she met Edward again; he was Morris's best man. It was also the first time she met Karen. She remembered it bothering her how her best friend Susan seemed to easily hit it off with Karen.

As the years passed by, she learned tidbits about Edward's life through Morris and Susan.

When Edward moved back to West Grey to take on his new position at KemKor Pharmaceuticals, she learned that Morris and Susan were invited to a party that Edward and Karen were throwing at their new property, called Pine Meadows. Though she didn't say anything to Susan, Charlotte wanted to go if for no other reason than a general interest in seeing how Edward may have changed since she'd last seen him—not that she really expected any big changes.

Two days after Susan had spoken to her about the party, she received a phone call from Karen inviting her. Charlotte accepted.

Before Karen's untimely death, Charlotte and she became friends in a small way. Though invited to several parties at their home, Charlotte only attended that one time.

Charlotte's Toyota Prius rumbled across a rusting iron bridge over one of the many convoluted paths carved out by the Saugeen River. When she returned to the gravel road, she noticed some horses standing under a tree near a pond.

Moss-covered rail fencing snaked beside stunted corn fields on one side of the road while either limestone boulder walls or white-painted wooden fencing lined the other fields that abutted the road on the opposite side.

The rollicking song of Bobolinks intermingled with the mooing sounds of cattle, which either grazed or lounged under the shade of trees.

Ahead, two horseback riders came out of Edward's lane and rode toward her.

She pulled her car to the side of the road and put it into park.

The field beside her was fenced with limestone boulders in various states of disrepair. On one of the rumpled hills behind the stone wall was an old, weather-beaten wagon that tilted on an empty front axle and was braced against a wagon wheel.

An SUV backed down the same lane the horseback riders had just come down, and because of the etching on its back window, she was sure it was the same Lincoln Navigator that almost dislodged her from the face of the cliff in the Gorge.

When the Navigator came to a skidding halt on the road, plumes of dust engulfed it.

A man with a ponytail, who sat in the passenger seat, began pointing in her direction. Then, he and the driver got into an animated discussion.

The black Lincoln Navigator began to slowly back down toward her.

Charlotte was about to put her vehicle into reverse when sunlight, reflecting off the rear window of the Navigator, momentarily blinded her.

At that point, all hell let loose!

The lead horse reared, sending the rider off its back and onto the road. When the horse came back down, its front hoofs landed squarely on the front of her car, setting off her air bag and stunning her, while the horse fell backward and onto its side. When it regained its footing, it pushed by the other rider and stood its ground between the car and rider.

The Navigator stopped reversing and thrust forward, spitting out a shower of gravel that stung the hindquarters and flanks of both horses.

Chaos swirled around Charlotte.

The still-mounted horse reared but remained firmly under the control of the rider.

Through the labyrinth of the spider web–shattered windshield, she could read "Idylwilde" across the Navigator's back window as it tore up the road and disappeared over the hill.

Suddenly the riderless horse's hind legs kicked backward with two short, powerful bursts, caving in her driver's door and setting off the side air bags.

Shit! She felt as if someone had just used her face as a punching bag. Crawling across the seat, she exited through the passenger door. The ground she expected to find there was three feet below her car, and she fell into the culvert with a thud, knocking the wind out of her. *How stupid of me not to remember how close I was!*

The boys' frantic voices drew Charlotte's attention back to the road as she remembered the fallen rider. As she got up and began to make her way back up to the road, the horse that had kicked in her driver's-side door jumped the fence on the other side.

Good riddance, she thought.

Kneeling beside the fallen boy, Charlotte checked his pulse and gently touched his face. "Are you okay?"

"I'm all right." His reply was tentative and weak. After a short silence, he quietly said under his breath: "I guess I should have been better prepared."

"What's your name?" Charlotte was concerned by his sleepy-like speech and feared he may have suffered a concussion or worse.

"Andres. My name is Andres."

He tried to move, but she discouraged him with her hand. "No! Lie still. Do you or the other rider have a cell phone?"

"The other rider—he is my brother, Camilo. I don't have one, but he does."

"Of course! You're Josh Green's boys. I'm Charlotte Bradley."

"I know."

Camilo, who had already dismounted and was holding the reins of his horse in one hand, walked toward them. Handing the reins to Charlotte, he dropped down on one knee and began to examine his brother from the neck down. Camilo's hands worked diligently as they skilfully explored the full length of his brother's frame. After he was done, he turned back to Charlotte. "He's okay. Nothin' broken. Badly bruised, some gashes, but no need for stitching or hospital." He turned back to his brother. "Are you ready to go?" he asked Andres in Spanish. Camilo placed one arm along his brother's shoulder and helped him to sit up. Then, using his other hand, he helped Andres to his feet.

"It's not stitches I'm worried about, Camilo. He could have a concussion. Please, call 911 so someone with more medical experience can check him out," she pleaded. She slowly began to pace back and forth in front of them before stopping and staring at Camilo. "Please! Or else *I'll* call! Unless … are you two in some kinda trouble?"

Camilo's cold stare unsettled Charlotte, and she backed up a couple of paces.

"I know what I'm doing," Camilo replied. He turned to his brother. "Let's get out of here before she asks too many questions," he said in Spanish.

"Who were those men in the Navigator?" Charlotte interjected in Spanish.

Charlotte loved these "gotcha" moments, especially when she was dealing with assholes like Camilo, and she let her Spanish language skills sink in for a moment before continuing. "Well, who were those men who just left Mr. Slocum's?" She stepped into Camilo's personal space, but he didn't budge from his position. "What did you mean by, 'Let's get out of here before she asks too many questions'?" she continued in Spanish.

Camilo said nothing. His cold, blank stare sent a chill up Charlotte's spine. *This guy's a bad dude.* It was a conclusion she had deduced shortly after climbing out of the ditch.

Camilo climbed onto his horse and then pulled Andres up behind him.

Pointing to her battered Toyota, he said, "Next time, you may not be so lucky."

"There won't be a next time!" she yelled.

Showing them the bird, Charlotte was disappointed that neither boy looked back to see it.

Charlotte walked toward the lane that led to Edward's home. Her face hurt like hell along with the rest of her body. Halfway up the drive, she noticed the door to his porch was wide open.

Chapter Sixteen

"EDWARD, ARE YOU OKAY? Can you walk?" Paul asked, kneeling down beside him.

At first the voice talking to him seemed detached and distant. When Edward finally opened his eyes, he felt relief to see Paul's friendly face looking down at him. "Yes—no. I don't know." Edward's reply was garbled; his mouth felt full of marbles.

Rusty began to lick Edward's face, and he pulled the Labrador close to him, hugging him. "Thanks, furry friend."

Paul and Richard helped him to sit up while brushing off his clothes with their hands.

"How's that?" Paul asked.

"I guess okay, but who really knows until I try standing. I suppose I don't have to guess how you found me," he replied, ruffling the top of Rusty's head.

Edward's speech had returned, and other than the bongo player in his head, he did not feel too bad. "Tell me, how did you even know I was down here?"

"We can discuss that later. Right now, you need medical attention," Paul said. He looked over to Richard and signalled to him to get a grip under Edward's arm. "Once you think you've got a good hold there, Richard, we'll lift him."

Richard secured his grasp under Edward's arm and braced his legs. When he nodded to Paul he was ready, the two lifted Edward to his feet.

"Okay?" Paul and Richard asked in unison.

"Think so. Just a little unsteady."

"Well, don't worry. We've got a good hold on you," Paul reassured him.

Perspiration trickled down their faces, their clothing soaked in sweat.

"That's one helluva nasty wound above your ear. How did you get it?" Richard asked.

"Please don't touch it."

"I won't," Richard replied, withdrawing his hand.

"Well?" Paul enquired again. "How did you get it?"

"I was shot at."

"You were shot at? By who?"

"By one of the guys I saw last evening."

"Oh! Was he alone?"

"There were two others with him."

Edward's legs began to buckle under him, and Paul and Richard quickly readjusted their grips on him.

"Think of us as your crutches," Richard suggested. "Do you think you can do that?"

"I sure as hell will try. Just give me a few minutes."

"Let us know when you're ready to walk."

Paul stepped closer to Edward.

"Tell me something. Would you be able to recognize the other two guys?"

Edward shook his head. "Too busy running for my life." He felt the strength returning to his legs, and he stood taller. "I think I'm ready now."

The group slowly made its way back onto the path.

"Why the hell were you burrowed under all those rotten leaves?" Paul asked.

The three of them slowly moved along the path, Paul and Richard occasionally adjusting their grips each time Edward stumbled.

"Camouflage."

"Come again?"

"To throw the dog off my sent. I thought they had returned with a dog."

"I see." A crease of a smile formed at the corner of Paul's lips. "So, other than the one shooting at you, you can't describe the others?"

Paul carefully maneuvered along the path, taking on slightly more of Edward's weight because of the slant of the path.

"No. After I recognized the guy out in front of them, I started running. Honestly, I was too damn scared to look back."

Edward stumbled again, but thanks to Paul and Richard's quick reactions, he recovered quickly.

"You okay?" Paul asked.

Edward nodded. "Keep going," he insisted.

"We got a call from Charlotte just before we found you. Seems your house has been broken into. Kinda coincidental," Paul said.

"I don't think so."

"You don't?" Paul rejoined.

"It's all connected with last evening," Edward continued. "That's why I was down here—to get samples from that effluent spill."

"But why break into your home?"

"I'd bet they were looking for my research notes."

"And you keep them there?" Paul asked.

"I do. But they're well hidden."

"I sure hope you're right. Well hidden often turns out to be obvious to the burglars. So where did you put them?"

"That's a little secret I'll keep to myself."

Edward clenched his jaw as he picked up his pace.

A half hour later, Edward was in the front passenger seat of the police van, working on his second bottle of water. He closed his eyes and leaned his head against the headrest as Paul fitted the seat belt around him.

"There. Comfortable enough?"

Edward nodded.

Richard returned from the back of the van with the first-aid kit, opening it. Paul opened a tube of Polysporin and spread the ointment along the wound above Edward's ear before bandaging it. He then handed him a couple of extra-strength Tylenol and told him to drink it down.

"There's really nothing I can do about that bump on the back of your head. How do you feel?" Paul asked.

"Do you need to ask?" Edward replied.

"No, I guess I don't. Hopefully, the Tylenol will help."

Edward finished his bottle of water and handed it to Paul.

After Richard had returned the first-aid kit to its proper location, he climbed into the van behind Edward.

Edward heard the panting and slurping sounds of Rusty in his cage, in the back of the van. To his surprise, Edward found the dog's sounds soothing and somehow reassuring.

"Whatever's going on, it looks to me that you're right in the centre," Paul said to Edward as he slipped his muscular frame behind the steering wheel.

"Yeah, I've really pissed off someone."

"That's one way to describe it."

Paul turned the ignition.

"What's another way?" Edward inquired.

"Somebody's out to get your number," Paul replied.

"I assume that means your appraisal of last evening and what happened has changed?"

"Uh-huh."

The van left the pebbled riverbank behind as it made its way up the embankment and onto the Valley River Gorge Road.

Paul turned onto the paved road in the direction of Markdale. "You know, that busted up puss of yours might get some sympathy votes for Blackwell," Paul said sardonically, a smirk on his face. "You are still goin' Saturday, aren't you?"

"You bet your ass I'm goin'. I've still got a few days to recover."

"I kinda expected you to say that. No harm meant. It's just I don't have a lot of nice things to say about politicians."

Paul made a quick call to Durham Police Central to fill them in and to arrange for officers to go to Edward's home.

"You mentioned Charlotte Bradley's name earlier," Edward said.

"I did. She called in the break-in at your place. Know her?"

"I guess you could say that. Why was she at my place?"

Paul shrugged. "Don't know." Clearing his throat, he shifted uncomfortably in his seat. "Why don't you lie back and relax. It shouldn't be too long before you're at the hospital."

"Sounds good." Edward shut his eyes. The gentle rocking of the vehicle and the hum of its engine soothed him.

"You know, Edward, I've been in this job too damn long not to have developed bullshit detection radar. I'll get to the bottom of whatever happened last night and today. Promise you."

"Thanks, Paul."

Edward's head rocked back and forth as he fell asleep.

Richard reached over the seat and tapped Paul on the shoulder.

"Quite a load of shit you just gave him," Richard whispered.

"If everyone keeps their story straight, keeping that promise should be easy."

"What are we going to do about him?" Richard nodded in Edward's direction.

Paul glanced at Edward, sleeping beside him, and said nothing.

CHAPTER SEVENTEEN

PAUL TURNED DOWN THE North Line Road toward Edward's home.

Edward had been given a complete bill of health by the doctor at the hospital. The wound above his ear had been cleaned and a new bandage applied. He also had been given enough Tylenol tablets with codeine and antibiotics to tie him over until he got his prescription filled.

Edward had been in and out of Markdale's Emergency Department within two hours. Other than a reoccurring headache when the effects of the Tylenol began to wear off, he felt fine. That is, fine for someone who had no doubt that he was still on the target list of the asshole who tried to kill him.

"Ya say somethin'?" Paul asked.

"Pisses me off! My entire CD collection was in that Wrangler."

"Interesting priorities," Paul said flatly. He looked somewhat askance at Edward. "I think there should be a lot more than that on your mind."

"Don't get me wrong—my head's spinning with the possibilities. But why would those jerks take my Wrangler, anyway?"

"My guess was to throw us off the scent. Whoever it was didn't count on someone seeing that it wasn't you who drove it off."

"Someone? Who?"

"Charlotte Bradley."

"Charlotte? Well, did she tell you who took it and where?"

"I wish she had. It would have made my job quite a bit easier."

Paul slowed his vehicle down as they passed a beat-up Toyota Prius at the side of the road.

"Any idea whose car?" Edward asked.

Stretching his neck, Edward continued to look at the Prius as they drove on.

"My guess, it's Charlotte Bradley's," Paul replied, turning into Edward's drive.

At the end of the drive were two policemen with Charlotte. They stopped their conversation to watch the police van as it pulled up and parked beside the cruiser.

Turning to Richard in the backseat, Paul asked him to exercise Rusty and then turned his attention back to Edward. "Edward, why don't you just rest here while I find out where things are at?"

Putting on his cap, Paul vacated the vehicle. By the time Paul joined the group, the three were already occupied patting Rusty and talking with Richard. Charlotte continued to fuss over Rusty while Paul and the other two constables stepped to one side to talk. A few minutes into their conversation, Paul looked over at Richard.

"I think you'd better get goin' with Rusty. Not long—just enough to stretch his legs. Remember to fill up his water bowl when you get back."

Edward watched from the comfortable coolness of the van as Charlotte joined Paul and the other two constables. He noticed that Charlotte kept shifting her attention back to him as she spoke to them.

Though Edward hadn't thought about it until now, he still found her attractive. He enjoyed watching her animated gestures as she spoke and the fluidity of her movements. When she took off her baseball cap and shook out her hair, he remembered when its soft, clean freshness once fell over him when they first made love as teenagers.

The first and only time they had made love was at his parents' cottage. In the shadow of adulthood, they had naively hoped their love would last forever. At the back of his parents' boathouse, as they had lain together, they had planned their future together, never once giving thought to how life might change and reshape them.

When Edward took the position at KemKor, he and Karen had hosted several social events to reintroduce him to the West Grey community.

To his delight, Karen had invited Charlotte to most of these events, but she had only attended once.

Though Karen, Susan and Charlotte had occasionally gone out to lunch or gone horseback riding, Karen often commented to Edward about Charlotte's aloofness, and that disappointed him.

Edward had every hope, after seeing Charlotte at Morris and Susan's wedding, that they would be friends.

"Forgive, not to forget," would be the mantel upon which to build their friendship. But as time and life would have it, friendship had become an elusive endeavor, and they rarely or ever spoke.

In a way Edward understood her actions though he had wished for something different. He came to the conclusion that Charlotte could not be a friend until she had come to accept that the person she used to share dreams with had changed and had now chosen to share other dreams with someone else.

Edward felt guilty for not returning Charlotte's phone calls after Karen died, but he just couldn't. Foolishly, he thought it would cast a blemish on his memories of Karen. He remembered meeting Charlotte shortly after he had begun working for KemKor and how those same old feelings had stirred in him. At the time, he had attributed his vulnerability to the troubles in his marriage.

When his relationship with Karen had improved, he had pulled out of groups and functions that he knew Charlotte would have likely been in attendance.

Charlotte looked back again, and he nodded his recognition and smiled. As Edward watched Charlotte, he felt a need to reconnect.

Paul motioned to Edward to join them.

After Edward was introduced to the other constables, George and Jim, Paul went over what he had gleaned from Charlotte and the report of the constables. After pocketing his notebook and pen, Paul turned his attention back to Edward. "Edward, your place's been trashed."

Edward's spirits dropped through the basement floor. He had expected the worse, but until he was told, he had hung on to the hope that maybe, just maybe, he would be lucky.

"You up to going in?" Paul asked.

Barking directed their attention to the field behind the barn as Rusty bounded across the field and onto the path toward them. Constable Richard Malone had given up the chase and, shaking his head, trudged his way along the same route the dog had just travelled.

Once the dog was back in its cage and water had been put in its bowl, Paul went around to the driver's side of the van and turned the air-conditioning up to full capacity. Then, yelling out to Richard to stay with the dog, he returned to Charlotte and Edward.

Other than saying "Hi" to each other, Charlotte and Edward stood awkwardly silent, waiting for Paul.

"Well, Edward, I guess we should go in. I need you to tell me what, if anything, is missing," Paul said. Paul preceded them onto the porch and waited for them at the open door.

Taking in a deep breath, Edward looked in. *Shit!*

Edward felt Charlotte's hand momentarily press on his.

Everything in the great room was either broken, turned upside down or piled in a heap.

For a moment, Edward couldn't bring himself to cross the threshold, and he popped another Tylenol with codeine into his mouth, swallowing it dry.

The forlorn look on the constables' faces told it all as they up righted the futon. Nothing was untouched except for the wood-pile beside the fireplace.

Paul's heavy hand fell across Edward's shoulders as he pressed him forward. "Edward. I need you to look around and tell me what's missing," he said, stepping around Edward and over the articles strewn across the floor. At the kitchen counter, he pulled out his notebook from his shirt pocket and flipped through it until he came to a blank page. Then he put it back in his pocket.

Edward tentatively stepped across the threshold. He was sure the expression on his face was similar to a deer caught in the headlights of a car. If it wasn't, it was damn close to it. "Look around? For what?" Edward felt so dejected. His home looked like a dump site. "Look, Paul, I still haven't got my head around this. Surely, you don't expect me to give you a full report this instant?"

Edward felt Charlotte's hand again as she gently gave his lower arm a reassuring squeeze. When she began to withdraw her hand, he quickly grasped it and was surprised not to meet resistance. "What I need at this moment is a stiff drink," Edward said loud enough for all to hear. He let go of Charlotte's hand and made his way across the mess to a cabinet in the far corner of the room and opened it. "God bless small mercies! It's all here! Come to me, baby!" Edward pulled out a bottle of Ardmore single-malt scotch and held it up as an offer. Charlotte nodded that she would have some, but the rest refused.

Edward had just passed Paul on his way to the kitchen when he felt dizzy and fell against the counter. Paul quickly grabbed him and relieved him of the bottle of scotch, placing it on the counter. He led Edward over to the futon and sat him down. "I think you'd be wise to lay off that scotch right now. I don't think it and the codeine are a good match."

Edward sat quietly on the futon, taking in the chaotic mess around him.

Paul took off his cap and, after wiping his brow with his sleeve, sat beside him on the futon. "You know, Edward," he said, sweeping the room with his hand, "we both know this is no coincidence. The stuff that happened to you down by the Gorge, I'd bet had everything to do with what you saw last night around Building 3C. But this … Well, it's a whole new story. Now, based on what Charlotte told me, the guys who broke in here were probably the same guys who shot at you. Do you have any idea why they would want to come back here?"

"Like I told you earlier, my research."

Edward slid forward and looked over the futon toward his office.

"By the looks of it, Paul, they took my computer."

Paul looked at Edward long and hard. "So you're still telling me you kept your results here and not at KemKor?"

"Both places, actually."

"And you're telling me it was on that computer they took?"

"No. I can say that with a hundred percent certainty."

"Where did you keep it, then?"

"That's still my secret."

"So you know for a fact it wasn't taken?"

"Actually, I don't know that."

Paul shuffled uncomfortably on the futon before standing up and looking down at Edward.

"George's going to stay at the top of the drive tonight."

"There's no need for that," Edward retorted.

"Edward, this is not open for negotiation."

"But—"

"Thank you, Paul," Charlotte interjected.

Paul was about to leave when he turned back. "When you get the serial numbers on that computer and anything else that comes to mind, get it over to me."

"Now, that could be a problem," Edward replied. "You see, I kept that stuff in my wallet. Karen and I always argued over the definition of a safe location. I argued wallet, and she the safety deposit box. Well, I guess this one is on me. My wallet was in the Wrangler. I just hope she put a copy in the safety deposit box."

Paul let out a deep sigh. "You'll check tomorrow then and let me know?"

"First thing," Edward confirmed. He stood up and wandered aimlessly about the room, kicking aside debris as he went. Suddenly he stopped and picked up the shattered frame containing Karen's photograph from under some paper. He carefully removed her photo and stood silently looking at it.

"Well, I'd better get going," Paul called out. He looked at his watch. "I should have enough time to get over to the Greens' before it's too dark."

"The Greens?" Slightly bewildered by the mention of that name, he walked over to Paul.

Paul cleared his throat before answering. "Charlotte here said she saw Josh Green's boys leaving this place on your horses. I know they exercise your horses, so there's no need to get into that. But it was another one of those coincidences I don't believe in."

"Surely you don't believe Camilo and Andres had anything to do with this?" Edward asked.

"I don't know what to believe. Right now, I'm following wherever a lead takes me."

After everyone had gone, Charlotte put together an icepack and held it at the back of Edward's head while they sat on the futon.

Through the large front window, the sun was a blazing red ball as it started its descent in the horizon.

"Do you think Janet will be long?" he asked.

"No, not much longer. Do you want me to phone again?"

"Only if you're in a hurry to leave."

"I'm not."

"Sorry about your car," Edward said. Taking the ice pack from her, he held it in place at the back of his head and stood up. "You know, I haven't a clue where to begin to start looking for my phone in this mess." He kicked aside the empty magazine rack. "And, quite honestly, I don't have the energy to start looking."

"Here, use my cell."

Edward took her iPhone, punched in some numbers and wandered off to his office.

After several attempts to reach Irving Grynberg, Edward returned to the living room and handed her the phone. "I can't reach him."

"Who?"

"Irving Grynberg. I don't know if you remember him, but he was a bud of mine during high school."

"Not really. Did you leave a message?"

"Yes, but I don't know what good that will do."

"What do you mean?"

"He never checks them."

"Oh. That could be a problem."

"I'll try again tomorrow." Edward's headache returned with a vengeance, along with a general malaise. "One more favour, Charlotte?"

"What's that?"

"Would you mind getting me a Tylenol? I think the pill container is on the kitchen table."

After he took his Tylenol along with a large glass of cold water, he let his head rest against the back of the futon.

"Don't get too settled there. Take that shirt off." Charlotte briskly helped him off with his shirt and held it up against the light coming in the front window. "This thing not only stinks, it's beyond filthy." She threw it toward the garbage bag at the end of the kitchen counter.

"Hey! The hamper's that-a-way," Edward exclaimed. He pointed in the direction of his bedroom.

Ignoring his complaint, Charlotte headed to the bedroom. A couple of minutes later, she returned with a wrinkled but clean shirt. "Put this on."

Charlotte picked up the garbage bag at the end of the kitchen counter and threw his shirt in it. Then she stuffed some of the garbage strewn about on the floor on top of it. When she looked back at Edward, half expecting a complaint, Edward was preoccupied with looking at the photo of Karen he had picked up from the floor.

SAN VICENTE DEL CALGUAN

Chapter Eighteen

ANDRES CLUNG TIGHTLY TO Camilo's waist as they cantered toward the path leading to their house. He knew Camilo would want to gallop the rest of the distance, and he wanted no part of it, especially because of his uncomfortably awkward sitting position behind him. Freeing one hand, he tapped forcefully on Camilo's shoulder. "Stop! Please! Stop! Let me off!"

Camilo ignored Andres's entreaties and dug his heels into the horse's side, commanding it to pick up its pace.

Jagged pain radiated outward from Andres's spine to his rib cage, and as the horse picked up speed, he slapped harder on Camilo's shoulder. "Goddamn it! Let me down!"

The horse came to an abrupt halt, lifting its front hooves high in the air.

Andres quickly grasped Camilo's belt for an anchor to stop from slipping off. When the horse's hooves came back down, Andres tried to readjust his position, but it was too late as the horse rose high in the air again.

Damn! I'm falling! Andres had only a split second to think. He knew the fall wouldn't kill him, but the horse's hooves might.

Stiffly angled across the horse's hind quarters, Andres was barely able to secure his position by holding on to Camilo's belt. Then the belt buckle broke, and he began to fall backward.

Camilo sharply swung around on his saddle and clamped his hand onto Andres's outstretched arm, holding him in place as the horse came back down.

"You're okay, little brother! I've got you!"

The horse jerked its head forward, showing its readiness to recommence its forward motion, but Camilo retained his command and sharply pulled back on the reins.

"Stand!" he commanded. "Stand!"

A few moments later, the horse, now standing still, showed its displeasure by sharply pinning back its ears.

"Let yourself down easy," Camilo said quietly. Camilo used both hands to secure the reins while he waited for his brother to safely dismount.

Relieved to be on terra firma again, Andres looked up at his brother and glimpsed a disdainful expression across his face.

Camilo circled the horse in ever-widening circles around Andres until, coming off the tangent, he then dug his heels into the horse's sides and cantered up the road.

Camilo was at a full gallop by the first bend in the road, reappearing and disappearing several times in blurred succession as he passed cedars and maples that lined the route. By the time he reached the third hill, he had become nothing more than a speck as he disappeared over its brim.

Dusk was well underway as Andres arched backward and tried some stretching exercises to work out the kinks from his fall earlier, but it only made the pain worse.

Gritting his teeth, he lumbered up the road. As he walked, Andres mulled over the incidents of the last few hours.

Andres hadn't liked the way Camilo had tried to intimidate Charlotte.

Intimidation was just one of many choices Camilo plied from his nasty bag of preferences—often against Andres.

Yet Andres was sure from the way she had stood her ground that Ms. Bradley hadn't been in the slightest way intimated by his brother, and that gave him deep satisfaction.

What bothered Andres the most was the break-in and the thought of being accused of betraying Mr. Slocum's trust.

He kicked at the stones as he walked.

Pain shot up Andres's back to the base of his head and he flinched. Stopping, he hunched over and waited for it to diminish. When the pain finally dissipated, he continued walking.

Night was quickly overtaking dusk. Ahead, the remnants of an old wall overhung with boughs of a maple tree offered a welcome respite.

Andres found a half section of the wall that was easy to perch on. While sitting on one of the flat rocks, he scooped up some gravel from the surrounding detritus and began to cast each stone aimlessly about, one at a time.

He thought about his birthplace, San Vicente del Calguan, in Colombia, and about a billboard that had been erected in the main plaza, facing the town church.

How old was I? Twelve? Yes—I was 12, he remembered. *What did it say? Now I remember. "Plan Colombia: los gringos ponen las armas Colombia pone los muertos." Strange I should remember that now. Maybe this heat's getting to me,* he mused.

While standing up and gritting his teeth in anticipation of the pain, Andres stretched the taut muscles across his back. He wanted to arrive home before dark, so he picked up his pace. Initially the pain slowed him down, but as he kept moving and trying to focus his mind elsewhere, the pain subsided somewhat. He cringed with the thought of how painful it may be getting out of bed next day.

His mind drifted back to that billboard in the main plaza, and he remembered asking his dad what it meant.

"It has only one message, son: No to gringo intervention in Colombia."

To this day, Andres had found his father's answer confusing, because he knew the literal translation was, "The gringos supply the arms, and Colombia supplies the dead."

He shrugged and attempted to jog, but he quickly gave up on that idea. When he came to the bridge at the bottom of the first hill, he stopped and leaned over the rail to watch the Saugeen River pass under it. After a few moments, he looked up at the sky. *I guess getting home before dark is out of the question.*

His mind drifted back to his family and their life in San Vicente del Calguan.

His family lived apart from the rigors of this frontier village because his father had been a high-ranking commander for the Revolutionary Armed Forces of Colombia, known as FARC. In the centre of town, during weekends, he remembered seeing smartly dressed, gold-chained coca buyers setting up small tables and putting one sisal bag with millions in local currency on their right-hand side and an empty bag on their left for the cocaine. Campesinos, peasant men and women of all ages, arrived from the surrounding region with small plastic bags of coca paste ready for sale. His dad, along with a large number of heavily armed men and women from his FARC unit, wandered among the tables demanding mordida, or coca taxes, from buyers. The campesinos had already paid his dad's unit earlier for each hectare of coca they had cultivated.

San Vicente was a village with gas fumes, manure-filled streets and river stench. Sometimes the smoke was so thick from slashed and burned forests that small planes were unable to land. When the small planes finally did land at the edge of the village, they were used to transport the coca paste to laboratories for processing into finished cocaine, which was later packed for export. Coca paste was a way of life and carried no moral weight; it was just the currency most people used for business. His parents often drove to Bogata to exchange coca paste for hard currency. It was on such a trip that his parents were killed in a car accident between Bogata and Villavicencio.

Six months later, through one of the local Christian missions, Camilo and Andres met Josh and Marta Green through their uncle Garcia. Working through their uncle and the Colombian authorities, the Greens were able to obtain custody of the boys. A year later, Camilo and Andres were on their way to live in Canada with Josh and Marta.

Andres's pain was now a dull ache that he barely noticed. He sighed deeply as he began his trek down the second hill.

I miss the Greens, he thought. *I wish they hadn't returned to Colombia.*

Six months earlier, Josh and Marta had returned to Colombia to continue their missionary work.

Andres was proud of his Colombian heritage and the country he had left five years ago. Living in Canada during that period had changed him.

He had come to realize that he no longer shared the same moral currency and goals of his Colombian family.

He kicked at the loose stones as he walked. When he came to the bottom of the second hill, the grade ahead seemed onerous, but after a few deep breaths, he labored on.

CHAPTER NINETEEN

DARKNESS HAD FALLEN AS Andres walked down the laneway to his house. He felt something reassuring, warm and welcoming when he looked up and saw the soft glow of light spilling through the windows onto the front veranda. Wedges of light streamed from the windows at the back of the house from the brick lean-to kitchen and the side where the doddy haus had been built. He was surprised that the Gothic-pointed window above the front door was in darkness since, on a normal night, he and his brother would be upstairs getting ready for bed.

Ahead of Andres, the laneway forked. One branch of the drive led to the house, while the other branch led to a large asphalt-covered surface in front of the egg-processing facility. Running off from the asphalt area was a winding pathway of sandy loam to the stables, located behind the facility. Three long, white-sided, red-roofed aluminum structures, forming a C, embraced the paved area. The loading docks at the egg-packing plant had refrigerated transport trailers in them, but only one bay was active with people.

Andres discerned the outline of four men in conversation, standing in front of the trucks. As he drew closer, he was able to recognize his brother, Uncle Garcia and Doug Irwin. Though he didn't know the other man present, he did know that that man, along with Doug and Camilo, had broken into Slocum's home earlier. Not wanting to know why these men were present at the farm, he backed up enough to make it clear that he had no intention of listening in and waited for his uncle to greet him. He was surprised that Camilo had not yet stabled his horse.

"Join us." Garcia invited Andres with a wave of his hand. "Camilo told me what happened. Are you okay?" his uncle asked, wrapping his arms around Andres and hugging him.

"Si, Uncle, I'm okay—really," Andres insisted.

Andres patiently waited for his uncle to finish examining him. Garcia turned him around and, running his hands up and down Andres's spine and around his ribs, he finally checked out Andres's head. "Maybe we should take you to the hospital, just to be safe."

"I don't need to go to the hospital. Really, Uncle, I'm okay!" Andres tried to back away and flinched under his uncle's pincher grasp.

Garcia frowned, his dark eyes probing him. "I just concerned. That's all."

He loosened his grip on Andres and gently pulled him closer, ruffling his hair and whispering into his ear.

Then turning to the others, Garcia said, "I was just telling my nephew here that he has good genes, just like his father." Garcia gave Andres a hearty slap across the back. Andres cringed in pain and did his best to hide it. "You say you okay, then okay it is. No hospital." Garcia let his arm slip away from Andres.

Camilo grabbed Andres's hands and pushed the reins into them. "Since nothing's wrong with you, here, take care of my horse."

Andres resented the demeaning way his brother treated him, especially in front of his uncle; doing it in front of these strangers made it worse. The punishing blows from his brother's fists over the years had made the tendency for Andres to take those reins automatic. *No more!* His mind screamed silently. *He can go and fuck himself.*

"Do it yourself," Andres exhorted, and he dropped the reins to the ground.

Flinching slightly in pain, Andres braced himself for what had become the inevitable as Camilo moved forward with clenched fists. The vein in Camilo's neck had enlarged with rage.

Garcia quickly stepped between them.

"Brothers no need to fight! Never!" Anger flashed on Garcia's face as he placed a strong resisting hand on each of their chests. "Family must stay together, no matter the price."

Garcia maneuvered his hands to their shoulders and pressed his thumbs deeply into them. The effect was what he wanted as the brothers backed away from each other. "Now, that's better!"

Garcia called out to Carlos, one of the men on the loading dock, and commanded him to take the horse to the stables.

Carlos, a large, muscular man with dreadlocks, jumped off the loading dock and ran toward them. When he reached them, he picked up the reins and began to run with the horse toward the pathway to the stables.

Garcia turned to face Camilo. Quietly, Garcia took a moment to measure his next words. He wanted his message to be concise, clear and full of searing impact.

"Never—ever—ask your brother to do something below his station in life. You are equals. Do you understand? Equals!" Garcia fanned his hands in the direction of the men on the loading dock before continuing.

"There are others whose station it is to do your bidding." He stared coldly at Camilo. "Have I made my point?"

Averting his uncle's eyes, Camilo bowed his head. "Yes, Uncle."

Garcia looked at his watch and then turned to Doug.

"Where's Chris? He should've been here 20 minutes ago. Surely he's finished at Rattray's by now?"

"I don't know, Mr. Urquiza." Doug shrugged as he glanced over at Ken, who was using the tip of his knife to clean the dirt from under his nails.

"Perhaps a little discipline wouldn't hurt, Mr. Urquiza?" Ken suggested.

"No, Ken." Garcia pressed Ken's hand and gestured to him to put the knife away. "If I think there's need for that, it will be I who will suggest it, not you.

A few moments later, Chris's Silverado pulled into the lot, dragging a U-Haul behind it. He parked at the edge of the paved area and got out.

Garcia motioned to the others to stay put as he slowly made his way across the parking area to meet Chris.

Andres watched his uncle and Chris quietly talking to each other as they walked a short distance away from the group.

Andres remembered when his uncle had immigrated to Canada.

A year after he and Camilo had arrived in Canada with Josh and Marta Green, Andres had learned that his uncle had applied for entry into Canada under business class as an investor. At the time, Andres never gave much thought to its meaning, but as the time drew close for their uncle to arrive at the farm, he had learned from Josh Green—and he couldn't remember why or how it came up—that their uncle had to have a net worth of at least eight hundred thousand dollars, 50 percent of which had to be invested with the Canadian Receiver General for five years. Never in his wildest dreams had he expected his uncle to be so wealthy. He had never thought of him on par with his dad as a businessperson, because Uncle Garcia had just been one of his dad's lieutenants.

When Andres had queried his uncle shortly after his arrival at the farm about his wealth, his uncle would stare intently at him through his dark brown eyes and say, "Never judge a book by its cover, Andres." Time proved his uncle had been right. Garcia's business acumen and wealth got Green Poultry and Egg Producers up and running, after several unsuccessful attempts by Josh Green.

Andres never prejudged anyone again.

Amazed by how quickly his uncle had integrated into this community, he had later learned that for many in the community, his uncle's handshake had become the only contract between them, and that the guest list at many functions had been considered incomplete without his uncle's inclusion.

When his uncle had been approved for permanent residency, word travelled quickly in the community. Neighbours had arrived in droves laden with home-made pastries, breads, pots of hot food, cold meats, salads and all sorts of delicacies. And, of course, liquor, homemade and bought, and lots of it! Anyone who could play a musical instrument brought it, making the night electric in song and dance. Simply put, the community had rolled out its best.

Andres remembered watching the mirth and merriment from his second-floor bedroom window, since children younger than drinking age were not invited. The celebration had lasted well into the next morning.

Andres smiled to himself when he thought of how little sleep he had gotten that night. Andres had tried several times to get closer to the festivities, but each time he tried, Carlos, who had been assigned to watch over him, always found him. Fed up with Andres's antics, Carlos had finally tied him to his bed.

The next morning, Camilo had gloated over him and threatened, as only a sibling would do, not to release him. But after Andres had agreed to pay Camilo his allowance for two weeks, his brother finally untied him.

Uncle Garcia had been sloshed when he had called them down. He communicated how deeply touched he had been by what the community had just done.

Andres had never seen his uncle so emotional—and he would never see him that way again. Before that moment was finished, a dark mood had settled around his uncle like a thick curtain. He remembered watching his uncle as he pounded his chest in hysterical laughter and yelled out, "El Zorro! El Zorro!"

As suddenly as it had begun, it had stopped. Standing tall and pushing back his shoulders, his uncle had negotiated his way across the room and disappeared into his bedroom.

Andres always wondered why his uncle referred to himself as el zorro: the fox. Garcia never openly labelled himself that way again.

Camilo jabbed Andres in the ribs with his elbow.
"Later, little brother—later. In the meantime, pay attention."
Garcia walked past them toward the egg-packing facility.
Chris hung slightly behind, visibly shaken.
As the others followed his uncle toward the facility, Andres felt awkward and uncomfortable standing alongside Chris, whom he knew wasn't one of his uncle's favourites. Andres stepped away from Chris.
Perception and allegiance went hand in hand in Andres's world, and he wanted no misconceptions about where his allegiance lay.
Indecisive as to whether to follow along or head to the house Andres's decision was made for him by his uncle, who yelled out for him and Chris to join the group.
Unlike his brother, who began working late evenings at the facility two years ago, Andres had never been allowed near it.

Andres's brother had been tight-lipped and threatening in his response to Andres's inquiries about what he did in the facility. It was a reaction that Andres found baffling and suspicious.

When Camilo thought his brother asked too many questions, his fists meted out a brand of corporal punishment that stilled further query from Andres.

As Andres walked toward the entrance, he wondered whether he had finally arrived, so to speak. *Is this my day of passage?* he asked himself. *Is this the day my uncle finally takes me into his confidence? Is this the day I will finally begin to learn the business?*

Excitement swelled up in Andres. He believed that he would finally have the answers to what his brother did in this facility during those late evenings. He believed this future would distance him far away from the village of San Vicente del Caguan.

Chapter Twenty

—⊂= =⊃—

ANDRES ENTERED THE EGG-PACKING facility along with Chris. Slightly ahead of them, Doug, Ken and Camilo followed Garcia.

Lingering behind, Andres watched as women worked at the egg processors while a handful of men, on forklift trucks, either brought skids of empty egg cartons to the front of the operation or picked up skids of cartons filled with eggs from the other end. The finished skids went immediately to either waiting refrigerated trucks at the shipping docks or into large coolers for later transport.

Andres found it strange that none of the women so much as registered the slightest interest or curiosity when they entered, whereas the men waved and yelled out greetings in Spanish above the din.

Garcia stopped and waited for Andres to catch up.

"Gentlemen," yelled Garcia above the noise of the machinery. "Camilo and I are going to show Andres around. As you know, it is his first time, and he has much to learn."

From behind Andres, Carlos stepped forward to usher Doug, Chris and Ken to the office at the end of the aisle.

Andres was surprised to see Carlos. *How the hell did he get here so quickly from the stables?* he mused. *He sure didn't come through the same door we did.*

As Andres walked with his uncle, the answer became evident. Diagonally, just behind where his uncle now stood, was a long, narrow hallway with a door at the far end. Because of Andres's angle of view a few moments earlier, a support column had hidden the hallway's presence.

Garcia came over to Andres and put his arm around his shoulders. "As I said, Andres, there is much to learn, but we'll take small steps." He directed Andres's attention to the centre of the complex. "Firstly, Green Poultry and Eggs is an in-line production. You look puzzled," he said, smiling. "Let me explain. It means that everything is done right here on site. In other words, we own the feed mill, hens, buildings, egg-processing facility and transportation vehicles. This must bore you. You already know this, si?"

"No, Uncle, it doesn't bore me. Please forgive me if I did anything to make you think that."

A dubious smile cracked Garcia's face as he reached out and ruffled the hair on Andres's head. "Then I should continue? Si?"

"Please, Uncle."

As Andres walked alongside his uncle, he noticed Carlos exiting the office and crossing to a door beside a large metal sliding door at the opposite side of the complex. Carlos knocked several times before it was finally opened, and he entered. The door slammed with such a heavy thud that it could be heard above the drone of the machinery.

Curiosity getting the better of him, Andres felt compelled to interrupt his uncle. "Forgive me for interrupting you, but that door over there, where Carlos just entered ..." Andres pointed to the door across the factory floor opposite to them.

"Carlos? I didn't see Carlos." After a brief silence his uncle continued. "Right now, Andres, I want your attention here. Not over there!" Locking eyes with Andres, Garcia stepped closer.

"Do you understand?" Furrows had formed at the bridge of his nose.

Startled by his uncle's reaction, Andres felt like a bug just about to be squashed. "I only—yes, Uncle, I understand." Lowering his head, Andres glimpsed at the door from the corner of his eye and wondered what lay behind it. Behind him, he heard his brother snickering.

Camilo sharply slammed his fist into Andres's ribs when his uncle turned his back.

"Damn! That hurt!"

Garcia turned around, his eyes darting between the two boys.

Andres glanced at his brother's smirking face. *I swear, your time will come!* Andres promised.

"Whatever's going on between you two, settle it later," Garcia said. Grasping Andres by the chin, he stared into his eyes. "Your attention is here, with me! Not your brother."

Andres could barely nod under his uncle's strong grasp.

Garcia let go of Andres's chin, stepped back and looked over to Camilo.

Other than the cacophonous churning of machinery, silence reigned between the three of them for a good few moments.

"You walk on this side of me, Camilo," Garcia directed. "Andres, this side." With Andres and Camilo on opposite sides of him, Garcia continued with Andres's lesson. "A layer house flanks either side of the plant. Hens in the layer houses are fed grain, brought to them by a conveyor system. There are about hundred to a hundred fifty thousand laying hens in each house." Garcia pointed to the end of the facility. "The eggs from the layer houses are transported by the conveyor belt to be washed with mild detergent and—se saneado?"

"Sanitized," Andres interjected.

"Hmm, yes, sanitized. Thank you, Andres. As a businessman in an English-speaking environment, it's always smart to improve on my skills."

Andres noticed three men, with weapons slung over their shoulders, entering through the same door Carlos had gone through earlier.

"Bored?" Camilo inquired.

Quickly realizing that he had not been circumspect enough when he had redirected his attention, Andres searched for a diversion.

Andres hated that loathing expression on his brother's face—and even worse, his uncle's attentive look as he waited for an answer, too. Finding his diversion, Andres nodded in the direction of a large piece of machinery where eggs entered before reappearing at the other end.

"What's that over there?"

Smiling, Garcia nodded approvingly. "Your brother *is* paying attention. Why don't you tell him, Camilo."

"That, little brother, is the automated computerized detection system that grades eggs," Camilo said. His smug, almost self-righteous demeanour irritated Andres.

"We're interested only in AA and A grades," interjected Garcia, "while others go to the breaker room." Garcia pointed in the direction of the door that continued to captivate Andres's curiosity. "There—now you know what goes on behind that door," Garcia added.

"Jumbo, extra large and large eggs are the only eggs we're interested in here," Camilo inserted. "But you already knew that."

Andres didn't already know that, and he clinched his fists, frustrated with his brother's continued sarcasm.

"Camilo, your brother knows very little if anything about this operation. He's just learning, so stop with the sarcasm." Garcia glanced over at Andres. "You look puzzled, Andres."

"I am, Uncle. What is a breaker room?"

"Let me, Uncle." Clearing his throat, Camilo began his description. "That's where the eggshells are cracked and the contents separated. Our operation does about three hundred thousand eggs per hour."

Still puzzled, Andres turned to his uncle. "Why is the breaking room kept so securely locked up? What makes it so special from the rest of the operation?"

Purposely, Andres left out the three armed men he saw entering that section earlier.

"Hmm." Garcia rubbed his chin thoughtfully as he scrutinized Andres. Then, glancing at Camilo, he took in a deep breath and let it out slowly. "Let's join the others. There's lots of time, Andres, for you to learn later."

Without any further exchange of words between them, they walked toward his office.

Andres followed the conveyor system as the eggs rattled across the facility's floor to an opening beside the large metal sliding door that Carlos and the three armed men had entered. He puzzled over why his uncle hadn't taken him to see that part of the operation. Patience was Andres's hallmark, keeping his mouth shut a virtue. He knew answers would come soon enough.

Andres entered his uncle's office behind Camilo. The smell of recently laid oak flooring met his nostrils.

When the door slammed shut behind him, he was surprised by how effectively the office was cut off from the cacophony of machinery on the factory floor.

Against one wall was an oversize brown leather couch where Chris and Doug sat. Ken was looking at a map of Ontario covered with an assortment of brightly coloured pins. Andres noticed a cut and some bruising under Chris's right eye that wasn't present earlier.

Garcia sat behind his desk. Opening the side drawer, he pulled out a bottle of Trago Aguardiente, kiwi flavored, and six shot glasses. He filled each glass.

Taking a glass, Garcia invited the others to do likewise. "This Colombian drink," he said, "is only for special occasions. Like now!" He raised his glass. "To our success!"

The group members present held up their glass. "To our success!" they all said in unison, and they threw back their drinks.

Andres coughed uncontrollably as the liquor passed the back of his throat. Tears streamed down his cheeks. He thought he would vomit as he began to gag.

The men laughed raucously as they slapped him on the back.

His uncle passed him a tall glass of water, and Andres gulped down its contents.

"Not a man yet," Garcia cackled.

Standing up, Garcia came around to the front of his desk and held out his arms to Andres, hugging him.

As he held Andres, Garcia motioned to the others to quiet down.

Garcia held Andres at arm's length and looked deeply into his eyes. Then, turning to Camilo, he directed him to take his brother back to the house. "Both of you—stay there!"

Andres felt Camilo's eyes burning through the back of his head as they walked along the path to the house. Camilo clearly expected to be part of that meeting, not babysitting his brother.

The sound of a vehicle coming down the road to the house redirected their attention. The limousine passed by the house, stopped at a right angle to Doug's Navigator.

Andres strained his eyes for a closer look.

Camilo grasped Andres from behind and propelled him through the open screen door onto the floor.

Payback had begun, and Andres curled up into a foetal position to protect himself from Camilo's punishing blows.

CHAPTER TWENTY-ONE

IT WAS ABOUT 5:30 Thursday morning when Edward was jerked out of a deep sleep.

Groggy, disoriented and in his recliner—sitting upright—he was befuddled by his present location. *I could have sworn I slept in my bed last night*, he thought. *How the hell did I end up here?*

While trying to focus his eyes in the darkened room, his attention was first drawn to the coffee table in front of him. Scattered across its surface were two large pizza cartons strewn with crusts and tomato-stained serviettes, and two empty and one partially empty bottles of Coffin Ridge Marguette. Located an hour northeast of Priceville, Coffin Ridge Winery was situated between Owen Sound and Meaford on the fresh water bay of Georgian Bay.

He remembered how massively tired he had been at supper, and as he massaged his temples, he vaguely recollected drinking far more wine than he should have during his melatonin rush.

On the other side of the coffee table, Charlotte slept in a foetal position on the unfolded down futon. The blanket that covered her was drawn up tightly around her neck.

Edward stood up and attempted, as best he could, to work out the kinks in his body by stretching. The grey morning haze of early light cast a thin veil over the room as he looked around.

Largely due to the help of Janet and Charlotte, the chaos from yesterday's break-in was replaced with some degree of normalcy. To Edward, the clean-up process had been more about trying to reconstruct his life—if only in a small way—than just putting things back in their proper place. He had approached each item as if it was a scene in his own personal movie, and as its director, he had decided what ended up on the cutting room floor.

On the table beside his recliner was the broken frame containing Karen's photograph. Edward slipped out her photo and held it against his chest. The morning chill sent a shiver up his spine. After placing Karen's picture on the table beside his recliner, he went to his bedroom. When he came back out, he wore a lightweight sweater to ward off the chill. Under his arm was a pillow.

Gently, so as not to awaken her, he lifted Charlotte's head off her hands and placed the pillow under it. When she moaned and turned over, Edward stood perfectly still. Once assured that she was asleep, he headed into the kitchen.

Passing by the kitchen table, he noticed a slightly crumpled up, folded newspaper lying on it. He quickly realized that it was the same paper from his office containing the pictures with Norman Rattray in them. In all of the commotion over the past 24 hours, he had completely forgotten about it.

Making a mental note to drop by the *Chronicle* later that day, he placed it on the counter that divided the living room from the kitchen and carried on into the kitchen. Placing ample coffee and water in the coffee maker, Edward turned the dial to strong brew and switched it on. As he faced out into the living room, he watched Charlotte's dark outline jockey for a more comfortable position on the futon.

He pulled out the USB memory stick that hung at the end of his string necklace. Giving it a slight squeeze, he let it drop back down behind his shirt. That memory stick contained the most important files to date on the sewage recovery and filtration systems. He had hidden the backup hard copy in a secret compartment he had designed and built at the back of the firebox.

Taking a pen-sized flashlight from the kitchen drawer, he headed for the fireplace. He carefully examined the back of the firebox. "So far, so good," he whispered to himself.

Placing the end of the flashlight in his mouth, he worked his fingers on either side along the back of the box until the flat rectangular piece on top loosened enough for him to slide it along its track toward him. When it slipped out, he placed it beside him. He took the flashlight out of his mouth and shone it into the cavity. *Thank god!* He sighed in relief. *Everything looks intact and untouched.* He took the binders and folders back to the kitchen and placed them on the counter. After several minutes thumbing through them, he was satisfied that nothing was out of place or missing. He closed them up and returned them to their hiding place.

As he slid the top of the compartment back in place, he glanced over at Charlotte. Her heavy breathing convinced him that she was still sound asleep. Tip-toeing past her, he returned to the kitchen and poured himself a mug of black coffee. The coffee smelled wonderful, and it delivered the punch he needed.

His stomach growled. Feeling an ephemeral twinge of guilt from having eaten only a few hours earlier, he still lathered two slices of whole grain bread with peanut butter and some sort of berry jam that he had bought during Flesherton's Split Rail Festival.

Darkness was lifting outside the kitchen window when he checked the time on the wall clock, which now worked thanks to Janet. "Just needed three triple-A batteries," he remembered her saying. "No excuse for that, Eddy." And, she was right—there was no excuse. Edward shook his head, disappointed with himself.

He pushed the remains of the peanut butter and jam sandwich into his mouth and proceeded to chew it while occasionally wetting it with his coffee.

"Coffee smells good there, Chippy. Hope you made enough for two?" Charlotte garbled through a long yawn. "You normally fill your jowls like a chipmunk?" She laughed when Edward exaggerated his cheeks even more. "Caveman." She finished a long, drawn-out stretch and sat up. She put her feet on the floor and quickly withdrew them back up under her blanket. "What do you store under your floor boards, ice? I think I'll stay put." She wrapped the blanket tightly around her as she looked under the coffee table and around the room from the futon. "By any chance, do you know where I put my sandals? And if you're not already aware of it, you're running your air conditioner at much too low a temperature."

Edward spotted Charlotte's sandals under the kitchen table. "That them there?"

"Oh, Edward, would you—? Please and thank you."

Chomping on his sandwich, Edward retrieved her sandals, dropped them on the futon beside her and returned to the kitchen. He poured her coffee in an oversize mug and then scooped two level teaspoonfuls of whitener into it along with a tablespoon overflowing with honey. After putting her mug on a tray beside his, he headed toward the living room, stopping momentarily to turn up the thermostat on the air conditioner.

"You remembered," she said, reaching out for her mug and taking a sip. "Thank you."

"Janet must have turned the air conditioner down before she left," he said.

"Not likely, Edward."

"Can you give me a hand here?" He nodded toward the pizza boxes on the coffee table.

"And, just now, I was thanking you for remembering the honey in my coffee," she said.

"That concoction in your coffee is not too hard to forget. To put it bluntly, it's gross! Civilized people prefer the moo bag and granular."

She smiled at him coyly.

After Charlotte stacked the boxes at the far end of the table, he placed the tray down in the empty space. "I prefer to think that *my* ingredients are creative—especially the honey. How's the saying go? Don't knock it till you try it." Looking up at him, she gave him a smug look before taking a long drink from her mug.

"Dee-licious!"

"Whatever turns your crank," Edward mumbled. He went to the kitchen, returning a couple of seconds later with the newspaper tucked under his arm. Placing the tray and pizza boxes under the coffee table, he came around and sat on the table, facing her. "You mind?" He nodded for her to take the newspaper.

Plucking it from under his arm, Charlotte put her mug on the table and opened up the newspaper. "Is there something you want me to see?"

"Actually there is—the article on Norman Rattray's suicide, on the bottom half of the page. It finishes up on the second page."

"You do know I've read this along with everyone else in West Grey."

"Just have a look at the pictures."

She looked over the top of the paper at Edward. "Ah, what am I suppose to be looking for?"

"Well, those two pictures on the second page—I know they were taken between eight and ten years ago. I was just wondering if you knew any stories associated with them."

"Stories? What kind of stories?"

"Well, for one thing, the land that KemKor now sits on used to belong to Ritchie's."

Charlotte folded the newspaper so that the pictures on page two faced up at her from her lap. "What does stand out for me was the explosion and fire at Ritchie's during their renovations."

"In what way?" Edward asked.

"It meant I couldn't buy my discounted frozen yogurt from their main office anymore. And I still can't."

Edward took in a deep breath and let it out slowly before reaching for his coffee and having a drink. "Anything else?"

"There was some talk that it was done on purpose, but nothing was ever proven."

"Did any names pop up?"

Charlotte finished her coffee and handed the mug to Edward. "Please. And, this time two tablespoons of honey." When she had a fresh mug of coffee in her hand, Charlotte continued. "You asked me if any names popped up. There was only one—William Wardlaw Rattray."

Edward sat beside her and took the newspaper from her lap to scrutinize the two photos more closely.

"What's so special about that location? There were lots of other properties that KemKor could have chosen from that were probably better."

"The scuttlebutt, as I remember it, had to do with his wife—or at least her ancestry."

"In what way?"

"Surely you haven't forgotten. That used to be the site of Parker Brick and Glass Factory. When it was just an old, derelict building, I remember playing in it as a kid before it was torn down."

Edward asked, "But, what's that got to do with anything?"

"Because Rattray's wife, whose maiden name is Parker, is the great-great-granddaughter of the owners of the Parker Brick and Glass Factory. Now are the pieces fitting into place? That's why a lot of people were suspicious when Ritchie's stopped their renovations after the explosion and fire and handed over the site to KemKor."

Placing the newspaper back on Charlotte's lap, Edward tapped his finger on one of the photos. "Any idea who Norman Rattray was looking at in this photo?" he asked.

"You're kidding, aren't you? My best bet, though, is that Shirley Cooper at the *Chronicle* would know. She probably took those pictures."

"Nadia said the same thing the other day." Edward looked into his cold, partially full coffee mug and stood up. "I'm going to dump this and get a refresher. Want one?"

"No, I'm fine."

"On another topic, Charlotte, why didn't you go home with Janet?"

"My guess is that by the time she was ready, I was dead weight."

Edward glanced at the wine bottles at the end of the coffee table. "We kinda drank a lot."

"There's no 'kinda' about it—we did. Paired with exhaustion, well …" Cupping her mug in her hands, Charlotte bent slightly forward. "Have you ever wondered, what if?" she asked.

"What if?" Edward repeated.

"Yes—with us."

Letting out a deep sigh, Edward started walking back to the kitchen. As he passed the table beside his recliner, he reached out and touched the picture of Karen lying on it. He had often wondered "what if," especially when his marriage had been going through rough times.

He poured his coffee and returned, sitting on the recliner opposite her. "I'd be lying if I said I never thought about you after we broke up. You were my first real love. How do you forget your first love? You can't. But outside of that, the "what ifs" never really entered my life. What can I say, our relationship had ended, and I moved on." Sipping his coffee, he stared across at Charlotte. "Why did you never get married?"

"I guess I never found Mr. Right. Let's just drop it at that."

"I wasn't trying to pry."

"I know you weren't."

Edward picked up the picture of Karen and looked at it quietly for a few seconds before returning it to the table. "Now I've got to live with the guilt of never saying or doing the things I should have said and done. Funny, isn't it? You think you have all the time in the world to make up for any wrongs you've done, and you rarely ever do." Edward shuffled forward on his chair and placed his mug on the coffee table. "The good memories are where I need to focus now. Whatever you and I had between us, I'm thankful for it. I have no regrets." He looked down and away before returning his eyes to her. "I hope we can be friends?"

Charlotte said, "We always have been—that won't change." Smiling, she shifted forward, extending her hand. "Hi! My name is Charlotte Bradley."

At first puzzled, Edward finally realized that it was her way of saying, "Let's pretend this is our first meeting and start over again." He replied, "I'm pleased to meet you. My name is Edward Slocum." He shook her hand.

The room brightened as the sun rose higher above the horizon. For the next two hours they chatted. The conversation started when they first met and filled in as much of the missing pieces for both of them up to the time he returned to West Grey. When it was finished, they knew there was still much more to talk about, and they agreed to meet again later.

Though time had passed quickly, it had been rich and full of potential.

"Do you have any idea why those men wanted you dead?" Charlotte asked.

"Right now, I'm working with two scenarios that I think may overlap. First, those men wanted me dead because of what they think I saw at Building 3C."

"My sister told me about that."

"Oh? Well, I think the lead man who had shot at me confirms this first scenario because I did see him on Building 3C's loading dock. I've given Constable Dickenson full details, including the description of the fella."

"But …? I'm sure I hear a 'but' coming. Mark me if I'm wrong."

"No, you're not wrong," he replied.

"Well, are you going to tell me?"

"The second scenario is too outlandish. There's not a shred of evidence to support it. That's why I never shared it with Dickenson."

Uncurling her legs, Charlotte loosely put her feet into her sandals and leaned toward Edward. "Outlandish or not, the fact that your thinking it gives it some sort of credibility. So, out with it."

"Rattray."

"Rattray?" Charlotte repeated.

"There, you see? I've barely started, and you're already incredulous."

Reaching across the table, she took Edward's hand. "I'm sorry. It's just that, well, it wasn't what I was expecting."

"What were you expecting?"

"I'm not sure—just not that. How do you figure he fits in?" Clasping her hands together, she placed them on her thighs.

Edward explained, "Next Monday, Rattray—I mean KemKor—gets the rights to my research on the filtration system, but not before a substantial payout to me—already agreed to when I signed on with KemKor, plus a percentage of any royalties on any sales still to be negotiated."

"Maybe I'm dense, but I don't get the connection." Sitting back in the futon, she crossed one leg over the other.

Edward stood up and walked behind the recliner and leaned over it. "If I'm dead, all of what I just said becomes null and void—except for the part where KemKor keeps the rights to the system."

"I've never heard of such a thing!"

"I put myself in this bear-trap the moment I demanded that there would be a time-limited exclusion clause, which would allow me to have full rights should I leave KemKor before the clause expired. Rattray obviously felt confident enough that I wouldn't leave for him to sign it. It had been during the excitement of signing that another document—one I really wish I had read—had been shoved under my nose to sign. And like some idiot, I signed it without exercising my due diligence."

Edward put his hand up to the bandage above his ear.

"Are you okay?" Charlotte said as she stood up and walked toward him.

"Nothing one of those Tylenols wouldn't cure. Anyway, I guess you can understand why I said nothing to Dickenson."

Charlotte shrugged, searched out the bottle of Tylenol and returned with a glass of water and gave them to him. "How do Camilo and Andres figure into this?" she asked.

"Hey! I never mentioned anything about those boys," Edward retorted. He turned and watched her as she passed him.

Charlotte stopped at the counter just outside the kitchen. "No, you didn't, but I sure will. It can't just be a coincidence that those boys were here when the break-in occurred. Like Constable Dickenson, I don't put a lot of faith in coincidence. Those boys never said anything about the break-in to me, even when they had the chance. That black SUV that backed down behind them was there at the same time they were. It's a QED, and I can't believe you don't see their actions suspicious. Anyway, whether you believe it or not, I do believe they're up to their necks in it."

"Maybe you're right; it's obvious." Edward took the Tylenol pill and finished the glass of water and placed it on the counter beside her. "I think the obvious questions are: What was being loaded into the van from Building 3C, and where was it taken? Did it only happen that once? And, if not, does it only occur on Tuesday evenings? And, why didn't the guards at the gate notice anything going on?" Edward fell against the counter. "Whew! I feel a little light-headed. I'd better sit down." Refusing help from Charlotte, he made his way to the kitchen table and, pulling out a chair, sat down.

Charlotte asked, "Are you all right?"

"Absolutely, but I get a feeling you're not done yet."

"You're right," she rejoined. "I'm not. A couple of more questions you might want to add are, why Elkhart didn't follow through with the activation of the surveillance cameras, and why no samples from the effluent valve were taken by your lab?"

"There you go again!" exclaimed Edward. "I don't know if he followed through. All I know is at that time it hadn't been done. Anyway, I took my own samples and sent them off to Irving's Lab by UPS before heading to the Gorge."

"Good for us; at least we have something hopeful! But what are you going to do about Monday morning? Rattray still expects you to show up in Legal."

"I know, I know. I haven't worked that out yet."

"Would you consider a little detour today?" Charlotte asked.

Furrows formed at the bridge of his nose as he scrutinized her. "What kind of detour?"

He got up and walked over to her. "KemKor."

"KemKor? What's cooking in that brain of yours?" He stood slightly back and folded his arms across his chest.

"Why wait? Let's see if Elkhart followed through. If he hasn't, then that opens up a whole lot of other questions. Also, Building 3C needs to be looked at from the inside, don't you think? Can you get keys?"

"You're kidding." He gently began to massage the area above his ear where the bandaged wound was located.

"Nope," she said simply.

"I guess … Yeah, I can get keys." He began to massage the back of his neck.

"Good, now let's move on." Charlotte returned to the futon and sat down. "Edward? Does the name 'Idylwilde' ring a bell? It was etched across the back window of the Lincoln Navigator that initiated the crap and corruption on my Prius." Edward shrugged and gave her a negative response. "Hmm. I asked Dickenson the same question," she said, "and he didn't know, either. I found that strange since, being a local cop in the area, I thought he would."

"Paul's only human. You can't expect him to know everything."

"Regarding West Grey, I do. But that's something we can mull over later. Do you have any idea how those men who shot at you knew where to find you?"

Edward said, "I can only assume I was being watched and followed." He rubbed his hand across his face in a washing motion and went into the kitchen. "If I'm right," he continued, "I find that more than a little disconcerting." Pulling a plate and a box of crackers down from the cupboard, he went to the fridge and got some cheese. "You know, secrets wither quickly in this community." He cut several slices from the brick of cheddar and placed them on the plate alongside the crackers. After picking up the plate, he headed back toward her. "The very fact that you're asking questions, Charlotte, will travel faster than a brush fire on a hot, dry, windy day. The wrong ears may hear it."

"I'll be discreet," she replied.

"I know you will, but that's not the point."

"Would you rather it stops here and goes no further?" she asked.

"No, but—"

"Then it's settled. It's my choice, not yours," she replied adamantly. "Do you have Italian heritage?"

"Pardon? How did we get there?"

"Your arms are quite expressive when you talk. That's all." She walked over to the wood box and pointed to its back. "I know this worked this time, but I'm not sure it will next time. Remember what you just said about secrets in the community."

"Maybe I should put them in the vault at the bank, for safe keeping," he replied. He reached over and snatched up a couple of crackers with cheese and popped them in his mouth. Suddenly it dawned on him that she must have watched him earlier when he opened the back of the wood box.

"Hey! I thought you were asleep!" he garbled, smilingly.

"Girls can feign anything, Caveman. Remember Meg Ryan's orgasmic scene in *When Harry Met Sally?*"

"Yeah, yeah. I guess I'm the Billy Crystal character? Don't call me Caveman. I liked Chippy better."

"That porridge-like mush bubbling between your lips makes you a caveman."

"Then don't look." He stuck out his chin and shoved the rest of the cheese and crackers into his mouth.

"Men just don't grow up," she said, but she took his advice and turned away. Getting down on one knee, she examined the back of the wood box.

"Are you sure putting them in the vault is the practical choice? I mean, don't you use them, in some fashion or other, every day? So why not let me take care of them?"

"Because if they tried to kill me, they might try to kill you," he replied.

Distracted by her feverish attempts to find the mechanism that opened the secret compartment, Charlotte didn't hear his response.

"Usually I'm pretty good at solving this sorta stuff. But, this beats me. Show me." Standing up, she kicked the side of the wood box.

"I'd rather not."

Charlotte turned and stared at Edward. "Open this damn thing!" She kicked the wood box again, except this time with her heel. "If you didn't want me involved, you wouldn't have told me as much as you did."

"I don't want the cops snooping around KemKor any more than they've already done, at least until I can figure out what the hell's going on."

"Eddy, I'm not going to do anything that will encourage that. I just want to get your stuff into a safer place." She began to pace the floor in front of the wood box.

A few minutes later, Edward had retrieved the binders and papers and dropped them down on the futon. By this time, Charlotte had stopped pacing and was staring at him. "You're kinda careless about how you handle your life's work."

Edward held himself back from jumping all over her about that remark, but instead he shrugged and checked the time on his wristwatch.

"Charlotte, I don't want you involved. I appreciate your suggestion of finding a safer place, but I'll do that—not you."

"Eddy, I'm the last person anyone would think had this. Think about it. Most people who know us don't see us as friends."

"Charlotte, if they came after me, they'll come after you," Edward repeated.

"That's only if they know, and they won't."

Edward chewed the inside of his cheek as he thought over what she had said. "Okay. But I hope you're not planning to hold on to them long?"

"Don't worry, I have no such intentions." She went over to the futon and gathered the binders and folders together.

"What are you going to do with them?" Edward asked.

"That now is my concern, not yours."

"You mean you're not going to tell me?"

"Smart boy. You just earned a star."

"Look, are you sure you're up to this?"

"You don't know me if you have to ask that question," she retorted.

Stepping back, Edward dug his hands deeply into his pockets and walked a short distance away. From the corner of his eye, he watched her as she neatly arranged the folders and binders. "It *was* great back then, Char."

Charlotte stopped what she was doing and straightened up, facing him. "We were different people back then. Now, I'm just a friend doing what friends do to help each other," she replied.

Edward scuffed the soul of his shoe across the floor several times.

"I think I'd better tell you something."

"Is it important?" she asked as she continued to organize the material on the futon so that she could carry it easily.

He cleared his throat. "I think so. I've asked your sister to check out accounting and shipping."

She stopped what she was doing and stared at him. "And for what?"

"To see if she can find anything related to Tuesday evening."

"Knowing you, you expect she'll do it surreptitiously. Well, I'll tell you there's not a surreptitious bone in my sister's head. You of all people must have known that. What were you thinking?" She sat on the futon. "Edward! You've got to stop her—and now. Promise me!"

Edward lowered his head and squirmed uneasily in his position. "Done!"

"So it is a promise?"

"It's a promise." Edward touched the bandage over his ear.

"You touch that area a lot. Are you okay?" Charlotte asked.

"It's just a little sore, that's all."

Slapping her thighs, she stood up. "Okay then, I'm famished. Got any cereal?"

"Cereal's in the corner cupboard, and if you want some bread, it's in the fridge. How about I fry up some eggs?"

"Sounds great! Make mine two, sunny side up," she replied.

They could hear a vehicle with a slight knock in its engine lumbering down the drive. "By the sounds of it, it's Janet," Charlotte said. "And she's on time—eleven o'clock." Edward helped Charlotte gather up the binders and folders. "At the moment, I've got Janet to chauffeur me around. But what are you going to do?"

"I'll call Bernard's in town. Knowing Tim as well as I do, I'm sure he'll dig out some kinda rental to send around."

Bernard's Used Cars and Auto Sales had been in the town of Flesherton, 20 minutes east of Priceville, ever since Edward could remember. Tim O'Sullivan, a good friend of Edward's, now owned it.

When Tim had bought the dealership, he'd decided not to change the name.

Edward hesitated to give her the last two binders. "Are you sure you can handle all that?"

Charlotte gave Edward an exasperated look. "Just put them on and get the door."

Charlotte cradled the binders tightly to her chest as they walked toward the door.

"Thanks for doing this, Charlotte."

"Right now, you're like my seeing-eye dog. So if you can get me safely through that door and off your porch without me falling, well, that will be thanks enough."

As they stepped onto the porch, the screen door slammed behind them.

A Ford pickup truck with a horse trailer hitched to it followed behind Janet's Camaro.

Poking his head out the Ford's driver window was Garcia Urquiza. Garcia's gleaming white tooth-filled smile was enhanced by his deep copper-toned complexion. On the seat beside him was Camilo.

"Hola, Señor Slocum!" Garcia called out. He brought his vehicle to a jarring halt within inches of the back bumper of Janet's Camaro.

"We're bringing back one of your horses, Tequila. My nephews said that Roscoe jumped the fence across the road. Looking for greener pastures, I think. Camilo and his brother should never have taken your horses off the property. They are sorry, Señor Slocum. Come on, Camilo." He roughly pushed Camilo's shoulder. "Tell him you're sorry."

"Sorry, Señor Slocum. It won't happen again." Camilo's apology was mumbled and he did not keep eye contact.

"The other boy will apologize too, next time he sees you," said Garcia. "The truth, Señor Slocum, is that the boys panicked when they found your house broken into. Their misplaced logic placed priority on protecting the horses. What can I say, stupido. I didn't know until late last night. I phoned Constable Dickenson this morning to report it and found out he already knew. So here I am." Then Garcia looked at Charlotte and shook his head. "How rude of me. Forgive me. How are you, Miss Bradley?" He scrutinized the folders and binders she was pressing to her chest. Opening his truck door, he stepped out and looked toward the Camaro.

"And you too, Miss Thompson. Your engine needs attention badly. Maybe one of my mechanics can fix it for you. Bring it around to my place anytime."

Janet poked her head through the open window and looked back at Garcia. "She's like me: old, pensioned, cantankerous and a lot of mileage, Mr. Urquiza." She patted the steering wheel affectionately, got out of her vehicle and walked to the back of the Camaro. Examining the short distance between their bumpers, she gave him the eagle eye. "Well, Mr. Urquiza, I'm pleased you didn't roll in any faster or stop any later, because we wouldn't be on speaking terms. But we are, and I'd be pleased if your mechanic can fix this old bucket. Many have tried and failed." She let out a raucous laugh as they shook hands.

"I'll inform my mechanics that you will be dropping around," Garcia said.

"Should I ask for anyone in particular?"

"No, they're all great."

Their attention was quickly diverted to Charlotte, who was stepping off the porch and lost her footing. She began to fall forward.

Edward barely had time to grab her shoulder while Garcia scooped her up at the waist to stop her forward motion. The binders punched him in the face, causing a nosebleed.

"Are you okay?" Garcia asked. He released his grasp on Charlotte and backed away.

"My ankle's a little sore, that's all. Thanks, both of you. Oh, Mr. Urquiza, your nose!"

"Just a little blood. Not a big deal." Garcia reached into his pocket and withdrew a linen handkerchief. After wiping away the blood, he bunched it up and pressed it hard against the errant nostril. "Let me get Camilo to help you with those binders." He gestured to Camilo with his free hand.

"No, no! It's not necessary—I can handle them," she insisted. Taking in a deep breath, she smiled at Garcia and then asked Janet to open the car door so she could put the binders on the backseat.

Garcia removed the balled handkerchief from his nose. "See, the blood has already stopped." He nodded toward the binders as he put the handkerchief in his pocket. "Important?"

"No, not really. It's just Ministry of the Environment stuff I took from my car." She tilted her head in the direction of the battered Prius parked in front of Edward's property.

"I hope I didn't come across curt, Mr. Urquiza, because I didn't mean to be. Between the damage to my car and lack of sleep, well, I'm sure you understand. Please forgive me." She placed the binders and folders on the backseat of the Camaro and shut the door.

"Of course!" Garcia shrugged and smiled. "Let me show my chivalrous side by escorting you to the passenger seat."

Not waiting for a reply, Garcia quickly moved ahead of Charlotte and had the passenger-side door opened before she arrived. Once she was in, he closed the door and rejoined Edward, who was standing with Janet on the driver's side.

"I've heard your introducing Charles Blackwell Saturday. I think he has a good chance at being our next premier," Garcia said.

"So do I," Edward replied.

"By the way, where do you want me to unload Tequila?"

"In the paddock, this side of the barn. And thank you."

"Don't mention it, Señor Slocum." Garcia looked back at the truck. "I'm sure my nephew can take care of that. Right, Camilo?"

Camilo gave his uncle a quick nod, stretched across the seat to the driver's side and pointed to the ground behind Edward. "Señor Slocum, there—on the ground behind you."

Edward's gut twisted into a knot, and a cold chill that even one of the hottest days couldn't melt travelled up his spine. Less than a metre from where he and Garcia stood, a page filled with equations and drawings lay on the ground.

BLACKWELL FOR PREMIER

Chapter Twenty-Two

TIM O'SULLIVAN, OWNER OF Bernard's Used Cars and Auto Sales, came through for his friend Edward in a way Edward did not expect. When Tim learned what had happened to Edward and that his Wrangler had been stolen, Tim lent him his own fully loaded Chevy Equinox without reservation—and rent-free. All Tim asked of Edward was that the vehicle be returned safe and sound and filled with gas.

When Edward hesitated to accept Tim's generous offer, Tim laughed at him and gave him the keys, pointing out that he already owned three vehicles and that one less in the driveway wouldn't be missed.

From the kitchen table, Edward picked up the sheet of paper that had fallen from one of the folders that Charlotte had carried out earlier. He carefully folded it and put it in his pocket. He hoped that Urquiza hadn't had a good look at the contents of the sheet while it lay on the ground, because if he had, Urquiza would have known that Charlotte had lied to him about the folders and binders being Ministry of the Environment property. And, that meant their secret was already compromised.

Before leaving his home, Edward put a call through to his administrative assistant, Charlotte's sister Nadia, on his cell phone. When she picked up at the other end, she was surprised to hear his voice. "Edward? I thought you'd be at Norman Rattray's funeral."

With everything that had happened to him over the past 24 hours, Edward had completely forgotten about it. She went on to remind him that all of KemKor's administrative staff and management were at the funeral in Toronto—a two-and-a-half-hour drive south of Markdale. As the conversation progressed, he also learned that his CEO had told

Chris Stedman, the security manager, to hire an extra five security personnel. After what had happened on the Tuesday evening, Edward wasn't surprised that extra security would be hired. What *did* surprise him was how quickly it had been done since, according to Nadia, Chris Stedman had already introduced the new security guards around the building that morning.

To Edward that was both good and bad news. The good news was that it meant the CEO and Elkhart and their cohorts wouldn't be snooping around while Edward, Charlotte and Janet checked out Building 3C later that day. The bad news was the possibility of Edward having to explain to new security why two non-personnel should be allowed into a restricted area with him—something that he had not worked out at the moment.

Usually he would not have worried because Jim Higgins, with whom he had a good rapport, was usually at the front desk at the time he hoped to bring the three of them through. Now, Edward had no idea who would be either at the front desk or at the front gate, and that bothered him. The potential of running smack up against a brick wall had risen immensely. Edward had no intention of checking out Building 3C without Janet and Charlotte. They were the only people at the moment he trusted to cover his back. And they needed passes to go onto the grounds.

The other part of the bad news for Edward would be trying to explain on Friday why he didn't attend Norman's funeral.

Edward looked at his watch. He had about two and a half hours before he met Charlotte and Janet.

Picking up Wednesday's *Chronicle* and tucking it under his arm, he headed out the front door of his home. The pressure of the moment pressed in on him, and he looked at his watch again.

As he sat behind the steering wheel of the Equinox in his driveway, he quickly went over in his mind what he needed to accomplish before he met Janet and Charlotte. First he would start with the *Chronicle* to learn what he could about the photo and KemKor's acquisition of the land from Ritchie's. Then he'd check out who was on duty at KemKor; he'd have Nadia do that while en route. And depending on her answer to his query, he'd come up with some kind of sterling explanation to get Janet and Charlotte onto KemKor grounds if it turns out that Higgins was not on duty as expected. Backing down his drive, he reached for his cell phone and called Nadia.

Twenty minutes later he parked the Equinox in front of the *West Grey Chronicle* in downtown Markdale and turned off the ignition. He picked up the newspaper from the seat beside him and got out.

Edward hoped that Shirley Cooper, who had been the photographer of the two photos in which he was interested, was not one of those who had headed to Norman's funeral.

He stepped inside the *Chronicle*. To his right, just inside the front door, was a half wall two metres long with a clear, lacquered pine countertop half a metre wide that ran its length. On top of the counter were a silver half dome-shaped bell and some pamphlets on the dos and don'ts of ads, as well as public interest stories and who to contact if you had a story to submit to the paper. Behind the counter were two desks cluttered with paper. In front of him, in an open area, were four other desks. The surfaces of the four desks looked like they had barely been used.

Edward rang the bell. When no one came, he rang the bell several more times and hung over the counter.

"Is anyone here?" he yelled out.

He heard a door open and shut, and the shuffle of feet along the hallway to the back of the building. "Hold your shirt! I'm coming." A burly man in his 60s rounded the corner of the hallway and headed toward Edward. "So what's your hurry, bud? I'm the only one holding down the fort today. So whatever you're looking for, I'll have to do." Plopping a small fan on the counter, he directed the fan so that its breeze directly hit his profusely perspiring bald head. He wore a beige, long-sleeved shirt with the sleeves rolled up above his elbows, grey pants held up with dark grey suspenders, and sandals.

"I think you've just answered my question before I asked it."

"Hey! Aren't you Slocum? Edward Slocum?" Edward nodded. "I thought so." He wiped his hand on his pants and extended it to Edward. "I'm Jerry. Jerry Hobbs." The two of them shook hands. "The only reason I know you is because I was the paper's photographer at the recent Canada Day celebrations. You and that Rat-tray were in quite a few of my shots."

"I take it you don't like my CEO."

"Not a bit—and that includes his brother Norm. That's why I'm not at that old codger's funeral like the rest of 'em. Anyway, you said something about having a question answered before you asked it. Never assume anything, Mr. Slocum. You know what they say about assume—it makes an ass out of 'u' and 'me.' So go ahead, ask it."

"Actually, I came here to see Shirley Cooper. But I guess she's gone off to the funeral, too."

"You obviously don't know Shirley. And, no she didn't. She's probably having lunch right about now in that nice screened-in gazebo of hers. What do you want with her, anyway? Maybe I can save you a trip."

Edward opened up the newspaper and placed it on the counter. "You know anything about these two photos?"

"Hang on there." Jerry searched under the pile of papers on the desk closest to the wall behind him and came back with reading glasses. "Need my seeing eye dogs before I can answer that question." He barely looked at the photos before he took off his glasses and looked up at Edward. "I know these photos very well. They're mine."

"But I thought they were ..."

"I know—Shirley's," Jerry interjected. "Back then, she worked the human interest stories and I ... well, I worked the crowds. See, right there in the lower right is my initial."

"You're going to have to make better *J*s than that, because it sure looks like an *S* to me."

"Listen, are you thirsty? I sure know I am. There's some beer in the back, if you'd like some."

"That would go nice right now," Edward replied.

Jerry took the newspaper and came around the counter. After placing the "Closed" sign on the front door, he locked it and led the way down the hall and through the door he'd come through earlier. The large hall they entered was a mixture of computers, stacks of blank newspaper, a printing press and filing cabinets lining the walls.

The two of them walked along one of the two aisles to the far end of the hall and turned left. In the corner was a large fridge, and beside it was an old oak desk with two oak swivel chairs.

"Welcome to the cocoon." Jerry dropped the newspaper that Edward had shown him on the desk and opened the fridge. Looking inside, he began to chuckle. "You know, I really don't need to do this. I've pretty well got it memorized by now. Anyway, I should, wouldn't you think? Since I'm the guy who stocks it with beer. What do you want? A Blue,

Canadian, Sleeman or one from one of our local breweries, Maclean's Ales? Hope you're okay with drinking out of a can or bottle."

"It's the only way to go. A Maclean's will do just fine." Taking the can from Jerry, Edward snapped off the tab from the Maclean's and took a drink. "Tell me, Jerry, a few seconds ago you welcomed me to the cocoon. Why the name?"

"I do some of my best creative thinking right here before I go out on assignment. It's the location where the metamorphosis of idea and image take flight, with a little help from my friend." Jerry held up his bottle of Canadian and then took a long drink. Putting the beer on the table, he took out his reading glasses and opened up the newspaper to look at the two photos on the second page. "Why the big interest in these?"

"Actually, it's more curiosity than anything."

"Curiosity? About what?"

"This photo here. As you can see, everyone around Norman is smiling—except him. Whoever or whatever he was looking at put that expression on his face. I'm still trying to decide whether its fear, unhappiness or both."

"And you want to know who or what he was looking at."

"That's part of it."

"Hum." Jerry got up, grabbed another beer from the fridge and returned to the chair opposite Edward. "What's the other part?"

"I understand there were a number of rumours around how KemKor acquired its present location."

Jerry rubbed his large hand across his unshaven chin several times as he stared at Edward in silence. He took in a deep breath and let it out slowly before putting his beer on the table and rolling his chair back.

"It depends on how you look at it and what you know. Now, that having been said, sometimes it's wise to let sleeping dogs lie, Mr. Slocum."

"I'm not sure what you're telling me."

Jerry stood up and looked down at Edward. "You see, Mr. Slocum, I really don't know you. And until I do, this conversation is finished."

"Maybe Shirley Cooper can help me." Edward placed his half-finished can of beer on the table and stood up.

"Maybe, but I'd suggest you leave her alone."

Edward knew it was time to leave.

As the two of them walked along the aisle toward the exit, Jerry turned to Edward and stopped. "I understand you're going to be at Charles Blackwell's launch for premier this Saturday."

"That's right," Edward replied.

"We'll talk again then. In the meantime, leave Shirley out of this. You'll note I'm not asking you—I'm telling you."

As the *Chronicle*'s front door closed behind him, Edward wondered what the hell he had just opened up.

Jerry watched Edward as he climbed into the Equinox and drove down the street. A couple of minutes later, Jerry uncapped another Canadian as he sat at his oak desk in the cocoon. After finishing the bottle and placing it on the floor beside him, he took a key from his pocket and opened the file drawer in the desk. The only item in the drawer was a large black binder thick with overflowing newspaper clippings and other documents.

Putting the binder on the table, he made a phone call.

"Shirley, I think it's time to find a safer place for this binder."

"What's the problem, Jerry?" she replied.

"A fella by the name of Edward Slocum was just here. Know him?"

"I know of him."

"Well, he's asking questions about 10 years ago."

"Any idea why?"

"He said it was curiosity. He was particularly interested in one of those photos published in Wednesday's *Chronicle*."

"Which one?"

Jerry picked up the newspaper and looked at the picture again. "Why don't I bring it around and show you."

"Have you had lunch yet, Jerry?"

"No, not really, other than the barley sandwich I've got in my hand."

"Let me guess—a Canadian ale."

"You've got it. You know me too well. Do you think we can trust this guy, Shirley?"

"Bring the binder, and we'll talk over lunch."

Chapter Twenty-Three

EDWARD PULLED INTO ONE of the parking spaces in front of Shoppers Drug Mart and got out. He still hadn't heard back from Nadia about which security guard would be at the front desk. Pulling his cell phone from his pocket, he was about to phone Nadia when a call came through from Charlotte.

"Hi, Charlotte! Wrong sister received my brain waves."

"It's Janet. What's this stuff about 'wrong sister' and 'brain waves'?"

"Ah, skip it—it's just silly talk. So you're using Charlotte's cell. Big step up there, Janet. Next thing I'll learn is you've gone techy on me."

"I'm full of surprises, Eddy."

"Where are you calling from?"

"My place. We're running a bit late."

"What's 'a bit late'?"

"Twenty minutes—at the most a half hour."

Edward looked at his watch; it was 12:45. "So closer to 2:30?" he asked.

"I hope that doesn't mess anything up?"

"Actually, as it turns out, that will work out nicely for me," he replied. The automatic doors to the Shoppers Drug Mart swooshed open as Edward walked in. Just inside the door was the cosmetics section.

"By the way, what have you been up to today?" Janet asked.

"Up to?" The salesperson smiled at Edward and began to walk toward him.

"Yeah—up to," Janet said. "I got this strange call from Shirley Cooper asking about you."

Edward waved off the salesperson and continued farther into the store.

"About me? What was she asking?"

"Oh, what I thought of you, that type of thing."

"I hope you were kind?"

He heard Janet chuckle on the other end of the line. "I think maybe I was a little too generous. So, do you have any idea why she called?"

Edward thought it had a lot to do with his recent conversation with Hobbs at the *Chronicle*, but he did not want to pursue that with her at the moment. "I've got to get goin'. Oh, one question—how do you know her?"

"We were chums a few years ago when we taught together."

"Were?"

"Well, things happen in life that distances people. Anyway, you've got to go, and so should I."

"One more thing," he added.

"For someone in a hurry—ah, forget it. What is it?"

"There's a slight change in plan."

"How slight?"

"Slight. Instead of the three of us going into KemKor together, I want you and Charlotte to go to the front desk and have security call me in my office."

"And why should they listen to us?"

"Tell whoever it is on duty that I'm expecting you."

"That's it?"

"That's it. I'll take care of the rest."

"Whatever you've got cookin', I hope it works," Janet said.

"That makes two of us. But, I'm pretty sure it will."

"Anything else?"

"Nope, that's it. See you later."

Ten minutes later, Edward put a wheelchair that he had rented from the Home Health Care section of the Shoppers Drug Mart into the back of the Equinox.

He gave Nadia a quick call, only to find out that she still didn't know who would be the security guard at the front desk between two and four that day and that was why she hadn't called him back. He thanked her and told her not to worry about it anymore, and that he would see her later.

Sitting in the driver's seat, Edward glanced back at the folded-up wheelchair and smiled. He was almost certain he had solved his problem of justifying temporary passes for Janet and Charlotte. With Higgins on duty, it just would have meant considerably less of an ordeal and a 100 percent chance of success.

Feeling a little hungry and in need of a coffee, Edward drove a short distance up Toronto Street to have a quick lunch at Side Kicks Café.

At two o'clock, Edward pulled up to the main gate of KemKor Pharmaceuticals. He did not know the guard on duty. Reaching into his pant pocket, he pulled out his wallet and held it out to show his ID.

The guard stepped out of his booth and came closer to the Equinox. Taking Edward's wallet, the guard carefully examined Edward against the picture on the ID.

"You look pretty banged up there, Mr. Slocum. A car accident?"

Reflexively, Edward's hand touched the bandage above his ear. "Just a nasty fall."

"I see you've got a wheelchair in the back. You going to need any help getting into the building?"

"To tell you the truth, I don't know. This is my first time."

"Let me call Harold. Where's your parking space."

Edward pointed to the parking location beside the steps to the side entrance.

"Who's Harold?" he asked.

"He's manning the front desk, and I can tell you right now he's bored out of his mind. This would be a welcomed diversion."

"But should you …?"

"Just park your car, and I'll get the wheelchair out and help you into it, then take you around to the ramp at the front where Harold will take over. See, neither Harold nor me have really left our positions, and we've helped one of KemKor's executives to boot. By the way, why aren't you at the funeral with the rest of your executive friends?"

"Not up to it."

"Of course—how silly of me. You must've had one helluva nasty fall."

"I'm lucky to be still breathing."

Edward couldn't have asked for it to turn out any better.

Harold met them at the front door and took over, wheeling Edward into the front foyer.

Edward told Harold he expected two friends about 2:30 to help him carry some work he had to do to his car, since he wasn't going to be in the next day. When Harold offered to get him assistance, Edward waved him off by suggesting the work was too confidential and his two friends were the only ones he trusted with it. To his surprise Harold did not query him further and just wrote down the names of Charlotte Bradley and Janet Thompson, promising to set up temporary passes for them. Harold told Edward that this was his first real job, and he was overjoyed to be able to help him in whatever way he could.

Harold's youthful naivety could not have been more opportune for Edward, and Edward told him that he would pass on his praises to his boss. Then he looked at the array of video feeds behind the horseshoe-shaped front desk and asked Harold if the surveillance cameras were functional around Building 3C. He was told it was a nonfunctional area, and no, they were not activated. This troubled Edward because it meant that his friend John Elkhart had not followed through as he had promised he would. Still, from his point of view, there was a silver lining to this particular cloud because if he could gain access to Building 3C, it meant that his going to and coming from Building 3C would go undetected.

As Harold spoke about his duties and KemKor's expectations, especially after Tuesday's alleged break-in—not realizing that Edward was the one who had reported the incident—Edward noticed a number of keys on hooks lining the far edge of the desk under the counter.

When a call came through on Harold's cell phone, Harold excused himself and walked a short distance away, his back toward Edward.

Edward worked quickly as he maneuvered his wheelchair to the open area beside the keys. Holding his breath as he scanned the keys, he hoped that Building 3C's key would be there. When he found it, he immediately checked the screens to see if the front desk was on one. The surveillance camera that included the front desk had started its scan of the far side of the foyer.

Reaching in, Edward lifted the key off the hook and shoved it into his pocket before making his way toward the elevator, waving over his shoulder to Harold as he passed him.

Life is indeed a yin yang, he thought. And at this moment, he rejoiced in being in the yang.

When the elevator doors opened onto the executive level, Edward wheeled out into a ghostly quiet and mostly empty corridor of administrative assistant desks outside closed offices.

Of the eight executive offices Edward passed by on the way to his office, only three administrative assistants were hard at work, though they were not too busy to let him roll by without saying hello.

Edward felt he didn't need to inquire as to why they weren't at Norman Rattray's funeral with the rest of their colleagues, because he figured they were either too young or too new to the region to have known him. He wondered why Nadia hadn't attended, but he came up empty-handed.

At the end of the corridor, he turned toward his office. He was surprised to find that Nadia wasn't at her desk and that his office door was wide open. Since Nadia's desk looked busy, he assumed she wasn't too far afield and wheeled into his office. Half expecting to find her there, he was disappointed when she wasn't.

Stepping out of his wheelchair, he sunk into the leather chair behind his desk and waited for the phone call that would soon begin his clandestine operation.

"Hi, boss!" Nadia poked her head through the open doorway, munching on a sandwich.

"I guess I don't need to ask where you've been," he replied. By the looks of the sandwich, he surmised she had got it from the vending machine in the lunchroom on the first floor.

Nadia pointed to the wheelchair. "Are you okay? I didn't think it was that serious."

She stepped inside the office, walked over to the wheelchair and let her hand glide across its back.

Edward said, "I get a little light-headed from time to time. I've been told it will pass." His hand touched the bandage above his ear. Letting her in on his little ruse would be foolhardy—the fewer who knew, the better. He glanced at his watch. "Why don't you tidy up your desk and take the rest of the day off."

"Are you sure?" she asked.

"Sure, I'm sure."

Nadia turned to leave when Edward got her attention. "One more thing—I won't be in tomorrow. I'll be working from home. Is there anything you need to leave me or tell me before you go?"

"No, not really. There's nothing that can't wait until Monday."

"Good. I'll clean out this in-basket and take whatever else I need. If something does pop up that's pressing, just text me or send me an e-mail, and I'll get back to you."

When Nadia turned the corner heading toward the elevator, Edward took out his cell phone and called Charlotte.

"Edward? How did you—? Never mind. We're just parking across from KemKor. We should be at the front desk in a couple of minutes."

"Charlotte, your sister's on her way out, and I don't want her to see either you or Janet."

"Oh! Gotcha. We'll park elsewhere and wait it out. See you in 10."

"Make it 15 to be sure."

He opened the side drawer of his desk, pulling out a few small sample collecting envelopes along with a handful of packaged sterile wooden tongue depressors. He put them in the breast pocket of his shirt.

Twenty-five minutes later, Charlotte and Janet walked on either side of Edward's wheelchair as they made their way along the back hallway toward the door leading out to the courtyard.

Once there, Edward lifted himself out of the wheelchair, folded it up, and placed it under the stairwell before following Janet and Charlotte into the courtyard.

A couple of minutes later, they approached Building 3C. Janet agreed to stand watch outside.

Using the key Edward had purloined from the security desk, he and Charlotte entered the building.

"We need light. Hold the door open so I can find the switches," he said.

Charlotte placed her foot against the door to stop it from closing. She stood in a fat wedge of light that didn't progress much more than two metres into the building. "I don't see how that helps much." When she received no reply, she called out, "Where the hell are you?"

She had no sooner asked than he turned on the lights.

"Shit. This is much farther along than I'd been told," he said. "You can close the door now, Charlotte."

As the door shut behind her, Charlotte stood wide-eyed, looking around.

"Something I don't get, Edward."

"And, what's that?"

"This is your project, isn't it?

"I think I know where you're going with that. The building and machinery falls under Elkhart's jurisdiction. My part doesn't come into play until the filters are in place and the testing begins. I'm not even allowed to enter this place without his explicit okay. That's why I don't even have a key."

"He's your friend. Surely he's not that pernickety?"

"John's under Rattray's thumb."

"So how did you get that key?"

"I stole it. Enough said. Let's look around."

"What are we looking for?"

"I'm not sure. Anything that might tell me what was going on here last Tuesday."

Edward went over to the stainless steel grinder. This was the location where the active ingredient for making pills was ground and mixed with a binding agent.

He looked inside. "It's as clean as a whistle."

He let out a long sigh, stood back and looked around. "Would you mind checking out the stamper while I have a look here in the dryer?"

"Not at all—if I knew what it was," Charlotte said.

The stamper formed the shape of the pill before it went into a coating solution. "That piece of machinery way over there."

"What am I looking for?"

"Powder residue. If you find any, call me. Oh, and one more thing— check both the upper and lower portions of the stamper."

Edward watched Charlotte as she headed over to the machinery before turning his attention to the dryer. Again he found nothing. He decided to join Charlotte.

Charlotte was meticulously checking each part of the machine. "Found anything?" he asked.

Charlotte didn't lift her head as she moved slowly along the machine, thoroughly checking each part. "If I had, you would have known," she replied. Suddenly she stopped and looked back at Edward. "Is this what you meant?" she asked, pointing to the section in front of her.

Edward came closer and bent down to get a closer look. He smiled and nodded. "That's what I meant."

He pulled out one of the tongue depressors, peeled off the paper wrapping and snapped the depressor length-wise so that it would be small enough to fit into the mould. Then, taking out a sample envelope, he gathered the powder on the end of the depressor, carefully fed it into the envelope and closed it. He put the wrapping and used depressor in one pant pocket and the sample in the other.

Charlotte, who had moved farther along the line, found some more powder.

Edward gave her a sample envelope and tongue depressor and patiently watched as she gathered another sample. When she was done, she handed him the envelope, and he placed it in his pocket along with the other sample.

Suddenly the door they had come through earlier slammed shut, and it startled them. Janet frantically ran toward them. "Two security guards are heading this way now," she bellowed. Her voice reverberated throughout the building.

Charlotte and Edward stopped what they were doing and quickly joined her. After turning off the lights and locking the door, they waited in silence.

Twenty minutes later, when they left Building 3C, all was clear.

On the floor beside the stamping machine was the paper wrapper and tongue depressor that Charlotte dropped when she was startled by Janet's unexpected arrival.

CHAPTER TWENTY-FOUR

WORKING FROM HOME WAS a luxury Edward had rarely afforded himself, and he wished that he had done it more often.

Putting his pen down, he rolled his chair back and looked up at the picture of Karen on the shelf above his desk. He wondered, if he had worked from home more often, whether it would have made a difference in their relationship. "Maybe she would still be alive if I'd stayed home that evening," he whispered under his breath.

Taking in a deep breath and letting it out slowly, he rolled his chair closer to his desk and picked up his cell.

Anxious to get the powder samples into Grynberg's hands for testing, Edward had left several messages on Irving's cell, home and business numbers, asking him to call him back. This was just one of several attempts to reach him that morning. *It's so unlike him not to return my calls*, he thought.

Pulling up his e-mail from his iPhone, he checked for messages. Other than a "Good morning!" and smiley face from Nadia, there was nothing that couldn't wait until he returned to his office on Monday.

Restless, he decided to drive into town before the Friday rush to drop off the wheelchair at Shopper's Drug and, on the way back home, make a detour to the Grynbergs.

It was a sunny, clear day; the northwest wind moderated the late morning's heat.

Forty-five minutes later, he drove up the Grynbergs' drive, parked his vehicle and got out.

"Anyone home?" he called out. The Grynbergs were avid gardeners, and Edward hoped to find at least one of them tending the vegetable garden at the back of their home.

There was no one there.

Climbing the few steps to the screened-in porch, he opened the screen door and entered. He let the screen door purposely slam behind him so that if there were anyone around, they would hear him. Walking to the kitchen door, he peered in the window and began to knock loudly on the door.

When no one answered his calls, he looked around the porch for something to write on. Finding some butcher's paper in the recycling box, he tore a piece off and quickly scribbled a note emphasizing the importance of Irving returning his calls, without saying why.

Throughout the rest of the day and well into the evening, Edward continued to leave messages during his breaks at each number he had for Irving.

When Edward went to bed that evening, he still hadn't heard from him.

Saturday morning was hotter than the day before, with no northwest wind to mediate it.

Dry, gritty air pushed at Edward's face through the open passenger window of Janet's Camaro as it cackled along Epping Road to William Wardlaw Rattray's estate.

Edward glanced at his watch; it was 11:30.

He hadn't heard a word Janet was saying when Charlotte and she broke out in laughter. Turning slightly, he feigned inclusion by nodding at them before returning his attention to the passing landscape. His thoughts at the moment circled around Irving and why he had not heard back from him. He was beginning to worry that something may have happened to him.

"That's a big, sorrowful sigh, Edward," Janet said as she drove over the bridge spanning the Saugeen River. "Anything you want to share?"

"Oh, I'm just thinking about my speech," he replied.

He was pleased that neither Janet nor Charlotte pursued the topic, and he fell back into his thoughts. *God, I hate giving speeches!*

Five years ago, his good friend Charles Blackwell invited him and Karen to join him for dinner at the local chapter of the Conservative Party. Edward knew a large number of the people present from his youth and through business dealings in his capacity as one of the vice presidents of KemKor. Shortly after their arrival that evening, Edward learned that the president's position for the local chapter was open due to illness.

How he had let Blackwell rope him into accepting the nomination for president was still hazy to him. What he did remember, though, was his wine glass was never empty.

It still amazed him how he had been able to juggle this position along with his other obligations. Or had he?

Maybe that's why Karen and I drifted apart, he thought. *I took on too much and didn't make room for us.*

After delivering his introductory speech, Edward was then expected, as the local president of the Conservative Party, to mingle and to shore up support for Chuck when and where it was needed. Most of the guests would already be converts, so he expected little to no work and lots of opportunity to slip away unnoticed.

Schmoozing at political functions and hosting dinner parties were not his strong suits; those had been Karen's forte. He had just tagged along with a smile and a few words, and he generally followed her direction. That was why he cringed at the thought of having to host a dinner party—aka barbecue—later that day for Blackwell. The guests at this barbecue would include provincial cabinet members, both provincial and local executives and a number of well-heeled supporters.

Damn! I wished I wasn't obligated to have this barbecue. He felt exhausted and hotter than hell. His blue dress shirt was already soaked in perspiration.

Blasted humidity! he complained to himself. *Everything clings to me, and I hate it. Anyway, I'm an idiot for wearing this strait-jacket.*

He wore a lightweight, pale-blue jacket, a dark-blue shirt with a blue, small, plaid tie and navy-blue pants.

Why doesn't Janet have air-conditioning in this old rattle trap? I should have gone in the Equinox and told them I'd meet them there.

After undoing the seat belt, he took off his jacket and handed it back to Charlotte, who received it without too much commotion, and then he redid his seat belt. Pulling down the visor, he checked his hair in the mirror; normally full, it had collapsed to a stringy, thin series of rivulets pasted atop his head. He tried to correct it with his comb but quickly gave up. *Too damn wet!*

"Well, well! Janet, look who's preening himself. Do you need some lipstick or face powder?" Charlotte joked, and she chortled. She reached across from the backseat and ruffled Edward's hair. "Oi, yuck!"

"Screw off!" he yelled as he pulled away to stay out of her reach. "Unless you've got something for this mess, Ms. Bradley." He pointed to his tousled hair and sweat-soaked shirt. "Ah, forget it."

"Actually, I do." She held up a small, portable hair dryer and DC adapter. "We girls always come prepared. Don't we, Janet?"

"I should have known," he chuckled, shaking his head. "Sorry for the outburst. It's just that I'm, well, uptight right now."

"Apology accepted. And for what it's worth, I'd feel the same." She handed him the hair dryer. "A little farther up this road we'll stop and give you time to spruce yourself up. Won't we, Janet?"

"Sure will," Janet said. "In fact, I'm going to turn down that lane ahead; it's well treed and hidden from view. Ladies like us are embarrassed by the dishevelled appearance of a man of your stature."

"Okay, okay! Enough is enough! I get it. You're making me regret that I didn't go in the Equinox by myself. It would have been a helluva lot cooler."

"Maybe so, but you would not have had our company. Now, be careful how you answer that, Edward," Janet cautioned him, smiling.

Before the Camaro had come to a stop and she had turned off the engine, he had already inserted the adapter into the empty lighter receptacle and was blow-drying his hair and clothing.

Politicians, for the most part, left Edward cold and mired in cynicism. He didn't mind—in fact he welcomed the opportunity to deliver the opening speech for his friend Chuck Blackwell. But deep down, he knew it was his need to believe that Chuck wasn't like most politicians. *If only Premier Bolsover hadn't been his mentor*, he reflected. *Maybe, just maybe, I wouldn't be so wary of Chuck. Yet Chuck does inspire creditable hope. Whatever Chuck learned from Bolsover, it's sure not apparent in either his politics or personal life. He appears to be a straight shooter. Yet, the job does shape the person—it's rarely the other way around.*

Smiling, Edward turned his attention back to Janet and Charlotte. "Thanks for putting up with me." He handed the dryer to Charlotte, who immediately began to blow dry her own hair and clothing. "I don't know what I would do without my Mycroft and Watson," he said.

"Mycroft and Watson?" bellowed Janet and Charlotte in unison.

"I think you've got that wrong," piped in Charlotte. "Just like a man, don't you think Janet?"

"Right on, girl!"

The two high-fived each other before Janet took the dryer from Charlotte.

"I got it wrong?" Edward perked up, surprised.

"Yeah! Don't you mean Sherlock and Mycroft?" Janet yelled over the sound of the dryer, pointing to Charlotte and herself.

A smirk creased upward from the corner of his mouth as he ran his hand across his chin. "Oh, I see. *I'm* Watson."

The three of them broke into raucous laughter.

CHAPTER TWENTY-FIVE

EDWARD LOOKED OUT ONTO the crowd as he delivered his introductory speech. He could see that their enthusiasm had not been dampened by the sauna-like conditions from the scorching sun.

Charles "Chuck" Blackwell, a tall, slender man, rose to thundering applause as Edward introduced him as the next premier of Ontario. Relinquishing his dress jacket and tie to an aid, Blackwell rolled up his sleeves and undid the top two buttons of his shirt as he walked toward Edward. After a brief handshake and hug, he stood at the podium and waited for the crowd to quiet down.

"Why are you here?" he bellowed out to them.

Chants of "Blackwell for premier" erupted throughout the crowd.

Brushing back his sandy-brown hair from his forehead, he held up his hands and waited for quiet. "We are here to have a say in our future. We are here to bring about the kind of change that is real, listens and is transparent. We are here to give voice to our future and the future of this great province of ours. That's what we're here for, and that's why I'm putting my name forward to be the next premier of this province."

The crowd erupted into an outburst of unrestrained hoopla as they raised their placards and chanted again. One sign read, "Blackwell: A Voice for the Future," while another sign read, "Essential Government: Blackwell for Premier."

He lifted the microphone from its cradle and stepped to the side of the podium. Again he waited for them to quiet down. Walking back and forth across the front of the stage, stopping occasionally to emphasize a point or ask a poignant question, Blackwell delivered his speech.

Edward watched in amazement as Chuck spoke without a prepared script in front of him. Edward couldn't help but feel the same high level of excitement and energy that he was sure the audience felt. As Edward watched him work the crowd, Blackwell reminded him of the Elmer Gantry character in the novel by Sinclair Lewis.

After he adjusted his position in his chair to alleviate the growing discomfort in his lower back and legs, Edward looked out onto the crowd. From time to time, he noticed that some members of the audience were pricked into a different catatonic state when approached by news media for photo ops and interviews. All the major newspapers and local news stations were here, including the *West Grey Chronicle*.

It was then that Edward saw the *Chronicle's* photographer, Jerry Hobbs. Hobbs was following reporters to the periphery of the crowd, where some high-profile politicians and businesspeople had gathered. Though, the canopy above the stage shielded them from the sun, it also acted as a trap for the suffocating humidity.

Edward glanced at the others on the stage. At the moment, he just wanted off the stage and hoped that Chuck's speech would soon be over.

His attention was suddenly drawn to Charlotte, who was standing in the front row bobbing a hastily made sign up and down. Straightening up, Edward squinted as he tried to make out the faint print on the sign. *Oh my god! Why the hell would she do that?*

He couldn't believe what she had written on the sign: "Fuck the old bastard and put in the new prick."

It's right in Chuck's face, his mind screamed. He collapsed back into his seat. *Why hasn't anyone removed her?* He looked around for reaction from others on the stage but found none. *I can't believe it. They're oblivious to it.*

Edward's attention was suddenly jolted back to Chuck's speech. Looking around him, Edward knew he wasn't alone. Chuck had alerted everyone as he spoke that he was about to say something momentous.

The media immediately left whomever they were interviewing and rushed toward the stage. Eager to get the best position for both interview and camera, they unceremoniously jostled each other.

Hobbs stood in the middle of them, trying to snap photos with his camera.

Blackwell returned to the podium and fitted the microphone back into its holder. The media continued to nudge and elbow each other as they impatiently waited for him to speak.

When Blackwell began to speak, it was slow and deliberate. "All vehicle fuels sold in Ontario," Blackwell began, "will have to reduce greenhouse gases emitted during their production and final use." Chuck hesitated long enough to let it sink in before he continued. "That is, gases discharged during the full cycle of the petroleum production phase will be counted." He slammed his open hand on the podium to give emphasis to his remarks.

Taking some tissue from the shelf in his podium, Chuck wiped his brow and face. He had just delivered a bombshell, and everyone, including Edward, sat up at attention in stunned silence. The import of how Chuck delivered those words couldn't be ignored.

The crowd broke the momentary silence by pumping their placards and chanting his name over and over again in cacophonous jubilation.

Thrusting their microphones forward, reporters called out hurriedly composed questions with the hope to capture a newsworthy reply that would scoop the others.

Finally, Edward and the other dignitaries stood up and joined in, clapping unrestrainedly.

At that moment, everyone knew that Ontario had just taken a different direction. It meant that for the first time in years, environmental initiatives and concerns would no longer be relegated to the backseat; they would now be in the forefront.

Everyone on the stage regained their seats to listen to the remainder of Chuck's speech.

Edward noticed that Hobbs was holding up a package, pointing alternately at the package and then in his direction several times.

Behind Hobbs, Edward became distracted by Premier Bolsover charging toward the VIP tent. Bolsover's driver jogged a short distance behind him.

When Edward looked back to the location where Hobbs had been standing, he was not there anymore.

The usual protocol surrounding the premier was out of whack—the driver- and passenger-side doors of his limousine had been left wide open and unattended.

The peremptory applause from stage members and surrounding crowd prompted Edward to join in, but his attention was focused on the animated conversation between the premier and KemKor's CEO, William Rattray, outside the entrance to the VIP tent—and Hobbs who was hurrying toward them, hastily taking pictures.

Bizarre, he thought. *Why would the premier's driver be included?*

As they spoke, Edward noticed Bolsover's driver step away to interject himself between them and Hobbs. After a few words, Hobbs handed him the camera.

Edward could tell by his actions that Hobbs was anything but pleased.

A few seconds later, Bolsover's driver returned the camera to Hobbs. Another exchange of words ensued between them before Hobbs turned and headed slowly back toward the stage area. Bolsover's driver watched him until he was well into the crowd before rejoining Rattray and Bolsover.

As the three of them continued to talk, they kept looking back to the stage.

Dutifully, Edward clapped along with the others, but he had no idea why; he remained focused on the entrance to the VIP tent.

John Elkhart and Garcia Urquiza stepped out of the VIP tent and joined the discussion. The premier's driver grabbed Urquiza's arm and appeared to forcefully usher him behind the tent while Bolsover, Elkhart and Rattray continued to talk, apparently unaffected by what just happened.

A few minutes later, Blackwell's speech ended, and Bolsover's driver appeared from behind the tent alone. After a short exchange of words with Bolsover and the other two, he returned to the limo and backed it down the drive toward the main road.

Rapturous cheers and clapping forced everyone on the stage to their feet.

Edward jockeyed to see around the person in front of him—just in time to observe what he thought was a venomous exchange of words between Bolsover and Rattray.

The stage began to fill up with well-wishers and news media seeking out Blackwell. Edward's last glimpse of Bolsover was him stomping off toward the entrance to the VIP tent and evaporating into it shadows.

Manoeuvring his way through the throng of people who had gathered on the stage, Edward finally made it near the steps.

Unfortunately for him, the congratulatory mass flowing up the steps made it impossible for him to go down.

Stepping back, Edward waited for a break along the railing, and once it came, he quickly ducked under, lowering himself the metre to the ground.

His feet had no sooner hit the ground than his arm was grasped. It was Jerry Hobbs.

"What the hell happened over by the VIP tent?" Edward asked.

"That guy took a nasty dislike to me taking their picture."

"What was he doing with your camera?"

"Erasing them." Hobbs cracked a smile. "But, I got several shots of them with this camera from over there," he said, pointing to the area in front of the stage.

"You're damned lucky he didn't confiscate all of them."

"I had to do some quick thinking and fasting talking. The bastard scared the shit out me. His eyes are so black that I wondered if he had any fuckin' pupils. Anyway, here—I hope this helps you." Hobbs reached into a pouch that was strapped to his waist, pulled out a folded envelope and handed it to Edward.

"What's this?" Edward asked.

"Pictures."

"What kinda pictures?"

"You'll know when you look at them. I'd shove them in your pocket if I were you. Look at them later—away from here."

Edward did what he was told.

"You know, Slocum, that prick really pissed me off."

"Let it go."

"No way! The prick showed me the butt end of his gun."

"He threatened you?"

"You could say that."

"Then let the police handle it."

"It would be my word against his, and he being the premier's driver, well, I'd bet my word wouldn't trump his. Oh, I almost forgot. Shirley Cooper agreed to meet you. Give her a call and set up a time. I'd suggest sooner than later. Since she's not listed, I wrote her number on the back of the envelope I just gave you."

"Thanks. So you're not going to the police on that other matter?"

"Not yet. I'll see what those pictures I took turn up first; a little investigative reporting on my part. I'd better get going. I think you'll find what I gave you will help. Off to work! Any questions, don't hesitate." Hobbs pushed his way through the crowd until he joined up with his news media colleagues.

Edward didn't have to go far to find Charlotte; she and Janet were beside him almost the moment Hobbs left him. "What did he want?" Charlotte inquired.

"Just to see if I could add something that might give the *Chronicle* a scoop."

"And did you?"

"I don't think so."

"Is that why you've got that sour puss look?"

"I didn't know I had one."

"Chuck did great! *Better* than great! It was what we all hoped for. Look around and get in the mood!" Charlotte said, trying to inspire him. She playfully punched at his arm and immediately regretted the gesture. "Oh, what a scowl you have. Look at it, Janet," she continued, pointing at him and resting her arm on the crown of the wooden stick that her sign was affixed to. "You look like you're about to rain on this parade. What's the matter?"

"You're what's the matter!" Edward grabbed at the sign, but she moved too quickly for him to grasp it.

Charlotte took evasive action behind Janet as Edward wrestled her for the sign.

Finally, Janet had had enough and fixed Edward to one spot. "Stop it you two! This is childish. Edward, what's this all about?" she growled.

"That!" he retorted, pointing at the sign.

Janet reached around her and relieved Charlotte of her sign. "What's wrong with this? I've never seen so much fuss kicked up over nothing. Well?" She pushed the sign toward Edward's face.

Edward stood in silence reading it. "Hum—um."

Charlotte came from behind Janet. "I thought it was quite original," she said snootily. She drew her finger along each line and read it out loud. "Pluck the old bastions and put in the new brick, Blackwell."

"I'll have to tell you someday," he replied sheepishly. "Let it suffice to say that I simply feel like an ass right now. Forgive me."

"For what?" Janet asked. She handed the sign back to Charlotte.

"Here, come closer and I'll tell you," Edward said.

After he told them, the two girls stood back, looked at each other and broke out in laughter. "Yipe! You're an ass, all right," Janet quipped, a broad smile on her face.

Edward noticed Elkhart and Rattray heading toward him. Once the crowd shifted against them, they quickly returned to the VIP tent.

Edward swatted absently at some pesky annoyance breezing across the top of head. When he couldn't ignore it any further, he looked up prepared to quash it, only to discover Chuck's beaming smile looking down at him, his hat swinging like a pendulum at the end of his outstretched arm.

Edward could barely hear him above the raucous jubilation of the crowd. "Join me at the stairs, big guy," Chuck yelled down. He returned his broad-rimmed Tilly hat to his head. "By the way, what happened to you?" He pointed to the scratches and the bandage above Edward's ear.

"Long story; I'll tell you later," Edward yelled back.

"Hey, Charlotte, Janet, thanks for comin'."

The words were barely out of Chuck's mouth when he was swept up by the people filing off the stage.

Scarcely having time to say his good-byes to Charlotte and Janet, Edward turned to Charlotte and reached into his pocket, pulling out the two sample envelopes containing the powder they'd found in Building 3C.

Out of the corner of his eye, Edward continued to monitor Chuck's progress by his beige hat bobbing above the crowd.

"Look, Charlotte, I don't have much time here, but I'd like you to hold on to this." Seeing some hesitation, he forced it into her hand. "Right now it's better with you." Not waiting for further discussion, he gave her a chaste kiss on the cheek and headed off to join Chuck.

Edward and Chuck jostled their way through the throngs of well-wishers. Chuck stopped every so often to pump flesh, pose for a strategic photo op, and exchange a few well-rehearsed pleasantries with key Party supporters. Edward found it a gruelling experience, especially when the media thrust cameras, tape recorders and microphones across him and over him to capture anything newsworthy from Chuck. Prisoner to their nauseatingly hot breathes and perspiring bodies, Edward learned everything he never wanted to know about what they recently ate or drank from their acrid odours. Everything was laid on and, per usual, gluttony reigned, especially in the booze department.

Foolish souls, Edward thought. *And on such a hot day.*

During the last few metres to the VIP tent, the crowd thinned out as Chuck's handlers were successful at corralling them away. Being the proverbial sardine in a sardine can was not Edward's idea of a good time. He deeply breathed in his new found freedom.

Chuck drew closer to Edward as they walked. "You know, Eddy, contrary to what you may think you see here, many of the Party members are quite entrenched in an opposing ideology; they prefer Bolsover's more laissez-faire approach. If they only knew how the old bastard manipulated them. And trust me, it's no laissez-faire—it's outright corporate favouritism. Unlike him, corporate tax cuts don't top my agenda; the environment and health care do. And there's a lot of bridge building and mending that must be done. Bolsover's confrontational policies weakened and compromised this province's social fabric and brought about a lot of unrest and turmoil among the unions."

Stopping, he turned to face Edward. "Now, here's the rub, whether I like it or not. I've got to choose my words and platform carefully, because I need their support. Though I'm looked upon as Bolsover's golden-haired boy, they still see me as too young and in need of more seasoning. Needless to say, I don't agree, and neither should they if they gave it any serious thought. In their world the status quo trumps change. So I keep my cards close to my chest and continue to shove my record in their face. You see, I know and they know that today's speech was a calculated political risk on my part. And so far, seeing the reaction, I've won out. Chalk one up for the good guys." He placed a checkmark on an imaginary board in front of him. "I intend to be a bane to the likes of your CEO and others of his ilk. No longer will his corporate lobbyists control the direction of this government as they have under Bolsover."

They continued walking toward the VIP tent. "Right now, Eddy, it's a cat and mouse game. They want to know where I stand on certain issues, and I'm not willing to give that all up until I'm good and ready. Please keep in mind, I need their support." Blackwell slowed his pace down and motioned to his aides to continue to keep the media away. "I know you don't think much of this soul-sucking business I'm part of, but whether you'd like to admit it or not, politics does make the world go round. Nothing happens without it, Eddy. When I'm ready to snap the trap on those bastards under Rattray's wing, I have to know its fool-proof and that they can't turn it back."

"What's all of this got to do with me?" Edward asked.

"A few, highly trusted people know what I have just said to you, like Leonard Palladin over there. To just call him my right-hand man is an understatement—he's much, much more. But I do ask that you keep what has just been said under wraps. In the coming weeks, you will hear a lot of things that may confuse you and possibly question your support for me. The stakes are high. Just hold tight! Patience's a virtue." A broad grin filled Blackwell's youthful face. "Even, if it does run contrary to your nature," he said. "Wait, until I or one of my associates contacts you. At that time, I promise you, everything will unfold. It's just my long-winded way to ask you to be part of my team when that time comes."

"Boy! You've taken a lot for granted," Edward snapped back. He kicked at the ground with a disturbed look on his face. "You know I hate politics. And besides that, I'm up to my ears with this project of mine for KemKor."

"All I'm asking you to do is to just think about it," Blackwell replied.

Edward and Chuck walked the rest of the way to the entrance to the VIP tent in silence.

As they arrived, Rattray came out holding a partially full champagne flute. Rattray's neck had a chameleon-like quality that either took on a blotchy red and sunburned appearance when he was angry or deeply distressed, or it remained unaffected when he was calm.

At the moment, Edward judged that Rattray was very agitated. He had come to recognize this about him when things didn't go his way during board meetings.

Rattray finished his champagne and summoned one of the waiters standing just inside the tent to serve them. Encouraging them to join him, which they did, he toasted Blackwell's speech and future success before he ushered them into the VIP tent.

Edward and Chuck gave their half-empty flutes to the waiter at the entrance. They had decided that there was too much political gymnastics remaining for them to compromise an already-winning start to their day.

CHAPTER TWENTY-SIX

EDWARD SLIPPED OUT OF the VIP tent unnoticed, and he started looking for Charlotte and Janet. He found them schmoozing with two couples at the barbecue buffet table. *How they're able to carry on any kind of a conversation is beyond me,* he thought as he walked toward them. Charlotte had just bitten into an oversize hamburger, and rivulets of juice and sauce flowed over her chin, while Janet's chin and hands were a blood-bath of sauce from each bite she took from her barbecued ribs. One of the men had retrieved a handful of paper napkins and was busily dividing them between Charlotte and Janet when Edward arrived. Edward recognized him immediately. *Why, it's Chris Power, Minister of ... something or other in Bolsover's Cabinet.* Edward was too damn exhausted to retrieve Power's title from his memory banks. And quite honestly, he didn't care. After a polite round of introductions, whatever conversation they were having before he arrived had gone flat, and the two couples graciously excused themselves to join festivities in the VIP tent. Edward nonchalantly looked along the long buffet table. Relative to the present fare gracing this buffet table, he had had a rather upscale meal in the VIP tent, but unfortunately he had left without dessert. He was making his way along the tables to the dessert section when Janet slipped in beside him.

"Well, Edward, how did everything go?" she asked. She tilted her head toward the VIP tent.

"Okay, I'd guess." Edward eyed a scrumptious-looking strawberry tart and was more interested in procuring it than talking to her at the moment. He began to pick up his pace toward it. "Actually, better than okay. I should have said really well!"

"Our company's not posh enough?" Charlotte jested. She ran up to him and gave him a gentle poke in the ribs.

"Not at all. It's just that procuring that last strawberry tart there takes main stage at the moment." He moved faster along the table.

Out of the blue, Nadia appeared in front of him and swiped the strawberry tart off the table.

"There's one procurement you lost—and to my sister, no less," Charlotte snickered. She waved at Nadia. "Well done, Sis!"

Tears of laughter streamed down both Janet's and Charlotte's faces as they clapped their hands in pleasure.

Nadia made Edward's loss all the worse by blatantly savouring each morsel as she walked toward him.

Screwing up his face to show his displeasure with her antics, he quickly turned his attention back to the table and surveyed the other tarts and cakes that were there. "Well, I guess it's the pecan, then. It's not my first choice, but it's certainly up there."

"Pecan tarts are really yummy too, Boss," Nadia quipped. She delicately popped the last piece of the strawberry tart into her mouth without as much as a hint of conscience.

If they're so damn yummy, he thought, *why didn't you choose it instead of the strawberry?*

Edward picked up the last two pecan tarts and put them on his napkin.

Twenty minutes later, the four of them travelled along the Epping Road in Janet's Camaro. As they were about to turn onto County Road 13, she brought the car to a gear-grinding halt.

"Dang hair! It keeps getting in the way while I'm driving. I should crop it off, or at least shorten it." She combed her fingers through her hair.

"Here, wear my sun-hat," Nadia offered. "I like the feel of my hair blowing about."

"So do I, honey, but not right now," Janet said with a grimace. Bunching her hair up under the hat, she secured the last delinquent strands of hair under its brim. She admired her handiwork in the rear-view mirror and said, "That should do just nicely. Thank you, Nadia."

Charlotte reached across the back of the front seat and flicked the straps on her hat. "If you're going to drive with your window down, Janet, I'd suggest you tie the straps together."

Janet tied them together in a bow under her chin. "There, it's done."

"Yeah, we're a regular 'Bonnet' and Clyde," teased Edward. He began to spray the car with imaginary gunfire.

"I see you've finally come to life. You've been brooding ever since we left Rattray's estate," Charlotte grumbled. She stretched across the back of the front seat and began to stroke Edward's hair. "Tell Momma what's wrong."

Nadia, who was sitting beside her, began to giggle.

"Nothing's wrong, and stop doing that!" Edward scolded. He pushed her hands away. "Have you still got those two sample envelopes I gave you earlier?" he asked. He continued to ward off her attempts to massage his head.

"Of course I do. Why would you think otherwise?" Charlotte gave up teasing him and slumped back against her seat.

"Well, where are they?"

"Here, in my pant pocket." She extended her leg and patted her pocket. "Do you want them now?"

"No, I can wait until I get back home," Edward replied.

"What sample envelopes?" Nadia asked.

Charlotte sat up and simply shrugged her shoulders.

"Eddy?" Nadia asked, bending slightly forward in her seat.

"What?" Edward replied.

"You didn't get those samples from Building 3C by any chance?" Nadia queried.

"And if I did?"

"Well, you weren't too careful about it."

Edward turned and looked at Nadia.

"For the sake of argument, let's say I did. How wasn't I careful?"

"During lunch yesterday, Allison—you know her, the one who from time to time works in security—well, she told me that there was evidence of another break-in."

"Did she tell you what kind of evidence?"

"Allison? Are you kidding? She's a temp, a secretary. She'd never be privy to that kinda stuff."

Edward turned around, took in a deep breath and let it out slowly. He was about to ruminate over what Nadia had just said when Charlotte tapped him on the shoulder.

"Earlier, that reporter from the *Chronicle*—well, you seemed evasive when I asked you about him."

"Hobbs?"

"Is that his name?"

"Uh-huh. He gave me an envelope," Edward replied.

"What did it contain?" Charlotte asked.

"Photos."

"Photos? What kind of photos?"

Squirming in the front seat, he reached into the front pocket of his pants and pulled out the envelope.

"Photos taken at the ground-turning ceremony for KemKor—you know, the one that was in the newspaper I showed you. I guess there's no better time than now to have a look at them." Opening the envelope, Edward dumped the 10 or so photos on his lap. Charlotte shifted closer to see them, but he said, "Why don't I pass each one to you once I've finished looking at it?"

"That'll work for me," she replied.

Edward began to examine each photo carefully before passing it back to Charlotte.

With only four photos remaining to look at, Edward was beginning to feel disheartened until Charlotte thrust the previous photo back in his face. "Isn't that Premier Bolsover's driver?"

Edward took the picture from her and examined it closely. The premier's driver was just one of many faces in the crowd. "You're right, it is. Now why would he be there? From my understanding, Bolsover wasn't part of that ceremony."

Handing her back the photo, he began to scrutinize the last set of photos.

He had hardly begun when he stopped dead. "Jesus! It's him!"

"Who?" Charlotte asked.

Edward held up the picture and pointed to a short, wiry individual with a ponytail who was standing beside Toler Ritchie, owner of Ritchie's.

"That was one of the guys who tried to kill me at the Gorge."

"Are you sure?"

"Of course I'm sure, Charlotte. You don't forget the face of someone who's trying to kill you."

"Let's have a look," Janet asked. Taking the photo from him, she looked at it for a few seconds and began to shake her head. "I've never seen him before," she said. "What's in the other two photos on your lap?"

Edward spread them out on his lap for all to see.

"I'd say by the look of that photo there, Bolsover's driver and the guy with the ponytail know each other," Nadia said.

Janet picked up the photo and held it up. "Toler sure doesn't look happy here between them."

"No, he doesn't." Edward confirmed. He took out his cell phone.

"Who are you calling?" Janet asked.

"Constable Dickenson, who else? Now I've got a picture to go along with the description I gave him." Edward put the important pictures from the group on top before putting them back into the envelope.

"From what I can see, you've got a heck of a lot more than that to show him," Charlotte piped in.

After Edward finished his short conversation with Dickenson, he turned to Janet. She smiled at him and, not giving him an opportunity to speak, said, "I'll drive you over to his office, and I won't take no for an answer."

She turned the key in the ignition, and a few seconds later the Camaro jolted forward onto County Road 13, pushing everyone back against the seat.

It was not without some degree of trepidation that Edward, Charlotte and Nadia watched Janet crunch through the gears with the intensity of a race car driver as the Camaro staggered up to the speed limit, its engine pounding out its rendition of flapping lips in a snore.

Janet glanced over at Edward. "You know, Eddy, there is another thing."

"And what's that?"

"You didn't look too happy outside that VIP tent. We put it down to being with that haughty-tot of an asshole, William Wardlaw Rattray." She dragged out Rattray's full name with a Southern dialect. "Anything you want to get off your chest? You do know whatever you say stays here. Isn't that right, girls?" Janet encouraged.

The girls quickly assured him that their lips were sealed.

"I know that. It's just that … Well, a lot has happened over the past few days, as I'm sure you know." He patted the envelope on his lap. "And I'm still trying to get my head around it."

"Indeed. A lot of things have been going on, and more." Janet said.

"What do you mean by that?" Edward asked.

Janet looked into the rear-view mirror. She cranked her stick shift noisily into third gear as the Camaro lumbered breathlessly up the hill outside of the town of Kimberley. "Stay with that thought, Eddy. Right now, I'm focused on getting this damn car up this hill." She began to rock to and fro ardently.

Edward, Charlotte and Nadia rolled their eyes, watching Janet's antics behind the wheel and after shrugging their shoulders, they joined in with the rocking. At the brow of the hill, the car picked up speed, and they flopped back against their seats cheering.

"Honestly, I don't know if that rocking to and fro helps," Janet said. Her cheeks were red from the effort. "But silly old me, I always do it anyway. Thanks for the support. Now, where were we? Oh yeah! First, let me pull over to the side."

"No! Keep going!" the three of them exclaimed in unison.

Janet was taken aback by their combined reaction, but she did what she was told. Sucking slightly on her lower lip, she continued. "Well, the cat will be out of the bag soon enough. But it's my choice when. Got it? My choice! What's said stays in this car." Once the three of them agreed, she turned toward Edward. "I thought you might have sniffed it out when you saw us talking to the Minister of Natural Resources."

"Who?"

"Chris Power, you nitwit!" Charlotte interjected from the backseat.

"Nothing more from the peanut gallery back there," Janet insisted, growling out one of her best teacher's command. She waited a few minutes before continuing. "In the next three weeks, Edward, my name will be put forward to fill the vacancy created by Ian McPherson's lengthy illness. I believe I have a lot to offer as this area's Member of Legislature."

"Well, I'll be damned! You've got my vote." Jubilant, Edward rubbed his hands together. "I can hardly wait to get on the campaign trail with you."

"And that comes from someone who loathes politics," Janet said. "I couldn't ask for a better person to support me. Thank you, Edward."

The Camaro turned onto County Road 4 toward Flesherton.

"I'll be late to your barbecue this evening. It can't be helped. There's just a little something I've got to do. And by the way, Chuck knows—it was he who asked me to put my name forward. I just procrastinated about giving him an answer. That is, until today, when Chris nailed me down. I'm glad you're on board too."

"On board? I haven't committed to anything."

Janet smiled and patted him on the hand. "Of course you haven't."

Chapter Twenty-Seven

$\Rightarrow\Leftarrow \Rightarrow$

WILLIAM RATTRAY SAT ALONE at a circular table in the back corner of the VIP tent. It was the only table that had not been cleared. While swirling the contents in his champagne flute, he watched the catering personnel as they packed the silverware, fine china and crystal glassware from the tables. The tables lined both sides of the VIP tent, creating a large central area free of tables and chairs that had optimized movement and closeness to Blackwell earlier. Large, tied-off garbage bags that contained the flotsam and jetsam of the day's consumption were scattered around its perimeter. On either side of the main entrance to the tent, the contents of the bars had already been packed into cardboard boxes to be carted away.

Shifting slightly in his chair, Rattray watched as the podium and the risers that had formed the stage were ported off piece by piece through an exit behind him.

To Rattray, politics was a crude kaleidoscope of back clappers, flesh pressers, power brokers, and mealy mouthed parasites speaking out of both sides of their mouths. They all tried to anchor their grapnel to the current rising political mule to benefit self and, more often than not, some corporate entity they owned or represented. He had no qualms about saying that he was better at it than they.

He finished his drink and refilled his flute with the last of the champagne from the bottle in front of him.

Blackwell's speech deeply troubled him. From his perspective there were just too many unknowns. He sipped his champagne. *Still, everyone has their weakness*, he thought. *Blackwell's extramarital dalliance is his.*

Holding up his flute, he looked at the bubbles rising in it before he took a drink. *Yes, that's my hammer and deal-breaker with Blackwell.* He drummed his fingers on the table. *Or is it?*

Bolsover's ego had been easily plied with money and the hint of power. Blackwell, on the other hand, was a different breed from the likes of Bolsover, and Rattray's problem was how different. He had to learn what turned Blackwell's crank, what made him tick.

He drained the champagne from his flute.

Just outside the main entrance to the tent, Rattray observed his wife, Diane, talking to Premier Bolsover.

At first he was dismayed by how close they stood to each other. When Bolsover loosely held her hand, Rattray's blood boiled. *He takes my money, and now he's trying to take my wife.*

Only lately had he come to suspect that Diane may be having an affair. Never in his wildest dreams, though, had Rattray ever suspected that it would be with Bolsover.

He watched as his wife and Bolsover disappeared from his view. A deep sense of hurt, jealousy and malaise washed over him as he replayed what he had just seen in his head.

Looking around him, Rattray found the waiter who had stayed close to him throughout the day and called him over.

"More champagne, Mr. Rattray?" asked the young waiter.

"How would you like to make a few hundred bucks, kid?" The astonished, acquiescent look on the young waiter's face told Rattray what he needed to know. "You know my wife and Premier Bolsover?" The young man nodded. "They were just at the entrance there a few seconds ago. I want you to follow them and tell me where they go and what they do. Do you think you can do that without them seeing you?" Again the young man nodded. Rattray peeled off two hundred dollars and gave it to him. "There's more if you can bring me pictures."

"I can get you pictures," the waiter replied.

"Bring whatever you get to the patio outside the library. You do know where it is?"

"Yes, sir, I do."

"I'll wait there until I hear from you. Just knock on the sliding doors. By the way, what's your name?"

"Rahim, sir."

"Well, Rahim, you'd better go and earn your money."

Rattray watched Rahim cross the open area and exit.

"Bolsover had better not be poaching in my territory or I'll crush him like an ant," he quietly promised himself through clenched teeth.

This had put a whole new dimension to his association with Bolsover, and Rattray needed time to think this through.

Standing up, he headed for the entrance. The outside heat was stifling.

Rattray took a cursory glance around the grounds for John Elkhart and Garcia Urquiza, and when he came up empty handed, he began to walk toward his house. Pulling out his cell phone, he called John, who answered at the first ring.

"Where are you?" Rattray asked.

"I'm enjoying a nice walk through your lovely woods. Is everything all right?"

Rattray climbed the few steps leading to the kitchen and opened the door. "Is Garcia with you?"

"Yes. Do you want to talk to him?"

"No. When you return, drop by the library. Both of you."

Rattray closed his phone and grasped it tightly in his hand as he shut the door behind him. He walked through the kitchen and into the hallway toward the library. Just before entering the library, he tried reaching Bolsover on his cell but got no answer.

The coolness of his house and the privacy of his library was an inviting respite from the stifling heat outside. He stopped at the baby grand piano and played a few bars from Chopin's *Nocturne*—the remnants of a spent youth forced upon him by his mother—but it soon dissolved into an angry cacophony as he hammered the keys with his fists.

What the hell does Diane see in that prat? No—I won't go there. It may just be my imagination. He shook off the thought. *Anyway, I'll wait for Rahim. Right now Blackwell should be my only concern.*

He took a glass from the bar, held it under the ice maker and dropped two cubes into it before reaching for the bourbon under the counter, filling his glass to just above the ice. He took a few sips and then walked to the sitting area in the middle of the room, ensconcing himself in one of the two couches. All he wanted was to savour his drink, lay his head back and relax, but his mind was too active and wouldn't let him. Sitting up, he retrieved the remote from the coffee table and turned on his Bose system. The melodic trumpet sounds of Wynton Marsalis playing "Taking a Chance on Love" floated through the room like soothing waves gently lapping along a shoreline, and he laid back his head again, closing his eyes and allowed the music to wash over him.

Rattray was startled by knocking at the library door and spilled the remaining bourbon on himself. "Damn!" Rushing to the bar, he grabbed a number of paper hand towels to soak up the mishap on his pants. "Come in," he bellowed gruffly.

John Elkhart and Garcia Urquiza entered the room, closing the door behind them.

"I hope we didn't interrupt anything, William," John said, smirking.

He scrutinized the unfortunate and embarrassing location of the wet area on Rattray's pants.

"I don't, appreciate your implication," Rattray replied, wryly. Turning off the Bose system, he walked pass them to the door, vigorously wiping the delinquent area on his pants. "Fix yourselves some drinks; I'll be back in a few moments."

When Rattray returned, he had on a fresh pair of pants and shirt. "Good! I see you've taken care of yourselves. Join me." He directed them to sit on the couch opposite him. After taking a cohiba for himself, he pushed the humidor toward them, but they refused. "Okay, let's get down to business." He cut off the end of the cigar, drew in the smoke and exhaled. "What impressions, if any, did you form from today's political event?" Smoke clouds hovered between them briefly until it was spirited upward and dispersed by the gentle drone of the revolving ceiling fan.

For the next hour, Rattray listened carefully as John and Garcia shared what they saw and voiced their concerns. When they were finished, he stubbed out his cigar and stood up. Taking the remote with him, he sauntered to the bookcase behind him and, leaning against it, mulled over what they had said.

"Your comments, John, on corporate culpability being a boon to KemKor are right. Especially in light of the fact that full rights to the effluent filtration system will be legally ours—I mean KemKor's—Monday. The problem may be the process of how a Blackwell government establishes, constructs and guides new bills to become law. In the Bolsover government we've managed to affect the outcome of decisions in those legislative committees that directly inputted to the final outcome." He put the remote on one of the shelves. "Garcia, does your inside man still believe he can ensure control over outcomes in those committees?"

"Si, Señor Rattray."

"No matter who it is in power?"

"No matter who is in power, Señor Rattray," Garcia emphasized. He looked somewhat perturbed.

"Our interests and the interests of our friends depend on that," Rattray replied. "There's no room for doubt at this time." He turned and removed a number of books from the shelf and put them on the window ledge beside him. In the vacant space was a small safe.

"I cannot tell you who it is or how it will be done," retorted Garcia, now standing, "if that's what you're asking."

"That's exactly what I'm asking, Garcia! But, for the moment, no matter." Rattray pulled out a DVD container from the safe and held it up. "This *is* tangible." He picked up the remote and pressed a button on it.

The section of the bookcase to his left shifted backward and then slid along a track into the wall, revealing a large, flat-screen television. Rattray took out one of the DVD discs and inserted it into the player. "Now, how long is it that we've known each other, Garcia? Let's see ..." Rattray scratched his head, feigning an attempt to remember. "Wasn't it two years before you acquired Greens' farm? A nice little operation you've got there. I've always wondered what it was you did to make it so lucrative."

Reflectively, Rattray rubbed his chin. "You see, I always get nervous about new boys on the block, especially when they're on *my* block and don't invite me completely in. Yet they want to use what I have—for example, your use of my Building 3C." Rattray cleared his throat and then reached behind him, pulling out a sizeable document from the safe. "I've known for a while that you've had an interesting past, Garcia. Oh, I can see by your expression that you're thinking, 'How the hell would he know?' Well, I know because I always do my homework before I enter into a business arrangement with someone." Rattray held up the document. "I must add, Garcia, that this report on you cost me dearly. Bad bunch of people you hang out with in Colombia." He handed the document to Garcia. "It's a copy of the original. And don't bother asking where the original is."

Garcia slowly thumbed through the pages of the document, lingering at some pages before continuing his perusal.

"I'm normally a patient man, Garcia, but my patience is wearing thin with you. Six months ago you started your Oxycontin operation in Building 3C." Supplies of Oxycontin on the street had dried up at that time because it had been outlawed. "I should have received a sizeable return on my investment by now, but I haven't seen so much as a nickel. Should I be thinking about dissolving our business arrangement? Or maybe I should let certain people know about your cocaine operation at the Greens' Farm."

"Señor Rattray, I can't—"

"I understand you'll need to discuss this with your colleagues," interjected Rattray. "But if I were you, I wouldn't be tardy about it. Forty-eight hours should suffice."

"Señor Rattray, though you and I cut that deal, it is not I who runs it."

"Quite honestly, I don't give a flying fuck who runs it! I want something tangible in my hands in forty-eight hours. Oh, by the way, I want a larger share of the operation. Now, that's part of the business completed. That is, unless you feel a need to add more, Garcia?"

Garcia looked down and away.

"Good! Let's move on and see what's on this DVD."

The images that exploded on the screen instantly captured their attention. At first, because of where the camera had been hidden, they didn't recognize the couple on the screen.

The couple had barely shut the door to what appeared to be a hotel room when they frantically began to remove each other's clothes. Their tongues hungrily sought out each other's mouth, necks and earlobes. The man guided her eager and compliant body toward the king-size bed, only her panties and his underpants still on.

At that point Rattray placed it on pause.

For a long moment the room rested in silence.

"Well, I'll be damned!" John said astonished. "It's Charles Blackwell."

"Who's the girl? She looks familiar," Rattray said.

John stepped closer to the screen to have a closer look. His face dropped as he stepped back. "That's—Slocum's wife, Karen," John replied disconcertingly.

"Well, well, well! Two fish for the price of one," Rattray replied. Gleefully he rubbed his hands together and restarted the video.

Karen and Charles's actions softened momentarily as he removed her panties and gently kissed her breasts, then her stomach and abdomen, before burying his face deeply between her legs. Though there was no sound, each of the men watching heard her pleasurable moans as she squirmed when he massaged her clitoris with his tongue.

Charles removed his underpants, and her pelvis lifted to accept his erect penis. Rocking gently at first, it soon became frenzied as they climaxed together. Withdrawing from her, Charles then laid beside her, holding her in his arms.

Rattray turned it off and smiled at them. He took in a deep breath and said, "After what we've just seen, I hope we can clear our minds for further discussion." He ejected the DVD, placed it in its holder and returned it to the safe before closing off the television by returning the bookshelf to its original position. "Well, gentlemen," he said with a broad smile on his face, "I would say Blackwell's in a bit of a pickle. Diddling a best friend's wife isn't kosher, and I'm sure if this got out to the public, they would lynch him politically. As I see it, the question is, how do we use it so that it featherbeds our other business interests without jeopardizing what we already have going?"

Rattray was distracted by a tapping sound at the sliding doors.

"I don't need an answer right now. Let's agree to meet in the usual location in four days. That would make it Wednesday evening, say at nine. Good, we agree, then. I don't mean to hurry you up, but I still have a lot to do."

Once he saw them off at the front door, Rattray quickly returned to the library to lock the safe and return the books to their location in front of it. Pulling back the curtain at the sliding door, he let Rahim in. "Well, Rahim, what have you got?"

"I think it best you see for yourself. I have several videos."

Rahim pulled out his iPhone and showed him the first video. He watched as his wife and Bolsover embraced, kissing each other deeply.

Rahim pulled up the second video. Diane and Bolsover walked along the path to the back woods, holding hands.

By the fifth video, Rattray had had enough. He could not watch their coital exhibition. "How much did you pay for this iPhone?"

Rahim told him, and Rattray reached into his pocket and put twice that amount in Rahim's hands before snatching the phone from his grasp.

"Now, tell me truthfully. Did you post this on the web?

"No, sir, I wouldn't do that."

Rattray got right up in Rahim's face. "Not on YouTube or Facebook?"

"I said I did not, sir."

Rahim backed away. The boy was obviously scared by Rattray's menacing demeanour. Scrutinizing him closely, Rattray finally backed off, satisfied.

"Consequences, Rahim. Every action has consequences. If this were to go viral, no telling what the consequences would be for you. Not pleasant, I can assure you. I've been told you have a lovely family. Do you get my drift?"

Rahim nodded. "Sir, nothing—I will say nothing."

"If you do, then it's nothing you will receive except a lot of heartache. I will pay you once I've reviewed it."

"How much, sir?"

"How much do you think it should be?"

"I do not know."

"Then Rahim, that's your homework before we talk again—namely, to come up with an amount."

After Rahim left, Rattray exited the library and went down the hall to his office. After he downloaded the images from the phone onto to his laptop, he dropped the phone on the floor and destroyed it with the heel of his shoe. Then, picking up his cell phone from the desk, he placed a call to Bolsover's driver, Antonio, and expressed his concern about Rahim.

Rahim completed his obligations to the catering company by loading the last few items onto their truck, and an hour later he headed toward his vehicle. He was pleased with how unexpectedly successful his day had been as he felt the money in his pocket.

While putting his key into the door to his car, he was startled by a man's voice behind him and turned to find a pleasant-looking gentleman smiling at him. The relief on his face must have shown because the man commented on it. Rahim thought it strange that he hadn't noticed him along the path to the parking area. His accent and certain words he used told Rahim that he came from a Spanish-speaking country. Using what little he could remember from his Spanish classes at high school, he was able to decipher from the gentleman that he wanted directions to the town of Maxwell. Rahim tried several times to give him directions in Spanish, but to no avail. Finally, using a sort of sign language, he successfully conveyed the message that he would get his road map from the car and show him. As Rahim turned to open his car door, an arm wrapped around him, pulling him backward, and he felt a prick in his neck.

Rahim had no time to react, and he fell to the ground dead.

Chapter Twenty-Eight

UNTIL GARCIA URQUIZA TOOK over Green's Egg Products, the eggs produced on the farm had been transported elsewhere for processing. Now, everything was produced and packaged on the farm. The operation suited his needs nicely. However, the noise from the conveyor system delivering grain to the 500-foot-long layer house to feed the more than 150,000 hens irritated him tonight. Two other layer houses, shut down for clean-up, wouldn't come back online for at least two more months. Though the lost production bothered him, it did not weigh as heavily on his mind as to how Rattray intended to use the investigative document that he held in his hand.

The occasional wisp of cloud marred the clear, star-studded night sky as the moon drifted lazily from its zenith to the western horizon. Garcia stopped and, looking up, silently named the constellations. Astronomy, a self-taught hobby since his youth, provided an enjoyable diversion that took his mind away from business.

Rattray has gone to great lengths and has spent a lot of money for this document, he reflected. *But why?* If there was one thing Garcia had learned about Rattray, it was that he never did anything without a reason. *What does he hope to gain from this?*

Curling the document into a cylinder, he tapped it against the open palm of his other hand.

"What else does the sonofabitch have up his sleeve than just a larger share?" he muttered to himself.

He let the report spring back to its original form. Then he walked along the path toward the burnt-coloured, aluminum-clad building. At the door, he stopped and listened to the crickets and hoped for a flicker of a breeze to cool him. The sound of an approaching car captured his attention.

Ten o'clock. Hmm, two hours late.

When the driver exited, they approached each other and embraced warmly.

"Antonio, it's not like you to be so tardy."

Antonio shrugged. "I'm sorry. My lateness couldn't be helped. I ran into some unexpected business." He held up a USB memory stick.

Garcia said, "You have my attention, Antonio." He reached out to take it, but Antonio quickly withdrew it out of reach.

"Later," Antonio said, putting the memory stick in his pocket. "What's in your hand there?"

Garcia sighed deeply and handed the document to Antonio.

"It was given to me by Rattray. I think its best you judge it for yourself."

Antonio looked at him long and hard. "Rattray never gives anything without some kind of price tag attached to it," he said. He slapped the document with the back of his hand. "It appears there will be much more to talk about than planned. Let's step inside where there's light so I can look at it."

Garcia led Antonio along one of the aisles to a large steel door with an eye-scanning device on the panel. Garcia then stepped forth and positioned his eye close to the scanner, and as the door slid open, he pointed out the numerous surveillance cameras surreptitiously situated throughout the building.

"How do you deal with government inspectors? Don't they get suspicious?" Antonio asked as he peered around the door to the large, active area beyond.

"As you know firsthand, the government is a poor employer, Antonio." Garcia stepped aside, letting Antonio enter first. "Their workers are overworked and much underpaid." He waited until the door closed behind him before proceeding. "I guess you could call us a surrogate employer who offers an alternative, wealthier future. Since they're not many, they are easy to monitor. Our Colombian experiences have taught us well in how to ply fear as a persuasive. Having our people inside their Ministry of Agriculture provides bonus protection."

He watched Antonio as he surveyed his surroundings.

The room was about the same size as the one they had just left. Men with sidearms attentively supervised preassigned quadrants where women filled egg cartons. Twenty feet above the floor was a grid of railed, metal walkways. Stairs and firemen poles were strategically placed along the length of the walkway to allow quick and easy access to any quadrant on the main floor level. Men with automatic weapons supervised these work areas from above. Women took some eggs off a conveyor system and dipped them into a solution before placing them into egg cartons alongside other eggs taken from a large system of trays beside them. Men scurried about on lifters to ensure a constant supply of egg cartons. Once the egg carton was packed and closed, it was placed on another conveyor belt, where it was sent for weighing before being placed on a skid with the others for shipping.

He directed Antonio to follow him to a large enclosure at the far end of the building. "I must thank you for sending Dr. Chavez."

Without saying a word, Antonio nodded and adjusted his grip on the document. "Garcia. When will I have time to look through this document of Rattray's?"

"Soon. Just humour me a little longer. This is part of the operation you have never seen."

Garcia opened the door to the enclosure and, stepping aside, allowed Antonio to precede him. "Over there, large and jumbo-size eggs enter. As you can see, the eggs are placed upright on one of those machines and punctured top and bottom. Then, their contents are sucked out, along the tube at the bottom, to one of those sterilized barrels. Once the barrels are full, they go out to the legit part of the operation for refrigeration and eventual shipping."

He then directed Antonio to another part of the operation. "The empty eggshells are now placed here where their interiors receive a sanitary wash and are dried." Noticing that Antonio was beginning to fall behind, he gently touched his elbow to speed him up. Having his attention again, he continued. "Once that's done, the shells arrive at this station, where a plug is placed at the larger end. The final stage is here, where the cocaine is blown in and the egg is completely sealed and weighed to ensure they are within the average limits of either a jumbo or large egg. Once that is done, they are on this conveyor belt and sent out to the women, who mix them with the real thing for shipment. The real eggs are the ones in the large trays beside them." He picked up one of the shells filled with cocaine and handed it to Antonio. "Here, check one out. Can you tell if the egg has been tampered with?"

Antonio looked closely at the egg and shrugged. "The egg looks normal," he said, handing it back to Garcia. "What are those women dipping the eggs in before they pack them with the real eggs?"

"That, Antonio, is a brew of old uncooked egg and chicken shit. Between the real eggs and these, it throws the dogs off the scent."

Antonio stood back and looked at the operation for a few minutes. "Very efficient, Garcia. Very!"

Garcia smiled at him before commenting. "It took almost a year to obtain this level of proficiency."

"I remember you telling me about your frustration. A lot of broken eggshells, if I remember correctly."

"Yes—a lot." He looked at Antonio before continuing. "How's your Oxycontin operation going?"

Without turning to look at Garcia, Antonio replied, "That's partly why I'm here tonight."

"Then we have much to discuss. Let's go back to the house. It will give you a better location to go over that document while you're enjoying a good cohiba and a glass of Trago Aquardiente."

Antonio looked down at the document in his hand then at Garcia. "We'll hold off on the cigar and drink until after we talk."

"Let's see if you feel that way once there."

They did not talk as they left the egg facility.

At the side door to the farm house, Antonio lingered at the threshold. He took in deep breaths and began to grin ear to ear. "Wonderful! Are you cooking what I think you are?" he asked. He sniffed at the aromas that drifted through the screen door from the kitchen.

"I asked Eduardo—he's a local chef who just happens to be a Colombian—to prepare a bandeja paisa platter. It may not be as good as you remember, but I think its close enough. Give me that document. It can wait," Garcia said, laughing. Taking it from Antonio, he pointed down the hallway.

"Go to the end and turn right. I have no doubt your nose will find the rest of the way."

Several minutes later, Garcia joined Antonio in the kitchen. Antonio was too preoccupied devouring the paisa platter to notice him.

The bandeja paisa was served in a large, oval-shaped tray containing red beans cooked with pork, white rice, ground meat, pork rind, fried eggs, plantain patacones, chorizo, arepa, black pudding, avocado and hogao sauce.

In a bowl beside Antonio was mazamorra with milk, sweetened with ground panela, which he drank between helpings of the paisa. When he put the bowl down and was about to tuck back into the platter, he noticed Garcia standing in the doorway holding up an unopened bottle of Aguardiente Antioqueno and two shot glasses, and he waved for him to join him at the table. "I have not tasted this since I left San Vicente del Caguan," Antonio mumbled. His mouth was full of food. After he chewed and swallowed it, he took a drink of the mazamorra with milk. "A wonderful gift! Wonderful!" He turned to Eduardo and bowed his head in admiration. "But, it should be you I thank."

"The zest with which you eat is thanks enough," replied Eduardo. He graciously bowed his head, looking to be somewhat embarrassed by the adoration. He was a mustached, middle-aged man with a thick head of black hair that was currently topped with a chef's hat that tilted slightly to one side. The size of the kitchen swallowed up this slight frame of a man as he fidgeted nervously with his hands.

Antonio said, "Eduardo! It's meant as a well-earned compliment. No need to be self-conscious of your art. Here, join us in a drink. Garcia, get us another glass."

A moment later, Garcia returned with another shot glass. He was disappointed to find that they had already been pushing back drinks without him; by the measure of the alcohol level in the bottle, he reckoned they had already thrown back at least three. Though somewhat perturbed by this, he chose not to dwell on it.

After several toasts to the chef, and their family and friends in San Vicente del Caguan, Garcia swept the bottle away and screwed its cap on. "Thank you, Eduardo." He stood up and pointed to the empty location at the table set aside for him. "Place my bandeja paisa platter there and let me escort you out."

"I have yet to clean up," responded Eduardo. He took off his chef's hat and twisted it nervously in his hands. "I never leave a kitchen like this."

"Well, then, this will be your first," Garcia responded curtly. "I don't mean to be unsympathetic, but Juanita will clean it up in the morning."

He took Eduardo's shot glass and placed it in the sink.

Eduardo reluctantly followed Garcia to the front door, where he was handed an envelope containing a handsome remuneration for his services. He heard the door lock behind him as he stumbled down the stairs in the darkness.

For a moment, Garcia watched Eduardo. Then he returned to the kitchen to enjoy *his* bandeja paisa.

An hour later, the two of them entered the cherry wood–paneled den situated off the hallway to the kitchen. Over stuffed with food and bellies fired up with liquor, they flopped down in the tanned leather recliners opposite each other. A half-filled bottle of Aguardiente Antioqueno dangled from the end of Garcia's fingertips in one hand while an empty shot glass was suspended from the other.

"Would you like a cohiba?" Garcia asked.

Antonio held up his hand in refusal as he got up and examined the tranquillizer rifle mounted on the wall. "When did you last use this?"

"Colombia. It took down wild boar—keeps the meat fresh. Humans, too—when there was a quiet need for information."

Antonio sat back down on the recliner opposite Garcia. "What I would like is some quiet time to look through that document Rattray gave you. By the way, where did you put it?"

"Over there on the computer desk. I'll get it." Garcia put the bottle and shot glass on the table beside him and retrieved the document for him. "I'll go for a walk on the property to work some of this dinner off."

"Uh-huh." Antonio was already immersed in the document.

"How long do you need?" Garcia asked.

"Twenty minutes should do."

A half hour later, Garcia reentered the room.

Antonio looked up at him from the recliner with a drink in his hand. He patted the document lying on his lap. "This is very thorough and extensive. It exposes our whole operation—including the Ottawa operation and the northern route. Any idea why he would have such a document compiled?"

"Only a guess," Garcia replied, pouring a drink.

"Well, let's hear it."

"Control, pure and simple. It's his way of saying, 'Don't fuck with me or else.'"

"My thoughts, too."

"Also, he wants a larger share of the pie. He asked me why he hadn't yet received his cut of the Oxycontin operation," Garcia continued.

"What did you say?"

"Nothing. I couldn't—it's your operation."

"What did he say?"

"I had 48 hours to put the money in his hands."

"Hum. There is another reason for this document," Antonio added.

"And what's that?"

"His insurance policy against someday disappearing. I could do with that cigar now."

Garcia put his half-finished shot glass down and went to a table beside the sliding door. He pulled out a humidor from its drawer and placed it on the small coffee table between them before sitting down. He decided against having a cigar himself but enjoyed watching Antonio light up and draw in a couple of obviously satisfying puffs. He sipped from his glass as he scrutinized him. "How *is* the Oxycontin operation doing?"

"Until last Tuesday, I would have said peachy," Antonio said.

"You're talking about Slocum?"

"How those assholes didn't kill him at the Gorge is beyond me. I'll have to send Juarez to finish the job."

"Are you sure that's a smart idea? According to Dickenson, Slocum really had no idea what was going on."

Antonio blew smoke ringlets into the air. "My men found evidence that someone was snooping around Building 3C. My bet is it's him and those two bitches he hangs out with because he signed them into KemKor the day we're sure it occurred."

"Charlotte Bradley and Janet Thompson?"

"If that's what they're called."

Antonio drew in the smoke from his cigar and released it in a slow, lazy cloud.

Garcia rubbed the rim of his glass back and forth under his chin. "What kinda options are you playing with?"

"In this case, I'll leave that for Juarez to work out," Antonio replied. He held out his glass for a refill.

Garcia retrieved the bottle beside him and filled both their glasses, placing the bottle on the table between them.

"By the way, where are Camilo and Andres?" Antonio asked.

"They're at a dance."

Garcia stood up, walked over to the sliding door and stared out, watching Antonio's reflection in the glass.

"What's that smirk on your face?" Antonio asked. He put his glass down and joined him at the door.

Garcia turned to face him. "Andres took Jennifer Blackwell to the dance."

"Charlie Blackwell's girl? Nice catch! So, you're sayin' *both* boys have the same interest?"

Putting his cigar in his mouth, Antonio ruminated over the possibilities of this opportunity.

Garcia opened the door, stepped out onto the deck and went over to his telescope to peer into its lens. When he heard the door close and the creaking sound of wood behind him, he knew that Antonio had joined him.

"She's really interested in Andres. Camilo's interest is strictly for selfish reasons—he just wants to outdo his brother," Garcia said, continuing to look through the telescope.

"No matter. This girl is potentially an ace in the hole we can't ignore." Folding his arms across his chest, Antonio chewed on his cigar. "Between her father's sexual liaisons with Slocum's wife and now this—it's just too good."

Garcia straightened up and turned to face Antonio. "How did you know about Slocum's wife?"

Antonio didn't answer. He just puffed on his cigar and stared at him.

"I see there'll be no answer to that. Am I right that you want to use Blackwell's daughter to further stain his character?" Garcia asked.

"Extra reinsurance never hurts," Antonio replied.

Garcia took in a deep breath and slowly let it out. "Camilo should set that up."

"Why not Andres?"

"He's too soft—he's not one of us."

After a brief silence, Antonio ground his cigar into the deck. "It's too damn hot out here," he complained. "Even my sweat's sweating. I'm going in." He opened the door and quickly stepped inside. "Hurry! The cool air's escaping!" he called back.

Once they were inside, Antonio pulled out the memory stick from his front pant pocket and held it up to Garcia. "You were interested in this earlier?"

"I still am. What's on it?"

"Rather than me explaining what it contains, why don't you have a look for yourself."

Antonio walked over to the corner computer table and inserted it into the USB port of the laptop. After a few adjustments, he stepped aside.

Garcia barely knew what to say when he saw the images on the laptop's screen.

"Why, that's—."

"Bolsover fucking Rattray's wife," interjected Antonio. "It happened this afternoon at Rattray's while he enjoyed the fruits of his labour." A hint of a grin creased Antonio's lips. "He paid one of his helpers to follow them. I followed the helper," he added.

Garcia went to the laptop and replayed the clip. "How long has this been going on? Does Rattray even have an inkling of this?"

"In a word, yes. Mind you, I think he just picked up on it today. He called me to take care of the little asshole who took these shots. We can use this when we deal with Rattray. And one more thing."

"What's that?" Garcia asked.

"Bolsover's been recording his conversations with Rattray. He's got quite a collection in his safe at home."

Garcia sat down in the recliner. "Can you retrieve them?"

"Just say when," Antonio replied.

"I think we may have our tit for tat."

"It should neutralize whatever Rattray thinks he can use as leverage."

Garcia and Antonio clinked glasses and emptied them in one gulp.

"And by the way, how many people know about this?" Garcia asked. He pointed at the screen with Matthew Bolsover and Diane Rattray frozen in a very compromising position.

"Three."

"Three?"

"You, me and Rattray."

Antonio sat down in the recliner opposite him.

"So Rattray's already seen this?" Garcia asked.

"He's seen it all right" Antonio snickered. "I watched the poor fella through his study window. Not a pleasant sight. I almost pissed myself with laughter when he ground the iPhone into the floor with his heel."

"You mean the phone of the guy who took those pictures? That makes four who know, not three."

"Only three."

"Oh—I see." Garcia shifted to the edge of his seat, his arms dangling across his thighs. "If Rattray destroyed the iPhone, how did you get this?"

"The guy sent a copy to his home computer. Why such a worried expression? I assure you that I wasn't seen when I broke into his apartment and retrieved the stuff. And before you ask, yes, I destroyed the hard drive."

"His body?"

"He won't be found for a long time. Stop being so nervous," Antonio said matter-of-factly. He pulled himself to the edge of the chair. "About that report of Rattray's, I'll put Juarez onto it. If there's anyone who can sniff out all the players, it's him." Antonio slid back and popped up the leg rest. "Damn comfortable! It still smells new."

"Juanita puts something on it to make it smell like that." Garcia began to massage the back of his neck. "One of our drivers, Drury Singh, tried to do a little independent work on the side and got caught smuggling marijuana across the Peace Bridge in Buffalo the other day. Thank god he wasn't driving one of our trucks."

"Still, he's one of our drivers. How large a shipment was he trying to get across the border?"

"I've heard at least 160 kilograms," Garcia replied.

Antonio shuffled about in his chair. "Jesus—that carries a mandatory minimum five years in the clinker." He ran his hand across his face as if testing the length of the bristles for a shave before he continued. "I've no doubts that the RCMP will be around here as part of their investigation. Just the fact that he was one of your drivers makes that likely. So you've got to be ready."

"I want him dead, Antonio. Now, before this goes much further."

"Done!" Antonio got up and walked to the window and looked out. "It'll be made to look like a revenge killing. They happen all the time in the pen. What do you think about Justice Minister Nicholson's new regulations to target organized crime in Canada? It opens up the authority's bag of tools. I figure as long as our technology stays ahead and we don't draw attention to ourselves, I think your little egg operation here and my Oxy will do just fine."

Antonio turned to face Garcia.

"Agreed, but the borders are becoming tighter every day. It could mean greater scrutiny to the egg products crossing the border," Garcia replied.

"Maybe, but I don't foresee a problem. One bright light for me was the lockout of dock workers at the port of Montreal by the Maritime Employers Association. Ships rerouted to ports in New York and Norfolk, Virginia, not only overloaded their docks but put a fly in the ointment for their under-staffed inspectors." Antonio rubbed his hands together to show his satisfaction. "Two rather large and important shipments of Oxy—complements of Building 3C—are already in our warehouse in rural New York because of that strike."

"What about the Virginia operation?" Garcia asked.

"Still waiting to hear."

Antonio returned to his chair opposite Garcia and sat down.

Garcia leaned toward Antonio. "How long do you think John Elkhart can keep Building 3C operating without attracting attention?" he asked.

"Well, if Slocum and those two bitches are out of the way—I'd say indefinitely."

"I thought that building was going to be used to test a new filtration system?"

"I guess Rattray will have to justify the use of another building."

"That video with Slocum's wife and Blackwell ..."

"What about it?" Antonio asked.

"Is there anything else about it that I should know?"

"Only that Rattray thinks he has the only copy."

Antonio leaned back in his chair.

"He doesn't?" Garcia asked.

"The other one's in Bolsover's study. You see, when he can't sleep, he likes to go to his study, take it out of his wall safe and watch it." Forming his hands around an imaginary cylinder, he rapidly moved it up and down between his legs.

"Not the greatest image for a premier. But how do you know this?"

"I've set up a number of cameras throughout the rooms in his house. Let's just leave it at that. If I think you need to know more, I'll tell you. Oh, by the way, I do have the combination to his wall safe."

"I thought you would." Garcia stood up and leaned on the back of the chair. "Get the contents of that safe," he said. "I'd hate to see them disappear elsewhere."

"Me too, so I'll get on to it," Antonio replied. "Were you able to find out where Slocum was hiding his research on that filtering system? If I remember right, Rattray offered, what, a quarter million if we retrieved it?"

"It wasn't going anywhere until Camilo and I went over to Slocum's ranch to return his horses. Without going into a lot of detail, a sheet from a bundle of binders Charlotte Bradley was carrying fell unnoticed to the ground. When Slocum noticed it, he tried to slough it off as a problem for his column."

"So you think she's got his research materials?"

"I'd bet my life on it!"

"Be careful what you bet," Antonio said. "This poker game we're playing has dramatically moved to very high stakes. Juarez will have to pay her a visit. As I'm sure you are aware, there's a lot more than that quarter million riding on what she may know."

"I know. Have you made any headway on the Northern Ontario route?"

"Some. A Marc Sharpe, a constable in the Kenora area, has built his own UAV. The federal authorities allow drones in remote, sparsely populated areas. So my problem right now is to find out how extensive an area they cover and whether they are a threat to us."

Garcia looked over at the paused image of Bolsover fornicating with Rattray's wife. "Those UAVs have not only been affective against the Taliban in Afghanistan but also in monitoring drug smugglers on the Manitoba–North Dakota border."

"I'm aware of that. That's why I need more time to get someone on the inside." Antonio raised his fingers to his lips to signal to Garcia to be quiet. "What's that noise?" he whispered. "It sounds like someone's in the house."

Garcia was about to rise to retrieve the memory stick and turn off the computer when the door burst open.

Camilo, Andres and Jennifer Blackwell stood in the opening. The boys' eyes were on the stranger who had been talking to their uncle while Jennifer's stare was fixed to the image on the computer screen.

CARMELLA

CHAPTER TWENTY-NINE

THE PHONE BESIDE HIS bed rang five times before Edward finally climbed out of a deep sleep to answer it.

"Yes?" he said over a long yawn.

"Oops! I thought you'd be awake by now."

Edward sat up in bed still trying to shake off the sleep. He looked at his watch. It was 9:30.

"Irving? It's about time. Where the hell have you been?"

"Long story. Anyway, what's so important that you had to leave all those messages?"

"Where are you right now? Did you get that note I left at your house?"

"I'm at the lab. Haven't been home in a couple of days. Like I said, it's a long story. Again, what's so important?"

"I need you to test something for me."

"You do realize it's Sunday?"

"Well, since you're already at your lab, maybe you won't mind doing me a favour?"

There was a moment's silence before Irving answered. "I guess I've got nothing better to do today. When can you get here?"

Edward had already left his bed and was in the washroom, looking in the mirror and sliding his hand across face trying to decide if he could get away without shaving. "I've got to shave, shower, have a bite to eat and drive there."

"So about three hours?" Irving replied.

"No more than that."

"See you when you get here."

"Irving, is everything okay? You don't sound like your chipper self."

"You've heard the saying, 'Life's a bitch and then you die'? Well, I'm in the bitch stage. Talk to you when you get here."

The phone went dead at the other end before Edward could ask him anything further.

Edward decided to shower and shave at the same time to speed up things, since cutting breakfast was non-negotiable. After stepping out of the shower and drying himself, he still wished he had been able to get some extra sleep.

The previous evening's barbecue for Blackwell and the other political and business dignitaries had gone better than Edward could have hoped for, especially without Karen to cohost it with him. Without the support of Charlotte and Nadia, and eventually Janet, who arrived later, he knew that he would have been the proverbial fish out of water.

Once all the guests had gone, the four of them had sat around and talked about the new responsibilities Janet would be taking on should she be elected as the new provincial Member of Legislature for the district. They also discussed the pictures Hobbs had given to Edward.

Constable Dickenson had wanted to keep the pictures, but Edward had been reluctant to do that because as far as he knew, these were the only copies, and he didn't want them getting lost. After some haranguing, Edward convinced Dickenson to scan them onto his computer. At first he had been hesitant to tell Dickenson the source of the photos, because he wanted to shield Hobbs from involvement until it was absolutely necessary, but he finally relented after push came to shove.

Edward had been excited for Janet. He enjoyed how energized she had become as she relayed all the work and responsibilities that lay ahead, as if it were fun. Though it wasn't his idea of fun, Edward didn't mind being roped in to help her. It wasn't just because she was a friend; he knew she was the right person to represent their district.

As midnight approached, Janet, who had not wanted her Camaro to turn into a pumpkin, offered to drive Nadia and Charlotte home. Charlotte had passed on Janet's offer and decided instead to stay behind and help Edward clean up the dishes and put everything back into some semblance of order.

Charlotte had stayed the night, setting up temporary residence in the living room on the pulled-out futon.

Dressed and famished, Edward had barely placed his hand around the knob of the bedroom door when he remembered that Charlotte was sleeping in the next room. Not wanting to barge in on her, he tapped lightly on his door. He hoped if she was awake, she would give him the all-clear so that he could carry on through to the kitchen for something to eat.

He opened the door slightly. "Charlotte?"

The smell of bacon cooking and movement in the kitchen assured him that she was already up and it was okay for him to enter.

"Good morning, Chippy! Coffee?" she called out.

"I could sure do with a mug."

He made his way across the living room to the kitchen to join her.

"How do you want your eggs?" she asked.

"Sunny side up."

"I love the smell of bacon and how it sizzles and curls up."

"It's hard to resist, especially when my stomach's growling the way it is," he admitted.

Fifteen minutes later the two of them sat across from each other at the kitchen table, hungrily devouring the stack of toast, eggs and bacon.

"This is great! Thank you, Charlotte."

He maneuvered an unbroken egg from his plate onto his slice of toast. "Charlotte, I've never known anyone who takes honey in their coffee."

"And, your point?" she asked as she soaked up the remains of the yolk from her plate with her toast.

"Just a comment, nothing more."

"We agree, then: I'm unique." She popped the slice of toast into her mouth, washing it down with coffee.

"We agree," he replied.

"When are you meeting Irving?" she asked abruptly.

"How do you know I'm meeting Irving?" He popped the egg and toast into his mouth and chomped down.

"Well, aren't you?" Charlotte passed him paper serviettes to clean up the egg yolk that dripped from the corners of his mouth. "Hmm. Here you are, caveman."

He put the used ball of serviettes on his plate. "So how did you know?"

"Deduction. You've tried numerous times to contact him. You got a phone call, and you rushed off to the shower. So, unless there's a woman in your life I'm not aware of it had to be him." She reached into her pant pocket and pulled out the two sample envelopes he had given her yesterday, pushing them across the table to him.

"You're going to need these, then. How long do you think it will take him to tell us what the white stuff is in these envelopes?"

"I'm thinking by the end of the day."

"We could have just easily given it to Constable Dickenson to test. It would have saved you that two-hour drive to Brampton."

Edward shrugged and took a drink from his mug. "You're right, I could have."

"I hear a 'but' in your answer."

"I can't put my finger on it, but there's something about that guy that bothers me. Let's just leave at that for the time being. It's probably my imagination getting the better of me anyway, especially after everything that's happened to me." He picked up the envelopes and tucked them into his shirt pocket. "Anyway, I trust Irving to find out what this is better than me or anyone else."

"What about the scrapings from the effluent tap?" she asked.

"I forgot to ask Irving about that. He should already have it. I sent it by UPS a couple days back. Mind you, I wouldn't hold my breath over it telling us much." He lathered a piece of toast with raspberry jam and took a bite. "You want more coffee?" he asked.

"No, and neither should you. You've got a long drive ahead of you."

He tore off a piece from his toast and began to chew it as he talked. "My bladder can handle it, if that's what you're getting at." Mug in one hand, toast in the other, he ate on his way to the coffee pot by the stove. "Hmm." Charlotte's eyes followed his trail of jam droppings and crusty bits to the counter.

"By the way, thanks for your help during last evening's dinner party," Edward said. "I think the Blackwells enjoyed its informality. After talking politics all day, he told me that it was nice to ratchet it down a few notches. Did you get any feedback from Sara?" He shoved the remaining toast into his mouth.

"She enjoyed the change of pace too. But I feel kinda sorry for her."

"In what way?"

"It can't be easy being the wife of someone running for premier," she replied.

"You mean the public scrutiny and all that stuff?"

"I guess that's what I mean."

"Chuck's been in politics a long time, Charlotte. I'm sure she's learned the ropes by now. She'll do just fine." He filled his mug and held up the coffee pot. "Last offer."

"Okay, then." She held out her mug. "By the way, on another topic, where are the photos you showed Dickenson?"

He filled up her mug and placed the coffee pot on a table coaster. "Right here in my pocket." He patted his front pant pocket and sat down beside her.

"I thought I'd show them to Irving. Who knows—maybe he can add something. He's lived in this neck of the woods for a while."

"When are you going to call Shirley Cooper?" She raised her mug to her lips and quickly recoiled. "Boy! That's hotter than I expected."

"You okay?"

"I'll live. I'll just let it cool for a bit."

"Her unlisted number is on the package of photos Hobbs gave me. I'm thinking once I've finished with Irving, I'll give her a call and see if it's all right to drop by today."

"May I make a suggestion?"

"Shoot."

"Have you put it on your iPhone yet?" Edward shook his head. "And, why not? For a smart guy you're not always engaged. You just said her number is unlisted. If something should go amiss and you lost that number … Need I go further? Here, let me put it on mine as well, for further backup."

After they were done, Charlotte picked up her mug and, sipping her coffee, perfunctorily perused the kitchen. Finally her eyes came to rest on Edward. "You know, I think my stepsister has a crush on you."

"Nadia? Don't be silly."

"Silly or not, I thought you should know."

She played with the thought of eating her toast but placed it back down on the plate. "I hope you told her to stop snooping around Accounting. I mean it, Edward! I don't want her involved. I have a real bad feeling about all of this."

"We've already agreed on that. So drop it!"

The two of them sat quietly across from each other, until Edward stood up. He placed his mug on the table and headed into the living room.

"Where are you going?" she asked. Receiving no reply, she sat back in her chair and waited.

When he returned, he placed a sheet of paper in front of her.

"What's this?"

"This fell from one of the binders when you were trying to put the lot into Janet's car. It must have happened when you tripped. After you left, Camilo noticed it lying on the ground. I'm pretty sure Garcia had a good look at it."

"Oh! That's not good." She picked it up and gave it a cursory read.

"No, it isn't," he replied as he sat down beside her. "I told him it was just something for my weekly puzzle column in the *Toronto Star*, but I don't think he bought it."

"Why do you think he didn't believe it? It looks like a lot of math gobbledygook to me."

"Just a hunch, that's all."

"You want it in any special folder?"

"It fell out of the red binder."

"You sound concerned about Urquiza."

"I am. If you know anything about him, it doesn't take long to realize he's a very smart man—and he's the boys' uncle. If those two boys are caught up in this mess, well, it becomes difficult to exclude him."

"It wouldn't be the first time a parent—in this case an uncle—didn't know what their kids were up to. You know, one of those parental blind spots."

"Perhaps, but somehow I doubt it. Urquiza strikes me as being too worldly to have one of those blind spots. Anyway, I hope this powder I have here in my pocket will be my ace in the hole."

She pulled her chair closer to him. "Ace in the hole? What are you talking about?"

I need it to buy time. Rattray has set up a meeting for me to see Legal tomorrow, and I'd like to scuttle it."

"Legal?"

"Rattray's after the rights to my project. It seems that when I signed the contract to join KemKor, I waived any fiduciary rights to the patents for my filtering system. It takes effect tomorrow unless I can prove the company acquired those rights through coercion or through knowingly committing an illegal act. For example: if they promised me Building 3C for my system—which they did—but knowingly stalled or lied about its use for illegal purposes, then the rights to my system stay with me. Unless—and here's the downer—I'm dead, and then it all reverts to the company." He looked at his watch. "I've got to get out of here. I'm already starting to run late."

As he reached the front door, his cell phone began to vibrate in his pocket. "Slocum here."

"Mr. Slocum, this is Leonard Palladin." Leonard was Blackwell's point man for the campaign and chief administrative assistant.

"Good morning. Quite frankly, you couldn't have called at a worse time. I'm on my way out. Could I call you back later?"

"No, that would be out of the question. As Jennifer's godfather, Mr. Blackwell and his wife, Sara, wanted you to know before it hit the evening news."

"You make it sound like the world is about to end."

"For the Blackwells, it may possibly be just that."

Edward walked back into the house and over to where Charlotte was sitting at the kitchen table. "I'm not sure I'm going to like the answer to this, but what's happened?"

"Their daughter, Jennifer, never arrived home last night. The provincial police and your local police, led by a Constable Dickenson, have been on it since three this morning. Though foul play hasn't officially been stated, it hasn't been ruled out."

Edward's shoulders slumped as he let out a deep sigh. "What can I do?"

"At the moment, nothing; just hold tight. My number should have shown up on your cell. Use it if you have any questions."

"I feel so helpless."

"At the moment we all do. Right now we've got our fingers crossed hoping it's just one of those bizarre things that teenagers do from time to time."

"She wasn't that kind of person."

"We know. I'll keep in touch."

Edward returned the cell phone to his pocket. His face was drawn and ashen as he bit on his lower lip. His head slung low, and he said nothing.

"Edward, what's wrong?" Charlotte asked.

He looked up at her and ran his hand across his chin. "Jennifer's missing. She didn't come home last night." He began to circle the kitchen one way and then another before coming to rest opposite the window at the sink. "Needless to say, Chuck and Sara are beside themselves with worry."

She went to him and wrapped her arms around his waist and pressed her face into his back. "Is there anything we can do?"

"Nothing. We just wait it out and leave it to the police." Undoing her hands, he turned to face her. "Knowing Chuck as well as I do, I expect he blames himself."

"Why would he do that?"

Shaking his head, he walked back to the kitchen table and sat down. "Running for the premiership puts him and his family in the spotlight and makes them open to all kinds of nutcases who have an ax to grind or political cause to gain."

"Are you thinking that Jennifer was snatched by a terrorist group or something?"

"Honestly, right now, I'm not thinking straight."

"Didn't she go to a dance last evening?"

"Yes." His lips pinched together as he began to massage the back of his neck. "If I remember correctly, she went with Andres. I think his brother, Camilo, drove them," he added.

"Andres and Camilo!"

He held up his hand. "Charlotte, I know where you're heading with this, but pull back. Paul's been on it since two or three this morning. Needless to say, I expect after he had spoken with Chuck and Sara that he headed straight out to the farm to wake them up."

Charlotte's back went rigid as she pressed her fists into either side of her waist.

"And?"

"I don't know any more."

"Those two boys were here during the break-in, and now this. I don't believe in coincidences," she said.

Edward shrugged and shook his head. "Neither do I, but what do you want me to say? That they're guilty of something or other? I'm not going to do that."

Charlotte sat at the edge of the chair beside him. "Okay. I can see it's a sensitive point with you. Let's change the topic. Janet's going to want to support Chuck and Sara in some way."

"I'd suggest she call Leonard Palladin before she does anything."

"Who's he?"

"He's the person I just spoke to. Everything goes through him at the moment." He gave her the phone number.

Charlotte said, "I'd better call Janet to pick me up. I'll tell her what's happened when she gets here. Right now, you'd better get going, or else Irving's going to give up on you and leave."

He glanced at the wall clock. "Damn, you're right." He scurried across the living room and picked up the keys for the rented Equinox from the kitchen counter. "I'm outta here! Keep me informed."

"I don't need to be reminded, Edward—it *was* my idea. Just you remember to keep your cell on. How do you ever manage to make it on your own?"

"Barely. Even less so since Karen's gone."

"I guessed that."

As Edward closed the door behind him, he smiled to himself. *Whatever happens today I'll be okay*, he thought. *I've got a good friend to share it with.*

Chapter Thirty

◁═══ ═══▷

"WHAT ON EARTH ARE you doing there?" Janet asked, nodding toward Charlotte's cell phone as she parked her Camaro at the entrance to the Valley River Gorge Road.

"I'm texting." Charlotte was too preoccupied to bother looking up.

Janet rolled her eyes. "I can see *that!* May I enquire as to whom you are texting?"

"You may," she replied matter-of-factly. Her eyes remained focused on her iPhone.

"Well, to whom?"

When Charlotte finally looked up, a crease of smile had formed at the corner of her lip.

"I'm texting Edward to let him know that we are about to begin our search for his Wrangler."

"Did he know we were doing this?"

"Are you kidding? Of course I didn't tell him. He'd have only discouraged it and told me to let the police do it."

"Come to think of it, that probably would have been the smarter choice."

"Where's your sense of adventure, Janet?"

"Oh, I've still got that—it's my life I would miss. Anyway, when do you expect him to read it? Surely not while he's driving to Brampton?"

Janet stretched her neck to see what Charlotte had written.

"Of course not!" Charlotte retorted. "I know it's illegal for him to talk or text while driving."

Her face had contorted into a wry expression as she pulled her phone to one side so Janet couldn't see.

Janet said, "Just askin'. No sense getting your knickers in a knot. I hope you're not expecting him to champion this little adventure?"

"At this point, does it matter?"

"I guess not."

Finally finished texting, Charlotte shoved her phone into her pant pocket and slipped out of her sandals to put on her walking boots.

Janet reached into a carton on the floor behind her and tossed a bottle of water over to Charlotte; she took another one out for herself. "Use sparingly, these are the last ones." She gave Charlotte's leg a gentle slap just before she exited the Camaro. "Let's get goin'."

Charlotte finished tying up her boot and by the time she looked up, Janet was already heading down the Gorge Road at top speed. "Hey! Slow down!"

Charlotte scrambled out of the Camaro and ran after her.

Juarez stretched and yawned before looking through his binoculars again. He had parked his Ford Explorer well enough back so that Charlotte and Janet were not likely to see him, but not too far back that he couldn't monitor their actions.

He had been ordered by Antonio to retrieve Slocum's documents from Charlotte and to kill both her and Janet—tasks with which he wrestled. He knew whatever he finally decided, it had to be convincing, or else it would not only expose him but collapse the whole undercover operation that had taken years to build.

A first-generation Canadian, born of Mexican parents, he had not been an easy boy to raise. Involved with local gangs and drug trafficking from an early age, he had been finally sent to a low-security prison under the Young Offenders Act for two years less a day. It was there he had met the prison chaplain who changed his life around.

It had happened in small stages, too subtle for him to notice at first. But by the time he left, he had acquired his high school diploma with honours and had his acceptance to study law at the University of Toronto. With his master's degree in hand, he had applied for and had been accepted into the Royal Canadian Mounted Police, better known as the RCMP. For him, it couldn't have been a better fit. It didn't take long for his superiors to recognize his talents in language, especially Spanish and French, and his street savvy.

After several years of participating in a number of high-profile undercover stings, he was invited to be part of a joint US-Canadian drug operation in Juarez, Mexico. Deeply embedded, he had worked his way up the cartel until he was noticed by its leader, Rafael Aguilar Guajardo. During this time, he was given responsibility by Rafael to set up more direct contact with drug sources in Colombia, namely the Revolutionary Armed Forces of Colombia—better known as FARC. He had aligned himself with Antonio and later, after he returned to Canada, Garcia Urquiza. Unexpectedly, as it turned out, it had been a wise decision because Guajardo was murdered in Cancun, and Amado Carrillo Fuentes took over the leadership. Fuentes, Antonio and Garcia were allies.

Juarez was the only name he went by. He had almost forgotten his birth name was Emilio Leyva, and he barely remembered his parents, whose funeral he could not attend and graves he could not visit. He had seen and done too much. He had become someone even he didn't recognize, and he wondered that when the time came for him to integrate back into society, whether he would be able to do it.

Stepping out of his vehicle, Juarez quietly closed the door behind him and wiped his forehead with the sleeve of his shirt. Then, unbuttoning both sleeves, he rolled them up until the thickness of his biceps stopped further advance just above his elbow. His sculptured bronze face was capped in jet-black glistening hair; his eyes were closely set and intense, and they were mounted on either side of a hawk-like nose. All of this sat on a tall neck and a lean, muscular body. Stretching, he undid his fly and urinated against the wheel of the truck.

Finished, he circumspectly perused his surroundings, attentive to any sounds or movements. Satisfied that there was no one else around, he reached into the truck, fetched the binoculars and looked through them. He saw Charlotte running off to join Janet, who had already disappeared down the Gorge Road. Throwing the binoculars onto the front seat, he walked around the front of the vehicle to the passenger side and, opening the door, reached under the seat and pulled out his Glock 22. He shut the door and ran toward the location Charlotte had just left. His pace slowed as he reached Janet's Camaro, where he opened the passenger door and rummaged through the glove compartment and the odds and ends in the backseat. Not looking for anything in particular, he couldn't pass up an opportunity to learn more about the car's owner and maybe her passenger.

He held up Charlotte's sandals. *Small feet,* he thought.

He returned the sandals to their original position. Other than the driver's ownership, a dried-up, half-used roll of Lifesavers and the remnants from a bag of mixed nuts, and a couple packages of Kleenex, there was nothing else in the glove compartment. A box filled with empty water bottles lay on the floor in the back, and a cowboy hat rested on the seat. Checking under the front seats, he found nothing useful. He stepped out and closed the door. Tucking his Glock in the nap of his back under his shirt, he slowly made his way down the Gorge Road.

Janet glanced back at Charlotte and shook her head. "Now, what are you telling him?" she asked.

"About the eyes you have in the back of your head," Charlotte said, smirking.

"Eyes in the back of my head? What on earth are you talking about, girl?" Janet tripped over a root at the side of the road.

"I'll tell you later. Just watch where you're walking?"

"*Me* watch where I'm walking?" Janet found it difficult to hide her pleasure as she watched Charlotte trip over the same root outcropping.

A few moments later, Charlotte stopped opposite to what used to be the entrance to Parker Bridge. The route, declared off-limits years ago, was overgrown and barely visible. Janet stood beside Charlotte scrutinizing the terrain on either side and along the defunct route.

"My friends Agnes Stoddart and her husband, Ray, fell to their deaths from that bridge," Janet said.

"Oh! I didn't know. I'm sorry. How? I mean, what happened?"

"While cycling across it, the part they were on gave way. Their deaths were declared an accident, and the region declared it a hazardous zone and closed it off."

"Wasn't there any talk about repairing it or replacing it?"

"Nope—at least nothing that I was aware of. Are you sure this is where Edward's Wrangler turned along?"

"It's my best guess. Remember, I was on foot, and it had a good start on me," Charlotte replied.

Janet kneeled down to have a closer look at the route. Branches snapped a short distance behind her. Startled, Janet quickly stood up and looked around, pressing her fingers against her lips to silence Charlotte.

A couple of minutes passed before Janet spoke. "I heard some twigs snap. It must have been some sort of forest dweller passing through."

"What kind of forest dweller?"

Janet ignored her question and replied, "There's nothing to fret about." She gave one last look around before she reexamined the route. "Well, Charlotte, good guess. To me, it looks like some vehicles have passed through here recently."

"Vehicles?"

"Uh-huh. Look further in, Charlotte. See how the grass is flattened down in several places? Whoever's using this route did a damn good job of covering up their tracks by brushing up the overgrowth from the shoulder here to a point 15 feet in. On a normal day, a passerby wouldn't have so much as an inkling that a route ever existed before. Except, of course, for those 'No Trespassing: Road Closed' signs posted there." She turned toward Charlotte. "Well, if you're ready, let's go and find Edward's Wrangler.

Following the tramped-down grass, 20 minutes later they came to a locked, hinged gate across the road. Beyond it, the road had been cleared and well maintained.

"A road? But why?" Charlotte asked.

"Your guess is as good as mine," Janet replied. "Why would anyone want to maintain a road that goes nowhere, except to a broken-down bridge?"

"Unless it's no longer a broken down bridge …?"

"Well, there's only one way to find out. Are you ready?"

Charlotte had barely nodded her agreement by the time Janet was over the top of the gate and lightly jogging along the route.

Five minutes later Janet came to an abrupt halt. At first Charlotte thought it might be a wild animal and dramatically slowed her progress, but, when she finally caught up to her, she understood and her jaw dropped wide open. It was the Parker Bridge, fully restored.

"Well, there's our answer. Now, Janet, I hope you're not thinking we should cross it." Trepidation dripped from every word out of her mouth.

"You bet I am! I'd bet my life on it that Edward's Wrangler lies on the other side." Janet stepped onto the bridge and, turning, held her hand out to encourage Charlotte to come forward. "Come on, slowpoke."

"You might be okay with betting your life but I'm not. Janet, I'm not comfortable with this."

"Neither am I, but I'm going across whether or not you come."

Shrugging in resignation, Charlotte headed toward the bridge but stopped cold when she saw the sheer terror on Janet's face.

"What's wrong?"

"I wish I hadn't bet my life just now." Janet pointed to a position behind Charlotte.

"What in blazes are you talking about?" Charlotte asked impatiently, following the direction of Janet's pointing finger. "Oh!"

"Ladies." Juarez stepped out from behind the trunk of a nearby maple tree and walked toward them, his Glock pointing in their direction.

Chapter Thirty-One

AS EDWARD SAT IN a small coffee shop at the corner of Queen Street East and Hurontario in Brampton, enjoying a large black coffee without sugar and a glazed cinnamon bun, he scrolled through the several messages that Charlotte had left on his cell phone.

An hour earlier, he had dropped off the sample envelopes containing the white powder he and Charlotte had collected from Building 3C to Irving.

Grynberg Laboratory was located on the top floor of a red-brick building on Hurontario.

Edward had to knock several times on the door before Irving finally opened it to let him in.

Irving's dishevelled appearance—most out of character for him—had briefly taken Edward aback. A slight-built man, Irving was definitely having a bad hair day, and he looked like he hadn't shaven in days. He wore a plaid, short-sleeved cotton shirt that had carelessly been tucked into his dark grey shorts in obvious haste. The single pocket in his shirt bulged with a row of pencils, pens and his glasses case. There was a slight hint of alcohol emitting from him.

Behind Irving, Edward could see into his office and spotted the mattress in front of his desk.

For a moment, silence reigned between them. "Where are those samples you wanted me to test?" Irving asked.

"Here in my pocket." As he handed them over to him, he asked, "Did you get the effluent scrapings?"

"I did. I didn't find anything out of the ordinary." While walking down the hall toward the lab, Irving turned to Edward.

"By the way, where are the downstream samples you were going to collect? I thought you would have brought them along."

Edward followed Irving into the lab. "Oh, that's right—I haven't told you."

"Told me what?"

As Edward watched Irving ready the equipment he needed to analyze the samples, he brought him up to speed with what had occurred to him.

"I sorta wondered what that bandage was about above your ear," Irving admitted.

"Now you know. Do you mind being distracted for a few minutes?"

"This shouldn't take too long. Sure. What do you want?"

Edward reached into his pocket and pulled out the envelope containing the photos and separated out the top three.

"I'd like you to have a look at these. Especially the two men on either side of Toler Ritchie. Tell me if you recognize either of them."

Irving looked at them closely for a few seconds before looking up at Edward. "Am I supposed to?"

"I take it you don't recognize them."

"Nope. Any idea when they were taken?"

"About 10 years ago, at the ground turning for KemKor. Why are you asking?"

"I just can't believe that much time has passed since Toler and his wife died. Time sure flies! They were a close couple. At least they died together."

After he handed back the photos, Irving refocused his attention to separating the samples into the test tubes.

"What did they die of?" Edward asked.

"If I'm remembering correctly, the coroner couldn't tell with any degree of certainty. There wasn't much left of either him or his wife after their house burned down." He stopped what he was doing and turned to face Edward. "I don't mean to be a spoilsport, but do you mind coming back in, say, an hour? Better still, I've got your cell number. I'll call you when it's ready. I'm just having some concentration problems at the moment. Maybe if I shower up and shave, it will help me concentrate better. Why don't you head to The Meeting Place Café? Now there's a place that should bring back memories for you. It's changed a little since you and Karen met there—actually, it's changed a lot—but I think you'll like it nonetheless."

"Irving, I saw the mattress on the floor in your office."

"I thought you had. My wife and I are separated—I think for good this time. I really don't want to talk about it right now. When I'm ready to talk about it, you'll know. For the moment that will just have to do. Like I said, the analysis shouldn't take long once I'm on it."

As Edward left the building and walked toward the café, he felt a deep sadness for his friend.

Though its name had never changed, The Meeting Place Café had gone through several owners and renovations since Edward had briefly hung out there as a teenager. The serving counter was in the original location, except that instead of the choice desserts and fancy sandwich combos being arranged behind the counter, they were now displayed behind a refrigerated glass enclosure that ran the full length of the counter.

He remembered the first time he'd met Karen. It wasn't until much later he learned that it was not only her first job but also her first day serving customers at the café.

Though they hadn't said much to each other as he paid her for his glazed cinnamon bun and coffee, he never forgot her. Days after that meeting, he and his family moved to West Grey, and until now, he had never returned to the coffee shop.

During one of his work terms while at university, he met Karen again at a cocktail party sponsored by the engineering firm at which he was interning. She represented some ad company that his employer had been considering for an upcoming promotion program. They had spent that whole evening talking, and by the end of it, he not only knew that he had to see her again but that his life had changed.

Unfolding the newspaper, he glanced over at the young girl behind the counter and wished it was within his power to turn time on its heels and start over again. He took a bite of his glazed cinnamon bun and washed it down with coffee.

Edward didn't know how to reply to Charlotte's messages. In a word, he was pissed off with her for possibly putting herself in harm's way. He decided not to answer her and give himself time to settle down rather than saying something in a text to her that he might regret. *Surely if she was in danger, it would have shown up in one of her texts.*

Already a fait accompli, he decided to wait it out and let fate take its course.

A high-pitched burp from a police car on the street startled him. Whatever thoughts he just had had evaporated, as he absently watched the flashing lights from the cruiser turn north onto Hurontario Street. A few moments later, a fire truck, horn blasting, entered the intersection from the south heading in the same direction as the police cruiser.

Now I know why I don't like coming to the city, he complained to himself. *Give me the quietness, fresh air and sanctity of the country anytime.*

He glanced at his watch. An hour and a half had passed since he had left Irving's lab, and for something he thought was routine, he was surprised he hadn't heard back yet.

More emergency vehicles rushed through to a destination slightly north of the café. The intersection had suddenly become a hub of activity as more emergency vehicles rushed north to their destination. Police began to close off the north-south route to ongoing traffic as they redirected along the east-west route.

Curious, Edward stood up and went over to the window facing the street. Black heavy smoke drifted skyward from one of the buildings north of his location. He didn't have to follow the smoke backward very far for him to realize that it was either Irving's building or one very close to it that was on fire. Without thinking, Edward burst out of the coffee shop and into the pungent, smoked-filled air, moving along the sidewalk toward the intersection.

He was surprised on such a hot and humid day to see a black man running toward him with the hood on his hoodie drawn over his head. The man slammed into Edward and knocked him to the pavement, but not before Edward felt a pinprick in his lower abdomen.

The man stepped over him and kept going.

Edward's heart rate began to elevate sharply, and he frantically screamed out for help.

CHAPTER THIRTY-TWO

SLIGHTLY DISORIENTED, EDWARD WOKE up on a gurney in a curtained-off area in the emergency ward of Brampton Civic Hospital. The nasal cannula connection to the oxygen source on the wall, the IV, and vital signs monitor leads hampered his movement. Except for the hospital gown, he was naked. Under the curtain surrounding him, he could see a number of brightly coloured Adidas scurrying about. Occasionally, black-laced shoes or brown leather slip-ons stopped outside his curtain before quickly moving on. The activity was frenzied as he heard voices calling for so many cc's of this or that medicine and calls to the lab to take blood work. He closed his eyes and tried to block it out.

The curtain separated, and a middle-aged woman pushed in a cart with a number of test tubes and other paraphernalia on it. Behind her was a nurse.

"I'm here to take some blood," the woman said. "How are you feeling?"

"Until you told me that, I thought okay."

She put on latex gloves, examined the hospital bracelet around his wrest and checked it against the information she had. "What's your name?" the lab technician asked.

"Edward Slocum."

"Good, everything checks out." She put a tourniquet around his upper arm and asked him to open and close his hand several times as she patted around to find the best location to withdraw her sample. "You can stop now, Mr. Slocum."

Edward looked away as she inserted the needle and began to withdraw blood.

The nurse adjusted his pillow and checked the monitors.

"Now, wasn't that easy?" the lab technician asked, releasing the rubber tourniquet from around his arm and putting it on the cart. "Now, push down on this cotton ball while I put a bandage across it."

Holding up the four vials of blood she had taken, she gave them a little shake and placed them in a tray on the cart before leaving.

"You feel all right?" the nurse inquired. "You look a little pale."

"I think so."

"Let me check that bandage above your ear," she said. "It looks like the wound opened up again. How did you get it?" She worked quickly to apply some ointment and a new bandage.

Edward closed his eyes. He had no intention of rehashing how he received that wound.

After she reinserted the prongs of the nasal cannula and refitted the plastic tubing behind his ears, she momentarily disappeared outside of the curtain, only to reappear a couple minutes later with a towel to wipe his face.

"How's that feel?"

"Good. Thank you."

Once she checked the oxygen flow, she disappeared through the opening in the curtain.

Edward's eyes followed the curtain track to the point through which the nurse had just exited, and he mentally began to count the number of hooks which held the opaque, light-brown curtain to its track. At 21 hooks, he was interrupted by a lean, tall, pleasant-looking East Asian, carrying a clipboard.

"Hi! I'm Dr. Khan, but you can call me Sal. Nice to see you awake." He looked at the tubing for the IV and glanced at the vital signs monitor, writing down something on the sheet attached to his clipboard. "How are you feeling?"

"Other than a little tired, I feel okay. What happened?"

"You ever had any heart problems?"

"Not that I'm aware of. Why?"

"You were admitted with a pretty severe case of tachycardia."

"Could you put that in layman's terms for me, Sal?"

"It means your heart rate was faster—much faster—than normal. It caused you to pass out. Luckily for you, medics were close by."

"I was okay until that jackass bowled me over on the sidewalk. Come to think of it, I could have sworn he jabbed something into me."

"Where?"

"Here," Edward replied, pointing to his lower abdomen.

Sal pulled down the sheet and began a fastidious examination of the region Edward had pointed to. A couple minutes passed before he said anything. "Aha."

"You find something?"

"Almost missed it. Thought at first it was a small pimple." Sal turned away and recorded what he found before turning back to Edward.

"There's a small puncture wound in your abdomen. You don't by any chance do drugs, do you?"

"Absolutely not! Why would you ask that?"

"Traces of a cocaine derivative were found in blood samples that were taken shortly after you arrived here."

Edward found Sal's stare unsettling. "I don't ... I—"

Sal's features softened, and he began to smile.

"I'm sorry. I didn't mean for you to think that I didn't believe you. Now that I've seen your abdomen, I'm wondering why someone would be trying to kill you. You do know I'll have to report this to the police, and they're going to want to interview you."

"Of course. It's just that I'd like to get out of here." Edward shifted uncomfortably in the bed.

"It shouldn't take long. They have a community office right here in the hospital. By the way, who's your family doctor?"

"Dr. Albert Salinger, in Markdale."

"You wouldn't by any chance have his address? It's no big deal if you don't; it just makes it easier if you do."

"If I knew where my wallet was, I could show you his card. Anyway, where are my clothes?"

"I'll have the nurse round them up for you."

"Any idea how long it will take before I can get out of here?" Edward asked.

"Medically, you appear all right. Though I am going to suggest to your doctor that you be put on a Holter monitor and be referred to a cardiologist for a complete diagnostic assessment. Also, I'll ask the nurse to give you some cardiac support material."

"I don't expect to keel over from a heart attack, Doc."

"Actually, Mr. Slocum, I don't expect that either. But it's better to be safe than sorry. Now, back to your question as to when you'll get out. Since I don't expect anything untoward from the recent blood samples, and assuming everything else stays as it is—normal—I'd expect it would depend on the police."

When the doctor left, Edward resumed putting his time in counting curtain eyelets. It was the only thing he could think of doing to keep his mind off learning that a second attempt had been made on his life.

"I hope you're decent enough, because I'm coming in." The curtain parted, and Irving stepped in, dragging a chair behind him.

"Irving! You have no idea how pleased I am to see you. How did you know I was here?"

Placing the chair beside the gurney, Irving sat down with a manila envelope across his lap. "I saw them put you in the ambulance. What happened to you?"

"Long story; we'll talk about it over supper some time. Was that your building that was on fire?"

"I'm afraid it was. Lost everything." He scratched the side of his head.

"Insurance should cover your loss. You'll be back on your feet in no time."

"If, that is, I have any insurance."

"What are you saying?"

"I think my business partner—namely, my wife—my soon-to-be-ex-wife—may have let the insurance lapse. Normally it passes across my desk, and I don't remember seeing it this year. Too busy with her boyfriend, I'd guess. Like I told you over the phone earlier, life's shit and then you die. I'll give the insurance company a ding and hope for the best."

Irving crossed his legs and adjusted the position of the manila envelope.

"How did the fire start?" Edward asked.

"I haven't a clue. As I was walking over to meet you, I heard this large explosion behind me. After that, you probably know just as much as I do."

"I hate to ask under the circumstances, but did you finish the testing?"

"Right here in the envelope."

"Well, what did you find?"

"Have you ever heard of hillbilly heroin, or killer?" Edward was surprised by the question and slowly shook his head in the negative. "Those are two nicknames for Oxycontin. And that's what that white powder was you gave me."

"But it's been outlawed."

"I know. It's been replaced by a harder tablet, Oxyneo. It's supposed to be harder to crush for snorting or injecting. When the street supply of Oxycontin dried up, it put its value up considerably. Where'd you find this stuff?"

"We found it in a pill-pressing machine at KemKor."

"KemKor? And, who's the other part of the 'we'?"

"Charlotte Bradley?"

"Wasn't she …?"

"Yes she was," Edward interjected.

"This stuff is highly addictive. In the wrong hands—well, I don't need to go further. Do the police know about this?"

"Most of it."

"What the hell does that mean?"

"It means that they don't know about the Oxycontin. Even I didn't know until now. I'll let Paul Dickenson know about it once I'm back in Priceville."

"He's with the town of Durham's police force, isn't he?"

"Uh-huh."

"I assume they collaborate with the provincial police?"

"As far as I know."

The curtain separated, and a nurse came in with Edward's clothes and the cardiac booklets that Dr. Khan wanted him to read. "Now, you know you're not to leave until after you've spoken to the police," she said.

"I won't," Edward promised.

After helping to detach Edward from the monitoring device and the nasal cannula, she left.

Irving looked at Edward with a flummoxed expression. "Police? You can't leave until you see the police? What's that all about?"

Edward took in a deep breath and let it out. "Don't press me on that at the moment. As I said a few minutes ago, it's a long story. I think I'll need to owe you at least two meals to go through it all, by the time it's finished."

Two hours later, Edward sat in the Equinox in the library parking lot, dialling Shirley Cooper. He had never met her, and he wasn't even sure if she could add anything to what he already knew about the pictures Hobbs had given him, but he thought it was at least worth a try. *Anyway,* he thought, *why would Hobbs have given me her phone number unless he thought she could?*

He hoped he would be able to set up a time to drop by on his way home this evening.

Shirley picked up on the fourth ring. After he introduced himself, he briefly told her about the pictures Hobbs had given him.

She wasn't very friendly or inviting over the phone, but Shirley agreed to see him later that evening, provided he didn't intend to stay later than nine o'clock.

Driving out of the parking lot, he was anything but thrilled with the thought of meeting Shirley later that evening.

He had been pleased with how quickly and well his interview with the Peel Regional Police had gone. He explained what had happened and described, as best he could, the person who had knocked him down. However, he didn't think the description he had given would be useful. To help them further in their report, he had given them Paul Dickenson's name. Between Irving's report on the seat beside him and the package of photos in his pocket, he felt he had a good chance to delay KemKor's acquisition of his filtration system tomorrow.

As he drove through the town of Caledon, 10 minutes north of Brampton, it suddenly dawned on him why there was another attempt on his life. He berated himself for being so stupid not to pick up on it. *If I'm dead, KemKor gets the rights outright tomorrow! And if it was from a heart attack, no one would question it.*

Suddenly time had become golden to him. He stopped for a red light. His hands became clammy when he thought of what happened at the Gorge and in Brampton. He began to wipe his hands on his pants and stopped at the pocket where the photographs from Hobbs were supposed to have been. It was empty.

At that moment, all he could think of was what Irving had said earlier: "Life's shit and then you die." He was negligent for not having noticed that the photos had disappeared earlier.

CHAPTER THIRTY-THREE

TEN MINUTES NORTH OF Caledon, Edward pulled to the side of the road and checked his cell phone for messages. There were none since Charlotte's last text earlier in the day.

After the recent attempt on his life and the explosion and fire at Irving's lab, he decided not to tempt fate further and immediately phoned Dickenson. When he started to relate to Paul what had transpired in Brampton, Paul abruptly interrupted him to tell him that Peel Regional Police had already contacted him, and he was aware of what happened.

He had no sooner begun to share his concerns for Charlotte and Janet and the location of their last text than Paul interjected. "What the hell are they doing down at the Gorge?"

"They think my Wrangler's hidden somewhere there."

"My men scoured that whole area and found nothing. Did she say where she thought it was?"

"In one of her texts, she said something about checking along the route to Parker's Bridge."

"I see. The bridge has been down for quite a while; the route's off-limits. No place there to hide your vehicle. It could be a nasty fall if they're not careful. Look, my partner and I will take a drive over there and check it out. Where are you right now?"

"About 40 minutes south of Priceville between Orangeville and Caledon."

"I've got your cell number, so I'll call back if I find something. Call me if you hear from them. Okay?"

"Okay."

"I'd like to drop by your place later this evening, if that's all right with you?" Paul asked.

"Can it wait? I'm dropping by Shirley Cooper's place on the way home."

"Shirley Cooper?"

"You seem surprised."

"I guess I am, in a way. She's not noted for being too social. How do you know her?"

"Through the McAlistairs," he lied.

"Susan and Morris?"

"Same."

Edward crossed his fingers in hope that Paul wouldn't check.

"Nice people. Now, tell me, Edward, why would you want to spend time with Shirley?"

"If you had eaten any of her cooking, you'd understand."

"Can't say I have, and quite honestly I'm not interested. Hope your evening turns out to be what you expected. I'll phone you tomorrow to set up a time to meet. Remember to call me if you hear from Janet or Charlotte. Let's keep our fingers crossed that all's well."

"Oh, one more thing. Have you got those pictures I gave you?"

"They're right here on my computer. Why are you asking?"

"No reason—just asking."

Traffic had turned out to be worse than Edward had anticipated, and when he turned into Shirley's drive, he was an hour later than he'd expected.

He parked in front of her house. Other than the sound of birds, the place was very quiet. Smoke bellowed from the barbecue at the side of her house. He got out of the Equinox and walked over to the barbecue. Frantically waving his hand to disperse the smoke, he opened its lid and peered in. *Whatever was planned for supper, it's burnt beyond recognition,* he thought.

Teary eyed from the smoke, he turned off the propane tank and went around to the front door still rubbing at his eyes.

The door behind the screen door was open.

"Ms. Cooper! Are you here?"

He got no reply.

His cell phone began to vibrate in his pocket. He pulled it out and noted that it was an unlisted number.

Disappointed that it hadn't been Charlotte, he answered it. "Uh-huh?"

"Get into your vehicle and leave now."

"Who is this?"

"It's Hobbs. I'm with Shirley. Just do what I say—now! I'll be in touch." The line went dead.

As Edward sped away from Shirley's, he glanced up into his rear-view mirror and saw a black Lincoln Navigator turn up her drive.

Everything was happening too quickly, and he could feel the control he thought he had quickly evaporating away. He had never felt fear like this before—fear that cut so deeply to the bone.

He pulled onto Toronto Street just south of Flesherton, stopping for a red light at the only traffic lights in town. When it turned green, he headed west toward Priceville.

His cell rang on the seat beside him, and it startled him, causing him to swerve slightly.

Apprehensively, he reached over and picked up the phone. When he answered it, his voice was hesitant and quiet. "Hello."

"Mr. Slocum? It's Leonard Palladin. I spoke to you earlier."

"I remember." He felt relieved to hear a familiar voice he trusted.

"Mr. Blackwell would like to see you."

"Tonight? Now?"

"Yes, tonight—now, if possible?"

Edward pulled the Equinox to the side of the road and put it in park. "Have they found Jennifer?" he asked.

"Where are you right now?"

"I'm between Flesherton and Priceville."

"So we'll see you in about 15 minutes? And Mr. Slocum, tell no one. Mr. Blackwell just told me to tell you that Ms. Bradley and Ms. Thompson are here."

"May I talk to them?"

"Soon enough. Just hurry up and get here."

Excited to know that Charlotte and Janet were safe, he put the vehicle into drive and floored the accelerator. Ten minutes later, he parked at the end of Blackwell's driveway. Picking up the envelope containing Irving's results, he got out and began to walk up the centre of the long drive to the house. Cars were parked on either side along the route. As he passed Janet's Camaro, he looked farther along the drive toward the three-car garage. Its door was open. His attention was caught by a single vehicle inside—a red Wrangler.

When his cell phone vibrated in his pocket, he ignored it because he was already running toward the open garage.

Before he reached the garage, the cell had stopped vibrating. He opened the door to the Wrangler and climbed in, looking around its interior. Except for his iPod and CDs, everything appeared to be more or less in their familiar location.

Stepping down, he closed the door and slowly began to walk toward the house.

His day appeared to be ending on a high note, and as he knocked on Blackwell's front door, he hoped that whatever lay beyond wouldn't dampen it.

He tucked the lab results under his arm when he heard footsteps approaching from behind the door.

A tall, lean, pleasant-looking man in his early 50s opened the door. "Good evening, Edward. You made it here in very good time, I see. I hope you enjoyed our little surprise for you? This house contains little joy at the moment, so it was nice to have something occur that was uplifting."

"I sure needed that little surprise. Thank you."

"Don't thank me. Thank those woman friends of yours."

"Charlotte and Janet?"

Leonard gave a slight nod and smiled. "Follow me. Mr. Blackwell is looking forward to seeing you."

The living room was abuzz with young men and women setting up computers and other high-tech devices while others worked the phones. At one end of the room was a large whiteboard filled with a multicoloured flowchart. In front of it was a small group of individuals being instructed in its use.

He and Leonard walked down a set of stairs that led along a hall to the back of the house.

The first door Edward approached was slightly ajar, and he could hear the agitated voices of a man and woman talking to at least one other person in the room. The man's voice was familiar to him, and he stopped to peer through the opening.

The man inside paced back and forth as he talked. When he saw Edward, he came to the door and closed it.

Hobbs?

"Mr. Slocum, perhaps later—but right now we need your attention here," Leonard called out.

At the end of the hall, Leonard had opened the door to Blackwell's office, and Janet and Charlotte were standing in front of his desk looking back at Edward.

As Edward entered the room, Leonard stepped back and quietly closed the door behind him so as to leave the four of them to talk in private.

It wasn't a large room, but the positioning of the furniture made it seem larger.

Charlotte, Janet and Edward immediately entered into a group hug before Blackwell stood up and came around his desk to shake Edward's hand. He directed them to a set of four soft-leather chairs arranged around a circular coffee table. He was the last to sit down.

"How's Sara holding up?" Edward asked.

Chuck sighed deeply before answering. "Not well. Actually, I'm barely holding my own." He softly bit on his lower lip as he rested his head against the back of the chair, looking at them.

For a couple of moments, silence reigned between them until Chuck spoke again. "I bet you were pleased to see your Wrangler."

"That I was." Edward addressed his attention to Charlotte and Janet.

"I've been told I should thank you two for finding it. I owe you big time. Thanks. But wherever did you find it?"

Chuck sat forward in his chair.

"Earlier, before you arrived, we went over what Janet and Charlotte can and cannot say at this time. I'll explain later. In the meantime, their story will be … should I say, somewhat abbreviated. Listen to it and ask your questions. Just don't be surprised to find some of your questions will be met with silence. Which one of you wants to start off?"

Janet's and Charlotte's eyes skirted between each other until Janet nodded to Charlotte to begin.

"My last text to you was just before we explored along the route to Parker's Bridge, wasn't it?" she asked.

Edward nodded.

"Well, Janet and I followed that route right up to the bridge and across to the other side."

"Hang on there. Did I just hear you correctly? You crossed the bridge?"

"You heard correctly, Edward," Janet interrupted.

Edward was confused. "But it's condemned. The county never thought it was worth repairing after part of it fell down."

"That's true," Chuck said, "but evil's hands went to work and repaired it."

"Whose evil hands? And why?"

"I'll answer the 'why' part of your question in a moment," Chuck said. "But first let Charlotte finish up."

"I don't know if you remember but there used to be a lumber mill on the other side. It was closed down sometime in the '50s. Janet and I were surprised to still find it in pretty good repair."

"Again, evil's hands at work," Chuck added.

"Anyway, that's where we found your Wrangler: in the lean-to. The problem—at least for me, not for Janet—was how to get it out of there without a key. That's when Janet taught me how to hot-wire a car." A smile crossed Janet's face as she shifted in her chair. "I drove it back across the bridge," Charlotte continued, "dropped Janet off so she could get her Camaro, and we drove over here."

Edward's eyebrows furrowed together. "So it was that easy? You saw no one? Encountered no one?"

Charlotte and Janet looked at each other and then over at Chuck.

Edward quickly picked it up. "I see. So it wasn't quite that straightforward. I guess this is one of those silent replies?"

"For a few more days," Chuck replied. "Also, over those next few days, your Wrangler stays here, hidden."

"I can't say I like that, but you have your reasons. Okay, I can live with that. But can you at least answer the 'why' part of my earlier question?"

Chuck stood up and walked behind the wing chair, resting his forearms across its back. "It's imperative that nothing that has been said or will be said leave this room. Are you all in agreement?" Assured of their acquiescence, he continued. "In a nutshell, the bridge was built to provide a quicker and more efficient route to transport Oxycontin produced in Building 3C. When their trucks use this route, they are two miles closer to their drop-off point and are not easily detected, since they don't travel public roads. Charlotte told me you brought samples to Grynberg Laboratories in Brampton? I take it that those are the results in that envelope on your lap. May I see them?"

Edward passed it over to him.

Chuck opened the envelope as he walked over to his desk, and after sitting down, he began to slowly thumb through each page of the report.

"Leonard!" he called out.

When he entered the room, Chuck gave him the reports and asked him to make copies. Leonard was about to leave when Chuck asked him in a cracked voice, "Leonard, have they—have they heard anything yet about my daughter?"

Leonard's reply was soft, barely audible. "No, not yet."

The four of them sat in silence, waiting for the report and their copies.

When Leonard returned with them, he and Chuck stepped outside his office, and they talked in whispers. Upon reentering, Chuck shut the door behind him and returned the originals to Edward before sitting in the wing chair across from him. "Do you still have the photos Hobbs gave you?" he asked.

Edward shifted uncomfortably in his seat. "No, I don't. They were stolen before I left the hospital. Wasn't that Hobbs I saw in room down the hall?"

"It was—and Shirley, too. They're here for their protection and to go over documentation that originally you were to get—actually this evening, at Shirley's."

"Documentation? What documentation?"

Chuck let out a long sigh and massaged his chin and lower lip as he stared at Edward. "Charlotte, Janet, please step out into the hallway with Leonard. It will only be for a few minutes." When they had left and the door was secured behind them, Chuck turned his attention back to Edward. "You mustn't breathe a word of what I'm about to say."

"Agreed."

"Before Norman Rattray died, he gave Shirley a signed confession laying out his part in the explosion and fire at Ritchie's. Also included is enough information to incriminate his brother William with ordering Chris Stedman to murder Toler Ritchie and his wife. Included is also a detailed section describing how that land where KemKor now sits was procured. Very nasty stuff."

"How did Shirley come to hold it?"

"Few if anyone knew, but she and Norman loved each other and carried on an affair before his wife died. Afterward, they decided to carry on with their relationship but kept it quiet. Now, tell me, do you have any idea who stole those pictures Hobbs gave you?"

"No, not really—but the Durham police have copies. Constable Dickenson scanned them into his computer," Edward rejoined.

"Dickenson, you say? Hmm. Someone obviously got wind of your meeting with Shirley this evening. Any idea who? Did you tell anyone about it?"

Edward took in a deep breath and let it out. "Other than Charlotte, no one. I didn't even tell Irving."

"Are you sure you told no one else?"

"Wait—I told Dickenson I was going there for dinner."

Standing up, Chuck said, "Thank you for your support and coming here on such short notice. I'd better get back to Sara. By the way, what are your thoughts on Camilo and Andres?"

"Camilo's a little on the rough side, but other than that they're good kids. Why?"

"Well, for one thing, they picked up my daughter and dropped her off after the dance the same evening she went missing. And second, according to Charlotte, they were at your place when your house was broken into. So, are you sure that's your opinion of them?"

"My opinion holds—it was just coincidence."

"Coincidence? You really believe that?"

Edward didn't answer as he and Chuck walked to the door.

"Did you know it was Dickenson who cleared them after he interviewed them?" Chuck asked. "I'm being rhetorical; I don't expect an answer."

Chuck opened the door and stepped aside for Edward to leave.

"I'm surprised Bolsover's not here, or at least his attorney general," Edward noted.

Blackwell scrutinized him long and hard before speaking. "Sometimes things are best left unsaid, and this is one of those times. Leonard?"

They shook hands, and Blackwell closed the door.

Silently, Charlotte, Janet and Edward followed Leonard through the hallway.

CHAPTER THIRTY-FOUR

MATTHEW BOLSOVER, THE SOON to be ex-premier of Ontario, sat at his desk in his air-conditioned home office looking down at the open binder of documents that needed to be read and signed before he reentered Legislature later that day. It was three in the morning.

Straightening up, he poked at the documents like a child deciding whether or not to eat his vegetables. Normally he would have been in bed sound asleep, but tonight he couldn't sleep. He was still stimulated after having had great sex with Diane Rattray an hour earlier. *Viagra is everything it's cracked up to be,* he thought. Resting his head against the soft upper cushion of his high-back chair, he let out a satisfied sigh. He had judged their sex as sort of ho-hum. That is, until tonight, when she reached nymphomaniac proportions. *Wow! My testicles still ache from the experience.*

He wasn't sure if he loved her and wondered if he wasn't playing out some sort of sordid fantasy, possessing something that belonged to the great Rattray. Yet he knew she loved him. He sat forward and turned another page in a document he really hadn't read.

He wasn't sure if he loved her or whether he even *should* love her. Their relationship was too dangerous for him. *Is she just a trophy?* he wondered. *Or just some fucking time bomb?*

Diane had told William that she was going to see her sister and do some shopping in Toronto, both of which she did. To add to her alibi, she had even booked a room at the Fairmont-Royal York and phoned Rattray from there to inform him she was staying over to enjoy its ambience and the Sunday spa. *Devious little bitch,* Bolsover thought. *How would I ever trust her?*

Quickly he signed the document that he had barely read, and he half-heartedly flipped over to the next one in his binder and tried to concentrate on its content.

I wonder how Chuck and Sara are doing? he thought. Leonard Palladin, Blackwell's right-hand man and jack-of-all-trades, had called him about Jennifer's disappearance. *I don't like the feel of this. I wonder if someone's using Jennifer to send Chuck a message, or to gain some sort of leverage.*

His mind briefly stalled at Rattray being a possibility, but he quickly dismissed it.

He looked over to the picture of Mitch Hepburn hanging on the wall. The bronze plate on the frame said that he had been premier of Ontario from 1934 to 1942. Somehow, since his childhood studying history at school, this guy had stuck in his head. He never knew why. Maybe it was his style of leadership, his flamboyance, his pizzazz. Though Hepburn was well before Bolsover's time, he felt he knew him after having read several books about him. *He was the only Liberal I ever liked.*

He got up and walked over to the picture and removed it from the wall, carefully placing it on the floor. Hidden behind the picture was a wall safe. Dialling its combination, he opened it and withdrew a rectangular teak box, hinged on the short side by gold-plated hinges. He lingered for a moment, looking at the DVD case containing the videos of Chuck and Karen's rendezvous at the Deer Run Motel outside of Shelburne.

Careless asshole. If he hadn't kept returning with her to the same damn motel room on the same damn day each month, we wouldn't have had them.

He looked at the large manila envelope containing the one hundred and ten thousand dollars lying under the DVD case. *Chicken feed.*

Returning to his desk, he placed the teak box on it and sat down, scrutinizing it like an archaeologist who had just discovered a lost relic. The corner of his mouth rounded up into a smirk as he congratulated himself on its contents. *Ten years of recording every goddamn meeting with Rattray.* Caressing the box like a greedy Scrooge, he was about to open it when he heard rustling outside his closed office door, followed by a soft knock.

He barely had enough time to place the teak box into his side drawer when the door opened.

"Antonio? What a pleasant surprise!" It was a lie he hoped his demeanour hadn't given away.

Ever since that first Christmas after becoming premier, Antonio had remained a fixture in his life. As his chauffeur and confidante, he had come to rely on his special skills to make things happen or disappear.

He wondered why after all these years of having safely tucked it away deeply in his mind that it would suddenly bubble to the surface now. Bolsover did not have to search further than the side drawer of his desk for the answer. As he had gathered incriminating evidence on Rattray, he had no doubt that Antonio had done the same thing to him.

Reluctantly, Bolsover was indebted to him and had arranged for Antonio's quarters to be located in what used to be an adjoining guest apartment at the far end of the premier's residency. Joined to the main house by an underground tunnel, it was once a luxurious apartment slated for visiting heads of state in the early part of the 20th century. Long since forgotten about and not part of public refurbishing finances, Antonio had had to spend much time and money to bring it up to liveable standards. So as a recognized occupant, Antonio had easy access to the residence and surrounding grounds, compliments of Premier Bolsover.

"I didn't mean to startle you. It's just that—well, I saw the light under the door and I thought I'd check," Antonio said, his bald head, craggy frog face and squat and stocky figure peering around the door. Without waiting to be invited, Antonio entered the room.

Deeply tilting back his chair and chewing the end of his pen, Bolsover watched Antonio's eyes take in the office, including the open safe and its contents.

"Everything's fine," Bolsover said, throwing the pen on the table. "As you are aware, late nights are part of my office, and tonight is no exception." Bolsover noticed the drawer containing the teak box, was still slightly ajar, and he shut it with his foot. "Now that I've told you my excuse for being up so late, what's yours, Antonio? It seems unusual for you to be wandering about so late at night." Signalling Antonio with the palm of his hand to hold his answer, he got up, closed the wall safe and rehung the painting of Mitch Hepburn. Then, turning to Antonio, he crossed his arms across his chest and indicated that he was now ready for his answer. *Shrewd little bastard!*

"Señor Bolsover, what can I say—I'm an unattached man. Need I explain further?"

"I hope she was good?"

Antonio smiled and nodded.

Unfolding his arms, Bolsover sauntered over to his desk and sat down. "Well, if there's nothing else, I've still got quite a bit here to finish before I head in today," he said, waving his hand across the binder and folders on his desk and picking up the pen. "And come to think about it, you don't have much time to sleep before you drive me to Queen's Park." Bolsover put on his reading glasses and glanced down at the next document in the binder before peering over the rims at him. "Did you forget, Antonio? This morning I've got to be there by seven. Should I arrange for another driver?"

"I think you jest, Señor Bolsover. No, no, I shall be ready." Antonio began to walk back to the open door when he stopped and turned to face Bolsover. "There is one other thing."

Bolsover pulled his chair closer to the desk and rested his arms across either side of the open binder. "What is it, Antonio?"

Antonio looked at Bolsover intensely before continuing. "You promised me Canadian citizenship before you left office." He walked over to Bolsover's desk and, knuckles pressing into its dark and shiny oak finish, leaned across it. "It would not be good if you have forgotten."

Bolsover pushed his chair back from the desk and looked up at him. "I don't appreciate your threatening tone, Antonio. So back off!"

Straightening up, Antonio stepped back from the desk.

"Thank you," Bolsover said as he rolled his chair closer to the desk. "My contact assured me that he has managed to circumvent the hurdles, and your citizenship is almost complete."

"When?" Antonio clenched his fists.

"I haven't been told a date yet, just that it will be soon."

Antonio looked down at the floor and then over to the Mitch Hepburn painting. Moving quickly around the desk, he spun Matthew's chair round to face him. "Like you, I have many secrets. The difference is, yours aren't secret—at least not to me." Straightening up, Antonio looked down at him disdainfully. "So don't try to jerk me around, or else your world will cave in on you like a house of cards, just like that!" He snapped his fingers.

"I told you, your citizenship is in the bag," Bolsover said. He pushed his chair back and stood up, walking behind it. "There was no need to threaten me!"

"I want to know when. And soon!"

"I'll make a call tomorrow to tie it down."

Satisfied, Antonio strolled toward the open door. "See you in a couple of hours," he said over his shoulder as he closed the door behind him. Moving a few paces down the hall, he took out his cell phone and dialed. When Rattray answered, he said, "It's as you thought."

"You're sure he's made a copy?"

"I won't be 100 percent sure until I see the DVD."

"Where does he keep it?"

"In his wall safe."

"Will that create a problem?"

"Not in the least. The fool taped the combination in one of the most obvious places to look—under the centre drawer of his desk."

"How soon will the copy be in my hands?"

"Before the end of the week."

"And the other thing I asked you to check?"

Antonio smirked to himself before answering. "Your wife's here."

"Hum." It was followed by a long silence. "Something else, Antonio."

"I'm listening."

"Your Oxycontin operation."

"What about it?"

"With everything that's happening right now, I think you should shut it down for a while."

"Getting cold feet?" Antonio asked.

"I guess you could say that."

"Let me think about it. How long did you have in mind?"

Rattray said, "Oh, we can talk about that next time we meet."

Sonofabitch wants a larger share of the profit, Antonio thought. "Anything more?" he asked.

"No, we're done."

Antonio walked along one of the hallways off the main foyer toward a door that connected him to his apartment via the underground tunnel. Stopping outside the door, he put in a call to Garcia Urquiza.

"I just spoke with Rattray."

"And?"

"He's become skittish about the Oxy operation."

"Oxycontin's street value goes up as we talk. As we have discussed, he wants a larger share of your pie just like he does of mine. What do you think?"

"Nothing has changed. We're in agreement on that one. But he does make a point."

"And what's that?" Garcia asked.

"Maybe with everything happening right now, it *would* be a good time to pull in our horns and wait it out until everything blows over."

"Paul hasn't heard anything through his network to indicate that there's any kind of problem brewing."

"Are you sure you can trust Dickenson's sources?" Antonio asked.

"Other than he's one of ours, he's a fuckin' cop. Why wouldn't I trust him? He's been right on the money so far. No, Rattray just wants a bigger slice of the profit from both of us. He loves to play head games."

"I'm still not sure Rattray's wrong in being cautious right now. The whole area is crawling with cops and concerned citizens looking for Blackwell's daughter. Before you know it, they'll be all over your farm looking for her. Remember, she was last seen with Camilo and Andres."

"Paul told me he had taken care of everything, so don't sweat over that," rejoined Garcia.

"Provincial Police trumps whatever Paul thinks he's taken care of. I wouldn't count on him having taken care of rat shit. Bottom line, we must get rid of her now."

Antonio's mind had been made up the moment Jennifer Blackwell and the boys had entered Garcia's home office after the dance.

"You made that quite clear earlier," Garcia said.

"So we agree?" Antonio walked a short distance down the hallways away from the door that led to his lodgings and waited for Garcia to answer.

"She must be moved first, Antonio. If Andres finds out, there's no telling what he'll do."

Andres—such a disappointment, Antonio thought. "Maybe Andres should disappear with her," Antonio added. He kicked at the doorframe as he mulled over what he had just said.

"I'll need time to think it through," replied Garcia.

Antonio opened the door and looked down the set of stairs. "Think quickly, Garcia, before it comes back and bites our ass, or I will."

"Tomorrow—we'll talk tomorrow. By then I will have worked it out."

"Tomorrow, then."

Antonio had had enough talking to Garcia and hung up. He was concerned that their operations were about to fall apart. Up until now, Garcia's cocaine and his Oxycontin operations had turned a tidy profit, and he had no intention in becoming empty pocketed because of Garcia's inability to act.

Putting the cell phone in his pocket, he closed the door behind him and descended the stairs. At the bottom of the stairs, exhaustion hit him like a runaway freight train. His normally high level of acuity compromised, he forced himself through the tunnel to his apartment in the adjoining building. He looked at his watch. He still had three hours before he began his duties as chauffeur for Bolsover. *Two hours is all I need to sleep.*

Normally cognizant of new security devices, Antonio had been too exhausted and too preoccupied to notice them. He had relied on Bolsover to keep him informed of such infrastructure changes. Tonight, Bolsover had forgotten to tell him.

CHAPTER THIRTY-FIVE

ANDRES PUNCHED AT HIS feathered pillow several times as he tossed and turned, trying to sleep. Finally giving up, he clasped his hands behind his head and stared up through the greyness at the ceiling. Except for his briefs, he lay naked on top of a thin sheet. Though the house was air-conditioned, his body was hot and clammy. In reaction to the cacophony of bird chatter and activity on the apple tree, he turned over onto his stomach and looked through the window behind his bed. The leisurely sway of the apple tree's branches scratched gently against the window pane. The horizon layered with crimson, pink and purple was pasted on a thin ribbon of azure sky as the veil between night and day slowly lifted.

Though he hadn't slept well, he wasn't in a hurry to get out of bed. He turned over onto his back, but feeling a chill sweep over his body, he climbed under the sheet. Below his room, he could hear his Uncle Garcia stumbling down the hall to his bedroom. *Too much Aguardiente,* he thought.

He propped up his head with the pillow and placed his arms loosely across his torso. *Finally! I got up enough nerve to kiss her. And on the dance floor, no less!*

After his uncle's friend had left with Jennifer to drive her home, his uncle's demeanour became nervous and fidgety, and that's when Andres thought it best to leave Garcia and Camilo alone and turn in for the night.

Awakened by loud voices a couple of hours later, he had peered out his window and saw the police car. He assumed it had to be Constable Dickenson since he often dropped by at the weirdest hours, night or day. Later, when he attempted to squeeze Camilo for information about the visit, all he got was an open palm in his face and pushed back into his bedroom, the door slammed after him.

Now, what was the name of that song? His mind churned as he sifted through the possibilities. *Of course! Ricky Martin. She's an avid Ricky Martin fan.* He hadn't known that until the dance last evening. "The Best Thing about Me Is You." *That's it! Now it's our song.*

His face beamed with the pleasurable memory of that moment, sighing satisfyingly. His uncle had told him that girls liked boys who remembered special occasions. *And, this was sure one of those high points!*

He rolled over onto his side, pulling the sheet up around his shoulders. The more he thought about that kiss the more he knew he couldn't take credit. *It was really she who kissed me.* He rolled over onto his back and clasped his hands behind his neck. *That's even better!*

Andres closed his eyes, trying to relive that moment when he and she kissed, but it was blocked by the incident in his uncle's office. The whole episode lasted no longer than two minutes but long enough to glimpse the porn on his uncle's monitor before they were unceremoniously ushered to the door and told to wait in the kitchen. He had never seen his uncle so angry. By the time his uncle and friend had joined them in the kitchen, everything had returned to normal. It had been then that his uncle suggested that his friend drive Jennifer home. He tried to picture the stranger and was surprised how easily his image flashed into his head.

Though Andres had curtains on his window, he rarely closed them, preferring the natural light to be his alarm clock during the summer months. A wedge of sunlight splashed across the foot of his bed, reflecting off the opposite wall and down his dresser. His blood coursed through his body from the increased heart rate, and he knew he could not lie there any longer. Sitting up and stretching, he was surprised by how restful he felt. He swung his legs over the side of the bed, slipped into his sandals, stood up and made a bee-line to his dresser and began to scrimmage through the drawers for a clean pair of jeans and a T-shirt. He had taken two extra-strength Tylenol the night before and was surprised at how good he felt physically. He winced as he touched the bruised area on his ribs from his fall from the horse.

Five minutes later, he was dressed and standing at the door to his bedroom. Looking back at his bed, he decided to return and stuff pillows under the sheet to make it look like he was still there. Satisfied with the result, he returned to his door and, opened it slightly, peered down the hallway toward his brother's room and listened intently for any rustling coming from his room.

As he carried his sandals, the old plank wooden floors crackled under his feet, and every few steps he stopped to listen. As his foot landed on the top step of the staircase, the wood snapped. *Damn! I forgot!*

Moans came from Camilo's room.

When he heard nothing more, he scurried down the stairs and, at the bottom, quickly put on his sandals. When he heard his brother's door open, he moved quickly away from the stairs and pressed against the wall. He could tell by his brother's movements that he had crossed the hall and had looked into his bedroom.

Moments later the toilet flushed, and he could hear his brother's bedroom door close.

Reassured by his uncle's snoring but still conscious to tread softly, he picked up his pace and quickly traversed the kitchen to the back door, grabbing an apple and a handful of red grapes from the basket on the counter. Unlatching the screen door, he stepped out onto the wrap-around veranda and softly closed both doors behind him.

As he took the apple from between his teeth, he bit into it while enjoying the gentle warm breeze that caressed his cheek as it channelled between the overhanging roof and deck.

Sparrows, cardinals and finches busily fluttered around the four feeders, and he threw his apple core toward the feeders and watched the birds scatter.

The giggles swelled up in him, and he muffled them with his hand. Stretching and yawning, he went down the steps. The horizon was slowly filling with the spreading rays of golden sunshine as it pushed back night's blanket and replaced it with pale-blue sky.

Seconds later, he was walking down the slate-stone pathway toward the drive that led to the egg factory. He had a slight limp after twisting his ankle when he had fallen from Edward Slocum's horse Roscoe. The back of his head was still tender to the touch.

He never thought that someone of Jennifer's status—daughter to the likely next premier of Ontario—would even give him as much as a notice. Ever since he first saw her in elementary school, he had had a crush on her. Over the years it had grown to something more that tore him apart inside when he saw her with other boys. He had wanted to ask her out, but he lacked the self-confidence.

When his brother got wind of his affections for her, Camilo described him as a "gutless, spineless, not worth a shit of a wimp," and he said, "What she needs is a real man." That's when Camilo went out of his way to add insult to injury by pursuing her. At first she didn't appear to be receptive to his brother's advances, and then all of a sudden things changed and she was seen everywhere with him. *Maybe everywhere is a stretch*, he thought, *but I never felt so crazy with jealousy*. It was at that point he knew he had to act or forever lose the opportunity.

When he finally got up enough nerve to ask her to the dance last evening, his only concern was whether or not Camilo had already asked her. As it turned out, he had. But the strangest thing happened. She suggested that they both be her date. He knew Camilo wasn't happy with the idea, and it looked like he was going to dig in his heels over the issue, but somehow she miraculously changed his mind to a more amiable position. *What the hell did she say to him?* Camilo made it clear to him beforehand that he was allowing only three dances. More than that, he threatened to beat the crap out of him. When he had finally got the opportunity to have that all-important dance with Jennifer, Camilo was nowhere near the dance floor. In fact, he wasn't even in the building, and that perplexed him because Camilo was highly territorial.

When Camilo did return, he had a dark and deeply foreboding look about him as he reached out to take Jennifer onto the dance floor. But she had pulled away and had grasped Andres's hand. Camilo's glare told the whole story for Andres, and he braced himself for his brother's style of retribution. When it didn't happen, he knew he would pay later, away from witnesses—especially Jennifer. But it didn't matter, because he had won the girl of his dreams. And better still, he knew he now had the strength to stand up to his brother's bullying.

As Andres turned onto the pebbled drive, he slowed his pace to watch the first signs of the morning shift drifting into view. One or two women at first, then larger groups of four or more, made their way along the pathway from a large two-story structure tucked in a grove of trees behind the layer houses. All Hispanic, they ranged in age from late teens to early 30s. Many already had their hairnets in place, though an equal number carried them in their hand. They all wore light blue dresses with the name of the farm on the back. Their footwear ranged from sandals and running shoes to a low-heeled, black-laced shoe mainly worn by the older females. In front and interspersed throughout were large, muscular men in T-shirts and jeans. To Andres, these men looked menacing, and he was perplexed by their presence. He couldn't recall having seen them before, not even during his first tour of the egg factory. Other than his recent tour of the plant, he rarely saw his uncle's employees. They might just as well have lived and worked in the same building as far as Andres was concerned.

Picking up his pace slightly, he walked down the slope toward the egg factory, heading toward the well-worn path that branched off at the bottom toward the woods. His mind drifted back to the guilt he felt surrounding the break-in at Slocum's farm. He knew there would be consequences for him, but he had no idea what they would be. Despair swelled up within him and he feared his future with Jennifer might soon come crashing down around him. Stepping onto the pathway toward the woods, he stopped. His eyes had welled up with tears. *I have to make this right! I just have to!* It was the "how" that he hoped he would have an answer to before the end of his walk.

Something out of the corner of his eye caught his attention. A small group of employees, stragglers, were making their way toward the egg factory entrance. What puzzled him was that they were not accompanied by men. In their late teens, the three girls out front were in intense conversation while a fourth lingered. She stood out because of her blonde hair. He surmised that she was trying to prolong her time outdoors as long as possible. She dragged her running shoes through the dirt and gravel, creating a small dust cloud; every so often she would bend down, pick up a stone or sometimes a handful and fling them at the metal siding of the factory wall. Andres's attention focused on her footwear, and he began to run toward her. Though he called out, trying to get her attention, she appeared not to hear him. When she did, he could see the panic in her eyes. She ran forward to catch up with the other girls who were about to enter the factory.

Reaching out, he grabbed her upper arm and pulled her back as the door slammed shut. There was no missing the terror in her eyes as she tried to pull away, but he held on to her tightly.

"Where did you get those?" he blasted in Spanish, pointing at her running shoes.

The red and white kangaroos on the running shoes were uncommon, and he was sure they belonged to Jennifer.

Barely giving her time to answer, he dragged her to one of the two picnic tables on the grassy area beside the pathway to the woods, and he forced her to sit down while he caught his breath. He was surprised that she hadn't screamed out. His eyebrows pinched together as he looked at her hard and long. Pointing at her runners, he asked her again in Spanish, except more calmly. "Where did you get those?"

She looked up at him intently with a bewildered look but did not reply.

He wasn't sure whether it was fear or something else he saw in her eyes, but he knew he had to calm her before he would get an answer. Sighing, he sat down beside her, making sure that their shoulders touched so that he could feel any attempt by her to escape. Until he got his answer, he had no intention of letting her go.

As he sat, he continued to look at the runners. He could discern the small hideaway pocket on the side of each runner. *Jennifer kept her house key in one of them, but which one?* He sat in silence trying to figure out his next move. It certainly had to be one that elicited her cooperation, but what? Watching her out of the corner of his eye, her demeanour suggested that she was still trying to digest what was happening, but— and this was a big but—the way her eyes skirted about told him she was still a flight risk.

Damn it! I don't have time for this, he thought. He tapped her thigh and commanded her, in Spanish, to place her leg across his.

She pulled back and refused.

Andres grabbed her leg and forced it across his to examine the hidden pocket. *Damn it! Nothing!*

He dropped her leg from his grasp and pointed to the other one. Coyly, she smiled at him and lifted her skirt to her crotch.

Jesus! She doesn't have panties.

Then, before he had time to react, the toe of her runner caught him under the chin, sending his head jerking backward with such force that he fell off the bench. He knew the second it happened, he had lost. Dazed, he groped for the bench to help him stand. When he finally got to his knees, she was standing at the door to the egg factory looking back at him, laughing. She reached into the top of her dress and pulled out a necklace. It took a moment for Andres to focus, but when he did, he could tell she was dangling a key at the end of it.

Fuck!

He cradled his head in his hands as he sat on the bench. He knew very well where the answers lay for his next set of questions. But how to ask Uncle Garcia was the problem.

CHAPTER THIRTY-SIX

CAMILO WAS QUITE SURPRISED to see his brother up and about so early in the morning, and it garnered suspicion on his part. Shaking his head and muffling malign laughter, he thought of Andres's pitiful attempt to feign his presence in bed by stuffing pillows under the bed sheets. He couldn't remember a time when he didn't feel some kind of contempt for him. He never understood where it came from, when it began, how it started or why. It just was.

Involuntarily, Camilo shivered in the coldness of the air-conditioning. He was dressed in a T-shirt with "G_ F_CK Y_ _RS_LF" and "Care to Buy a Vowel" written across its front, black shorts and blackstrap Naot sandals. *Damn it, I'm freezing!* Backing into the hallway, he looked about for something to cover his upper body and retrieved a light jacket from the clothes tree farther down the hall.

Upon returning to the kitchen, his attention was directed to the kitchen window door by something being thrown at the bird feeders. He traversed the kitchen just far enough so as not to be seen by Andres, and he peered above the lower frame of the window in the door. Andres was standing on the top step of the veranda, yawning and stretching. Camilo's lips twisted in a smirk. His eyes never left the back of Andres's head as his hand wrapped around the handle of the carving knife in the knife block on the counter beside him. Rage boiled within him. *It would be so easy,* he thought, *and so satisfying to slit your throat.*

He wouldn't give in to that temptation because he needed him alive for the penultimate of satisfactions—watching him crumble when he learned that Jennifer was dead. *How dare you take her from me! Damn it,*

I loved her! She was mine! Mine, you snivelling little prick! You sealed her fate! I could have saved her, but now I won't!

He remembered how much attention his father had bestowed on Andres when they were growing up. As far as he was concerned, Andres had always been typecast as having more leadership potential, which was the role model Camilo, as the older brother, had to emulate. And he had resented it deeply. *Wrong choice, old man! I'm glad you're dead!*

His mother, whom he tried to love, gave him little attention in return. *I'm glad you're all dead.*

He watched his brother meander down the path toward the egg factory.

Saturday night, when he had left Andres with Jennifer Blackwell on the dance floor, Camilo cut a soon-to-be lucrative agreement with Donato in the parking lot. Donato would supply the meth, and he would provide the distribution network.

Methamphetamine, a versatile drug, could be used four different ways. It could be injected or slammed, smoked, snorted or as a suppository sometimes known as a butt rocket, booty bump, potato thumping or turkey basting. If placed in the vagina, it was called shelving. The point to the suppository was for increased sexual pleasure, and that was going to be Camilo's marketing ploy.

He knew his age group, many who would never have thought of buying meth, would buy for just that reason—as a sexual enhancer. *Hard to pass up going over the top when you're already horny as hell,* he thought. *And that's what I count on.* Though meth was relatively easy to make, he had to not only ensure a high-quality product and a secure network, but he had to discourage production by others. Since it was his uncle who suggested that trafficking in meth would be a good way to get his feet wet, he knew he would have very little trouble seeking guidance from him. Before that happened, he knew that thought and preparation had to go into his business plan before he dared to approach his uncle.

Tired of standing, Camilo backed against the counter beside the sink and, positioning his hands securely at the edge of the counter, pushed down and lifted his torso onto it. Pulling his legs up and wrapping his arms around them, he comfortably positioned himself to watch his brother through the window. He could see the staff coming into work. *Whores!* The men who escorted the women had taught him how to use meth for sexual pleasure. Often he watched them from a concealed enclosure inside a building he came to call "the sex hut." At first he just watched, but once the business significance of what he was watching dawned on him, be began taking video images with his cell phone. He wasn't sure the women knew they were being taped, but the men sure did—they were the ones who encouraged it. *Wow! Donato blew his load when he saw them.* He sniggered. *What a selling point! What a deal breaker! Marketing'll be a breeze.* His eyes drifted away from his brother to a point farther back along the pathway the workers had come from. *Carmella!*

He watched Carmella as she lingered behind the others, kicking up dust and splaying stones against the sheet-metal wall of the factory. He caressed his chin and smiled, his shoulders noticeably rising and falling as he breathed deeply. She had been the first he had tried the meth on. He sighed, biting down on his lower lip. A couple of his uncle's men had brought her to the sex hut and readied her. She had already been shelved before his arrival. *What a ride!* He had never had sex that good before. And based on this experience, he knew that he had a marketing strategy that would be a winner long before he met Donato that night at the dance.

When his uncle's friend had offered to drive Jennifer home the other evening, he had been forewarned by his uncle of the real intent of the offer and the reason for it. He stroked and pulled at his chin intensely, a red-spot forming at the point of contact between chin and fingers. He had been directed by his uncle to wait outside until his uncle's friend returned. When he finally showed up, he was told to remove Jennifer's body from the front seat and to secure her in the root-cellar at the side of the house. His heart stopped, fearing the worst when he first saw her, until he noticed the rhythmic motion of her chest. He was told she was in a deep sleep and would remain that way for a while. As he removed her from the vehicle, he inquired what would happen to her and was told to mind his own business and keep his nose out of it. An hour later, out of the blue and in a matter-of-fact way, his uncle told him that her fate had not yet been decided.

Abruptly, his attention was redirected to Carmella as his brother ran toward her shouting. *What the hell is he pointing at?* Opening the window so he could hear, he slid off the counter. He watched as his brother forced her to sit at the picnic table and lift her leg. Camilo's eyebrows knitted together in consternation. *Jesus! She's got Jennifer's runners on. How?* Beside himself, he finally understood what his brother was doing. *He's looking for the goddamn key Jennifer hides in the outside pocket of the runner. If he finds them, he'll not only know that those runners are Jennifer's but that something had happened to her.* About to run out the door to intervene, a hand grasped his shoulder, pulling him back.

"Don't do that!" his uncle said vehemently. "Carmella can take care of herself. Watch!"

No sooner had the words left his uncle's mouth, when, to Camilo's astonishment, Carmella's foot rose, striking his brother squarely in the chin and knocking him onto the ground. His uncle's raucous laughter startled him. *Bizarre,* Camilo thought, *for him to take it so lightly.* He watched her run toward the egg factory and turn, holding up something that was around her neck before disappearing behind the factory's closing door. *What the hell was she doing?* His uncle's heavy hand across his shoulder pulled him away from the window.

"I told you so, didn't I?" he kept repeating between bouts of halting laughter. "Did you see that? Ka-pow!"

Camilo didn't know what to say. At the moment he was more focused on what it was around her neck, and how she had come to wear Jennifer's runners, than joining in on something he didn't in the least find funny. He was pretty sure his uncle hadn't appreciated the gravity of what had just transpired. Presently his uncle was in a good place, and he had learned from many bad decisions on his part not to upset the proverbial apple cart. His uncle's mood had a tendency to change quickly, often with devastating consequences, especially after a night of drinking Aguardiente. And Camilo couldn't afford to upset him, because he had business to discuss with him. So, deciding to replay the incident in his head, he saw its comedic relief and joined him with light laughter. As their jovial moment subsided, he noticed Garcia was staring out the window. "Is there a problem, Uncle?"

"Eh? No. No problem, at least not for me," he said, smiling at Camilo. "But your brother, well, that may be a different story. As you can see," he said, pointing at Andres while putting his arm across Camilo's shoulders, "he is in much meditation."

"Uncle?" he asked softly.

"Uh-huh."

"You do understand what just happened?"

"Of course!" Garcia stepped back and looked long and hard at Camilo. "You have a horny brother hoping for some fluff."

"No, Uncle."

"No?" the older man replied sceptically.

"She was wearing Jennifer's runners. And Andres was trying to prove that."

"Oh!" For a moment, his gaze became distant. "But they are just runners. How can they prove anything?"

"No, Uncle, they're not just runners. They're Kanga-ROOS." He walked away from his uncle and then turned around to face him. "Her parents bought them for her on their recent trip to Australia. In West Grey, they are one of a kind. And here's the kicker: she wore them last night." He let it sink in for a moment before walking closer and continued in a raised voice. "I can't believe you didn't notice them. They were bright red with white trim and laces with a kangaroo on the sides. Hard to miss!" The last thing he wanted was to come across disrespectfully. Still, he knew his last comment may have just crossed the line. "Sorry, Uncle." He bowed his head slightly.

His uncle looked at him intensely, a sternness pasted on his face. Then, like a cloud passing by the sun, his features softened and brightened as he nodded his acceptance. "My interest, dear nephew, was in what Jennifer saw, not with what she was wearing."

Camilo replied in a softer tone. "I understand that, Uncle." Nervous, he moistened his lips with his tongue before continuing. "But those Kanga-ROOS are uniquely connected to Jennifer. I know that, my peers know that, and almost everyone who knows her knows that." With his hands open, he shrugged his shoulders, trying to emphasize the obviousness of what he said. "We've got to get them off Carmella—and, more important, find out how she got them."

Garcia stepped closer to Camilo, placing a hand on his shoulder. "Who cares how she got them? The point is she's got them." He gave him a gentle pat on the cheek. "And we know where to find her and their owner." He went over to the coffee maker and turned it on. "I'm 15 minutes early but I just can't wait," he explained, looking back at Camilo. Satisfied that the coffee maker was working properly, he returned to Camilo. "Any concerns you may have, I'm sure can be easily resolved.

Eh?" he reassured him. "As for Jennifer, she was so doped up she could have been stripped bare on the cold stone floor, and she wouldn't've known. You know that. So, she's definitely not a witness to who took her runners." Not waiting for all the coffee to percolate through, he poured himself half a mug, savouring its smell and taste, and then he turned his attention back to Camilo. "Everything stays nice and tidy and right here on the farm, the way it should be. Ah? But there is one thing."

"Uncle?"

"It needs a credible explanation that your brother will buy into." Seeing that the coffee pot had filled, he refilled his own mug. Taking in a deep breath, he continued. "I've known for a long time, and so have you, that he's been in love with Jennifer. It was mean-spirited of you, you know, to try to take her for yourself." He took a long drink from his mug, his eyes never leaving Camilo's. "I put it down to sibling rivalry and figured that in time, it would resolve itself. Well, I guess it did—but not in your favour." He smiled sardonically. "And now you want revenge. You want to exact a price for your loss. Don't deny it; I can see it in your eyes." He took a few more sips. "But if you want to be a businessman, and I assume a successful one, you must never let your emotions rule you. His love for her makes him vulnerable to a different persuasion, and it's one that could hurt us quite deeply if not handled correctly. She can't be found here. Our immediate problem is your brother. What to say to allay his suspicions? I'm at a lost."

Agitated, Camilo began to pace the floor. He needed to find an answer. He combed his fingers through his long, black hair and then gathered it in a heap and dropped it as he turned to his uncle.

"Antonio—that was his name, wasn't it?"

"Yeah. So?" Garcia replied, looking at Camilo somewhat askance. He placed his mug on the counter.

"He's our excuse."

"Go on."

Camilo stopped pacing. "Jennifer loves to run barefoot; even Andres knows that. She was complaining about her feet being hot and sweaty after the dance last night. So much so that she took off her runners and stuck her feet through the open window of the car to cool them down." He stopped pacing and looked at his uncle. "She almost forgot the runners in the car when we arrived here last night. Don't you see?

Who's to say that she didn't do the same when Antonio let her off last night? When Antonio returned here, that's when they were swiped by Carmella."

"Good, I like it." Garcia reflected on what his nephew had just said for a few seconds before continuing. "But the police must not know about Antonio. As far as the police are concerned, you and your brother drove her home. At the moment, Andres doesn't know that part of the story."

"The first part takes care of the immediate. Andres knows nothing else. As for the rest, it buys us time to work it out." Camilo felt proud of himself, and when he looked to his uncle for endorsement—to his chagrin—his uncle was preoccupied elsewhere.

"Your brother returns along the pathway with much purpose. Let's hope your story holds."

"Uncle," he said, tentatively touching his uncle's upper arm, "it won't be us who tell him. We know nothing about those running shoes other than the obvious, and we can't possibly suggest an answer." He stepped around his uncle to watch Andres coming up the path.

"Who, then?"

"Antonio. It must be Antonio who tells him that they were left in his car. And, when he went to return them, they had disappeared."

"That should give us time to decide what to do with your brother."

"I can take care of that," Camilo said, and he slammed his fist into the open palm of the other hand.

Now, Shut Up and Follow Me!

CHAPTER THIRTY-SEVEN

LOADED FOR BEAR AND searching for answers, his sports jacket flung over his shoulder, Edward stepped off the deck of his house and into a wall of heat. It was barely seven on Monday morning, and already the sauna-like conditions heralded another scorcher for the week. He wished he hadn't had to take his jacket to work, but the air-conditioning at KemKor had been revved so high lately that it made it uncomfortable to work in his office without one. Dressed in a white short-sleeved dress shirt, red tie, dark brown pants, matching socks and slip-on shoes, he hurriedly made his way to the Equinox, climbed in and flung the sports jacket along with the package containing Irving's test results on the seat beside him, and put the key into the ignition. Before turning the air-conditioning to full blast, he lowered all the windows to provide an escape route for the hot, uninviting air that was about to be emitted from the vents. Initially a blast furnace, the vents quickly converted to blowing cooler, more refreshing air, and he let it riffle through his hair for a couple of minutes before closing the windows. Placing the Equinox in reverse, he slowly backed down the drive onto the North Line Road, and a few minutes later he turned onto the Glenelg-Artemesia Townline toward Markdale.

As he drove, he reflected on his conversation with Blackwell the previous day and the attempt on his life in Brampton. He hated the thought that John Elkhart was in any way involved, but with the illegal Oxycontin production now confirmed in Building 3C, he had no choice.

How the hell did they get the people they needed to produce that stuff and get it off the KemKor grounds without so much as a whimper from security? he asked himself. Elkhart had to know this was going on. *I just can't believe that no one saw anything this unusual without reporting it.*

What nailed it down for him as to Elkhart's guilt was what he had learned shortly after he was hired: the "transition of rights upon death" clause in his contract was Elkhart's doing as well.

Or was it? he mused. *Rattray could have directed him to do it.*

After being at Blackwell's the other day, Edward's instincts told him that something big was about to go down and he feared that he might either say or do something that might jeopardize it or give it away. *But give it away to whom?*

Until he knew differently, he decided to treat everyone the same at KemKor—guilty. Other than all this stuff spinning around in his head, he still had to work out how to stall Legal and get them to agree to a continuance so that he could hold on to the filtration rights long enough to prove criminal intent on KemKor's part.

Still, he continued to have difficulty accepting John's involvement in all of this. He couldn't believe that John had pulled the wool over his eyes for this long. *Damn it! John's a friend! Surely I'm right about that?*

He decided to take a chance and test the waters. He would solicit John Elkhart's support for continuance. And he hoped he wouldn't give away too much to get it.

As Edward walked through the doors to KemKor Pharmaceuticals and passed the security desk, he put on his sports jacket and tucked the manila envelope under his arm. In front of him were the elevators. Along one hallway were a number of offices and a door with a sign above it titled "Security Division." Along the wall to his right were a couple of other offices and a stairway to an oak door on the second floor. Under the staircase were two brown leather chairs and a large, round, wooden coffee table with a number of magazines strewn on it; behind that was the hallway leading to Lab and Quality Control. In an alcove opposite this was reception, which was where he headed first.

After some small talk with Lorraine at reception, he asked her to call up to Mr. Elkhart's office to set up a morning meeting. As it turned out, John's morning was wide open, and his administrative assistant asked him, via Lorraine, to choose a time slot and an approximate length for the appointment.

After a quick calculation, Edward replied, "How about an hour and a half from now?" He scratched his head and massaged his chin meditatively before adding, "Ask her to set aside an hour."

The message was relayed by Lorraine and his 9:30 appointment was confirmed. When he inquired about Mr. Rattray's morning schedule, he was told that his admin assistant was not yet in and was not expected for at least another hour. After thanking Lorraine, he turned and slowly walked away, reviewing his immediate priorities.

He knew that he didn't have to do what he was about to do, but he felt compelled to clear his mind of at least some of the doubts he had about John. And that was the rub, because it could very well reveal just the opposite—and if it did, it would dramatically change the contents of that 9:30 meeting later this morning.

Taking in a deep breath, he reviewed his immediate agenda with the hope that John had followed through on everything he had said he would.

First, he would visit security. He needed to learn if any additional information about that white van had turned up. Also, he wanted to satisfy himself that the surveillance cameras were operational in the area surrounding Building 3C and to find out when that occurred, if at all. Next on his agenda would be Lab and Testing in the Quality Control Division. He wanted to know if John's requisition to test the effluent taps had been received and acted on—and if so, when the results would be available.

Edward was about to begin the first leg of his morning, namely to visit security, when he heard a familiar voice. "Mr. Slocum! Wait!" Nadia called out, running toward him. She wore a short, white dress with laced-up gladiator sandals. "Boy! I'm sure glad I caught you," she said.

Pulled back by her tug, Edward's eyes took in all of her. *Wow!* He couldn't help but notice the lascivious way the young men looked their way as they came through the front doors to the building.

Feeling protective of Charlotte's sister, Edward pulled her off to the side. "What's so important that it couldn't wait?" he asked in a whispered tone, still looking about.

"I've been to Accounting." She brushed aside a wisp of hair that had fallen across her face.

Looking at her askance, he waited for the penny to drop. When the light bulb in his head finally went on, he understood what she was talking about. "Forgive me, Nadia. I must seem somewhat addled. But really, I'm not!" Tapping his head, he continued. "Just got too many things rolling around up here this morning."

"Well, addled or not, do you want to hear what I found out?" She rubbed the back of her neck. "I'm getting a crick in my neck looking up at you. Do you mind if we sit down?" She pointed to the two leather chairs under the staircase.

"Can we talk about this when I get back to my office?" He looked at his watch. "Right now I'm tight on time."

"Well, I guess that won't be today," she retorted.

"What do you mean, it 'won't be today'?"

"Last Friday, Mr. Rattray had me book your whole day off. Something about Legal?" She brushed back the same errant hair strand from her face with her hand.

"Forget about that, everything's changed. I'll be back in my office later this morning." He checked his watch again. "I really must go!" Pulling the manila envelope from under his arm, he gave it to her. "Nadia, please put this in my office. I really don't want to carry this around with me at the moment. I'll be by to pick it up for my 9:30 meeting with Mr. Elkhart."

"Sure. Any particular place?" she asked, taking it from him and casually examining it before letting it hang at her side.

"On my desk should be fine."

"Consider it done, Boss," she replied, smiling. Brushing back her hair with her hand, she headed up the stairs. From the corner of her eye, she watched him disappear through the door to security.

Charlotte yawned and stretched before opening her cell phone to check the time. *Ach! I've been awake for three hours!*

Ever since she had given Juarez the hardcopies to Edward's research, she had been wrestling with the dilemma of how to put Janet, Edward and her together at the bank's vault for its safe keeping without exposing what had happened to them and how they rescued his Wrangler.

Juarez had needed these documents to protect his credibility as part of the RCMP's undercover operation. Though he had been ordered by Garcia to kill both her and Janet, he figured he could work out something to buy enough time until the operation went down in a few days.

Damn it! Our original plan would have worked. She combed her hands through her satin black hair, stretched again and thought about her present dilemma. *Only Janet and I were to place it in the safety-deposit box. Why couldn't Edward have stayed with the original plan? Why did he have to insist that he be there?*

She hoped that the massaging effect from a shower might tease out a solution before she called Janet.

As she walked toward the bathroom, her cell rang. "Good morning, Janet."

"I think I might have a solution to our problem," Janet said. She sounded quite excited on the other end of the line.

Charlotte groaned. "I've been up since the middle of the night trying to find a solution, and you have one just like that?"

"Well, there is a certain thing about age and experience, dearie. Anyway, aren't teachers supposed to have all the answers?"

"Out with it, Janet," she chortled, shaking her head in disbelief. "What have you come up with?"

She heard Janet snicker. "Tell him I went to Ottawa and took his documents."

"You're going to Ottawa?"

"No, silly! He just needs to believe that. And remember, all we need is until the middle of the week. Juarez promised us that they would be back in our hands by then."

Charlotte sat on the futon. "Never thought about that," she said. "It should work provided he keeps his promise."

"I'm sure it's in safe hands, Charlotte. If you can't trust the RCMP, who can you trust?"

"Where are you going to stay?"

"Hanover, with my cousin's family. That way I'm no more than 40 minutes away from either you or Edward if something should go awry and you need me."

"I'll need a car."

"I'll take you into Flesherton. Say, about 10:30? You can rent one from Bernard's." After a few seconds of quietness, Janet continued. "Does that work for you?"

"It does." She got up and walked into the kitchen and poured herself a glass of milk before heading back to the living room. "You're still on for snooping around Green's property, aren't you? When do you think would be a good time?" Charlotte asked.

"Oh, are you sure that's wise after our meeting with Blackwell?" Janet asked.

"You're talking about the upcoming police operation."

"I am. And, I sure don't want us to mess it up," Janet replied.

"We won't. But time could be running out for Jennifer, and it may be too late by the time they act."

"Don't you think Juarez would have said something to Chuck if his daughter was there and in harm's way? It would be amoral not to say something."

"Maybe you're right, Janet." Charlotte hesitated for a few seconds before continuing. "Putting aside for the moment what I've just said, aren't you in the least curious about what goes on over there?"

"I might be curious about what lies beyond death, but it doesn't mean I'm in a hurry to die."

"Who said anything about dying? Look, we'll get in and snoop around a bit, and if there's nothing, we'll get the hell out. Now what's the harm in that? Or must I go alone?"

"And let you trip over your own shoelaces? No way, I'll go with you. But it must be tonight while I've still got nerve. Anyway, there's no moon."

"Tonight was what I was thinking, too. When and where shall I meet you?"

"East Road about 10. We'll walk in from there."

"Thanks, Janet."

"For what?"

"For just being there."

"My head got so wrapped up with this evening, I almost forgot. Bernard's rental. Don't forget to call ahead and set it up."

As she hung up, Charlotte wished she could have left well enough alone and just let the police do their job, but her instincts strongly took her in a different direction. No proof or anything near solid evidence supported her choices or insights; it was just a hunch. But she knew if she didn't follow it, she would regret it for the rest of her life.

Charlotte's cell rang, and she lifted it up. "Edward?"

"Hi, Charlotte! I don't have long. Do you mind going ahead without me?"

"No, Edward, I don't mind. Janet and I are capable of safely securing your documents in the bank's vault without you."

"I'll tell you about everything over supper. It will be my treat. Drop by later at my place."

"Depends."

"On what?"

"When you get home."

"I'll aim for five. Will that work?"

"Then I'll be happy to have supper with you."

"It sounds like you have plans for later in the evening. You care to share?"

"It's no big deal. It's just that I've promised to help Janet with something."

"You wouldn't consider breaking it, would you?"

Charlotte breathed deeply and waited a moment before she answered. "Can I take a rain check on that?"

"Of course you can—as many rain checks as you need. But what's so important?"

She wanted to tell Edward what she and Janet were going to do that evening, but she knew that he would only rain on their parade.

"It's just girl stuff, that's all."

Tonight, logic and commonsense would be thrown to the wind.

CHAPTER THIRTY-EIGHT

EDWARD'S MORNING STARTED BADLY. Not only had the head of security, Chris Stedman, gone on holiday for two weeks, but no one, including Doug Irwin, Chris's assistant, knew diddly squat about what Edward was talking about. It took all of his strength not to explode in anger.

"Doug, have the surveillance cameras been activated in the Building 3C area?"

Until today, Edward had never had the occasion to speak to him, though he had seen him often in the building and on the grounds. In fact, he couldn't recollect Doug showing up at any company dos, even the Christmas one. From Edward's point of view, whenever he did see Doug, Doug always seemed oddly harried and exhausted.

"No, sir! I can't do that without authorization from Mr. Rattray. You do understand that it was he who ordered them turned off in the first place?"

Doug was taller than Edward and had a slightly potbellied frame. Perched on his long, furled forehead were rimless oval glasses where wisps of untidily kept grizzled hair lay. He wore lightweight jeans and a yellow T-shirt with the company logo, "KK," on the breast pocket.

"Surely Chris left something about Mr. Elkhart rescinding that order?" Edward said. *Chris Stedman is becoming a thorn in my side.*

"Sir, even if he had, only Mr. Rattray can rescind it," Doug replied uncaringly. He adamantly crossed his arms across his chest.

Trying not to show his exasperation too much with this obviously hardheaded individual, Edward decided to pursue a different line of questioning. "Were the tapes reviewed from last Tuesday regarding the white van?"

"Tapes? White van? Hmm …" Doug protruded his lower lip slightly as he reflected on it.

"Eh, no, this is the first I've heard about a white van. If a report had been done, it should either be on my desk or Chris's. But I don't recollect seeing one. Let me check."

Pulling his glasses down from his forehead and positioning them on his nose, he walked over to his desk and rummaged around for a few minutes before inputting something on his computer. Then he entered Chris's office and did much the same thing.

Edward watched him exit Chris's office empty-handed, scratch his head and slowly walk back to him. *This doesn't look promising,* he surmised.

"Nope, there's nothing, Mr. Slocum." Doug took his glasses off, fogged them with his breath and cleaned them with tissue from a box on a nearby desk.

"There's no report?" There was incredulity in Edward's tone that he couldn't mask.

Doug placed his glasses on the top of his forehead and casually looked around the room. "No report, Mr. Slocum," he repeated.

"Well, would you please put together one for me and have it on my desk later this morning? I'll give you the time parameters I'm interested in for last Tuesday."

"I can't do that, sir."

"Whose authorization do you need now?"

"Yours would do," he insisted. He scratched the side of his cheek and looked back toward Chris's office. "It's just that those tapes have already been erased."

Beside himself, Edward stood in the hallway outside security. He couldn't remember when he was this angry.

When he thought of that nitwit Doug lecturing him on company policy and procedure for cleaning security tapes after 48 hours, he felt like putting his fist through his head. No matter how many times he tried to tell him that security had been alerted to the importance of those tapes within the 48-hour window, Doug kept quoting Section B, subsections 8, 9 and 10, absolving himself of any responsibility.

Edward was beginning to worry that they were already cleaning up any traces of evidence, and by his snooping around he may have inadvertently expedited the process. He wondered why Dickenson said nothing about the surveillance tapes or the logs at the guard hut, during his investigation. He knew someone was lying, and right now he put his bets on Doug if for no other reason than he didn't like the sonofabitch.

Distracted by the elevator doors opening farther down the hall, he heard the familiar but unwelcomed voice of David DeLuca from Legal calling out to him.

Can my day get any worse? he asked himself. *Yup! There's Lab yet to visit.* Shaking his head forlornly, he sighed and turned toward the elevator. He felt like a little kid who had been caught with his hand in the cookie jar. He definitely didn't want this meeting this morning, especially not now!

What the hell do I say? I guess like any other resourceful person, I'll make it up as I go.

"Did you get lost?" David said sarcastically. "No, I think not; the place is too small for that," he chortled. He wore a white dress shirt, red tie and buttoned-up, powder grey–striped, three-button suit with a matching handkerchief in the breast pocket. "Rattray did warn me that you might be reluctant to meet this morning."

"I guess he didn't tell you?" Edward replied.

"Tell me? Tell me what?"

"The meeting has been put off indefinitely."

"Indefinitely?"

"Yup, until the glitches are worked out."

DeLuca looked at him disbelievingly. "What glitches?"

"It's in the third-level centrifugal filtering system," Edward lied. "It may mean that all those years of hard work could be down the drain."

David's eyebrows spiked. "Sounds serious. I'm surprised Rattray didn't tell me this—it affects the transference clause in the contract. When did you find out?" He stepped closer to Edward, his eyes fixed on his.

"Ah, Saturday, at Rattray's," Edward said.

"Saturday? Oh, of course—that was Blackwell's launch party. A brouhaha, didn't you think?"

"You were there?" Edward asked.

"Of course I was. I wouldn't have missed it for anything. Local boy makes good and all that stuff. In fact, I was in the VIP tent. I even sat at the same table with Rattray. Funny thing, though, he didn't mention a word of this cancellation. In fact, he reminded me of my meeting with you. He didn't speak of any glitches." David scrutinized him even closer for reaction.

Edward shrugged. "It was probably the timing of when he spoke to me," Edward said.

"Hmm. Probably." DeLuca began to massage his chin thoughtfully. "I'd better call Mr. Rattray and get this straightened out."

"You do that." *The way he's looking at me, I know he doesn't believe a damn word I just said.* He looked at his watch. "Look, David, I've got a busy day ahead of me."

"Yes, yes, of course," he replied.

As he walked away, Edward glanced back and saw David take out his phone.

Edward stopped by reception and asked Lorraine to call up to Rattray's office. He knew it was a long shot that the administrative assistant was in, but he had to give it a try anyway. He wasn't surprised when Lorraine told him that she still had not arrived.

He needed to get to him before DeLuca did, and he couldn't do that unless he knew Rattray's schedule. *Having just laid a load of horse manure on him to buy time,* he thought, *I hope DeLuca doesn't have a direct line to Rattray. The fact that they sat side by side at the same table in the VIP tent makes that possible. How the hell did I miss him there?*

Shrugging, he thanked Lorraine for her assistance and said good morning to Marilyn Ferguson, whom he had just noticed poking through the magazines on the table behind him.

As he headed down the hall leading to Lab and Quality Control, he didn't like that feeling in the pit of his stomach. He figured it was akin to how Custer must have felt at the Little Big Horn when realizing he had been ambushed. With Tuesday's surveillance tapes now missing, it meant that his credibility and the credibility of the package, now sitting on his desk, depended heavily on what Lab and Testing had turned up.

Ahead, the set of heavy doors that separated him from Lab and Quality Control looked intimidating, and for a brief moment, he held his breath and crossed his fingers. Slamming his hands against the push bars, the pair of doors swung open to a long corridor with rows of windows on either side looking onto the lab and testing areas. After stepping across the threshold, for a split second he hesitated as the doors swooshed shut behind him. At the end of the hallway were the offices of Bob Littleton, manager of Lab and Testing, and Ronald Boswell, manager of Quality Control. Both offices shared a common area.

The request to test the effluent valve and Building 3C fell into both men's jurisdiction. Edward decided to start with Boswell, not only because he knew him from his university years but because he always found him amiable and approachable. Though he had a good working relationship with Littleton, he always found him edgy and a little too abrasive for his liking. And abrasive wasn't what he needed right now.

Entering the common area, Edward noticed that Boswell's door was slightly ajar, whereas Littleton's was wide open to an empty office. On a small cart in the space between their offices was a coffee maker with a splash of murky liquid remaining. As he drew closer to Boswell's office, the soft murmur of voices he originally discerned upon entering had turned into a heated exchange. As he pushed the door open wide, both men stopped talking immediately. Littleton swung around, spilling some coffee and scowling at Edward.

"This is a surprise! What brings you down here so early in the morning, Eddy?" Boswell asked, taking a couple of tissues from his side drawer and handing it to Littleton. Boswell stood up and moved around his desk. Before extending his hand to greet Edward, he wiped it on his trousers.

His question made Edward's heart sink as he shook his hand. "Depends," Edward replied. *Damn it! He doesn't know. John never called him. Sonofabitch!*

Littleton, who amply filled his chair, extended a limp handshake without standing up, still giving him a wary look.

"Depends?" Boswell queried. "On what?"

Boswell regained his seat behind his desk before giving Edward his attention again. "I'd offer to get you a chair, Eddy, but as you can see, there's not much room. As for coffee"—he nodded at the mugs on his desk—"those are the only two mugs."

Edward brushed off his concern. "It depends, Ron, on whether you received a call from Elkhart last Wednesday."

He noted the cursory glances firing between Boswell and Littleton.

"Why would either one of us get a call from Elkhart?" Littleton piped up. "The only time he calls one of us is when there's a problem. And I don't know of any lately." He placed one leg across the other, glancing over at Ron Boswell. "Do you, Ron?"

"Give me a moment. I need to shake these cobwebs loose. It's still too early for me." Finally, Boswell shook his head. "No, I don't think so. No, eh, none!" He rested his arms on his desk. "Eddy, if I recollect rightly, this is the first time you've visited this neck of the woods." His smile left as quickly as it arrived. "Your voice and expression tell me it must be pretty important," he continued. "So, what's up?" He sat back in his chair and shot a reproachful glance at Littleton before turning his attention back to Edward.

"I need you to do something that should have been started Wednesday."

"Wait a minute, here!" Littleton's foot slipped from his knee and thumped to the floor as he grabbed the arm of the chair and swung around to face Edward. "*You* need? You hotshots think you can just prance in here and dictate to us? Well—"

"I'm not dictating anything!" Edward interjected. "I'm asking for help."

"Bob, cool your jets! You want to get fired? I'm sorry, Eddy. What the hell's got into you, Bob, talking to Mr. Slocum that way?"

For a moment, nothing was said.

"I'm sorry, Mr. Slocum. I had no call to talk to you that way. It's just I'm fed up to here being treated like shit by the likes of Rattray and others of his ilk—that is, until they want somethin', and then it's all wine and roses."

Boswell angled his chair toward Edward and then sat back down, crossing his legs at the ankles and folding his arms across his chest. "Now that that is all out of the way, we're all ears."

Edward clicked his heels and picked up his pace toward the same double doors that he had dreaded entering. He had shared Grynberg's findings with them, and they agreed to send a team to gather samples from both the effluent valve and Building 3C later that morning or early afternoon. He had no doubts about what they would find. Better still, they had agreed to keep it all hush-hush until the results were fully in.

Marilyn Ferguson and David DeLuca, engrossed in conversation, walked toward him, and to Edward's astonishment they passed him, barely acknowledging his presence. About to go through the same set of doors he had entered through earlier, he heard Marilyn call out to him. "Edward. We've just found out that Mr. Rattray won't be in today." A serpentine smile sliced across her face. "No one seems to know where he is or how to get in touch with him." Her eyes narrowed. "You wouldn't by any chance know, would you?"

Slowly, DeLuca turned and looked over his shoulder, as if bird droppings had just landed on it, and he waited for his answer.

With a slight shrug, Edward said, "No, I wouldn't." He waited for a reply.

Turning to DeLuca, Marilyn Ferguson carried on a short, private conversation with him while every so often peering back at Edward. Then, without so much as an adieu, the two of them continued along the corridor.

As the doors slowly closed behind him, Edward watched as Marilyn and David were greeted and ushered into the office area by Bob Littleton.

Edward massaged his neck.

What the hell are they doing down here? he asked himself.

He glanced at his watch: it was 9:15. *I've only got 15 minutes before my meeting with John.*

Edward headed back to his office, except now it was with a heavier step. Everything pointed to Elkhart's involvement, and he had to reassess the contents of his meeting with him.

Nadia was nowhere to be found, and the door to his office had been left wide open. As he stood at the entrance to his office, he took a cursory glance around. His in-tray had been added to, and his out-tray was empty, the contents now stacked on her desk; the day's mail was piled in the middle of his desk, per usual. In the middle of his doorway, he stopped cold. Quickly he returned to his desk, pushed the letters aside and searched frantically through his in-tray. The manila envelope he had given her earlier that morning wasn't there.

I was sure I told her to leave it on my desk. He chastised himself for letting the envelope out of his sight. *How stupid of me! How fuckin' stupid!* His pace quickened as he headed down the hall toward the coffee room with the hope of finding her there. Panic rippled through his body.

"Where's Nadia? Has anyone seen Nadia?" he asked everyone he saw. They backed away from him as if he were a leper. Everyone saw her at her usual time; none had seen her since. Rounding the corner, he looked into the coffee room, which was empty.

It was 9:30. On his way back to his office, Edward literally bumped into Natasha Whitfield, Rattray's administrative assistant, as she came out of his office.

"Oops! Sorry about that." He released his grip on her.

"I'm glad you've got good reflexes, or else I might have been on my backside looking up. What's the hurry, Eddy?"

"You haven't by any chance seen Nadia, have you?"

"Actually, I have, about 15 minutes ago."

"Where?"

"She was with Chris Stedman."

"Stedman?"

"Yes. They went down the back stairs." She pulled Edward aside and looked around to make sure no one was within earshot. "Between you, me and the barn door, that guy gives me the willies," she said.

"That's not like you, to say something like that about a fellow employee, Natasha."

"Maybe not, but, he's an exception."

"My, my, what's he done to warrant such a negative report from the likes of you?" Edward asked.

"Nothing to me! She pulled him closer. "Have you ever noticed that teardrop tattoo under his right eye?" she whispered.

"Yes. So?"

"It means he's murdered someone."

A smile curled at the corner of his lip. "Natasha, where are you going with this? You know everyone goes through a thorough police check before they begin working here. It would have shown up then."

She replied, "Maybe so, but someone on this one slipped up big time. Do you remember the company picture last year?" Edward nodded. "Well, my cousin, James, who's a Toronto cop in the 23rd Division, noticed him right off. And, sure enough, it seems he belongs to some sorta gang."

"Gang?"

"James knows more about that kind of stuff than I do. I'll e-mail you his number once I'm back in the office. That way if you want to learn more, you can."

"Hang on a minute! Why didn't you report this to Personnel?"

"I did. But nothing happened."

"Nothing? That's not like Sylvia. Did she get back to you?"

"You mean other than to thank me?" Edward nodded. "No." She tilted her head slightly and smiled. "I guess you've heard Rattray is not in today. Nobody knows where the heck he is or how to get in touch with him. A fine pickle that puts me in. I'm his admin, and I'm out to lunch on the matter. Oh well! I think life's about to take a nasty turn for him."

"A nasty turn?"

She waved off his query with her hand. "Forget I even said that," she said. "Do you have any idea where Chris might have taken Nadia?"

"I was about to ask you that," he replied. "You look concerned."

"I am. I didn't like the look in Nadia's eyes. When you get back to your office, call James. By the way, are you busy this evening?"

"Why are you asking?"

"Oh, just asking."

"I don't have anything special planned."

"Could you keep it that way?"

"I guess. Sure, I'll keep it open."

Edward had a lot on his mind as he headed back to his office to lock it up before his meeting with John. He remembered as he looked at his keychain that he had the key to Nadia's desk file drawer. *I wonder ...* Holding his breath, he fitted the key in, turned it and pulled the drawer open. Sure enough, the manila envelope lay across the file hangers.

Though copies of its contents had been made by Blackwell, he felt safer having the originals back in his hands.

CHAPTER THIRTY-NINE

AT THE REAR OF the building, John Elkhart had a nice, spacious corner office that looked out onto the manicured courtyard of KemKor Pharmaceuticals and the distant hills of the Beaver Valley. Edward looked forward to his monthly meetings there because the views through the expansive array of windows were stunning, unique living murals that presented vibrant and rhythmic depictions of the ebb and flow of nature's paintbrush at her best on the landscape.

Elkhart's administrative assistant, Lola Albright, had her desk located just outside Elkhart's office, in the reception area. Across from her was a neatly arranged round table with some magazines on it and two chairs. In the corner was a brewing system for coffee, tea, latte and cappuccino.

"Hi, handsome!" She always reminded him of Jill Marie Jones, who played Toni Childs on *Girlfriends*. Compromise, especially in marriage, was up there with love and honesty. Watching *Girlfriends* with Karen had been one of those compromises. "You're a hard man to get a hold of. Go ahead and help yourself," she said, nodding toward the brewing system, "while we try to agree on a rescheduled appointment." She pulled out her day timer.

He waved off her gesture. "Heh?" He pressed up against her desk. "I thought I already had an appointment? I know I'm late, but I'm not that late."

Looking up at him, she registered a half smile. "No, no, it's not that!" she said, redirecting her attention back to her calendar book. "Well, it is kinda about that, but it's not."

"Now I'm really confused. Please, Lola, just get to the point." He placed the manila envelope that he had tucked under his arm on her desk.

She gave him a chagrin smile as she looked up at him. "He's not here." Her eyes settled on the manila envelope.

"Excuse me?" Edward said as he picked up the envelope.

"Shortly after you booked this morning's appointment, Mr. Stedman and Nadia showed up. And, between you and me, she didn't look too happy. Well, anyway, the two of them headed into Mr. Elkhart's office unannounced and shut the door. At first it was quiet in there, but soon their conversation became quite heated. Actually, there was quite a bit of yelling going on between Mr. Elkhart and Mr. Stedman."

"Any idea what it was about?"

"Mr. Slocum, you know I can't tell you that." Smiling coyly at him, she winked, still eyeing the envelope. "I can take that package off your hands, if it's for Mr. Elkhart."

"No, that's all right."

Edward slipped the envelope under his arm and stepped back from her desk.

"I see." She cleared her throat. "Anyway, no sooner had the yelling started than a call came in from Ms. Ferguson."

"Oh?"

Tilting her head, she examined him as if he were a bug under glass. "Is that a problem?"

Why the hell was she calling John? he asked himself. "No, not really. Please, go on."

"There's really not much more to add. I sent the call through to Mr. Elkhart, and everything became quiet again." She began to relocate some folders on her desk. "Quite honestly, I think I may have already told you more than I should have. I'm sure you wouldn't like it if Nadia ran off at the mouth about your affairs." She tilted her head toward Elkhart's closed door. "Well, neither would he."

"Fair enough," he said, sighing deeply.

Tired of standing, Edward pulled over one of the chairs, placed it in front of Lola's desk, sat down and put the envelope on his lap. For a moment, the two of them just sat there looking at each other.

"Sometimes, Lola, there are exceptions. And, right now, this is one of them."

"What do you mean?" she asked.

"Do you trust me?"

Lola sat back in her chair with a concerned look on her face. "Of course I do," she said.

"Then you know that whatever transpires between us stays between us and goes nowhere else." She nodded her head. "I need to ask you a few more questions," he said.

She shifted uncomfortably in her seat. "Fire away, then."

"When their voices were raised, was there anything that stood out that you might remember, like a name or location, that sorta thing?" he asked.

She thought for a few moments and then rolled her chair closer to her desk. "Funny you should ask. There were two things. The name Garcia came up a couple of times. Now, I found that strange—that's why I remembered it, because the only Garcia I know owns the Greens' egg facility just outside of town. And, I thought, why would KemKor Pharmaceuticals be all hot and bothered over an egg facility? The other thing that came up was that Nadia was being raked over the coals regards something in accounting. Now, I really found that strange since she didn't even work in that department." She slumped back in her chair and crossed her arms.

"Is there anything else?" he asked.

"Now, let's see. Not really, except that ..."

She slid forward and looked out into the hallway before turning her attention back to him. "You never know," she said, pointing to her ears.

"Except what?" he asked, impatiently, moving his seat closer until his knees pressed against the face of her desk.

"Well, after Mr. Elkhart's call from Ms. Ferguson, the three of them came out of the office. That's when he told me that something had unexpectedly come up and that he had to go down to the Lab. That's also when he told me to try and reschedule your appointment for 11:30. By the way, is that time okay?"

She picked up her pen and waited for his reply.

He nodded his agreement, relieved that he now had more time to review the intent of his meeting with John, especially in light of what he had learned this morning.

Recording it in her day timer, she turned her attention to the computer and tapped on the keyboard. "There, done!" Smiling, she looked up at him. "I always like a paper trail, just in case these things break down."

"So, after John—that is, Mr. Elkhart—requested the rescheduling of my appointment, the three of them just left? There's nothing else?" Edward asked.

She began to chew on the nail of her thumb. "Nooo. When they were standing in the hallway, I remember Mr. Stedman telling Mr. Elkhart not to be late at Garcia's."

"Who was Nadia with when they separated?"

"Mr. Stedman."

He drummed his fingers on her desk then, knocking a couple of times with the knuckle on his forefinger, he picked up the envelope.

"I'll be back at 11:30, then," he said resignedly.

Upon reaching his office, Edward slammed the manila envelope on his desk, flopped down into his chair and swung around, looking aimlessly out the window. He formed a fist and pressed it against his mouth. *What the hell have I done!* The phone on his desk began to ring. He let it ring several times before finally picking it up. "Slocum here."

"Mr. Slocum, it's me, Natasha."

"Hi, Natasha."

"Are you all right?" she said.

"What can I do for you?"

The pen between his fingers began to pulsate back and forth like a metronome hyped on steroids.

She asked, "Have you checked your e-mail?"

"Not yet."

"I've sent you James's work number."

"James?" His pen flew across his desk and disappeared over the edge.

"Are you sure you're all right? You don't sound like yourself."

"I'm okay." Getting up, he retrieved the pen and regained his seat. Silence reached through the connection between them. "Really, Natasha, I'm all right!"

"Well, okay then. I hope he will be able to help you learn more about that teardrop tattoo under Stedman's eye. It probably wouldn't hurt asking him about Stedman. Nothing lost and everything to gain, that sorta thing. I doubt that he would tell you anything, but you never know; James's always full of surprises. To break the ice, tell him his little Kenenstatsi gave you his number."

A few minutes later, Edward logged onto his e-mail. Natasha's was at the top of a very long list of messages that filled his daily routine. He opened it. The phone number for Detective James Joseph Brant appeared in bold print. *Hmm, interesting.* Minimizing his e-mail box, he googled the name Kenenstatsi. *Well, I'll be damned! It's a Mohawk name. I never knew she was from Mohawk descent.*

The "Joseph Brant" in her cousin's name was the name of a very famous Mohawk chief who had the city of Brantford, Ontario, named after him.

Bringing up his e-mail again, he wrote down the phone number on a pad of paper—nothing else—and erased her message. Circling the number a couple of times, he tore it off, sat back in his chair, held it up in front of him and began rocking back and forth.

A few minutes later, Edward got up and wandered to the window and looked along the main street to the intersection. He had no idea how long he had stood there when the ringing of the phone sent a shock through his body. Quickly returning to his desk, he picked up the receiver. "Slocum here." It was Lola, Elkhart's administrative assistant.

"Oh, Mr. Slocum, I feel bad that I have to do this again to you."

"Do what?"

"Change your appointment again. I just got a call from him."

"Do you know if he's in the building?"

"It was a call from his cell, and no, he didn't say."

"When is it this time?"

"Five o'clock. Mr. Elkhart assured me that there would be no more changes."

Edward eyed the stack of folders in his in-basket and the phone number in his hand. His chest heaved as he took in a deep breath. "I've got more than enough to keep me busy until then."

"I'm sorry, Mr. Slocum."

"So am I, but it's not your fault."

He wondered whether he should cancel the meeting outright but decided against it for fear of raising any more suspicion than he was sure he had already done.

Replacing the receiver, he opened his side drawer and pulled out the Owen Sound and Area phone book. Turning to the blue pages, he wrote down the number for the Durham police services on the same piece of paper as Detective Brant's number. He looked at his watch.

After dialling Durham police services, he asked for Constable Paul Dickenson, who wasn't there. He left his number and stressed with the duty officer that it was imperative that Dickenson call him back this afternoon. When he hung up, he called Detective Brant's number; it was the same thing. He left the same message, except this time he added his home number.

Sighing deeply, he looked through the open door at Nadia's empty desk. *What did you learn in Accounting that you couldn't wait to tell me?* He began tapping his fingers on the desk as he thought. *How does Stedman fit into all of this? Why didn't he do what John asked him to do regarding the surveillance video? It should never have been erased!*

Suddenly the drumming of his fingers on the desk irritated him and he stopped. Grabbing a folder from his in-basket, he absently thumbed through its contents before closing it and throwing it on his desk.

How do I prove to the police that Nadia was taken under duress by Stedman? And Garcia—now Lola mentioned his name. Why would he even be part of this equation? He shook his head and began to rock back and forth again, chewing on the end of his pen. *How do I muster support without coming across like some raving, paranoid idiot?*

Picking up his cell, he called Blackwell's private number. The voice at the other end wasn't Chuck's.

"I'm sorry. I must have the wrong number," Edward said. He was about to hang up when the person at the other end interrupted.

"No, Mr. Slocum, please don't hang up. You've got the right number. It's Leonard."

"I thought this was Chuck's?"

"It is. It's just—well, with everything happening around Jennifer, I'm sure you understand. Right now he's with Sara. What can I do for you?"

At first he wasn't going to say anything to Leonard about Nadia, but he reconsidered when he thought back to the other night and how closely Blackwell and Leonard appeared to trust each other. "It's Nadia. For whatever reason, Chris Stedman's taken her. I've already put a call in to Dickenson."

"And what did he say?"

"I'm waiting for him to call me back."

"Mr. Slocum, what I'm about to say may sound strange, but please say nothing to him about what you just said to me. In fact, tell no one on the Durham police force."

"But she could be in danger."

"All I can ask is for you to trust us right now."

"It sounds like you already knew about this."

Leonard did not answer Edward. "Is there anything else, Mr. Slocum? All I *can* say is that it will soon be over."

Hanging up, Edward flung his pen across the room and went over to the window. *Damn it!*

He was concerned about the people he cared about, and he hated feeling helpless and out of the loop. For the first time in his life, he not only didn't know what to say or do, but he didn't know whom to trust, and it deeply frustrated him.

His eyes drifted to the intersection where Karen died. *For once, I would just like to look out this goddamn window and see nothing else except the street below.*

Turning away, he pulled his cell phone from his pocket and slowly walked back to his desk. Calling up the address page, he highlighted a number and called it. His heart rate shot up until it went to message. Taking in a deep breath, he left his message. "I'm sorry, Charlotte, but our evening together has been screwed up. John unexpectedly rescheduled our meeting until much later." He looked at the folders on his desk. "They'll be lots to talk about when we get together." Hesitating, he felt the swell of words he needed to say. "Um, I miss you—I'll miss you this evening." He turned off his cell, returned to his desk and sat down. Crossing his arms, he stroked his chin.

Where's she going tonight that was so important? he asked himself. *I guess like everything else today, I'll find out later.*

He reached for the folder on his desk and was about to open it when the phone rang. Halfheartedly, he picked up the receiver. "Slocum."

"This is Detective Brant, 23rd Division."

Edward felt a rush of energy course through him. "Thank you, Detective, for returning my call."

There was a long silence.

"Do I know you?" Brant said.

"No, you don't. But, your cousin Natasha suggested I call you." Edward stood up and sat on the corner of his desk. "She said to tell you that your little Kenenstatsi sends her love."

"She's all right, I hope?"

"She's doing just fine." He picked up his letter opener and rolled it in his hands a few times before placing it back down. "By way of introduction, I'm one of the executive vice presidents at KemKor Pharmaceuticals."

"She hasn't done anything wrong or somethin'? You're not firing her?"

"No, no, nothing like that, she's one of our most valued employees." He picked up the letter opener again and began to tap its point on his desk. "Look, I'm just going to drop a name and one of his physical characteristics. Chris Stedman. Teardrop tattoo under his right eye."

"Okay. What do you want me to do with that?"

"Tell me what you can about the tattoo and Chris Stedman."

"No can do. You must know that." Edward heard muffled tones and what appeared to be paper being shuffled about on the other end of the receiver. "You know where my cousin lives?"

"Yes." Edward looked down and realized he had bored a small hole into his desk top. He swore to himself as he quickly released the letter opener from his grasp.

"I'll meet you there at seven this evening."

"I may be a little late," Edward replied, trying to stuff the fine wooden pieces back into the hole.

"As long as it's not a lot late, I'll wait for you."

Edward was about to explain why he might be late when the receiver went dead at the other end. *Well, that was kinda rude,* he thought.

Recognizing that it was a useless effort to refill the hole he had bored into his desk, he swept the remnants across the table and into the waste basket with his hand. He looked at the pile of folders in his in-basket.

Whatever they contained would just have to wait; he was in no mood to go through them. He took in a deep breath and slowly expelled it, his shoulders slumping in the process. He sat back in his chair, chewing on his lower lip as he tried to think through what he should do next. Lifting the phone, he called Elkhart's office. It rang several times before Lola picked up.

"Lola, it's Mr. Slocum."

"Now don't tell me that you're going to cancel the five o'clock appointment."

"No way," he chuckled, shaking his head. "By any chance, has John returned to his office?"

"No, sir, he hasn't."

"And you still don't know where he is?"

"I should, but this is one of those rare occasions when I don't have any idea. I'm sorry."

"There's nothing to be sorry about." He picked up his letter opener and twirled it between his fingers before quickly placing it down. "I'm going to ask a favour."

"If I can. What is it?"

"All I want you to do is to remember back to this morning when Chris Stedman and Nadia showed up in John's office."

"I've told you all that I remembered."

"Please, just take a moment and try to remember. I'm particularly interested in where Stedman may have taken her."

"Well, I told you about the heated words in Mr. Elkhart's office about something Nadia did in accounting. Now, as you know, that threw me since she doesn't work in that department. The only other thing that stands out is hearing Mr. Urquiza's name mentioned when the three of them were in the hallway."

"How was Urquiza's name mentioned?"

"Hmm? Let's see. Something like 'not to be late at Garcia's.' No, it wasn't that—it was, 'Don't be late at Garcia's.'"

"Again, who said what to whom?"

"It was Mr. Stedman talking to Mr. Elkhart. I hope I've helped?"

"You have no idea how much."

Edward replaced the receiver and tilted back in his chair. *Damn! How did I miss that? The answer to the question, Where does it impact? Somehow it impacts Garcia. And I bet that's where Stedman took her.*

He redialled Elkhart's office again. This time, Lola picked up on the first ring. "Lola, I need another favour."

"What this time?"

"I want you to call Garcia Urquiza's number and ask for Mr. Stedman."

"What am I suppose to say."

"Nothing. If he answers, just hang up."

"And if I'm told he's not there?"

"Ask when he's expected. Tell them it is an important company matter and that he must call your office."

"And if he calls then, what am I to tell him?"

"Hmm. Now that could be a problem. Wait! Tell him you got a call from Rattray's office on ... Help me out here, Lola."

"I'll figure out something. This better not cost me my job."

"It won't; I promise. I'll man up if push comes to shove. Tell Natasha what you're doing beforehand."

"Are you sure about that?"

"Just tell her that it has to do with Stedman and that I asked you to do it. I have no doubts she'll be on board."

"You'd better be right!"

"Lola, you have so little faith! Please, call me immediately once you have an answer either way."

After hanging up, he sat back in his chair and rocked back and forth.

Why Garcia? What interest would he have in KemKor? That one I'll have to mull over.

He pushed back his chair and, picking up the newspaper from the side table, headed to the sitting area. Choosing the wing chair closest to the bookshelves, with a telephone on the table beside it, he opened to the front page and gave it a desultorily look before stretching his arms out and flipping through the pages. The headline of an article on the back page anchored his attention: "Ten Arrested in Massive Meth Raid in West Grey."

Oh my god!

Camilo Green's name stood out among the arrested. Edward folded the paper over and continued to read the article.

> Early Sunday morning, the Ontario Provincial Police (OPP) and Durham police executed five search warrants for properties just outside the Town of Durham. Aided by the RCMP and Canadian Border Services Agency, $2 million in crystal meth and $1 million in anabolic steroids were seized.
>
> The operation resulted in 10 arrests, including Constable Richard Malone of the Durham Police. Constable Malone is alleged to have leaked information to the targeted personnel of the investigation. Further seizures and arrests are expected in the near future as the investigation spreads across the province.

When the phone rang, he dropped the paper at his feet and picked up the receiver.

"How did you know he was there?" Lola asked.

"It was just a hunch."

"Mr. Slocum, you're still on for five o'clock, aren't you?"

"More than ever now, Lola."

"By the way, Mr. Slocum, Natasha was more than pleased to help. Who would have guessed? I've always thought of her as uppity, if you know what I mean?"

"No, I don't. But life's full of surprises."

"Oh, there's something else. She wanted me to ask you if you liked carrot cake."

"Tell her I sure do. With lots of icing! Thanks, Lola."

The newspaper crunched under his feet as he got up and crossed the room to his desk. He had no sooner sat down than his phone rang. It was Constable Dickenson.

"Paul! I thought you may have forgotten about me."

"Honestly, Eddy, I'm up the wazoo with this recent meth bust. I guess you've heard about it by now?"

"Yes, I just read about it." He glanced over to the newspaper on the floor.

"You know, Eddy, the hardest part was arresting a fellow officer. You heard right! It was me who had to arrest him. I had been the best man at Richard's wedding. You know, you think you know someone ... Well, you don't need me to finish it. I'm sure you know how it ends."

"I'm sorry, Paul. I read that Camilo Green was picked up."

"He was, but he was released about an hour and a half ago. In fact, I drove him back to Greens' Farm. His uncle Garcia was none too happy, I can tell you that. Just got back to the station a few minutes ago, and that's when Loretta here told me you called. What can I do for you?"

"Oh, nothing really. I just called to see if there were any new developments in Jennifer's disappearance, and something else."

"I wish there was." There was a moment's silence before he continued. "What's the 'something else' you want?"

"I'm wondering if you could make a copy of those pictures I gave you. You know, the ones you scanned into your computer." Edward felt uncomfortable with the lengthy silence at the other end of the receiver. "Are you still there Paul?"

"When do you want them?"

"I could drop by tomorrow, if that's okay," Edward replied.

"Like I said earlier, this is a busy time. Right now between the Blackwell case and now this meth bust, I'm drowning in paperwork. Give me a few days, and I'll drop them by your place."

"That'll work. There's no real big rush."

"So, is that it?"

"That's it."

As Edward hung up the receiver, he was surprised that Dickenson hadn't asked him why he needed a copy of the photos, since Dickenson knew he had the originals. The only conclusion he could come up with— especially after he factored in his earlier conversation with Leonard—was that Dickenson knew that the originals had been stolen. And that meant he was probably somehow connected with their theft.

Chapter Forty

⚍⚍ ⚎

AT FIVE O'CLOCK EDWARD walked along the hallway to John Elkhart's office and entered the reception area. He found Lola Albright packing up to go home; she had a disturbed look on her face when she looked up.

"I feel so horribly embarrassed, Mr. Slocum."

Edward looked at John's closed office door and back at her, and he quickly figured out what was troubling her. "It's not *you* who should feel embarrassed, Lola."

"It's not like him not to call. I was going to call you, but I waited as long as I could with the hope he'd show up. I'm sorry—I waited too long."

"Don't fret over it; I needed the exercise."

"Do you want me to set up an appointment for first thing tomorrow morning?"

"No, that's okay. I'll try him at home later this evening."

He had no intention of calling John at home, but he said it to make her feel better. Right now he felt like he was in the middle of a hornet's nest with nowhere to run. Whatever was going on, he knew it was big and out of his control. He had to trust that Blackwell, Leonard and whoever they were working with knew what they were doing, and that everyone he cared about would be returned safe and sound.

As Edward left KemKor with the manila envelope containing Irving's results and walked toward his vehicle, he thought about what Leonard had said to him earlier: "It will soon be over." *What will soon be over?* he thought. His sixth sense told him that it included far more than just the

Oxycontin production in Building 3C, and he was sure that by the time he spoke to Leonard, he had already known that Stedman had taken Nadia. *But how? And do they already know where Jennifer is?*

Opening the door to the Equinox, he threw the manila envelope containing the report onto the front seat, climbed in behind the steering wheel and turned the ignition.

He looked at his watch. It was only 5:20, and his meeting with Detective Brant at Natasha's home was more than an hour and a half off. He pulled out his iPhone and called Charlotte. *Hurry up and pick up! I need to talk to you!* He sighed when it went to message, and he hung up.

Edward turned onto the North Line Road and saw plumes of dust in the distance from a receding vehicle. He sped up with the hope that if it were Charlotte, he'd be able to catch her and explain why he had missed their dinner date. But by the time he was opposite his drive, the dust had already settled and the vehicle was long gone.

His stomach felt like it was in a twist as he thought about Nadia and Jennifer. He hated depending on someone else to act, and he couldn't help but feel that time was their enemy at the moment. He hoped he was wrong.

Edward hung his car keys on the key hook in his entranceway and was on his way to the liquor cabinet in his living room for a scotch when he saw there was a message on his phone system. As it turned out there were two messages. One was from Natasha resetting the time to 6:30 instead of 7:00, and the other was from Paul Dickenson requesting him to call him back.

After drowning the ice in his glass with scotch, Edward flopped into his comfy chair in the living room and put his feet up on the ottoman. As he sipped his scotch, loneliness scratched away at him. It was the same helpless loneliness he felt when he had learned of Karen's death, and he knew that life's cruel injustices had the potential to play it out again—except this time with Nadia and Jennifer. Suddenly he felt exhausted, and he put his glass on the table beside him. His watch indicated it was only 5:40, and he closed his eyes. A power nap would give him a brief respite before he headed off to Natasha's to meet Detective Brant.

When his cell phone began to vibrate in his pocket, he almost knocked over the side table with his scotch on it. Standing up, he pulled out his cell and saw that it was from Natasha Whitfield.

"Hi, Natasha!"

"Edward, are you still coming?"

Combing his fingers through his hair, he looked at his wristwatch. *Shit, it's 6:45!* "Forgive me, I must have dozed off."

"I wondered if you got my phone message."

"I got it. I'm really sorry."

"No harm done. James was late, too. He just arrived."

"James?"

"My cousin, you know, Detective Brant. Edward, throw some cold water on your face and then get over here. Wait a second!" Edward heard muffled conversation before Natasha got back on the phone. "He wants you to bring that analysis report completed by your friend."

"How did he know …? Never mind. Anything else?" Again he heard quiet, indiscernible conversation. "He said that unless you've got something else, that's it."

"I'll think about it while I'm washing the cobwebs out."

Refreshed, 10 minutes later Edward was in the Equinox driving over to Natasha's. Beside him were Grynberg's report and a brown envelope. In the brown envelope was his diary of events from the moment this roller-coaster ride began for him last Tuesday. Though today's events were not recorded, he figured he could fill that in later—provided, of course, her cousin was interested.

Natasha met Edward at the door with a large, welcoming smile and escorted him into the living room, where her cousin sat in the far corner of the couch. When she introduced him, James nodded without saying a word or extending a hand. He wore sandals, no socks, faded jeans and a buttoned shirt with the top three buttons undone, revealing an amethyst at the end of a leather necklace. He had broad shoulders and a stocky build but didn't appear fat or overweight.

Upon entering the living room, Edward felt James's eyes follow him. He sat in the chair opposite him and mustered up a smile.

"I'll be back in a minute with goodies. James, tea or coffee?" Natasha asked.

"Coffee's fine," James replied.

"Edward?"

"The same, please."

Silence fell between the two men. In what was obviously a well-used chair, Edward shuffled about trying to find a comfortable mould he could slip into, but he was unsuccessful. Tucking the two envelopes beside him, he smiled at her cousin. *Damn, I bet this is how a bloody criminal feels when he's just about to be interrogated!*

Edward quickly rose to offer his assistance when Natasha returned with carrot cake, plates, forks and hot cups of coffee on a tray. She shooed him away and placed it on the dining room table. After Natasha served each of them a piece of carrot cake—corners with lots of icing—and a small piece for herself, they took their cake and coffee back to the living room. She placed her coffee and cake on the coffee table and went to the table beside James. She pulled out a hide-away table from below it and placed it in front of Edward. "There, put your dessert and coffee here." She sat down on the couch beside James and nudged him with her elbow.

James was well into his carrot cake when her jab to his ribs caused him to look up.

"This is really great, Kenenstatsi!" he said.

"I guess you're going to want another before we've hardly started ours?"

"I didn't have supper, and I'm starving."

"Whose fault's that? I offered a fridge full of choice when you arrived, and you turned it down flat."

He lowered his head and gave her a sheepish look. "Kanenstatsi, you know my philosophy. Life's short; eat dessert first."

"Hmm! James, I don't know how you do it. With the life you lead and your eating habits, you should be the size of a cow. Why didn't I get those genes?" Natasha joked.

Picking up her plate, she carved out a small piece of cake with her fork and popped it in her mouth. Then she placed the plate down on the coffee table and sat back, folding her arms across her chest. "Well, have you sized him up yet, James?" she asked.

James casually looked over at Edward and then back at Natasha. "Uh-huh. Anyway, this dossier tucked in beside me here has more information on him than even he can remember." He held out his empty plate to her, and she took it.

"Dossier? On me? Why would you need, little alone have, a dossier on me?" Edward asked, shuffling in his chair.

"Believe it or not, Edward, it's good news," Natasha interjected. She gave James a stern look before getting up and heading to the dining room to cut him another piece. "Do you want some more, Edward?" she asked, stopping in front of him.

"Please." He handed her his plate and shifted his attention back to James. "You still haven't answered my question," Edward said.

"Edward, I don't travel two hours to have a meeting with someone I know squat about, and to talk about someone—in this case Stedman—who happens to be an item of interest to my investigation. That's it, nothing else, so don't get your shorts in a knot."

"Okay, that's fair."

Edward noticed that James's features had softened somewhat and that a broad grin had replaced the remnants of a scowl. A couple minutes later, with drinks refilled and sizeable chunks of well-iced carrot cake from the two remaining corners on the men's plates, Natasha regained her position on the couch beside James and initiated the reason for their get-together.

"I assume those envelopes contain what was asked for?" Natasha asked, pointing to the packages beside Edward.

Edward looked at James, expecting some interest, but he was surprised to find his only interest appeared to be in finishing his cake.

"They are," Edward replied, placing them on the coffee table in the space between them.

Mouth still full, James said, "You seem surprised. Or is a better word 'confused'?" He turned and smiled at Natasha. "There's a lot to tell him and so little time," James said, looking at his watch. "So let's begin. Which one of these envelopes contains your friend's report?"

"That one there," Edward replied, pointing to the manila envelope.

James picked up the envelope, pulled out the results and began to read through them.

"What's in this one?" Natasha asked, pushing aside the plate with her cake on it, picking up the envelope and opening it.

"Except for today's entry, my diary of events since it started."

"Whatever you've got in there, Edward—I hope you don't mind me calling you Edward?" James interrupted, peering over the top of Grynberg's report.

"Not in the least."

"Good—I hate formalities. Anyway, whatever you've got in there is only a small piece of the big picture, but it may turn out to be a very important piece." James redirected his attention to the report.

Natasha said, "James, his diary is quite detailed."

"As I said, the only entry missing is today's," Edward added.

James glanced at Natasha. "Edward, believe it or not, today has already been filled for us." He placed the half-open report on his lap and pointed to the document Natasha was reading. "Tell me, would you be willing to swear to the accuracy of this stuff in a court of law?" James asked.

Boy, has this taken an unexpected turn. "Of course I would."

"I'm hearing a 'but,' Edward." James closed Grynberg's report and placed it on the table beside him. "Well? Am I right? Is there a 'but'?"

James and Edward locked eyes. For a moment, no one said anything.

"James?" Natasha nudged him. "I think we may be moving too quickly."

"Too quickly is an understatement," Edward complained. He stood up and wandered toward the dining area before turning back. "Look, unless you can get Nadia and Jennifer back safely, I'm not committing to anything."

"We know where they are, and at the moment, they're safe." James rested one leg on top of the other. "Now, please, come back and sit down."

"How could you possibly know that?" His eyes shifted between James and Natasha.

James glimpsed at Natasha and took in a deep breath before continuing. "We have someone embedded with them."

"Embedded?"Edward asked, sitting down on the edge of the chair. "Who's embedded? Exactly who are you two?"

Natasha replied, "We can't tell you *who*, but we can answer the rest. I'm Captain Natasha Brant, Canadian Border Services Agency, and

James, here, is really my brother. He works for the Special Division on Crime and Drug for the Ontario Provincial Police."

"Hang on a minute. Let me get my bearings. You're not cousins?"

Edward slumped back in his chair. "No, we're not cousins."

"So you're not Natasha Whitfield?"

"I am. It's the name I went by before my separation."

Edward moved to the edge of the chair again. "So why is someone from the Border Agency an administrative assistant to the CEO of Kemkor Pharmaceuticals?"

"Right now all we ask is that you be patient. Hopefully, if all goes well, you'll have answers to a lot of your questions before this night is through."

"If all goes well? James, Natasha, there can't be any 'ifs' here. Surely you know that."

"We do. This is the toughest time in any operation," James said. "I can assure you they're safe and will be protected at all cost."

Natasha added, "You see, Edward, when I gave you that number to call James, it was one part of a code to say that it was either me or someone I trusted. By giving you my Mohawk name, Kenenstatsi, he knew beyond any doubts that you were the real thing and, therefore, okay."

"I see." Edward let out a deep sigh. "And you can assure me they're safe?"

James uncrossed his legs. "At the moment, yes. I know you're worried, but they are being protected. They should be back home before the night's finished." James gathered the contents from both envelopes and walked over to Edward, placing his hand on his shoulder. "To get back to my earlier question, are you prepared—and there can be no buts here—to testify in court to the accuracy of this material and anything else you should be asked?"

"Yes, yes I am."

"Good!" James glanced at his watch. "You'll have to excuse me. Natasha will fill you in with whatever she can. I'm afraid you're going to have to stay here, at least until we feel it's safe for you to return home." He gave Natasha a peck on the cheek. "Be safe, Sis. See you in about three hours." He was already on his cell phone as he opened the front door and closed it behind him.

Natasha said to him, "I'm sorry for the inconvenience, Edward. But it must be done. Do you want some more coffee or a sandwich before I head off?"

"Coffee and a sandwich sounds great." He followed her into the kitchen.

"I'll brew a fresh batch." Opening the fridge, she crouched down and began to search through the meat drawer and crisper. "Is ham okay? Cheese and lettuce?"

"It all sounds wonderful. Thank you." He sat down at the kitchen table. "I guess I fell into one hell of a hornet's nest?"

"You could say that. Do you want mayonnaise on your bread?"

"Sure." Edward drew imaginary circles on the kitchen table with his index finger. "Natasha?"

"Yes?" Cutting the sandwich in half, she placed it on a plate and brought to the table. "Cat got your tongue?"she said, looking down at him.

He looked up at her smiling face and chuckled feebly. "I think you know me better than that."

"I do. So what's your question?" She returned to the coffee maker and, after filling it with water, opened the cupboard to find the coffee container. "Forgive me, Edward; I'm on the clock right now. I *am* listening, so shoot. What do you want to ask?" She began to scoop the coffee into the filter.

"Can you tell me what's happening tonight?"

She turned on the coffee maker and breathed in deeply before turning round to face him. "We're raiding the Green Farm tonight."

"We?"

She pulled out the kitchen chair and sat down beside him. "It's a consortium of RCMP, OPP, my agency and the Durham police. Paul Dickenson and three of his men are going in first under the pretext of questioning Camilo further over the meth bust. Paul figured that since he's on good terms with Garcia Urquiza, it would be a much softer approach than having all guns blazing and not knowing what's at the other end. Once he reports his findings to us, we go in. What's the matter?"

"You don't by any chance know Leonard Palladin, do you? He works for Charles Blackwell."

"Why are you asking?"

"Well, earlier today he told me not to share anything with Durham police."

"Why would he tell you that?"

"I thought you would know the answer to that."

Natasha stood up and walked over to the coffee maker. "Do you fish, Edward?" she asked without turning around.

"Only as a child."

"Then you probably learned how important the bait is to catch the right fish." She poured him a mug of coffee and placed it in front of him. "Edward, I can see by your expression you want to ask more. Don't. With patience comes knowledge. Anything *else* you want to add?"

"It's only a feeling."

"Feelings are good. They help guide us through life."

Edward took a drink from his mug before he continued. "I sure hope I'm wrong about this feeling, but I have a strong sense that Charlotte and Janet had every intention of snooping around the Green Farm tonight."

"How strong is your sense?"

"Basically 100 percent."

She went to the kitchen counter for her cell phone and dialed James. "This may step up the timing of this operation considerably," she said to Edward. Then she said into her phone, "James we have a snafu."

CHAPTER FORTY-ONE

"SLOW DOWN! I CAN'T see a thing out here!" complained Charlotte, frustrated and trying to speak in a whisper while she swatted at mosquitoes and attempted to keep up with Janet, who barrelled ahead through the tall grass. Barely five minutes had passed since she and Janet had left their vehicles on East Line to begin their trek across the back field of Greens' Farm. The moonless sky and lack of familiarity with the terrain had made the journey treacherous for her. *How the hell can she move so fast?* "Damn!" Her foot caught another rock, and she crumbled onto the ground for the second time. Brusquely rubbing her shin, she looked up at Janet, exasperated. "That really hurt this time." Her jeans were slightly torn and were slightly wet in the region she was rubbing. *I bet I've broken the skin.*

"I thought you had the eyes of an owl?" Janet snickered, holding out one hand to help Charlotte up while the other slapped at a mosquito about to feast on the side of her neck. "Gotcha!" Gathering it between her fingers, she flicked it off.

Charlotte ignored Janet's extended hand and continued to massage her leg.

"Had you already reconnoitred this route?" Charlotte asked suspiciously.

"Come on, take my hand."

Finally, Charlotte gave in, took Janet's outstretched hand and rose to her feet. "Either you did or you didn't. I can't think of any other reason why you're able to move through this damn field so quickly."

"I walked it yesterday, before dusk," Janet confessed, shrugging. Sheepishly she stepped aside revealing a readymade trail of stamped-down grass. "I just wanted to see if it had changed much since I was a teenager."

"You can't be serious, Janet. Look around. Surely you'd expect change over a hundred years."

"I'll ignore that last statement of yours, smartass. Anyway, can't a person reminisce? You see, I used to work this farm every summer in my youth, when it was hayed. I must have walked every inch of this field and the others, tossing square bales onto wagons. Back then, the Palmers owned it." Janet pointed ahead. "See those spots of light in the distance? Well, that's where we're going. And I'd like to get there before sunrise."

"Don't get snarky!" Charlotte snarled. "Just walk slower, trailblazer." Charlotte became preoccupied with mosquitoes dive-bombing her head.

"Enough sarcasm! Did you spray yourself with repellent?" Receiving no answer, Janet shook her head in disgust, reached into her rucksack and pulled out a small can of Bug Off. "Close your eyes and stand still while I spray you."

Emptying the can, Janet placed it back in her knapsack and swung it over her shoulder. "Hopefully that will do the trick," she said. "Now let's get goin'. If you need to, grasp the straps on my knapsack."

Fifteen minutes later, they broke through the waist-high grass onto a clearing and crouched down to get their breath. A hundred metres in front of them was a large, high-peaked, two-story structure outlined against the star-studded sky. Light emanated from the two upper-level windows and the row of windows on the first level

"That place gives me the willies," Charlotte complained. She shivered involuntarily with the thought. "It looks like a witch with a hat atop its sinister, smiling face. What is it, Janet?"

"Well, it used to be a bunkhouse and conference centre. I have no idea how it's being used now. Josh and Marta Green had it built shortly after they bought the property from Palmer."

Adjusting her position so that one knee rested on the ground, Janet placed her backpack beside her.

"The Greens were quite religious, you know. I don't remember the name of their religious affiliation, but they used to have regular gatherings of some kind in that building," Janet added.

Opening her backpack, Janet pulled out two black woolen balaclavas.

Charlotte looked at the balaclavas in disbelief. "You've got to be kidding? I'd drown in my own sweat in one of those."

"Our dark clothes won't stand out, but our faces sure will. Put it on!" Janet pushed it out at her.

Reluctantly, Charlotte took it. She was about to pull the balaclava over her head when Janet stopped her with her hand.

"Shh! Stay still." After a couple of minutes, Janet motioned for Charlotte to follow her back into the tall grass. Janet evaporated into the darkness.

Then, as suddenly as she disappeared, Janet's disembodied hand shot out of the wall of grass, frantically obvious in its intent, her command like the sting from the cracker on a bullwhip.

"Move your ass, now!"

Getting caught up in her own feet, Charlotte fell in beside her. "What a klutz!" she berated herself, somewhat embarrassed.

"What part of shh don't you understand?" Janet whispered.

"What was the big rush?" Charlotte muttered.

"You obviously hadn't noticed."

Charlotte followed the direction of Janet's extended index finger. Four individuals, three men and a girl, could be seen making their way along a lighted path to a low-lying structure about 200 metres from the large structure. The girl began to struggle with the men on either side of her until the man behind her hit her with something. Limp between the two men, they dragged her the rest of the distance.

When they disappeared into the structure, the lights along the path went out.

"Shit!" Charlotte rose with the intention of intervention and rescue, her mind racing with how quickly she could cover the distance between her and them before she was seen. But she fell hard. Something had ensnared her.

"Don't be stupid!" Janet hung on to Charlotte's ankle for all she was worth.

"Let go of me!" she pleaded. She tugged at her foot, trying to release it from Janet's grasp. "Damn it, Janet! She needs help now! That could be Jennifer!"

Janet raised her hand to her mouth for silence. "I know it *could* have been. But then again, Charlotte, it probably wasn't." Janet's voice was low, almost timorous in texture.

"How do you know?" Charlotte snapped back.

"I don't. But what I do know is they don't know we're here, and that gives us the advantage—an advantage you were about to squander. Be sensible. Let's give away nothing, wait it out and then check out the building." After feeling Charlotte's leg relax, Janet let go. "Thank you."

"How long?" Charlotte asked. She lay on the ground looking back at Janet, biting at the bit.

"How long?" Janet repeated.

"How long do we wait?" Charlotte asked.

"Until we're sure that we can cover the distance without being seen."

A few minutes later, balaclavas covering their faces, the two of them made their way across the open field to a line of thick copse behind the building to where the men and girl had been heading. The faint glow of light from the front room painted the two back windows.

Janet and Charlotte cowered down. They could hear someone opening the windows. The pungent smell of cigarette smoke soon filled the air. They tucked even more tightly into each other, barely breathing, fearful of being heard. After a few minutes, they mustered up enough nerve to peer at the windows. A stream of cigarette smoke drifted out of the screened window, furthest from them. They scrunched down again. A few moments later, they heard one of the men call out. The person at the window replied grumpily. They could hear him scuffle his feet before his footsteps receded into another room in the building. Muffled, whimpering sounds, like a dog that had been hit by a car, drifted from within, violating the stillness of the night air.

Janet felt sick to her stomach and threw off her balaclava as she moved away from Charlotte. She knew there was nothing she could do. Wiping her sleeve across her face and forehead, she sponged the perspiration. Again she was assaulted by the sounds of whimpering, and again chills ran up and down her spine. She continued to wipe her face dry. The need for her to do something was overwhelming. *I mustn't give in! I can't!* she screamed to herself. *It would be foolhardy!* She looked at Charlotte. *She doesn't understand. We're no good to her if we get caught!* Her brain churned with what-ifs and maybes.

She was too preoccupied to notice that Charlotte had put her own dangerous plan into motion.

Charlotte was already starting to move forward when Janet noticed it.

"Jesus!" Janet exclaimed under her breath as she grabbed for Charlotte and missed. She tried again, this time hooking her fingers into Charlotte's waistline. She could feel the fabric ripping away in her grasp but she continued to pull back.

Charlotte fell back, hitting the ground with a resounding thud. Immediately, Janet placed her hand across Charlotte's mouth. She held her breath and waited. Nothing. She felt relief—no one had heard.

"Are you okay?" Janet asked. "Sorry about that. I really didn't know I had that kinda strength. You are okay, aren't you?"

"Hmm," Charlotte replied, stifling her growing anger. Pushing away Janet's hands, she spoke in hushed tones. "I'm not sure if I'm okay. I'll be damn lucky to be able to walk, let alone run out of this place." She sat up rubbing her neck and head. "Why did you do that?" At first, Charlotte thought she had wrenched her back, but after a few stretches she was relieved to find that she was okay. "I've even got a goose egg forming," she continued, rubbing the back of her head. "Here, feel for yourself." She tilted the impacted part toward Janet.

"Why did I do that?" Janet repeated. "You're a smart girl—I'm sure you can figure it out for yourself, if you just took time for once and thought it through." Her eyebrows furrowed sharply together, and she looked hard at her friend. "Let me spell it out, then. Read my lips." She enunciated her next words. "We are in one helluva dangerous situation here. We can't get caught if we want to help her."

"Do you think I don't know that!" retorted Charlotte. She was barely capable of keeping her voice below a whisper because she was hurt by Janet's aspersions. "I'm not like you, Janet. I have to do something." Charlotte recovered to a crouched position, still rubbing the side of her head.

"Our goals are the same, Charlotte. It's just that we go about them differently." Janet took off her backpack and handed it to her. Then, picking up her balaclava, she put it over her head, pulled it down over her face and stood up, slightly hunched over. "Before we go any further here," Janet said, "let me check out the area around this building and along the pathway they came. And while I'm at it, I'm going to see what that former bunkhouse and conference centre is used for now. Okay? I won't be long." She bent down, picked up Charlotte's balaclava and handed it to her. "Charlotte, do you think you can come up with a signal I can use to identify it's me? Also, you'll need one to alert me to danger."

Standing up and careful not to be seen, Janet scanned along the back of the dwelling several times.

After taking in several deep breathes, Charlotte replied, "We'll use the call of the Great Horned Owl." Janet hunched back down. Grasping some soil, Charlotte let it sift through her fingers. "Normally," she continued, "the Great Horned Owl makes only four 'Ho-ho hoo-hoo,' but sometimes it makes five: 'Ho-ho hoo-hoo-hoo.' Four it's all clear, and five from either one of us means danger."

"It works for me," Janet replied. She pulled back her balaclava and wiped her face with some tissues from her pocket. "Look, if all we can do to help that girl is to snap a picture or two with your iPhone, then that's all we do. We won't do her or ourselves any good if we're caught." She jammed the soggy tissues back into her pocket.

"Yeah, and I'd better be ready to run like hell," tittered Charlotte.

"And yeah, run like hell," Janet replied resignedly. *But to where?* she thought. "I'll try searching for another escape route just in case. There's no tellin' if the trail we came in on will still be available." Hunching down, she squeezed Charlotte's hand. "Believe it or not, Charlotte, I feel the same way you do. You and I, we'll get this job done. We'll help her. Just try to be patient." Breathing deeply, Janet mustered up as much courage as she could before pulling down the balaclava over her face. Then, as stealthily as possible, she made her way through the copse.

Climbing the short incline to the pathway, Janet deposited in the back recesses of her mind any discomfort she might have felt about the ease with which Charlotte had acquiesced to staying put and to acting as lookout. Right now, she wrestled with more important matters, and there was no room to second-guess now that common sense had prevailed.

CHAPTER FORTY-TWO

"HO-HO HOO-HOO." HUDDLING IN the bushes, Janet emulated the call of the Great Horned Owl again. "Ho-ho hoo-hoo." No reply. *Something's happened*, she thought. In the distance, she could make out several beams of light moving through the field that she and Charlotte had come through earlier. Removing her balaclava, she pushed it into her back pocket and wiped the sweat from her face with her sleeve. The footpath between the conference centre and cabin was clear. Moving closer to the pathway, she tried again. "Ho-ho hoo-hoo."

"Ho-ho hoo-hoo."

Finally! Checking, once again to ensure the walkway was clear, Janet scurried across and rejoined Charlotte. About to scold her for tardiness in not replying sooner, Janet's words evaporated before she even began. On the ground beside Charlotte, a video played on her iPhone. Slumping down beside her, she wrapped her arms around Charlotte and, while she held her, reached out and turned off the phone. *Why, oh why, did you look through that window?* She cradled her in her arms.

The flashlights, strung across the field, were getting closer.

"Charlotte, we can't stay here," she said softly.

"They were raping her. I know they were. The men blocked my view." Charlotte's voice, cracking and barely audible, escaped through the sobs. "Camilo—he …"

"What about Camilo?"

"He was one of them."

Janet's shoulders dropped heavily with a sigh. "Charlotte, I need you to stop crying and to look up." Janet pointed toward the field. "We must leave—now!" Janet urged. "Pick up your phone and make sure it's secure on you. It may be our only evidence." Janet was in the process of slinging her knapsack over her shoulder when she stopped. "Charlotte, what are you doing?"

"I'm sending a copy to Edward, just in case."

That "just in case" sent a chill up Janet's spine.

The lights went out in the cabin behind them, and voices mixed with laughter were heard outside.

Janet placed her hand over Charlotte's mouth and pulled her close. "Shush!"

Floodlights lit up the path between the conference centre and cabin.

Shit! Janet looked back at the approaching lights in the field.

"Follow me when I give you the okay. And for god's sake, stay close to the ground and in the shadows."

Slowly, Janet made her way to the corner of the cabin and crouched down. Peering around the corner at the pathway, she saw three men and a barefooted blonde girl between them being escorted toward the conference centre. At the rear, Camilo lingered, looking out to the field and fussing with something in his hands. He hung them over his shoulder and walked into the fullness of the light. *Running shoes?* she asked herself. The red and white running shoes, a kangaroo emblazoned on the side, stood out in the light. *Why on earth would he have running shoes?* Then it dawned on her. *Why, the little bastard's collecting his trophy.* She gritted her teeth and growled under her breath.

As long as Camilo continued to plant himself in the walkway, looking outward, she knew that she dare not motion for Charlotte to join her, so she waited. Camilo was steadfast, and the flashlights in the field were almost to the edge of the tall grass. A bellowing voice called out in Spanish from the bunkhouse and conference centre. A babble of voices closed in from the field side. Panic washed over her body like a tsunami. She watched Camilo edging toward the centre while he looked out to the field. Suddenly he bent over and picked up a black object from the path. *Strange! What was so important that he needed to pick it up?* She flattened herself against the cabin wall. *Go on, you little shit! Get movin'!* And as if he had picked up her prompt, Camilo began to run toward the centre.

Immediately Janet signalled Charlotte. No sooner did she join her than the floodlights went out along the path.

Securing her knapsack over both shoulders, Janet grabbed Charlotte's hand, and the two of them scampered up the incline and across the pathway, melting into the thick bushes on the other side.

Unexpectedly, the floodlights went back on. The door to the centre busted wide open, and Camilo and two men rushed through. The verbal exchange between them was loud and agitated until Camilo pointed along the pathway. The men left him and called out toward the field.

"Put your balaclava on, girlie," Janet commanded, "and let's get the hell out of here. Now! Stay close to the ground and in the shadows. Shit!" *My balaclava's not in my pocket. So that's what the little bastard picked up.*

"What's wrong?"

"Never you mind! Hightail it to the tree line at the top of that hill; I'll be right behind you. Remember, girlie, do it quietly, not like a herd of elephants."

"What do you think I am, an idiot or something?"

"At the moment, Charlotte, I wear that toque."

Baffled by Janet's reply, Charlotte apparently decided not to pursue it as she looked up the slope to the tree line. It was at least a 200-metre trek to the top, and she was paralyzed with fear.

"Unless you want to end up in that cabin like that poor girl, I would suggest you move your ass pronto!" Janet said as she grabbed Charlotte's hand and pulled her along, climbing the hill.

At the top, they crouched behind an old maple tree, out of breath. After giving each other a high-five, they watched as the commotion along the pathway below them ignited into pandemonium when the men from the field joined Camilo and the other two men.

Janet pointed to the automatic weapons the men were carrying.

"We have a whack of trouble," Janet said, shifting her weight to the other side. "I don't know about you, but this scares the piss out of me."

"Me, too!" Charlotte replied, biting softly on her lower lip. "What the hell have we stumbled into?"

"Your guess is as good as mine. But one thing's sure—there's a helluva lot more going on here than what happened in the cabin down there."

Cones of light suddenly stretched out from the walkway below, their beams searching and crisscrossing each other as they meticulously swept the tree line.

When the hunters' lights swept to another sector, Charlotte whispered, "I hope you've got a plan B, because I sure don't."

"I know the lay of the land, so that's got to count for something. You worry too much." Janet's concerns were as great as Charlotte's, but she tried to hide them.

"Do you blame me under these circumstances? As long as I'm not laid *in* the land, we've got a handshake on whatever you come up with. Hey! Since when did it become do as I say and not what I do?" Charlotte asked indignantly, pointing at Janet's uncovered face.

"Since I got careless. Now, shut up and follow me!"

"Oh, I see!"

Ten minutes later, they stepped out onto the manicured back lawn of what used to be the Greens' farmhouse.

"Whoa, girl!" Janet whispered, out of breath. She stopped Charlotte with an outstretched arm.

As they were hunched over, getting their breath, Charlotte noticed movement at the front of the house and quickly flopped to the ground, dragging Janet with her.

"Ouch!"

Janet looked at her. "Ouch?" she asked.

Flipping onto her side, Charlotte began to dig into the front pocket of her pants. "Damn! And double damn!"

Expletives dripping in whispered consternation erupted as Charlotte whipped off her balaclava and began to claw at the ground.

This can't be good, Janet thought. Looking up at the house and back at Charlotte, she asked, "What's wrong?"

"Everything! We're screwed!"

Charlotte pulled a substantial rock from beneath her and held up her broken iPhone.

"Screwed? How? You did send a message off to Edward with the video, didn't you?"

"I couldn't."

"But I saw you."

"I couldn't get a signal. I was going to try again up here."

She dangled the shattered phone in Janet's face before jamming it back into her pocket.

Scrutinizing Janet's backpack, she queried, "You wouldn't by any chance have a …?"

"You've got to be kidding," Janet replied, flattening herself on the ground. "I guess it all falls on us getting the hell out of here." Suddenly she lifted her head. "Shh!" Janet pointed toward the egg factory. "Get down, and put on your damn balaclava!"

A number of women exited the egg factory and went along a pathway on the far side that sloped down into the woods, where they were swallowed whole in its darkness. Shortly afterward, another group of women appeared coming up the same pathway, accompanied with several armed men. Running ahead of them was Camilo. *Well, if it isn't the little shit.*

Janet was about to draw Charlotte's attention in his direction when she noticed Charlotte's clenched fist and knew that she had already seen him. They watched him until he disappeared around the side of the house. The door to the egg factory opened, and the women were paraded through it while another man stepped outside and lit up a cigarette.

Crisscrossing light beams and voices scattered throughout the woods behind them moved relentlessly closer.

They'd be here by now if they knew we were here, Janet thought. *To them, I'd bet there is no "we." One balaclava equals one person. That's it! That's our advantage!* She wanted to tell Charlotte, but it would have to wait. *We need a safer location.* Janet's attention returned to the egg factory. *Whatever is in there, I'd bet it's not the product of chicken feed.* She watched as the man paced back and forth, smoking his cigarette. Time was at a premium. Her stomach tied in knots as the voices behind them drew nearer. She had made up her mind. The side of the building offered good cover. Once there, they would decide their best route of escape to find help. *Hurry up, asshole! Finish your goddamn cigarette!*

The man outside the egg factory stretched and then looked at his watch. Taking a few extra puffs, he threw what was left of his cigarette on the ground and stamped it out with his foot. Stretching again, he turned and reentered the facility.

"There's no time to waste, dearie. We're heading there." Janet pointed to the location she had chosen beside the egg factory. "Now!"

Crouching low, they began running toward the egg facility.

Janet felt something bite her neck, and she stumbled and fell. Dazed at first, she shook it off and recovering to her feet, began to run—but she knew her pace had slowed dramatically. She felt groggy and her vision was blurred. She could barely see Charlotte ahead of her. The light ahead was blinding. *There's not supposed to be a light. My legs!* She fell to the ground like a rag doll. *Shit, it was a trap!*

Removing his night-vision goggles, Garcia lowered his tranquilizer rifle and directed his men to retrieve her.

CHAPTER FORTY-THREE

CHARLOTTE REACHED THE EDGE of the egg factory and disappeared into the darkness alongside it as the floodlights came on at the front. Losing her footing, she stumbled into a shallow stony culvert used for rain run-off that ran the length of the building. She grimaced in pain. Unexpectedly, floodlights from somewhere above went on, lighting the tall grass and copse beside her. *Thank god!* She was still deep within its shadow's wedge. For the moment, she welcomed her immobility but understood its hazard if she lingered too long. Frozen to her spot, senses peaked, she listened.

The commotion behind her was oppressive because she now knew that Janet had not entered with her. Slowly she raised her head and, straining her eyes, tried to peer ahead through the layers of blackness that cloaked the stony route she was now destined to follow. *Ahead there is something, but what?* She squirmed slightly to look back. In the pool of light, two men stood in animated conversation while, beyond the light's edge, a number of black amorphous shapes trudged toward the farmhouse.

When the floodlights from the farmhouse became activated, she gasped. *Janet! Oh my god! They're carrying Janet.* Janet's advice echoed in her mind, "We won't do her or ourselves any good if we're caught." Throwing her balaclava to one side and more resolute than ever, she began digging one elbow in and one toe for thrust as she surreptitiously slithered along the stony spine of the drainage system toward whatever it was jutting out from the side of the building.

After a couple of minutes of pushing and pulling her body over the stones, she stopped to catch her breath. Muffled sounds and a thin slice of very weak light emanated from a slightly ajar door ahead. *Shit! I've been crawling to this? Now what do I do?* She settled down to consider her options. Peering back through the darkness, she noticed that several shapes had now gathered on the lawn area and were beginning to fan out in her direction. *Well, I guess going back's out.* She glanced at the tall grass bathed in light. *That's definitely not an option.* Drawing in a deep breath, her ribs ached pressed against the stone. *The back of the building's out. Too much damn light! Jesus, I can't believe what I'm thinking.* And without further thought, she was through the doorway, her nose butting hard against the steel toe of a man's work boot. Tears quickly flooded her eyes as she contained the expletives she wanted so much to scream out.

"You certainly took your time about it," the man whispered, chuckling softly. "Do you normally slide through a door as if you're stealing second base?" He bent down and removed a metal bar that had kept the door open.

They would have been plunged into darkness if it hadn't been for a small pen light balanced on a barrel behind him.

"Juarez? How did you …?"

"We'll talk about that later. Right now your nose is bleeding." Moving beside her, he handed her a clean cloth from his back pocket. "Use this to catch the blood. Now, sit up and bend forward. Here, I'll help you."

"I don't need your help!" Brushing off his hand, she sat up crossed-legged and bent forward as directed.

Standing up, he looked down at her and shook his head. "I think you do."

"Do what?"

"Need my help." He crouched back down beside her. "That is, if you want to get out of here alive." He extended his thumb and forefinger toward her nose, but she swatted it away.

"Do you think I don't know how to stop a nosebleed?" She pinched the soft part of her nose just below the bridge.

Juarez stood up. "I'm just trying to help." His eyebrows knitted together. "You do know to pinch it for at least five minutes? I'll take that nod as a yes. Okay!" He rubbed his hands together in a washing motion.

"Do you think you can be quiet here until I return? And that means staying put—no poking around. Get it?"

"Where are you going?"

He held his forefinger to his lips. "Shh!" Grabbing the pen light, he shoved it in his jean pocket and exited through a door a few metres away.

Shit! I can't see a thing! Her legs were beginning to go numb, and she carefully unfolded them while waiting for her eyes to adjust to the darkness. Slowly letting go of her nose, she felt around the nostrils for wetness and, finding none, wiped the area with the cloth that Juarez had given her. Then she felt again. *Good! Nothing!* Not having any idea how long she would have to wait for Juarez's return, she decided to find a more comfortable location. Sliding along the floor, she headed toward the door she had come through earlier and leaned against it. *That's better!* Crossing one leg over the other and folding her arms across her chest, she closed her eyes and settled in for what she expected would be a long wait.

A frantic rattling sound assaulted her ears as her body lifted with each pounding sensation against her back. Angry voices and barking dogs unceremoniously ejected her from her dreamscape, and her eyes blasted wide open to meet a fully lit room and two burly men, their automatic weapons trained on her. Behind them was Juarez. Something pricked her arm, and she moved her other hand to flick whatever it was away and came face to face with Garcia crouched beside her, a syringe in his hand.

"Stop pounding out there! We've got her," Garcia yelled out in Spanish, standing up and kicking at the door.

Groggy, Charlotte tried several times to open her eyes, but the salty puddles of sweat clinging to them stung, and she squeezed her eyes shut. She shook her head forcefully, which splayed a salty brew from her face. It was an action she quickly regretted. Dizziness and disorientation initially filled the void followed by a lava flow of stale, damp, acrid air. She felt an overwhelming need to puke, and after several fruitless retching attempts, she fell back against the stone wall in a cold sweat, her hands tied behind her back with a zip tie.

"Charlotte! That nausea is only temporary. Force yourself to breathe deeply."

"Janet?" Her eyelids, now slits, tried to focus on the figure that haphazardly made its way toward her across the dirt floor. "Is that really you?"

"It's really me, dearie. Now do what I told you. Breathe deeply. That's it, that's my girl! Now again, and again. I know it smells like shit in here, but believe it or not, you'll get used to it." Janet shook her head. "I never thought I'd ever hear myself say that."

Her legs and hands tied, Janet squirmed her way across the dirt floor and propped herself up beside her. "Thank you for not puking," she said. "It would have made things *sooo* much worse in here."

Charlotte's face screwed up as if she had just bitten down hard into a lemon. "No kiddin'," she mumbled.

"That Novocain-like effect will wear off, too."

"Where are we?"

"My guess is, it's the Greens' old root cellar.

"I thought its venting system would be better than this."

"What venting system? By the looks and feel of it, this hasn't been used as a root cellar in a long time." She glanced over at Charlotte. "Are you okay otherwise?"

"I think so. You?"

"Dearie, as best I can at this age. But I'm not so sure about them." She nodded toward two bodies curled up on the floor opposite them, at the far end of the enclosure. "One of them is Jennifer Blackwell. I don't know who the other one is." She tilted her head in the direction of a large barrel beside the steps. "At least they were generous enough to leave us some light."

"By the way it's flickering, I think their generosity is about to run out."

"That, Charlotte, is symbolism I can do without."

"Have you been able to talk with Jennifer?"

"Not a word! She just mumbles like you did when they first dumped you in here."

Staring at the other girl, Charlotte said, "You know, Janet, I'd bet that was the girl in the cabin down by the bunkhouse and conference centre."

"What makes you say that?"

"It's just a hunch."

Charlotte's gaze travelled down the young girl's body, settling at her feet. She shuffled forward to have a closer look.

"Just what I thought! It is her. She's got a gold ring on the second toe of both feet."

"Is she all right?"

"No! I'm sure she's not."

Shuffling back, she nuzzled her head against Janet's shoulder.

"I feel so helpless. Janet, she looks horrible. They both do."

"We've got to get them and us out of here! And pronto!"

Charlotte pushed against Janet. "Kinda obvious, isn't it? But how do you intend to do that?"

"I'm working on it." Janet twisted at the bindings around her wrists. "These damn things are cutting the circulation off to my hands." Looking at the fading light source by the steps she said, "Don't be offended but you generate too much heat." She shifted slightly away.

"None taken." Charlotte continued to stare at the two girls. "Whatever's going on here, it's centred in that egg factory. Don't you think?" she asked, turning to Janet. "You don't need guns to protect an egg factory. Unless it's …"

"Unless it's super illegal and highly profitable," interjected Janet. "But, right now, my mind is elsewhere, like trying to get out of here." Digging her heels into the dirt floor and pushing backward, Janet slowly eased up the stone wall until she stood on her own. "Phew! I'm sweating like a stuffed pig. Charlotte, can you see if they used zip ties on my wrists?"

Shaking off a drop of sweat that had settled just above her eyelid, she peered around at Janet's wrists. "Yes. So?"

Janet bent over and raised her arms as high as she could behind her back. Then pulling her arms apart with all her might, she came forcibly down on her tailbone. She repeated this action several times until the zip tie snapped.

"Where the hell did you learn that?" Charlotte asked.

"YouTube," she replied, untying the rope around her feet. "Now, let me see if I can find something to free you up."

"You never cease to surprise me, Janet."

"Good! It keeps things interesting that way."

Janet searched the shelves and paraphernalia scattered on the floor throughout the cellar.

"Out of all the choices on YouTube, why that?"

"You know Liz Hartman?"

"Uh-huh."

"It was her daughter, Mikayla. You see, she loved escape tricks. Well, one time when I was babysitting her, she found a whack of them on YouTube and insisted we both try them out. That was one of them. Ah, this should do." She held up a piece of broken glass she found by the steps and returned to Charlotte, cutting through the zip tie that bound her wrists. "I'll leave you to untie your feet." Returning to the stairs, she picked up the light and went over to attend to Jennifer.

After freeing herself, Charlotte joined Janet. "Do you think she'll be okay?" she asked.

"I don't know." Janet looked around the cellar and then nodded toward the other girl. "See how she's doing."

When Charlotte turned her over, she was surprised to find her staring up at her.

"I'm a friend," Charlotte said. "Don't be afraid."

Smiling, Charlotte gently wiped away the girl's hair from her face. When she touched her forearms, she felt her shiver.

"You didn't by any chance come across something when you were snooping about here that I might use to clean up her face," she said to Janet. "She's been pretty badly beaten up."

"Except for these empty potato sacks here, there's not much. But I could take another look around."

"No, they'll have to do."

After rolling up a number of the sacks into a pillow and placing it under Jennifer's head, Janet threw the extras over to Charlotte.

"The girl appears terrified," Janet said. "What's she staring at?"

They followed the girl's line of vision and froze.

Two men stood in the darkness at the top of the stairs.

A Thoroughbred
Bloodhound
Following a Scent

CHAPTER FORTY-FOUR

THE TWO MEN AT the top of the stairs to the root cellar were motionless, their faces cloaked in the shadows.

The heavyset man turned to the leaner one. "I told you we should have kept someone in here to keep an eye on them."

Charlotte's and Janet's attention were drawn to the landing at the top of the stairs as the two men stepped into the dimming light. One of the men was Camilo.

"But they were zip-tied. Who the hell gets out of that?" retorted Camilo.

"Apparently *they* did."

"Now what do we do?" asked Camilo, following the other man down the stairs.

"The obvious—we secure them." Descending the stairs, he took a wad of gum from his mouth and flung it at Janet. "Shit."

"Nice try, asshole. Too bad you missed." Janet scrutinized the man who had just thrown the gum, detailing every characteristic. "Well, if it isn't little dung and big dung."

"Big dung is one of KemKor's finest," Charlotte said caustically, "Chris Stedman."

"Now, Charlotte, I've heard that name before. Refresh my memory," Janet said. Her fists were clenched as she faced Chris and Camilo.

"He's KemKor's head of security," Charlotte said mockingly.

"Ah! I remember Edward mentioning the name now. So I guess you *can* say he's a big dung."

Janet stared at the two men, her stance more aggressive as she prepared to lash out to defend herself.

Cautiously, Stedman stepped onto the dirt floor, his Glock primed and at the ready. Camilo remained on the step behind him. "Shut your hole!" Stedman commanded.

Janet ignored him. "Have you got a shoe fetish, Camilo? Is that why you carry Jennifer's runners around your neck? Or, do you just like the smell of female feet? Yummy!"

Camilo lunged toward Janet, kicking out at her.

"Bitch!" he yelled. "No one talks to me like that!"

She felt Camilo's foot graze her cheek, but she evaded the full impact of his blow and latched onto his ankle like a trap, twisting his leg, and forcing him face down onto the dirt floor. Pouncing on him, she firmly placed her knee into the small of his back and swung the red and white runners around so that the tied laces caught him under the chin. She pulled back like reins on a horse while her forefinger and thumb on the other hand dug into either side his gullet. "Drop the damn gun, or I'll rip his gullet out and snap his back!"

"You move pretty quick for an old bat," Chris said. "But are you faster than a bullet?"

He aligned his Glock with her head.

"Fuck! Do what she says!" Camilo screamed out.

Stedman took a step closer to them. "I don't think so," he said. "What will it be, old bitch?"

"Old bitch, am I?" Janet pulled back harder on Camilo's chin and dug her fingers deeper into the sides of his gullet until she heard him gurgle.

"Well done, Chris! Don't give any ground."

Startled by this new voice, Janet relaxed her grip slightly.

Charlotte's and Janet's eyes shifted to the top of the stairs.

Garcia pushed Nadia forward, his knife pressed against her throat. "Chris, get that light from them and put it back here at the bottom of the stairs." Turning his head slightly, he called out behind him. "Juarez, bring another light—a good one—before this one in here burns out. Now!"

Grabbing the back of Nadia's hair, Garcia forced her head backward and carefully eased her down the steps to the dirt floor. "Janet, let my nephew go."

"Janet, he's bluffing! Don't do it!" Charlotte cried out.

Panic consumed Charlotte's body, her eyes locking with her sister's terrified expression, when she realized what she had just said. *What an idiot! I've just gambled with my sister's life.*

Garcia pressed the blade against Nadia's throat, drawing blood.

"No!" Charlotte screamed, rushing forward. Stedman's extended forearm caught her at the neck, sending her to the floor hard and gasping for air.

"Asshole!" Janet yelled. Her arms flung out at her sides like wings while Camilo's head hit the floor with a thud. Pressing her boney knee into his back, she heard a pop as she stood up and went to attend to Charlotte.

Camilo writhed on the floor in pain, screaming a generous selection of profanities.

Garcia's forehead and neck reddened as his eyebrows knitted together. "That wasn't nice, Janet." He glanced at Stedman. "Shoot her."

"Wait! I can reset it! I just need a couple minutes. Don't shoot!" Janet thrust her hands high above her head, waiting for Garcia's reply.

Juarez, who had just entered at the top of the stairs, was accompanied by a shorter individual who stayed well back in the shadows.

Pushing Nadia forward with him, Garcia took up a position beside Stedman and patted his forearm. "A couple of minutes." Then, he nodded toward Janet. "You're on the clock, so you'd better make it quick."

Several minutes passed by as Janet tried to get Camilo to lie still. When he finally did, she quickly corrected her malfeasance.

Carefully, Camilo rolled over onto his back and looked up at her. "God, I hate you, bitch!"

Though his back was still tender, the excruciating pain had gone. Pushing himself to a sitting position, he twisted slightly one way and then the other. Apparently satisfied with the results, he stood up.

"Are you all right, Nephew?"

"Not quite." Bending down, Camilo grabbed Janet by the hair, forcing her face close to his. When she spat on him, he smashed his fist into her face. He was about to kick her when he was pulled back by Juarez.

"Get your fuckin' hands off me! Later, bitch, later!"

Camilo drifted over to where Jennifer lay on the ground.

"Help me!" Charlotte screamed, her arm cradling Janet's head as she knelt beside her. "Please!"

"Juarez, get the first-aid kit out of the house and bring some towels and a bucket of ice."

When Juarez reached the landing at the top of the stairs, he was stopped by the person he had entered with earlier. They spoke to each other for a few seconds before leaving together.

Having no further use for Nadia, Garcia let her go and folded up his blade. "Let's get something straight," he began. "If you don't already know it, right now in this place, I'm god. So don't piss me off! Your lives depend on it. Get it?"

"Mr. Urquiza? What would you like me to do?" queried Stedman.

"Stay here until Juarez returns and relieves you. Then join me in the study. If any one of them so much as twitches the wrong way, kill her first." He pointed at Janet.

At the top of the stairs, Garcia turned and began to survey the cellar floor for anything obvious that could be used as a weapon by either Janet or Charlotte or the young girls. His eyes quickly came to fall upon Camilo, who was kneeling beside Jennifer, fondling her breasts and running his hand up her skirt.

"Camilo! Come with me, now!"

The door behind Garcia opened. Turning, he expected to find Juarez but was surprised to find Andres.

Reluctantly Camilo rose to his feet, and as he brushed by Stedman, he said to him, "Later. I'll enjoy her later." Getting a nod of agreement from him, he continued to saunter toward the stairs, occasionally looking back at Jennifer, who was slowly regaining consciousness.

Camilo's foot had barely touched the first step when Andres flew out of the shadows, slamming him into the ground. The impact knocked his breath out. Andres straddled his brother's chest, pinning his arms down with his legs as he pummelled him about the face and eyes.

Camilo could taste his own blood, and the anger swelled up in him to overflowing. He spat in Andres's face. That split second of surprise was all he needed to give him the advantage as their positions reversed. As he lifted his fist high, his arm was grabbed from behind. He looked back to find Juarez's eyes bearing down on him as he was dragged away from his brother.

"Fuck off! I'll kill the bastard," Camilo yelled out deliriously several times as he tried to get loose from Juarez's grip.

Finally he gave up struggling and peered at his brother on the floor through his swollen eyelids. When Andres rose to his feet and started walking toward him menacingly, he braced himself.

The distance between them had to be just right for maximum impact, and when it occurred, Camilo's foot exploded off the floor into Andres's crotch. He watched with gleeful satisfaction as his brother crumbled to the floor in agonizing pain. "Only the beginning, you little shit! Do you hear me? Only the beginning!" Camilo turned and ran up the steps, pushing by his uncle as he exited into the darkness.

Garcia shook his head in disgust as he looked at Andres writhing on the dirt floor.

"For the moment, Chris, remain here with Juarez. As for my nephew lying there, see what you can do for him." He looked at his watch. "I'd better get back." Reaching behind him, Garcia removed a new roll of duct tape from its hook and threw it down to Juarez. "Use this to bind and gag them. Don't bother tying Carmella or Jennifer. Bring them to the house along with Andres when you're relieved."

Garcia left the room, closing the door behind him.

Stedman sauntered over to Andres, who was now lying quietly on the floor. Assured that Andres was all right and that Juarez had his back, he got up off his knee and crossed the room toward Carmella, who was crawling toward the red and white running shoes.

She looked up at Stedman's broad, toothy smile and smiled back. *Such a small reward for the many times I've serviced you. You understand,* she thought. Still smiling at him, she reached out to the laces that joined the runners.

Stedman ground his heel into her hand.

Carmella's shrieks sent a battery of cold shivers throughout the hell that this root cellar had become.

Charlotte attempted to go to Carmella's aid, but she was restrained by Janet and Nadia.

"Bastard! Fucking bastard! Someday I'll rip that silly grin from your face," Charlotte screamed at Stedman.

"I don't think so," Stedman retorted. "Unless, that is, you can do it from the beyond."

Despair stared back at Charlotte from Janet's and Nadia's eyes. She looked toward Juarez, who had stepped back beside Andres and was whispering something to him, and her adrenalin picked up with renewed hope.

"Hey, Juarez, nice little piece, don't you think?" Stedman called back, nodding toward Nadia. "After we secure these two"—he held up the duct tape and pointed to Janet and Charlotte—"we should have some pussy. Juarez?" When he turned around, the blows came so quickly he had no time to react, one to the temple snapping his head back, the other shattering his windpipe.

Juarez said, "Hurry! There's so little time. Janet, are you able to move? Good! That's your job, Charlotte, to take care of her." Juarez turned toward Andres. "Help me move this piece of shit over there." He pointed to the far corner. "No one should see him until they're well into the room, and by then, it will be too late."

Watching them drag Stedman to the corner, Nadia asked, "Is he ...?"

"You're not going to be bothered by him ever again," Juarez interjected.

Juarez helped Andres cover Stedman's body with empty potato sacks and baskets.

"Charlotte?" Juarez said with a disconcerting look. "Do you know how to handle a gun?"

"I've fired one, if that's what you mean."

Carmella continued to moan.

"That's what I mean." Juarez quickly went to the first-aid kit and pulled out a bottle of water and a couple of pills, helping Carmella to swallow them. "You must keep her sedated until she's safe. As you can see, her hand's severely mangled. Here, take this bottle of water and the rest of the pills from the kit. Charlotte, get Stedman's gun, there on the floor. Kill any sonofabitch that gets between you and freedom. Do you think you can do that?"

She stared at the Glock in her hand for several seconds. "I don't know," she replied. "How else can I answer?"

"There's a strong likelihood you may just have to do that, if you hope to get everyone out alive."

Janet walked over and stood beside Charlotte.

"May I, dearie?" she asked, holding her hand out for the gun. "Unlike you, I've handled weapons most of my life. I've been a hunter and know what it's like to kill a living creature."

"It's not the same," Juarez injected.

"I know it isn't, but I also know I can pull the trigger when I have to."

Charlotte handed the Glock to Janet.

"Let's hope you don't have to and the cavalry gets here in time," Juarez said.

"Cavalry?" Nadia asked.

"If everything is still on schedule, this place will soon be crawling with cops," Juarez replied.

"Wouldn't it be safer for us to just wait it out until it happens?" Janet queried.

He replied, "Things always have a tendency to get fucked up. No, I think it's better to get you all out of here now." He glanced over at Andres, who was kneeling beside Jennifer. "Andres, are you ready? Have you got your story straight?"

Andres smiled back at him and nodded as he helped Jennifer to her feet. "Nadia, do you mind?" Carefully he handed Jennifer over to her. "It will only be for a moment."

"What's this about keeping your story straight?" Nadia asked, manoeuvring her arm under Jennifer's to brace her up.

"Later," Andres replied, turning around and reaching into the front of his pants.

"Hey!" exclaimed Janet and Charlotte in unison.

Turning back, his face beaming, Andres held up a scrotum guard, which he flung into the corner beside Stedman's body. "Considering the number of times I've been kicked in the nuts by my brother, I decided a long time ago to protect myself and feign the rest." He regained his position beside Jennifer.

Janet muffled her laughter. "The way you writhed on the floor sure fooled me," she said.

"Jennifer, can you walk on your own?" Juarez asked.

"I can stand on my own. I'm all right, really!" she reassured them.

"Good," he replied.

Picking up Carmella, Juarez carried her toward the steps. "We haven't got much time."

Andres ran up the steps, opened the door and disappeared through it. A few moments later he returned. "It's clear, but we'd better move it."

"We're heading for the pickup parked just outside. Once under the tarp in the back, lay perfectly still—not a word. Andres will know what to do once the time comes."

Juarez quickly ascended the steps. Once Juarez and Andres had finished arranging the tarp over the five women, they strategically placed cartons containing eggs and cages with hens in them in the flat folds of the cover.

"Remember, not a word or any movement!" Juarez said to the girls. "You'll be out of here soon." And he closed the gate on the truck.

"What are you doing out here? Aren't you supposed to be inside?" Camilo asked, stepping out of the shadows.

Andres began to step away from the truck and walk toward his brother.

"No, Andres," Juarez whispered to Andres, "I'll take care of this." As he walked toward Camilo, he called out over his shoulder, "Andres, head off to the Thornton farm, pronto! Just hightail it back here once it's done. Now, get going."

"Hey, hold the fuck up on that! He's not going anywhere. You heard my uncle earlier." Camilo picked up his step toward Andres but stopped when he realized that Juarez had positioned himself between him and his brother. "Anyway, why are you out here at all?" Camilo asked.

"What's the big deal, Camilo?" Juarez inquired. He carefully approached the boy so as not to alarm him, his hands waving expressively in front of him. "Stedman and I haven't been relieved yet. It will only take but a few minutes for your brother to deliver this and return."

Juarez glanced back at Andres and wanted to call out to him. *Get in the damn truck and leave!*

"What's this?" Camilo pointed toward the truck.

"Eh?" Juarez pretended not to understand his query as he continued to move closer to Camilo. *Leave, Andres! You mustn't see what I'm about to do.*

"What's he delivering?"

Camilo moved toward the side of the truck, where his brother stood.

"Eggs, some chickens, that's all." *Shit! Stay put, Camilo,* Juarez thought.

"Can't it be delivered tomorrow?" Camilo slowly moved along the side of the truck, his hand surfing over the tarp, boxes and cages.

"Get off it!" Juarez interjected. He changed direction to come up behind Camilo.

Looking back at Juarez, Camilo retorted condescendingly, "I'm not asking you."

Camilo turned his attention back to his brother. "Well, what's the rush? Why not tomorrow? Tongue tied? That's not like you." He turned around and faced Juarez. "Anyway, shouldn't you be heading back?"

"I thought you might want to come along. Stedman's probably got Nadia well greased by now, if you get my drift."

A smirk curled at the corner of Camilo's mouth. "I'm not used to seconds."

"So are you saying no?" A broad smile erupted on Camilo's face. "Then, let your brother do his business, and come with me." Juarez was about to walk back to the root cellar with Camilo when he noticed that a figure had come round the corner of the house and was walking toward them. *Shit!*

"Juarez?"

The person was small in stature, his stride exuding confidence. Unfortunately for Juarez, it was an outline of someone he was all too familiar with. "Antonio?" He looked at the truck and saw movement under the tarp—sizeable movement. *Fuck!* Quickly taking up a position beside Camilo, he wrapped his arm around his shoulders and, though the boy resisted, he steered him away from the truck toward Antonio.

"Camilo. Andres. To the study," Antonio commanded.

Camilo looked back at his brother.

"If you think what happened earlier is finished, little brother, you're sadly mistaken."

Antonio clipped Camilo up the back of his head. "Not like a snail, like a rabbit."

As Andres was about to pass him, Antonio reached out and grabbed him by the arm. "What were you doing there by the truck?"

"I—I was—taking eggs—chickens to the Thorntons."

"Thornton?"

Antonio noticed that Camilo still lingered. Still holding his grip on Andres, he turned and kicked Camilo, striking him in the thigh and hip. "Go! Now!" When the screen door slammed against its frame, he turned back to Andres. "Now, who or what is Thornton?"

"They're on the next concession." Andres wanted to pull away but knew better.

Antonio drew Andres closer. "Who told you to do this?"

"I—it was ..."

Clearing his throat, Juarez stepped forward. "I guess that was me."

Antonio released his hold on Andres. "You?"

"I didn't see the harm. Our relief hadn't arrived, and everything was secure in there," Juarez continued, thumbing over his shoulder to the root cellar. "I thought the timing was right." Glancing over Antonio's shoulder, he saw Charlotte's head momentarily peering over the tarp before disappearing under it again. *What in god's name is she doing?*

Antonio folded his arms across his chest, the index finger of one of his hands tapping against his lips. "Hmm. How long would it take you to deliver this and get back here, Andres?" he asked, pointing to the back of the truck.

Andres kicked at the ground a couple of times before answering. "Fifteen minutes, tops."

"Let me have a closer look." Draping his arm around Andres's shoulders, the two slowly began to walk toward the back of the truck.

"Antonio?" Juarez said.

Antonio dropped his arm from Andres's shoulder and turned around. "Is there a problem?"

"I've already checked the truck. That's one of the reasons I was out here."

"One of the reasons?"

"Well, we can talk about that once the boy's gone." The corners of his lips curled up into a smile. "Anyway, right now the kid's on the clock." He pointed to his watch.

"I suppose you're right. But then again ... No, forget it." He ruffled Andres's hair. "Get out of here, but make it quick. Let's see if you can make it back here in 10 instead of 15.

Opening the door to the cab, Andres climbed in behind the steering wheel and turned the key in the ignition. He was about to back out when a black Lincoln Navigator pulled in behind him. *Shit! They must be the relief.* Juarez and Antonio had already disappeared from view on his passenger-side mirror as he heard them greet the new arrivals. The maple tree ahead of him made an exit difficult but not impossible. *It must be now!* Putting the truck into drive, he slowly eased forward, picking up speed as he passed the old maple. Sharply he turned the steering wheel, the truck just missing the corner of the root cellar, and he pressed down on the accelerator, causing the backend to weave and kick up dirt and stone as its wheels hit the gravel drive. He fixed his eyes ahead as he passed the three men standing by the Navigator. When they were finally in his rear-view mirror, he breathed deeply as he turned onto the long drive leading to the main road. Once on the main road, he and Juarez had discussed what he had to do next.

"Why's the kid in such a hurry?" asked Doug Irwin as he stepped out of the Navigator. He flicked off the ash from his cigar. "Wherever he's going, I sure hope he makes it."

"He will," Antonio replied, smiling, as the passenger door to the Navigator swung open and the other man gingerly stepped out. "Ken, I'm so pleased to meet you again." He wrapped his arms around him. "We will have some Aguardiente and talk once our meeting is finished. Right now, you and Doug go with Juarez." He looked at his watch and then absently glanced at the drive Andres had just torn along. Watching the three of them heading toward the root cellar, he called out. "Juarez!"

"Yes, Antonio?"

"Make this transfer quick. I want you and Chris in the study pronto!"

"Got it!"

As Antonio walked back to the house, he pulled out his phone from its clip on his belt and pushed in a number. "Gervasi!"

"Yes, sir!"

"There's a truck heading your way."

"I see its lights."

"Stop it and check its contents."

"Anything else?"

"Call me only if you find something." Putting his cell away, Antonio opened the screen door and headed down the hallway to the study.

As Juarez walked back toward the root cellar, Doug stepped in front of him while Ken stayed behind.

"Hey! We're not running a race here!" Juarez said. Riled by Doug's unexpected insertion in front of him, he knew he was losing control of the situation and had to act quickly. When he attempted to step to one side, he was discouraged by Ken. *This is not good*, he thought. Stopping, he looked at both men warily.

"What's going on?" Juarez asked. *I must get them inside!* he thought.

"Going on?" Ken rejoined. "Nothing's going on. Is there anything going on, Doug?"

"Nothing that I'm aware of," Doug replied.

Juarez gauged his foes. *Doug's a known factor. His poor conditioning and reflexes won't be a challenge for me. But, this other guy's a whole different story.* His trained eyes scanned Ken's lean and muscular physique for weaknesses and came up empty. *This is really not good.* "Tell me, Ken, what are those tattoos about?" he asked, pointing to the tattoos that filled Ken's arms to his shoulders. *Damn! I need time to think this out.*

"What's it to you?" Ken retorted.

"Just askin'."

"You'll know soon enough," Doug piped in, pulling Juarez forward.

"Know? Know what 'soon enough'?"

Doug opened the door to the root cellar and pulled out his Glock. "That we know you're a fuckin' cop."

Janet and Charlotte were trying to administer a sedative to a very reluctant Carmella when Jennifer alerted them that the truck was slowing down. When the truck stopped and she heard men's voices, Charlotte placed her hand over Carmella's mouth to keep her quiet. "Janet, we must keep her still and quiet," she said in a hushed tone.

Flanking her on either side, the two of them wrapped a leg around one of Carmella's to prevent them from moving, while Charlotte tightened her hold across Carmella's mouth to muffle her moans and keep her head still.

Janet tightened her grip on the Glock at her side. *Kill any sonofabitch that gets between you and freedom.* Juarez's comments kept playing over and over in her head. Profuse beads of sweat dropped off her forehead as she waited. At first, it appeared that only one person had stopped them—someone by the name Gervasi.

The gate on the truck was unlatched and dropped.

Janet braced herself as the crates on top of them were removed and the tarp covering them was pulled back.

Adrenalin exploded in Janet's body as she tightened up, all her senses directed to the men in front of her. When she started firing she didn't stop until her gun was empty.

Gunshots and automatic weapon fire echoed in the distance.

It was now or never. Juarez swung around to find Ken facing in the direction of the shot. Juarez grabbed his head and twisted it sharply, snapping his neck. From the corner of his eye, he saw Doug raise his gun, and he swung around, pulling Ken in front of him as he fired. He thrust Ken's body at him, and as Doug tried to recover, Juarez turned with a high roundhouse kick, catching him with full impact on the chin. Doug fell like a stack of potatoes. Rushing forward to finish him off, he quickly realized that the coup de grace had already been delivered. His kick had broken his neck. The house and its perimeter were alive with activity as he lifted Ken's body over his shoulder. Stepping over Doug, he reached down and latched onto the back of his T-shirt, pulling his body along to the open door of the root cellar. He dumped Ken's body over the rail of the landing and onto the dirt floor, and he turned to retrieve Doug when a bright light blinded him. His hand was reflexively in the motion of shielding his eyes when the shot rang out.

Janet barely heard her gun firing or the automatic weapons that sprayed the cab of the truck.

The whole incident took eight seconds.

She didn't know how long it took, and she didn't care. Time had stalled, or nearly so, and was now jettisoning her back to its normal state. She heard and felt her rapid heartbeat and breathing as she dropped her weapon at her side and sat up.

She had shot the man who was on the cell phone in the face. Two other men lay on either side of him, T-shirts crimson against their chests.

Tears formed in the corner of her eyes as she looked away and began to shake. Jennifer put her arms around Janet and let her cry into her shoulder.

Charlotte, who had jumped off the truck when the shooting had stopped, was reaching through the driver's side of the cab searching for a pulse in Andres's neck. He was covered in blood. *Thank god!* Carefully she opened the door and slid him across to the passenger side while applying pressure to his chest wound.

"Help!" she screamed. "Please, help!"

Janet pushed away from Jennifer when she heard Charlotte's cries for help. "Keep an eye on her," she told Jennifer and Nadia, pointing at Carmella.

Ignoring Janet's request, Jennifer leaped off the back of the truck along with Janet and ran to the passenger side of the truck.

"Jesus! He isn't …?" Jennifer cried out.

"No! Get in here!" Charlotte screamed.

Vehicles were already visible along the route from the farm.

Janet ran to the driver's side, clambered in and restarted the truck. When she looked into the rear mirror, she tensed. The headlights were closer than she thought. Then, out of nowhere, a figure crossed her line of vision. "What the hell's that?"

Charlotte soon had her answer when she looked through the broken rear window. It was Carmella running barefoot through the field in the direction of the approaching vehicles.

"Where's my sister?"

Jennifer jumped out of the cab, ran to the back and climbed in. "She's okay! She's just dazed."

Nadia was lying partially under the tarp with a bloodied nose.

"Hang on, I'm about to take off," Janet yelled out. Gritting her teeth, she floored the accelerator.

The truck lunged forward like a racing greyhound, its rear end fishtailing as it hit the gravel road to Markdale. Within minutes the road behind and in front of them was filled with sirens and flashing lights of police cruisers.

Janet looked over at the earnest look on Charlotte's face as the younger woman continued to apply pressure to Andres's chest wound.

As the police cruisers sped by, Janet pressed even harder on the accelerator until she could go no farther.

Flashing lights from the police roadblock momentarily blinded her, and she brought the truck to a skidding stop.

The police ran forward, guns drawn.

"Hold on! We're not the bad guys. They're back there," Janet pleaded.

Getting to her feet, Jennifer stood up in the back. "Dad?" Quickly jumping off, she ran to the front of the truck and embraced the man who had just stepped out from behind the lights.

While Blackwell and his daughter hugged, Leonard Palladin supervised the paramedics who were taking Andres from the truck to the ambulance. Placing Charlotte and Janet in a cruiser, he directed the driver to follow the ambulance. Another law enforcement officer went along to take their statements.

Carmella scurried across the lawn to the side of the farmhouse. Pressing close to the wall to stay well within its darkness, she made her way along it until she could get a clear view of the root cellar. The door to the root cellar was open. What little light emitted from the cellar defined the outline of a body lying near its door. Taking in several deep breaths, she clenched her teeth as her hand throbbed with pain. She held it up close to her chest, as if it were in a sling, hoping to relieve its pulsating agony. Though she heard voices, they were distant. The lighted house was empty.

She quickly traversed the distance to the root cellar and, stepping over the body, closed the door behind her. She was pleased to find that she was not in darkness. A lamp, hanging from a nail on each of the two wooden pillars, provided the light source. Her eyes scoured the dirt floor, looking for the treasure that drove her to return. *They're still here!* She bolted down the steps, missing one and almost falling. With her good hand, she hooked her fingers under the tied laces that joined the red and white kangaroos and held them to the light, like a jewel appraiser examining a precious diamond. *I must wear them, now!*

For Carmella they weren't just a pair of shoes. They represented a way of life and family she never had. Though she knew nothing of Jennifer and her parents, those shoes had become a fixture in her mind for the imaginary home that nourished the unconditional love and security for which she hungered. They represented the perfect family and the world she believed existed and wanted so badly to be a part of. In her home she would not be a thing; she would be a significant person to its life rhythms. She would be loved and wanted for no other reason than herself. And it was for that, and that alone, she had returned to reclaim the red and white Kanga-ROOS: to keep her dreams alive.

She worked earnestly with her good hand, her blouse and skirt acting as a cloth to clean the dust and dirt from each shoe. Satisfied that she had done her best, she sat on the floor and, using her teeth and good hand, began to work at undoing the knot that joined the runners. As she worked on the knot, her eyes casually scanned the room. Suddenly she stopped what she was doing and focused on an area in the far corner. The knot came undone, and the runners fell to the floor as she stood up. She walked over to the disarrayed baskets and potato sacks. *Where is he? I know he was dead. This was where they put him.* Panic chilled her spine. *Whoever took Stedman is coming back. That's why the lights are on.* She hastily returned to the location where the red and white shoes lay, and she flopped on the floor, placing her feet into the runners. She tried to tie the laces, but without the use of her other hand, she found the task impossible. Any attempt to use the hand that Stedman had crushed with the heel of his boot was met with excruciating pain. Since the runners fitted snugly, she decided to tuck the laces down each side of the shoe. Wood softly splintered behind her. She froze to her position as she heard the creaking sound of feet pressing down on each step.

"Well, well, Carmella. I thought I'd never see you again. Let me help you tie your runners." Camilo came round to face her. Kneeling down, he pulled out the laces that had been tucked in from one runner and tied them in a bow. Then he repeated the same for the other. "There! "

She had seen that sinister smile from him and others too often. *No more!* Her mind screamed out.

With her good hand, her fist caught him squarely in the eye and he fell back. The thrust of her foot pounded into his chest. She scrambled to rise but fell back. She attempted again and made it to her knees. She frantically shuffled across the floor toward the steps and the railing, hoping to use it to pull herself up. She had hardly begun when she felt his grasp around her ankle. Flailing out at him with her other foot, she was unable to find her target as he pulled her back across the floor.

"Camilo! What the fuck are you doing?" Garcia rushed down the stairs and pulled him away, slapping him about the face and head. "Leave her! We must get out of here—now!"

When they were gone, Carmella made her way up to the landing.

As she peered outside, she saw a helicopter land on the back lawn and a number of black outlines exiting from it. The commotion from flashing lights and sirens polluted the usual stillness of the night, and she decided that this was her time to escape. Something touched her leg, and she looked down. The blood-splattered head of the man she thought was dead looked up at her, calling out her name. She cringed, backing away in horror. "I don't know you. Who are you? Stay away!" He said something to her in Spanish. "What did you just say? Say it again?" she implored him in Spanish. She did not get a reply. "You must open your eyes and tell me!" Still, there was no reply. The commotion of people and squad cars had picked up and she knew that her time had come; it was either now or never. She disappeared into the darkness, the red and white Kanga-ROOS securely on her feet.

After being questioned by Natasha Brant, Janet and Charlotte left the Owen Sound General Hospital early next morning. Though Andres had survived the operation, he had lost a lot of blood and was still listed in critical condition. Charlotte decided to go back to Janet's and try to get some sleep while they waited for an update on the boy's condition.

CHAPTER FORTY-FIVE

TWO EVENINGS HAD PASSED since the raid on the Green Farm. Earlier in the day, Edward had driven Charlotte back to the hospital with the hope of learning something about Andres's condition, but they left four hours later without so much as an encouraging word.

The curtain above the kitchen sink slapped furiously against the frame. Heavily sodden with water from the rain, the curtain hung heavy and still when Edward closed the window. Gathering some paper towels from its holder by the sink, he mopped up the water on the counter and floor and threw the pulpy mush into the waste receptacle. He placed extra paper towels under the curtain to catch the drips.

Lightning rolled across the atmosphere in tune with rolling waves of thunder as large splats of rain pounded against the windows and roof. Boughs snapped by the wind's strength were sent racing into the fields. Branches of trees thrashing about in the wind scraped the sides of the house like fingernails across a chalkboard.

A damp coldness spread across the back of Edward's shoulders as he watched the fury through the window and shivered. For a split second, he thought he saw the reflection of someone moving in his office. Startled, he quickly turned around.

It's lightning playing tricks with my eyes, he thought The lights flickered as a jagged bolt of lightning ripped through the night sky. *Damn, I'm soaked!*

Unbuckling his pants, he hopped on one foot and then the other as he removed his wet jeans. Then, flinging his pants over his shoulder, he went to the bedroom looking for a dry and cozy replacement.

Wearing a tracksuit and closed-toe sandals, he headed to the kitchen in search of something to eat but stopped on the way at the liquor cabinet in the living room for a scotch. Drink in hand, he continued on to the kitchen.

Another burst of lightning pierced the night sky, and the lights in the kitchen and living room flickered.

He opened the side cupboard and took out the jar of peanut butter and put it on the counter beside him. Then he picked up his scotch and sipped it as he looked out the window. His mind drifted back to Karen and the puzzling "what if" discussions that had begun about a year after he took on his position at KemKor. Often, those discussions popped up out of nowhere. They were the kind of "what ifs" that ranged from death to having an affair and to going through a divorce. In other words, they were heavy, mind-blasting discussions, and he remembered how much he hated them. He reflected on the brief period before her accident when the "what if" was pushed beyond his endurance. He wondered if she was having an affair and whether this was her way of testing the waters. Not able to stand it anymore, he had finally come right out and asked her. *That was two weeks before her accident,* he recalled. She had just laughed at him and brushed his query aside. *Still, she had been pregnant. And she had never told me. Why?* He scratched the side of head and took another sip from his glass. *Why would she keep something as important as that from me?*

Breathing deeply, he put his glass down and stared long and hard at his reflection in the window. *Unless ... It wasn't mine.* It tormented him that he would never know. He swept his hand across the counter, smashing his glass against the side of the sink. Emotionally numb with the thought, he stared at the broken glass in the sink. Finally when he looked up, his eyes focused on the mirage-like quality of a reflection in the window. It was John Elkhart standing in his office doorway. He closed the curtains and for a moment didn't move.

"John, I don't remember: Do you take your scotch with or without ice?" he called out.

"Just a little water," John replied, stepping into the office doorway.

"You don't need that," Edward said, nodding in the direction of the gun in John's hand as he went to the liquor cabinet for a bottle of Ardmore and two glasses.

"Let me decide that."

Edward returned to the kitchen and put the bottle and glasses on the counter. He watched as John walked toward him and stopped short of entering the kitchen.

John continued to point the gun at Edward as he adjusted a large manila envelope under his other arm.

"How much water?" Edward asked.

"Just a spurt." He watched Edward head over to the tap and back. "Place it here." He pointed to the end of the table closest to him. "Now, if you don't mind, I'd appreciate it if you'd take your drink and sit at the far end."

Edward placed the scotch bottle in the centre of the table and sat down.

"I've always liked this table. Mennonite, isn't it?" John pulled out the chair and sat down, placing the envelope to one side.

Edward nodded. "Do you have to keep pointing that thing at me?"

"I guess not. I feel safe enough now." He placed his gun on the table. "You look like shit, Eddy."

A car door slammed. Edward's and John's attention froze. Hurried footsteps across the front porch stopped as the person rang the door bell several times and hammered at the door.

Grabbing his gun, John took up a position behind the partial wall leading to the living room beside the front door. He peered through the curtained side window and began to smile.

"Open up the goddamn door. I'm getting soaked," Charlotte yelled, pounding on the window before returning again to press the door bell.

"If I were you, Eddy, I'd do what Charlotte asked." He slipped his pistol into the pocket of his hip-length leather jacket.

Edward got up and opened the front door.

When Charlotte entered, she began to batter Edward about the head and shoulders with a soggy, doubled-up newspaper she had used for an umbrella. "You sure took your time about it," she said petulantly, glaring at him. "Where can I lay out this newspaper to dry? There's something in it I want you to read."

Not waiting for an answer, she headed for the roll of paper towels beside the sink and, unfastening it, returned to the table to layer sections of paper towel between the pages of the newspaper, to help it dry out.

Walking over to her, Edward softly placed his hands on her shoulders.

"Have you heard anything further about Andres?" he asked.

With a forlorn sigh, she tried to smile as she shook her head no and continued to insert the paper towels between the pages.

After the last two pages of the newspaper were done, she turned to face Edward. "Oh, John!" she exclaimed, flabbergasted, looking at Edward and then John, then back at Edward. "I thought we were alone," she said to Edward.

"That's what I was just about to tell you."

Charlotte looked down at the puddles of water forming around her. "Well, you two, I'll have to change into something dry and hang these up somewhere before socializing further," she said, indicating her dripping wet clothes. Turning to Edward, she added, "Have you got something I can put on?"

Edward took in a deep breath before answering. "There are a couple of boxes at the back of the closet in the bedroom. You may find something there." Charlotte looked at him with a puzzled expression. "They were Karen's. And, it's all right. Unless you're uncomfortable doing that? Otherwise, check through the drawers until you find something of mine that works."

"I'll stick to rummaging through the drawers, please and thank you." She headed off to the bedroom and shut the door.

John turned to Edward. "I hope she won't be long. There's not a lot of time."

"What do you mean?"

"Be patient. We'll wait for Charlotte."

Ten minutes later, Charlotte appeared from the bedroom in an oversize cotton red tracksuit with a double white line running down both the arms and legs. She wore floppies on her feet. Her hair, normally in a ponytail, hung loose to let it dry.

"Have you got something I can hold these pants up with?" she asked Edward.

"I've got some string in the kitchen, if that will do."

"I guess it will have to. Where is it?"

"The set of drawers over there. Third from the top."

After she had tightened and bowed the string around her waist, she returned. She was pleased to see that Edward had put a bottle of honey brown ale on the table for her.

"I feel like the rabbit that's arrived late for the Mad Hatter's tea party. What's going on?"

She took a swig from her bottle and sat down beside Edward at the far end of the table from John.

Edward said dryly, "Your guess is as good as mine. Since he's got the gun, it's his show."

"A gun!" Charlotte exclaimed. John took it out of his pocket and placed it on the table beside the manila envelope. "Do you really think you need that, John?"

The lights in the kitchen flickered as the battery-driven wall clock's minute hand slipped into the next position.

Holding up his gun, he dropped out the magazine before ejecting the bullet in its chamber. "Does that help?" He put both magazine and bullet into his pocket.

"It still doesn't explain why you needed it," Charlotte said. She let go of Edward's arm and sat more relaxed in her chair.

"I'm hoping you'll understand once I've told my story. Maybe once it's finished, you'll forgive me." He moved to the middle of the table opposite the front door and directed them to sit opposite him. "Thanks, Charlotte, for not giving up Juarez."

"How is he? Is he all right?" she asked. "You know, if it wasn't for him, I wouldn't be here now—and neither would Janet, Jennifer or my sister."

"Quite frankly, I'm not sure he made it." John shifted forward in his seat. "Look, Edward, Charlotte as well as Janet knew that Juarez was a RCMP agent. He informed them the day the girls went looking for your Wrangler, and it was confirmed by Blackwell later. I don't know the whole story of what Blackwell told you, but I do know he wasn't aware of me."

Edward took a drink of his scotch. "I feel like my charter flight just flew off without me."

Unclasping his hands, John sat back in his chair and let out a long sigh. "Like Juarez, I've been under deep cover, too. Maybe too long. I work for a different agency than he does. At the moment, my agency thinks I've gone rogue—stepped over to the wrong side of the track."

"Why are you here?" Charlotte asked. "Surely you haven't stepped over? Or have you?"

John pondered her question before answering. "Sometimes, you have to do things—nasty things." He stared at his scotch glass as he tilted and swirled it about. "Edward, whether you know it or not, you're going to be a key witness in the upcoming trial. And what I'm about to give you is going to expose a major criminal activity and destroy more than a few reputations."

"Hang on here, John. Why me? Aren't you or Juarez going to testify? It makes more sense that way."

"Under normal conditions, I would agree. But these aren't normal conditions."

"How are they not normal?" Edward asked. "You've got the bad guys, you lay out your evidence during trial and voila, the bad guys are behind bars. C'est fini."

"Believe it or not Edward, West Grey is only a very small part of a much bigger organization that stretches all the way to our capital in Ottawa, and beyond. For example, when I arrived here tonight, I had no way of knowing what had been said to you. There's a cruiser sitting at the entrance to your drive with two cops in it, supposedly assigned to protect you."

"Supposedly?" Edward asked, feeling disturbed.

"Yes, supposedly. In West Grey this crime syndicate includes members of that same police force sitting out there protecting you. I just don't know if the two guys sitting out there are part of it. But I can tell you that a number of their informants are planted in policing organizations right across Ontario and well beyond this province's boundaries." He pushed the manila envelope toward him and sat back in his chair. "I've invested too much of my life to give up now. I'm that close to breaking it wide open. I can't give up my cover! I've reached too high up in this organization to call it quits."

"But, what do your superiors say? Don't you have to march to their tune?" asked Charlotte.

"And if they're out of tune, what do you do then? Bottom line is, if I show up for trial, my cover is shot and the higher ups in this crime syndicate go unchecked."

"At least you get these guys. Maybe you should be satisfied with that," Edward suggested.

"Maybe. But the big fish are so close to being netted—provided I can stay alive long enough to reel them in." He sat forward in his chair. "In that envelope is a folder that contains enough hard documentation to shut down this part of their operation and put the bad guys behind bars for an awfully long time. That's the good part of this story." Hesitating, he cleared his throat. "Also in there, in a white envelope, there is a bad part that has the potential to destroy you, Edward. Hopefully, you'll choose wisely about what to do with it." John sighed and took a sip of his scotch before continuing. "As you know, Edward, life's not always a stroll through a meadow. The trouble with living in a world of lies is that you may go ahead, but you can never go back."

"I'm not sure what you mean," Edward replied.

"Unfortunately for you, the evening you discovered that Building 3C was being used ... Well, that's when you were dragged in unawares into my world. In that envelope there's something that affects you directly. The unscrupulous bastards we nabbed had other plans for it. Now, it's up to you to decide its fate. The DVD's in this envelope are recordings of what has already happened; it can't be changed. But it can change you. How it changes you, depends on your choices." Sitting back in his chair he took in both of them. "You've got a smart girl there to help you choose wisely. Hopefully, you'll make good use of her."

Silence fell like a curtain between them.

"Before I leave," John continued, "I promise to give you the name of a person to talk to. He is expecting you. The envelope will also have the name of a motel written on it. You can either do nothing or view the contents of the envelope. It's up to you. I hope you chose wisely." He straightened up and smiled precariously. "Right now I need yours and Charlotte's attention."

Pulling out a folder from the manila envelope, he removed the elastic band around it and fanned through its contents before looking back up at them. Then, turning the manila envelope upside down, he dumped out the small white envelope.

As he inserted the white envelope into his jacket pocket, he said, "You'll get this before I leave."

John looked at his watch before he continued. "What I'm about to tell you must be shared only with Assistant Attorney General Thomas L. Robarts and no one else. He is expecting you. If you have any concerns or problems after I leave, speak to either Leonard Palladin or Chuck Blackwell."

"Why not the attorney general?" asked Charlotte.

John bit his lower lip. "Please, just do what I told you. In time the rest will fall into place."

"How will Robarts know that this information came from you?" Charlotte asked.

"Before I leave, I will give you something that I know he will find irrefutable."

"'Skill comes so slow, and life so fast doth fly,'" Edward quoted. "It's funny, isn't it? All these years, John, I thought I knew you—and I didn't know a damn thing. Tell me, does Terri know about you or about any of this stuff? Or is she even your wife?" He sat back in his chair, waiting for an answer. "By that pensive look of yours, I think I've already got part of the answer."

John took in a deep breath and looked pensively at his empty glass. "She's my wife—and no, she doesn't."

"You sure do live in a world of lies and deception. How do you live with yourself?" Edward asked.

John pushed his lower lip out as he apparently ruminated over how to answer Edward's question so that he would understand. "I can see, by the way you're now holding Charlotte's hand and looking at her, that you care about her. How far would you be willing to go to protect her? Kill someone? Put your life on the line?"

Edward slowly released her hand as he sat forward and clasped his hands together on the table. "I'd go to the ends of the earth to protect her," he replied.

"Our military and law enforcement agencies do that every day, Eddy. Except they protect hundreds of lives they don't even know to ensure that, for most citizens, their day is full, relatively safe and uneventful. Don't judge me because I haven't told Terri. That's up to her, to judge me when the time comes—not you. I'm pledged to duty, mission and family.

My daily choices are governed by that exact order. No exceptions! You and thirty million like you are damn lucky that I and others like me do this job." Their expressions satisfied him that he had made his point. "Now, let's get started. I don't have much time."

He pulled out a stapled document from the folder. "You've heard of San Vicente del Caguan?" An erudite smile creased John's face. "I bet you didn't know that Camilo's and Andres's dad was the head of the Revolutionary Armed Forces of Colombia—FARC for short—in that region?" he added, surveying the two of them. "No, I didn't think you did. Here's something you may or may not be interested in: five years ago, the Human Rights Ombudsman's Office in San Vicente recorded 17 politically motivated killings and 78 more killings from the surrounding municipalities."

"What's that got to do with the boys?" asked Edward.

"Do either of you read Spanish?"

"I'd like to say yes, but I think you already know the answer to that."

"Oh, how I remember those painful attempts at university, Eddy." A toothy smile filled John's face.

"I do," interjected Charlotte.

"Good." John handed the document to Charlotte.

Moving closer to the table, John continued. "Now, the number of killings was, in all probability, much higher because of the next to impossible ability to gain any information from many of the rural areas. Here's where the kids come in, Eddy. FARC recruits children into their ranks. What these children have done or seen is open to speculation, but it doesn't take much of an imagination to figure it out that Camilo and Andres were probably up to their yin-yangs with FARC because of direct family ties. And that especially goes for their uncle. Now, here's the kicker. Up until five years ago, the international community paid very little if any attention to the area. Then a strange thing happened." He pulled out another document and pushed it toward Charlotte. "A bunch of Iranian officials, said to be meat experts, arrived on the scene with the intention of creating an Iranian-Colombian joint venture for the creation of a meat plant in San Vicente del Gaguan, worth some three million US dollars." He pushed away from the table and began to walk around the kitchen and living room area, looking out the windows.

"What's wrong?" asked Edward.

"I thought I heard something." He looked at Charlotte, who was engrossed with perusing the documents written in Spanish that he had given her.

He located his chair about half an arm's length from the table and sat down opposite them, quietly watching Charlotte as she turned each page.

The clock on the kitchen wall marched out a full minute before John decided to continue.

"The Iranian-Colombian joint venture expected to process 20,000 tons of meat per year. According to US intelligence, not only is it not a meat-producing area, because the cattle are affected by a bovine virus, but the meat-producing centre is on the other side of the country. The key here is that the Islamic Republic was investing in a well-known cocaine-producing region. Let's remember that Iran traditionally gets its meat from Argentina, Ireland, France, Turkey, New Zealand and Australia."

"I'm not sure where all of this is going," Edward said flatly. "That's another world away. How does it affect us?"

"Be patient, Eddy; I'm getting there. According to a statement by Hamid Reza Asefi, the Iranian Foreign Ministry's senior spokesperson, the meat project was being carried out by the Iranian private sector and not the Iranian government. US intelligence and other sources have confirmed that the real reason for this so-called meat centre was to coordinate activities of the FARC and Hezballah to combat American forces in Colombia—and more important, to profit from the cocaine harvest to balance their revenue shortfalls. Surprise, surprise, most of the drugs are brought into the United States via Mexico. Interesting enough, the Iran-backed, Shi'a-based Hezballah has a strong base in Ciudad del Este, at the borders with Brazil and Argentina. Now we've reached the Canadian connection."

The lights flickered in the house as Charlotte stopped what she was doing and looked up.

"Thank you for joining us again," John said, smiling. Coughing a couple of times to clear his throat, he continued. "I'm sure you're wondering how their meat contract fits into all of this. Simply put, the cocaine is marked as meat and sent back to Iran. Then, through a network of Canadian troops, reporters and anyone else they can bribe to act as mules, they shipped it through the back door to North America via Canada. Unfortunately for them and fortunately for us, it met with only limited success. So the problem became how to get it into Canada. You see, they wanted to break away from the traditional route of drug trafficking via Mexico into the United States. As you know, that route had become very messy—too many killings and too much unwanted attention. Around the time the Iranians were negotiating for the meat centre, Josh and Marta Green returned home from their first missionary trip and, soon after, Camillo and Andres joined them. Shortly after that, their uncle Garcia began to make periodic trips to see them."

Scratching his head, he cleared his throat. "A few important things happened during this time: KemKor Pharmaceuticals set up its operation in West Grey, and Garcia Urquiza took over Green's Egg Products, and he not only expanded here in West Grey but also set up a distribution centre in Timmins. I'm sure that at some time, you must have wondered how the Greens were able to grow their business so quickly. I can assure you it wasn't Garcia's acumen for business, if you get my drift."

John stood up, stretched and remained standing. "Now, let's connect the dots. As you are aware, Josh and Marta returned to resume their missionary work but disappeared. Well, a month ago, we found their remains a few miles outside of Ciudad del Este." He began to pace around the kitchen. "Until now, that information has been kept under wraps so as not to set off alarm bells in the cartel. If their operation worked in Canada, it meant that the United States would be sandwiched between Canada and Mexico. Sweet, isn't it, if it works?"

He pulled back the curtain and looked out the window over the sink. "My job, along with Juarez and others, is to make sure it doesn't happen." Eyeing the peanut butter jar on the counter, he looked over his shoulder at Edward. "Do you mind if I have some, Eddy?" Getting no reaction, he opened the cutlery drawer, pulling out a spoon. Opening the jar, he scooped out a heaping spoonful and popped it into his mouth, savouring the bolus of peanut butter before swallowing it. Again he looked at his watch. Pouring himself a glass of water, he washed down the remnants of the peanut butter before continuing. "Here's how it works at the moment. The cocaine comes into Vancouver by container and is then flown by small aircraft across the country, refuelling at the smaller airports along the way. Here's a list of the suspected small airports that Juarez and I have been able to identify." He handed them three sheets from the folder and returned to the counter below the kitchen window. "Because law enforcement has been beefed up along the Mexican border, drug trafficking using the southern routes has become more of a challenge for the cartels. That's why they've looked north to Canada, where the border still tends to be more porous.

"Other than feeding the needs of the local markets, most of the Oxycontin produced at KemKor's ends up in the hands of the small airport owners for trafficking purposes, for the use of their airstrip." John walked back to Edward and Charlotte, who were still sitting at the table, and sat down. "Now, don't forget that this is only a very small piece of a very large pie." He pulled out a photocopied section of a map from the back of the folder. "You probably didn't know, Edward, but KemKor was planning to expand their operation in Timmins."

"Timmins! What the hell for? That's got to be a good 700 kilometres north of here. The market's in the south."

"In a nutshell, it's pretty isolated and police activity is sparse. The cocaine is delivered to the airport in Timmins by small plane, where it is picked up by Green's trucks and transported back to West Grey for processing. These rogue planes are nearly impossible to track when flying at low altitude with their transponders off. The finished product is split into two parts to optimize getting it across the US border. One way the product is taken by Green's trucks back to Timmins, where it is flown out by small plane to Guelph and finally off to Sandusky, Michigan. The other is where its stuffed in cleaned-out eggshells or put in tightly sealed bags and placed at the bottom of egg yolk barrels, and then taken to be sold across the border to specially designated marketplaces and restaurants. How they got the okay to do that, we're still working on."

John pulled out a pen from the inside of his jacket and took out the white envelope from his side pocket. He placed it on the table and began writing something on it. "I sure hope your memory's still like a sponge, Eddy, because if anything should happen to this folder …"

"Nothing will happen to it," Edward interjected.

John wasn't listening as he stood up and slammed the magazine into his gun and chambered a bullet. "What the fuck! Sirens?" he said.

"It was me, John. I'm sorry—I didn't know. I phoned them from the bedroom when I was changing. The newspaper article—" Charlotte pointed to the newspaper drying on the table. "It painted you as a criminal. It said you were dangerous and one of the kingpins of the cartel. It said you were responsible for at least 20 murders. Is it true? Did you?"

John grabbed up the newspaper and quickly perused the article before throwing it on the floor. "I'm not a cartel kingpin. Sit down!" John backed up to the entrance of the office, his gun still pointing in their direction. "On the back of that white envelope, Eddy, is the name of a motel. Just mention it to Blackwell." He continued to back into the room until they couldn't see him but could hear his voice. "If he's the kind of man I think he is, he will fill in the rest. What you do with it after that is your choice. As I said earlier, choose wisely. The rest of your life may very well depend on it."

A cold wind rushed into the kitchen from the office.

"John, are you still there?"

"Yes." His voice was surreal and faint on the wind.

"Karen. Her car accident. What …?"

"My report, beside the folder. Read it."

"John, tell me."

Nothing but a damp breeze and the flapping of curtains emanated from the office.

Edward entered his office and closed the window before he rejoined Charlotte.

Charlotte pulled the folder closer to her and opened it. On top was one half of a torn picture. She looked at it closely. *It looks like Juarez and John.* She glanced at Edward, who was preoccupied reading John's report to notice, and then at the picture again. *I'm to give this old, dog-eared picture to the assistant attorney general? He's gotta be kiddin'.*

Suddenly Edward shouted, "Charlotte, Karen was murdered. Charlotte! Did you hear me? Karen was murdered!"

Barely five minutes had passed since John had left through the window in Edward's office. It was as if the fury of wind and rain had been taken away with him. Distant sirens, once surreal as they undulated through moisture-soaked atmosphere, were now clarion and crisp as they drew nearer.

Charlotte placed her hand on Edward's and squeezed it lightly.

Moments passed until his hold on the document softened, and he looked away, surrendering it to her. Sliding the document toward her, she thumbed back to the beginning of the section Edward had been reading.

> Time: 2200 h
> Date: July 9th
> Location: Boardroom of Advertising Agency Moyer-Hayes and Roussel
> Present: William Rattray(CEO KemKor), Garcia Urquiza (Owner Green's Eggs), Doug Irwin (KemKor-Lab), Chris Stedman (KemKor-Security), an unknown (Darth Vader's voice on Skype) and, me, John Elkhart.

The title of the agenda was "Profit Optimization in a Competitive Marketplace." The title seemed innocent enough until she read the note in the margin. "Purpose: Illegal trafficking of Oxycontin." *Why did they have the meeting at Moyer-Hayes and Roussel and not at KemKor or Rattray's?* As she read on, she soon had her answer.

> Timothy Moyer, Richard Hayes and Rudolf Roussel are not the owners of the advertising agency. For a price (I do not know the amount), they agreed to enter into a contract (non-public) that created the illusion that the company was in their names. As far as Revenue Canada was concerned, they were the only owners. Since the company was far off the radar, it provided a legitimate front for the actual owners, for money laundering and safe meetings. Rattray, one of the owners, had become paranoid of late and insisted that all meetings be only in this location because this conference room and surrounding areas were swept regularly for bugs. Garcia often carried the meetings, so my guess is that he is also an owner. As for the third owner, I'd put my bet on the Darth Vader voice on Skype as the big honcho, since backs stiffened when he spoke. But I'll let the forensic accountants unravel that part of the story.

> Hopefully, Interpol will have tracked the person behind the Darth Vader voice on Skype by the time you read this report.

Police sirens blared along the gravel road and into the drive. When the sirens stopped, car doors slammed, and she could hear Paul Dickenson barking out orders. Time was running short. She knew it wouldn't be long before they barged through the door. Earnestly she flipped through the pages of the report, searching for the poignant passage. Then she found it. It stood out like a sore thumb. A large asterisk highlighted the following paragraph.

> Unbeknown to us, Karen Slocum was in the building at the time of the meeting. We had no idea how long she had stood in the doorway to the conference room before she let her presence be known. According to my watch, that was about 2330. When asked by me why she was at work so late, she told me that she was finishing a project for one of the firm's major clients. I must add, at this point, that the tension in the room was thick enough to cut with a knife. She must have picked up on it too, because she apologized for interrupting us and backed out of the room quickly, closing the door. Silence reigned for a good while after she left. Finally, the Darth Vader voice on Skype asked all of us to leave and wait in the hallway, except for Garcia Urquiza. Ten minutes later, Garcia opened the door, and we continued with our agenda until 0200 (the full report, below).

> I would be remiss if I did not include the following. Late the next evening, after she left work, Karen died in an accident at the intersection of Toronto Street and Main in Markdale when a rear-end collision by one of Greens' trucks pushed her into an oncoming transport, travelling at high speed. I do not believe in coincidence, and I believe Karen Slocum was murdered that evening. The reason is obvious. The witness to the accident was Chris Stedman. The investigators at the scene were well-known to all who

attended that meeting. The police report labelled it as an accident, and our court system, based on *their* evidence, agreed. I believe that as you continue to read my report and review the incriminating documentation, you will agree that there is a need to review this case in particular, and the handling of it by the police present at the site of the "accident."

Boots thundered across the veranda. Then there was silence.

"Charlotte, they can't see it! They can't see any of this!" He forced the white envelope into his pant pocket.

Usurping the document from her grasp, he placed it back in the folder and then slid the folder into the manila envelope. Breaking out in a sweat, Edward's gaze swept the room, looking for an appropriate hiding place.

Suddenly, the doorframe at the lock shattered, and the door exploded open. A man with a steel cylinder battering ram rushed through followed by Paul and two others with guns drawn. Paul motioned to Charlotte and Edward to stay put while his men fanned out throughout the house. When the "all clear" was assured, Paul and the others holstered their weapons. After a short discussion with the men, Paul approached the kitchen table. Behind him, the others left, closing the door as best they could.

Pulling a chair out from the side of the table, Paul dragged it to the door and secured its back under the door knob. "There! That should keep it closed against the wind, at least until it's fixed," he said. Turning, he looked at the two of them long and hard.

"I wished you hadn't dragged it like that." Edward nodded toward the score marks on his wood floor and then to the splintered doorframe. "Who pays for this mess?" he asked.

Not answering, Paul pulled out the chair at the head of the table and, turning it around, straddled it, resting his arms across its back. "Friendly discussion?" he asked, pointing to the empty bottle of beer, the scotch bottle and two glasses. A smile curled at the corner of his mouth. "Edward, I don't mean with Charlotte. I mean with John."

Edward's eye contact with Paul was momentarily broken as Edward noticed Charlotte slide the half torn picture, hidden under her hand, toward her.

"Now, you shouldn't hide things from the police," Paul said, grabbing her wrist and removing the picture from under her palm. "What a dog-eared old photo! And it's been torn in half." He sat back down and examined the photo. "Where did you get this?" The way their eyes skirted back and forth to each other answered it for him. "John?" His lower lip protruded as he hung over the back of the chair and placed the photo on the table in front of him. "What other little goodies did he leave?"

If he had blinked, he would have missed it. Edward's hand gave it away, and his attention was drawn immediately to the large envelope on the table. He shook his head. "You're making it too easy."

When he reached for it, Edward's hand fell on it first. "I can't let you do that!"

"Do what, Slocum?" Glowering, Paul's hand dropped to the grip of his sidearm. He tightly gripped Edward's wrist while keeping Charlotte in place by hooking the toe of his boot around the bottom of her chair.

"What's the matter with you two?" Paul's expression softened. He released his grip on Edward's wrist and pulled his hand away. "I get it, don't touch!" He let out a long sigh and began to chew on the end of his fingernails as he sat in silence with the two of them staring at him. Finally he turned to Charlotte. "Something I just don't get. You see, from my perspective, you two were pretty palsy with John while he was here. So why did you call me?"

"I didn't know he—I read it in the newspaper." She pushed the soggy newspaper toward him. "That's why I came here, to show Edward."

"Go on."

"Not much to add," she continued as Edward pulled the envelope closer to him. "I called you when I was changing out of my wet clothes."

Edward laid his forearms across the envelope and clasped his hands. "I see. But, what changed?" Paul asked, hoisting a brambly eyebrow as he picked at his front teeth with his forefinger.

"Pardon?" Charlotte began to massage her lower neck, the carotid artery pulsating rapidly under her fingers.

"What changed? Something had to have changed after that call to me. You don't just sit around buddy-buddy after a call like that unless you're—"

"Whoa! Now, stop right there!" Edward interrupted. "We weren't aiding and abetting any criminal."

"I think he knows that, Edward," Charlotte said.

The back of Paul's hand ran along his jawline from one side to the other several times until his broad face creased in a smile. "True, I do know that." He picked up the photograph. "Where's the other half?"

"Safe!" Charlotte replied, defiantly. "And I'd bet you'd like to know who's in the other half."

His hard, staring eyes sent chills travelling up and down her spine.

"Where is it?" He pulled out his Glock.

"We haven't got it." She crossed her arms tightly across her chest and looked away.

"Then who does?" He pointed his weapon in her direction.

Turning back to him, she replied, wryly, "Robarts."

"Thomas L. Robarts?"

"That's him," she retorted smugly. "The assistant attorney general."

Paul began to laugh mockingly as he rubbed the slide of his weapon back and forth across the side of his face.

"What's so funny?" they asked simultaneously.

Paul stopped laughing, his face void of expression. "In time. But, right now, I'm interested in knowing why the fuck John left this torn photograph."

The time between them passed in silence.

Finally, Paul's attention was redirected to the envelope Edward was protecting, and a smirk formed at the corner of his mouth. "Shove it this way," he commanded.

Edward's grip tightened on the envelope until Paul pressed his weapon against the side of Charlotte's head. "You wouldn't dare!" Edward yelled.

"Oh, you mean because of the police officers outside? They do and hear what I tell them to do and hear. Is that plain enough?"

Reluctantly, Edward pushed the envelope across to Paul.

Removing the weapon from the side of Charlotte's head, Paul stood up, turned the chair around and sat back down.

Placing his Glock beside him, he dumped the contents of the envelope in front of him. "My, oh my, John has been a busy person." Pouting, he formed a sorrowful expression. "Too bad it's all for naught." He placed his hand on his weapon. "Now, if you two would be so kind as to not create a problem, I'd like to go through this."

They watched as Paul approached each document like a thoroughbred bloodhound following a scent. As he finished with a document, he either flung it on the table or dropped it on the floor beside him.

Looking down, she noticed that the toe of Paul's boot was no longer around the leg of her chair, and she slowly began to slide her chair back.

"Sonofabitch! You fuckin' Judas!" Paul bellowed as he stood up.

Charlotte froze.

Paul's chair had fallen over, and he kicked it into the living room, shattering one of two aqua blue lamps that Karen had bought shortly after she and Edward married.

"Hey!" Edward shouted, half up on his feet.

The men outside hammered on the door frantically and yelled out, "Is everything all right in there?"

Pointing his Glock in Edward's direction, he bellowed, "Sit down!" Walking to the door, he released the back of the chair from under the doorknob and opened it. After a brief discussion with one of the men, he closed the door, securing it again with the chair. Turning, he pointed to the scattered documents on the floor and table with his gun hand. "Charlotte, gather up this shit and put it back in the envelope, including that photo." He began to pace the floor.

When she finished putting everything back into the envelope, she stepped forward and offered it to him. "Just place it there on the table," he demanded, pointing to the head of the table. "Then sit the fuck down."

A momentary cool, damp breeze from the office crossed the back of Edward's neck, and he guessed from Charlotte's reaction that she'd felt it, too.

Secure that there was no threat, Paul took a few strides into the living room and pulled out his cell phone.

"Unless you want the back of your head blown off, drop it!" Elkhart commanded.

He had reentered through the same window he had exited earlier and now stood in the opening to the office.

"Somehow I knew you weren't far off. Nice setup," Paul sneered.

"Nice setup? What the hell's he talking about, John?" Edward's eyes moved wildly between the two men.

Paul said, "Well, you see, Edward, you and Charlotte here were used as bait." Moving slightly to one side, he placed the cell on the coffee table while training his weapon on Charlotte. He turned slightly so as to survey John's position.

"Bait?" Edward clenched his fists.

"That's right! The two of you were just squirmy little worms at the end of a hook," Paul jeered.

"Paul, put the gun down!" John said.

"I don't think so." Paul moved a few steps diagonally so as to have all three in his line of vision. "If your finger even twitches on that trigger, she's dead." He glanced at the chair braced under the door knob. "We've got a bit of a stand-off here, John, don't you think? So, why don't you just relax that finger of yours? No? Well, under the circumstances, I guess I can live with that. Did you get that?" He chortled. "I can live with that."

"Stay away from that door."

"You've always been able to outguess me. Too bad Garcia and Antonio didn't see you for the Judas you are."

John stepped away from the office doorway and farther into the living room.

Paul's grip on his Glock tightened.

"Come no farther, John, unless you prefer messy," he directed, his eyes skipping between Charlotte and John.

"No one wants messy," John replied as he scanned the room with a practiced glance.

"You do know that that report is useless." Paul took a quick few steps closer to the table.

"Not in the right hands." John followed him along the sightline of his weapon.

"Robarts is one of ours."

"Now we know that for sure. Thank you."

"We? Oh, I see." He sighed. "The place is bugged."

John nodded.

Paul moved a few steps closer to Edward and, placing his hand on Edward's shoulder, bent closer to his ear, his eyes constantly swinging between Charlotte and John. "Slide that envelope over here."

Edward swung the envelope up, smashing Paul squarely on the nose, and Paul's gun fired as he slammed backward against the wall, blood gushing from his nose and the wound in his shoulder when John fired. Paul fired a second time in John's direction and readied for a third attempt when his throat exploded into a pulsating, gurgling flow of blood as John fired. Paul hit the floor dead.

"Oh my god! Charlotte!" Edward dived across the table to her. She had been shot below the shoulder, and Edward applied pressure to stop the bleeding.

John had been hit and was lying on the floor facing them when the front door was lifted off its hinges, and Detective James Brant and four SWAT members busted in.

Once the place was secured, the paramedics entered to attend to John and Charlotte before quickly loading them into the ambulances.

Edward wasn't allowed to travel with them in the ambulance, and Detective Brant directed one of his men to drive Edward to the hospital. As he sat beside the police officer following the ambulance, he hoped that the paramedic had told him the truth.

"They'll be all right. They're in good hands."

TIME WILL TELL WHATEVER TIME WILL TELL

Chapter Forty-Six

THE CRIME SCENE TECHS had finished their part an hour before Edward returned from the hospital, and it felt great to slip under the sheets of his own bed.

Edward rolled one way and then the other, trying to sleep. He turned on the light. *Shit, it's 3:20!* Throwing off the covers, he swung his legs over the edge of the bed and rested his head in the cups of his hands. Wearing only boxers, he enjoyed the invigorating coolness of the early morning air. He picked up a novel by Stieg Larsson, *The Girl Who Played with Fire*, from his side table and headed to the living room. After turning on the floor light that hung over his chair, he placed the book on the table beside it and continued on into the kitchen to make a pot of coffee.

There's too much swimming through my mind, too much to think about. He put two extra scoops of coffee into the filter, and closed the lid and turned on the coffee maker. *There! Strong enough to stand a spoon up in it!* His eyes drifted to the bloodstains on the floor. He quickly looked away. *It's been a couple of days since the raid on the Greens' farm,* he thought. All information about it had been closed down tighter than a pickle jar, not so much as a peep in the newspaper, radio, TV or any of the social networks. *It doesn't make sense. Why would anyone clamp down on it this heavily?* He let out a deep sigh.

Deciding to usurp the percolating process, he poured himself a mug and headed back to read the Larsson novel. Soon after sitting down and picking up the book, he gave up and just sat back drinking his coffee.

When the ambulances had reached the Owen Sound General Hospital—40 minutes north of Markdale—both Charlotte and John had been rushed inside. By the time Edward had arrived, they were already in the operating room. Three hours had passed before he learned that Charlotte's operation had gone well and that she was in post-operative care, but he would not be permitted to visit her until further notice. There was no word about John, and none was expected for a few hours. So, Edward decided to go home when Natasha told him she would call him once she knew.

At 4:30 he thought, *Damn it! Call!* An involuntary shiver made him realize how little he had on, and he pulled the throw around his shoulders. *I must be ready for the call. I must!* He glanced back at the clock in the kitchen. *Soon, it has to come soon!* Slowly standing up, he dragged himself to his bedroom to shower and to get dressed.

It was 4:50 when he exited his bedroom. He wore a lightweight blue short-sleeve shirt, faded jeans with a rope belt and sandals. Still there was nothing on his cell phone or home phone message system. Removing the chair from under the handle of the broken front door, he poked his head out. "Have you heard anything from the hospital yet?"

The policeman assigned to him shook his head.

Disheartened, Edward secured the door again. The rain had stopped hours before but the winds were still blustery.

His eyes drifted back to the bloodstains on the floor. *I have to do something!* his anguished mind thought.

He got a bottle of bleach and a scrub brush from under the sink in the kitchen, and he began to scrub earnestly at the bloodstains where Charlotte had lain.

At 5:30, both his cell phone and farm phone rang simultaneously. He rose so quickly from the floor that he neither noticed nor cared that he had knocked over the bleach bottle.

"Edward, get back here," Natasha told him.

With the cell pinned between his shoulder and ear, he headed out of the kitchen, grabbing his spring jacket off the coat tree beside the front door. "I'm on my way."

The police SUV cruiser had barely come to a stop when Edward bolted out of the passenger side, leaving the door wide open, and scurried around the back of the vehicle heading for the emergency entrance of Owen Sound General Hospital. Just inside the entrance Natasha and James Brant accosted him.

"Where is she? How is she?" He began to push his way to Enquiry.

"Slow down, Edward! Catch your breath," James said, grabbing him by the arm and stepping in front of him.

Edward grasped James's shirt with both hands. "Get the hell out of my way!" But James didn't budge.

Natasha softly touched Edward's forearm and got his attention. "Edward, we have to take you to her. You can't get onto the floor otherwise."

Slowly, Edward released his grip on James. "Is she okay?"

"Though she's heavily medicated, she's okay." Putting her arms around his shoulders, she hugged him. "She'll be okay."

"And John?"

Natasha released herself from Edward. Her look was forlorn as she glanced at James.

"He didn't make it." James found it difficult to keep eye contact with him, and for a brief moment he looked away. "You've known him for a long time, too."

They began to make their way down the hall toward the elevators.

"John and I met at university. But after last night, I wouldn't say I knew him. No, I really didn't know him." Edward was surprised with the amount of police presence in the area, and he was about to ask about it when he decided against it. "Now tell me, where is she?"

"She's in Intensive Care, but as I just told you, she's doing just fine." Natasha pushed the button beside the elevator.

"Her mother's with her at present," James said.

"Her mother?" Edward asked, somewhat taken aback.

"Yes. And what an irascible, cantankerous old lady she is! My condolences go out to Charlotte."

James held the doors to the elevator open until Edward and Natasha stepped inside before following.

"Don't you breathe a word of what I just said, Edward," he said, pushing the button for the second floor. "You seemed surprised."

"I am, because her mother has been dead for quite a while."

The elevator stopped on the first floor, and the door opened but no one was there.

"Cripes!" James began to frantically push on the second-floor button.

"Calm down! Other than your earlier comments, describe this person to me." As the elevators doors were closing, Edward listened to James's description of the woman, and he began to laugh.

"What's so funny?" James enquired.

"It's Janet, isn't it, Edward?" Natasha was nodding her head and smiling.

"Yep! And of course, James not being a local, she conned him." When the doors opened, Edward held the button until James and Natasha exited, and then he followed. "What the heck is going on?"

They had walked into a beehive of activity—a medical emergency—as medical personnel rushed down the hall toward the curtained-off area that Janet had just exited. A number of uniformed officers stayed their positions along the hallway, encumbering both the medical team and Janet's progress. The air turned blue with the exchange of harsh words. At the nurse's station across from them, a nurse stared harshly at them as well as at Janet, who was trying to make her way through the melee. Rounding the counter, the nurse came to them and, pointing at the set of double doors, told them in a commanding tone to wait on the other side, in the lounge. She assured them that she would come and get them once everything had settled down.

Though Edward had no intention of taking on this General Patton type of personality, he lingered, enduring her menacing look as he waited for Janet. The doors had already slammed shut on the other two when Janet reached him. He had never held nor been held as tightly as in that moment, oblivious to two more doctors pushing by them. "Is she all right?" he asked.

"Of course she is. She'll be as fit as a fiddle once she's fully recovered. It's Andres they're fighting to save."

"Andres?"

From the corner of her eye, Janet could see the nurse approaching. "I think we'd be wise to vamoose, Eddy, and talk in the lounge."

For a good 15 minutes, Janet spoke to Edward nonstop about the events leading up to Charlotte and her being captured, and their escape from the Green Farm.

Detective James Brant listened intensely while recording it on his cell phone. He seemed surprised that Natasha wasn't recording anything. He looked over at her somewhat askance and shrugged his shoulders.

"I already have it," she said, smiling smugly at her brother.

"When did you do that?" he asked with a hurt expression.

"A couple of nights ago."

"A couple of night ago?"

"Yep. The Agency stationed some personnel in Emergency. We figured that when the shooting started at the Green Farm that this was where the wounded would be sent. Needless to say, everyone was taken by surprise when the ambulance showed up with that wounded kid in it, along with Blackwell's daughter."

"Blackwell's daughter? Is she here now?"

"No. A heavy cloak of secrecy was cast over the whole thing. Twenty-four hours later, after the doctors okayed her, she was sent home under heavy surveillance."

"And I'm just finding out about it now?" He closed his cell and clipped it onto his waist.

"Don't get your feathers in a ruffle, big brother. What can I say? The Border Agency is on top of things like this—and a whole lot of other things you don't know about."

"Get that silly, smug look off your face, sis. No need to gloat. This is neither the time nor the place for that competitive streak of yours." Turning to Janet, he gave her a stern look. "Why did you lie to me earlier?"

"Who said I lied?"

Edward interjected. "Do you mind me butting in to ask a question?" He stood up and moved to the empty seat closer to Natasha and James.

Natasha turned around to face her brother. "James, why don't you pursue that with Janet later, eh?"

"Okay. But don't you think for a moment you're off the hook."

Surreptitiously, Natasha winked at Janet. Then she said, "Go ahead, Edward."

Edward straightened up in his seat. "As you've just said, it's been a couple of days since the raid on the Green property, and what I find perplexing is that there's not been so much as a word about what happened anywhere. Now, in this age of Twitter, Facebook and whatever, I find that outright strange and suspicious. Also, the fact that this hospital is still salted throughout with all kinds of security, uniformed and otherwise—well, I find it more than troubling, I find it outright conspiratorial. So what's going on?" Edward looked back at Janet, who had moved to the chair beside him.

"Hmm. I'm not sure what to say, if indeed I can say anything," Natasha answered.

James glanced at Natasha and nodded. "It's okay, Sis."

"At 3:00 this afternoon, Premier Bolsover and Assistant Attorney General Robarts will make a joint announcement tendering their immediate resignation from office."

"Is that all that happens to them? They resign and walk away from it free?" Edward asked. He looked away from them to the set of double doors.

"Once they step away from the podium and away from public view, they'll be cuffed and taken away," James replied. "Edward, I don't like it any better than you do. If I had my way, they would have been cuffed during the public announcement, for all to see. But their lawyers worked out this deal, and—well what can I say, it's life."

"Lawyers! Let's hope it's not another Homolka-type deal their lawyers worked out," Edward inserted.

"The state should never have done that—but they didn't have all the evidence, and they were just concentrating on Bernardo. A lot of people believed she was as much a deranged killer as he was," Natasha added.

"Well, whatever happens, happens," Janet said. "A lot of things happened in my life that I never understood. But you know something, it always seemed to work out in the end."

A nurse came through the set of doors looking for Edward.

A few moments later, Edward was standing beside Charlotte's bed holding her hand. She had more tubes emanating from her than an octopus had tentacles. He squeezed her hand gently before bending over to kiss her on the forehead.

"Mr. Slocum?"

Edward turned to find the nurse standing just inside the curtain. "Yes."

"We've only just recently removed the respirator, so don't be surprised if she has difficulty speaking. It's only temporary. Just don't tax her."

"I won't." When the nurse left, he turned his attention back to Charlotte, whose eyes were still closed. He brushed a strand of her hair to one side with his hand.

"Mr. Slocum, I'm sorry to bother you again, but I thought you might want to sit down." The nurse passed him a metal fold down chair with padded seat, the kind one often found in church basements for recitals. She smiled. "It's the best I can do."

"That's thoughtful, thank you." When the nurse was about to leave, he quietly called out to her. "Wait!"

She turned and waited for him to continue.

"Andres Green. Is he okay?"

"Are you family?"

"In a way, I guess I'm family. When he came to Canada, I helped him learn English. I'd still like to think we're close."

Taking in a deep breath, she turned and, poking her head out the curtain, looked both ways before she drew her attention back to Edward. "He's okay. It's not unusual to have a few bad spells with someone as severely wounded as he, but he's young and strong. I'd bet my paycheck on it that he'll come through just fine."

"That's great news! Again, thank you."

When she left, he unfolded the chair and, pulling it as close as he could to Charlotte's bedside, sat down. He held her hand, resting his head against the side bars until his hand felt like it was cramping.

"Hey! No sleeping on my watch allowed." Charlotte's raspy voice was barely a whisper as she tightened her grip on him.

"Ouch! Let go!" He stretched his hand a couple of times before stretching across the rails and kissing her full on the mouth. "One thing's for sure, you haven't lost your grip."

"Is that your feeble attempt at a pun?"

"You should rest that voice of yours."

"Then give me another kiss."

After a lengthy embrace, he sat back down. "How do you feel?"

She looked at all the tubes. "Considering? I guess as best I can; just unbelievably sleepy." She tried to move on her side to face him but quickly gave up. "Do you mind? I just want to see your ugly face better."

Edward stood up. "Is that ugly enough? Now rest! You can barely keep your eyes open. I'm not going anywhere."

She nodded and beckoned him closer. "Have you heard anything about Andres?"

"He's going to be all right. Now save your voice. Sleep." He pecked her on the forehead and began to stroke her hair.

She had already drifted off to sleep before he decided to leave.

When he returned to the lounge, a young person, her back turned to him, was talking with Janet, Natasha and James. When she turned around, he could hardly contain himself. "Nadia!"

Chapter Forty-Seven

WITH PILLOWS PROPPED UP behind him in his bed, Edward swirled the ice around in his scotch glass as he waited to catch up with what he had missed earlier that day on the CBC evening news.

He had spent most of the day with Janet, sitting by Charlotte's bedside. Other than brief attempts to open her eyes and incoherent mumblings, she never regained that momentary spurt of energy exhibited when he'd first visited her in recovery. He felt exhausted, not physically but emotionally.

He eyed the white envelope with Blackwell's name written on it, along with the name of a motel. It had been left by John.

It's up to you to decide its fate. What's happened can't be changed but it can change you.

When his cell phone began to vibrate on the side table, he rubbed the edge of his glass back and forth across his lips, trying to decide whether he wanted to pick it up. Taking a drink, he reached over and lifted it off the table. The caller wasn't identified. Against his better judgment, he answered it, saying, "Panella's Pizzeria and Spaghetti House."

He immediately heard laughter from the other end. "Since when did you open up an eye-talian restaurant, Edward?"

"James?"

"Good ear! I didn't think we talked enough for you to know. Natasha and I didn't know whether to see you before or after the evening news. What are you drinking?"

"How did you know I was drinking?"

"By the chinking sound. I assumed it was ice in a glass."

He looked at his glass; the ice had already melted. "How did you ...? Never mind, I just remembered. My house is still bugged. Where are you?"

"We're sitting outside in the car, waiting for an invite."

"We?"

"Yeah, Natasha and me."

Edward swung his legs across the bed and stood up, heading out of the bedroom toward the front door. "I'm removing the chair from under the door knob as we speak." He poked his head out the front door and waved them in. "Hey, James? When's that door going to get fixed, and who pays for it?" He went about preparing fresh coffee for his unexpected guests.

"As soon as you choose the carpenter and send us the bill," James called out, looking at his watch.

"Don't worry about the coffee right now. The TV's in your bedroom, isn't it?" Natasha asked. "The news should be starting just about now. And I'm sure you don't want to miss the replay of the 3:00 resignation addresses of the premier and the assistant attorney general. Eh?"

Twenty minutes later, Edward turned off the television with the remote "Why don't we go into the other room," he said, nodding toward the living room

As he was about to follow Edward, James noticed the white envelope on the bed. Picking it up, he looked at it for several seconds before handing it to Edward. "Expecting guests?" he asked.

"Eh?"

"The name on the envelope, it's a local motel, isn't it?"

"Yes, yes it is. And, no, I'm not expecting guests."

"Hmm. It looks like John's handwriting," James continued.

"John's? Not very likely," Edward replied.

"I guess I could be wrong. Is it advertising then?" James asked.

Edward dropped the package on the side table. "No, just a favour. Would either of you want a drink?"

Natasha elbowed James hard in the ribs. "He's going through enough, James, without you acting like a cop."

James leered at his sister as he rubbed his side. "We're off duty, or at least I am," he said. "I'll have some of what you're drinking, if that's okay?" He followed Edward into the living room.

"Natasha, what about you?" Edward asked.

"Coffee will be just fine." Natasha leaned against the doorframe, one leg across the other, her arms casually folded across her chest. "How's Charlotte?"

"Okay, I guess. Tomorrow should be better." He handed James a half-filled glass of scotch. "You want ice?"

"Whoa! I didn't need that much." Edward reached out to take the glass from James. "Not to worry, I can savour it that much longer. It just needs a little water, and I can get that." James walked to the kitchen sink and turned on the tap.

"Leave it on; I'll need it to make coffee for your sister." He crossed the kitchen floor to the cupboard beside the stove and pulled out the coffee filters and coffee container.

"I'm sorry about all of that," Natasha said, nodding toward the bedroom as she joined them in the kitchen. "James gets carried away playing detective and asks too many questions."

"Natasha," Edward said simply. Putting down the coffee scoop and turning off the tap, he came over to her. "It's no big deal, honestly, so drop it."

Ten minutes later, the three of them sat in the living room. Natasha and James sat at opposite ends of the futon, and Edward sat across from them in his recliner.

"You know, I understand half of what happened in that news conference—namely Roberts's resignation since Paul disclosed that the other evening—but the puzzler to me is why Bolsover resigned, too. From what you told me in the hospital, it strikes me that you two knew well ahead of the media and general public that he would. Well, am I right?" Losing his appetite for scotch, Edward placed his glass on the table beside him.

"Not quite. In Bolsover's case, it didn't all come together until just a few hours before the news conference," Natasha replied, sipping her coffee and crossing one leg over the other.

James took a drink from his glass and placed it on the coffee table in front him and sat back. "Our recording of Paul's statement incriminating Robarts and John's report snagged him. Oh, by the way, there'll be a team around tomorrow to remove the bugs."

Edward's eyebrows pinched together. *I wonder how long? Ah, who cares! It's history.* "Why the premier, then?"

James rubbed his chin. Shifting forward with his hands dangling over his knees, he cleared his throat. "Needless to say, when we raided the Green Farm, we found a lot of incriminating evidence that had been left behind in their hurry to escape. A lot of it is still being processed and will be part of the Crown's case once everybody is captured."

"You still haven't answered my question," Edward said. *Escape? Who escaped?*

"All I can say is that a number of tapes were found along with a video. This evidence hopped straight to the top, no go-betweens. There was a quiet meeting over lunch with the premier, and what normally would have been a news scrum on the day's proceedings in the House for him turned into his major announcement and very public arrest.

"Who found the evidence that nailed him?" Edward asked.

"I did," James replied.

"What about Rattray and Garcia?" Edward queried.

James looked at his watch. "Rattray should be in the process of being arrested. That package Hobbs gave Blackwell cooked his goose good. Unfortunately, we're still trying to find Garcia and another fella by the name of Antonio, who was Bolsover's chauffeur. According to John, Antonio was one mean dude. He and his brother ran the cartel. Antonio took care of the Oxycontin, and Garcia the coke."

"And Camilo?" Edward asked.

"Don't know. He was the sonofabitch who shot Juarez."

"Wasn't Juarez the fella who saved Charlotte's and Janet's life?"

"The same. He died at the scene, but not before he told us that it was Camilo who shot him. He was one of our best agents!" James slapped his thighs and stood up. "John left you his report. May I have it?"

Edward saw Natasha glance at James as she placed her coffee mug on the table.

"Look, Detective Brant, I promised John I would deliver it. It's safe and sound. I'll bring it to the attorney general first thing tomorrow morning."

"Suit yourself." James walked to the front door and removed the chair from under its knob. "Once you've fixed this, send me the bill, and I'll see what I can do." He stared at the bloodstains on the floor around the table and farther out. "The same goes for the floor. No promises, though." Opening the door, he stopped and turned. "You won't be heading to the attorney general without armed escort. You know that?"

Edward nodded.

As Natasha passed him, she smiled and gave his arm a gentle squeeze. "Right choice, Eddy." She followed James out the door.

When Natasha climbed into the car beside James, he turned to her.

"Why did you say that to him?" he asked.

For a moment, she sat silent.

"I know your ambition, James," she said, staring ahead out the window. "This time you need to share the spotlight."

His face dropped. "Oh, you still remember. I thought you forgave me?"

"I did, or at least I thought I did. Disrupting the coke operation of the Posse Gang in Toronto was a big deal for me. You pulled the rug from right under my feet. I never understood why you would do that to your own flesh and blood. You knew how hard I had worked on it and how important it was to me."

"I told you it would never happen again, and it hasn't. I told you I was sorry. What else can I say? That I'm a self-centred asshole? There, I said it."

"That's the first time you admitted to it. I guess that will have to do—at least for the time being."

CHAPTER FORTY-EIGHT

EDWARD HELPED CHARLOTTE OFF with her coat and knitted hat, and he hung them on the clothes tree along with his by the front door. "Not a bad day for October. How do you feel?" he asked.

"I love the chill in the air. The sun's just a welcomed bonus."

"Why don't I start up a small fire and open a bottle of Coffin Ridge Marguette?"

"It's sounds scrumptious!"

Rubbing her hands together and up and down her arms, she watched him gather the kindling, logs and paper.

A few minutes later, she sat cross-legged in front of the fire, wine glass in hand. "Edward? Aren't you going to join me? What are you doing in your office?"

"I'll be right out!"

When he finally joined her, he had a white envelope in one hand and a glass of wine in the other. "I thought I'd wait for the appropriate time to do this."

"To do what?"

He showed her the unopened envelope with Blackwell's and the motel's names written on it. Before sitting down beside her, he carefully placed it where the flame was bluest.

"Any idea what was in it?" she asked.

"It doesn't matter."

They clinked glasses, and she placed her head against his shoulder.

The flames peeled away the envelope, and two DVDs fell out. Hungrily the flames licked at them, twisting and shrivelling the discs until their potential to do harm dissipated with them, and they became nothing more than harmless, meaningless flakes among the fire's embers.

"Edward, have you heard from Chuck lately?"

"The last time was at the hospital. One of the times I visited you. It was just before he stepped into his new role as interim premier. Why?"

"No reason. Just wondering." She took a drink from her glass and returned to watching the fire. "He sent Janet and me quite a lengthy letter thanking us for rescuing his daughter." Picking up the bottle of Marguette between them, she poured some into her glass. "More?"

He held out his glass. "Funny thing, though."

"Funny? What was funny?" she said as she placed the bottle beside her.

"When we last spoke, he said he had something pressing to tell me—something about Karen and him."

"Whatever it was, it can wait." She placed her glass down beside her, took his glass and placed it beside hers. Sliding closer to him, she turned his face to her and kissed him on the lips.

"That was a pleasant surprise."

"Do you think we have a chance?" she asked.

"Time will tell whatever time will tell." And he took her in his arms and kissed her deeply.

CPSIA information can be obtained at www.ICGtesting.com
Printed in the USA
LVOW122135281112

309074LV00001B/1/P

9 781475 951325